If We're Being Honest

If We're Being Honest

·······················

CAT SHOOK

CELADON
BOOKS
NEW YORK

IF WE'RE BEING HONEST. Copyright © 2023 by Shook Not Stirred, LLC. All rights reserved. Printed in the United States of America. For information, address Celadon Books, a division of Macmillan Publishers, 120 Broadway, New York, NY 10271.

www.celadonbooks.com

Library of Congress Cataloging-in-Publication Data

Names: Shook, Cat, 1993– author.
Title: If we're being honest : a novel / Cat Shook.
Other titles: If we are being honest
Description: First edition. | New York : Celadon Books, 2023.
Identifiers: LCCN 2022018153 | ISBN 9781250847546 (hardcover) |
    ISBN 9781250847553 (ebook)
Subjects: LCGFT: Domestic fiction. | Novels.
Classification: LCC PS3619.H6525 I4 2023 | DDC 813/.6—dc23/eng/20220425
LC record available at https://lccn.loc.gov/2022018153

Our books may be purchased in bulk for promotional, educational, or business use. Please contact your local bookseller or the Macmillan Corporate and Premium Sales Department at 1-800-221-7945, extension 5442, or by email at MacmillanSpecialMarkets@macmillan.com.

First Edition: 2023

10 9 8 7 6 5 4 3 2 1

For my sister, Mary Martin, and my brother, Patrick

THE WILLIAMS FAMILY

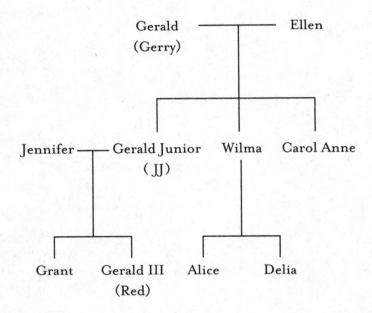

Gerald
(Gerry) —————————— Ellen

Jennifer ——— Gerald Junior   Wilma   Carol Anne
                    (JJ)

Grant   Gerald III   Alice   Delia
            (Red)

Prologue

They didn't mean to, but the cousins stood in order of age: Alice, then Grant, Delia, and Red. They stared at the house they had known all their lives, buzzing like an anthill, people mingling indoors and out, despite the thick June Georgia heat. They watched the new arrivals, all dressed in black, carry casserole dishes and pots and plates topped with aluminum foil. They could only guess how much food had already been dropped off inside. It was past time to go in.

The cousins were grown-ups, at least by age. Most of the time, it felt like their group text was the only thing that connected them. But they were fastened together by more than that: shared blood and their memories, an invisible twine snaking itself through and between them, tying them all together.

Chapter 1

Gerry Williams's funeral was a shit show.

Before it even began, deciding who would eulogize Gerry, the beloved eighty-two-year-old patriarch of one of Eulalia, Georgia's oldest families, proved difficult. Ellen, Gerry's wife of sixty years that past November, hoped their middle child and older daughter, Wilma, would do it, but Wilma wasn't one for attention, and felt that taking the task could be interpreted as her claiming to be closest with her father (which she wasn't, necessarily) or smarter than her siblings (which she definitely was). Her older brother, also named Gerald but nicknamed Gerry Junior and called, however inaccurately, JJ by everyone who knew him—and even those who didn't but were fans of *Keep It Up*, his afternoon sports radio show on 97.7 The Jam—felt like he *should* do it, but had private concerns he would get visibly emotional in front of the crowd, and that certainly wouldn't do. According to JJ, he was now the "man of the family," which made every Williams except for Ellen roll their eyes. Gerry and Ellen's thirdborn, Carol Anne, was completely out of the question for more reasons than can be listed, but chief among them: she was usually under the influence of drugs and/or alcohol; Gerry's lifelong marriage could not be detangled from his identity, and Carol Anne had already been married four times (though her parents only knew of three); and she couldn't go more than five minutes without mentioning her acting career, which didn't really exist.

Which left the grandchildren. Delia, Wilma's younger daughter at twenty-seven, had a disqualifying romantic situation or, more specifically, a complete lack thereof. Her boyfriend of four years had just dumped her, and she had barely talked about anything else since. And no one, herself included, wanted Gerry's eulogy to devolve into a speculation of whether her ex, Connor, had cheated (there were signs, but no proof). Wilma had raised Delia and her older sister, Alice, in Atlanta, and both had moved to New York City after graduating college. Though, unlike Alice, this left Delia with a disdain for Eulalia she was unable to hide, and all wanted to avoid the eulogy becoming a rant about how sexist the "Welcome to Eulalia" billboard was (a smiling blonde woman standing in a kitchen, wearing an apron, holding a pie) or about how the Chick-fil-A playground was listed as a "tourist attraction" on the bulletin board downtown.

Alice, the oldest grandchild, seemed like a decent option: she was widely considered to be the smartest in the family because she was a writer and had even had a book published. She loved her grandfather deeply and could have remained poised throughout, but there was no way his eulogy could exclude significant heaven talk, and Alice was decidedly and openly not religious, a fact which kept her grandmother up at night.

Gerald III, JJ's second kid, called Red for his carrot top, was chief contender. He worked at a youth ministry in Nashville, so he was used to public speaking and invoking Jesus without irony. But the pressure here was too much, and Red's chronic fear of disappointing others and his resulting anxiety rendered him ineligible.

Carol Anne had no children, so that left Grant, JJ's older son. Grant was the only family member who actually wanted to do it, and also the clearest nonoption. While he was affable, charming, and a dutiful grandson, most things he did in life were in an attempt to bed women or grow his client base (he was a personal trainer; these two goals often overlapped), and there was worry that his grandfather's funeral would be no exception. He tried to make the case for himself to JJ and his mother, Jennifer, JJ's wife of thirty years, arguing that a lot of the people at the funeral would want to hear from him anyway, given that Grant was currently living out his fifteen minutes of fame hot off a season of *The Bachelorette*. The episode in which he was eliminated had just aired, so he felt he had the sympathy of the nation on his side, with an uptick of 120,000 Instagram followers to prove it.

(The only person who was truly saddened by Grant's nationally televised elimination was his aunt Carol Anne, as Grant was sent home when the remaining five contestants became four. Had he made it to the top four, he and his family would have been featured on the hometown-date episode. Carol Anne had preemptively bought a plane ticket from LAX to Georgia the moment she realized it was possible she could be featured on television, plotting to pull Grant aside and engage in a long, tearful conversation about how she could tell he had found the one in Lindsay, the twenty-three-year-old "Outfit Planner." Her agent's phone would surely be flooded with calls once America saw her on-screen gravitas.)

It was decided that Fred Clark would deliver the eulogy. Fred was Gerry's lifelong best friend and business partner. He was a pseudo uncle and great-uncle to the rest of the family and would be the next best thing to actual kin speaking at the funeral. When JJ called to ask Fred if he would do it, Fred didn't speak for a good minute. JJ thought maybe he ought to repeat himself, before Fred replied, in a crackly voice wet with tears, that he would be honored. Ellen was humbled by Fred's agreeing. Even though she was pretty sure nothing could beat the numbness she had felt since the first night in over sixty years she'd lain down to go to bed without Gerry beside her, she knew it was no cakewalk to lose a best friend, either. Linda, Fred's wife, had been Ellen's closest friend (by association but also by genuine connection). She had died of breast cancer ten years earlier, and that loss had hit Ellen much harder than any member of her family cared to realize.

The Williamses were all seated in the first pew in Eulalia's First Baptist Church, in which all the grandkids had been baptized, even though by the time Wilma had Alice and Delia, she did not consider herself Christian, or religious in any way really (unlike Alice, she kept this to herself). Wilma was struck then, and again now, that the smell of holy water in the church was somehow fresh and stale at the same time.

Pastor Tom had been the one to dunk all the grandkids, and he was running the show the day of the funeral, as well. When it was time for the eulogy, Fred slowly weaved his way to the pulpit, stumbling a bit and clearing his throat with the rattle of a drum line before he began to speak. The Williamses—particularly Ellen, who still saw Fred regularly—were surprised to see how disheveled he looked, tie loose, white hair sticking up in odd places like a toddler just waking from a nap. Even though he had to be shaken with grief over losing his best friend, and he was the same age as Gerry (which is to say: old), Fred was considered something of a Eulalia miracle: he still stood up tall and rode his bike around the neighborhood daily. Unlike Gerry, he was also very shy, so Ellen and her daughter Wilma thought nerves could explain his stumbling, the volume of his throat-clearing, and his untidy appearance. JJ and Carol Anne were too wrapped up in their own grief to notice.

As was her nature, JJ's wife, Jennifer, immediately suspected something more sinister. And she was right to, because as soon as he started speaking, it became clear to the rest of the Williams clan that Fred was shithoused, even drunker than Grant had been at his high school graduation party a decade prior, which had ended with Alice and Red throwing buckets of water on the bushes outside JJ and Jennifer's house to dilute the vomit before anyone from the previous generation could notice. Jennifer's suspicion was confirmed when Fred pulled a flask out of his jacket pocket, took a swig, wiped his mouth sloppily, and leaned so close to the microphone it looked like he was trying to kiss it.

"I'm Fred," he said, his amplified voice so loud the Williamses all jerked back like a spark had been lit in their faces, momentarily shocked out of their grief. "Thank you to the Williamses-eses for asking me to speak today." He nodded in their direction before letting his eyes lazily drift to the ceiling and breathing a massive sigh. Ellen had never seen Fred drink. Gerry had told her that Fred's daddy had been a major alcoholic (the abusive kind, not the fun kind, like Ellen's father had been), and Fred had vowed never to touch the stuff, even though he and Linda never had any kids to abuse, anyway.

"The Williamses-eses are the nicest family around town. Ellen has one of the kindest hearts of any woman I've ever met. And I like Ellen the most of anyone because she's quiet, like me." He pointed his index finger at her like they were old buddies in the pub telling war stories. "She gets it," he said, slurring. Whatever he had consumed thickened his Southern accent to an unrecognizable drawl. "And Gerry and Ellen had such good kids. They were such beautiful kids. JJ could smile and throw the football, and Wilma was so sweet and artistic." Wilma cringed; she never handled praise for her photography well, even in situations that weren't already awkward. "And Carol Anne, well, she's always been her good ole Carol Anne self. A star. Sort of." The family nervously averted their eyes while Carol Anne smiled and nodded, understanding this to be a compliment.

"And all these grandkids, these gorgeous grandkids," he said, eyelids half closing. "Alice, Grant, Delia, Red. He loved all of 'em so much, Gerry did."

All four grandchildren had cried more than once since they had gotten the news of their grandfather's passing five days earlier, but none of them shed a single tear now, so disturbing was Fred's drunkenness.

Horrifyingly, Red felt nervous giggles coming on, but was saved and silenced by a wave of anxiety so powerful that had he been standing it would have knocked him to his knees.

"Gerry . . ." Fred trailed off, leaning against the podium unevenly enough that Alice almost went up to the pulpit to prop him up. He bent his head down and leaned on his fist, and Delia was strangely reminded of how she always held her head when she was in pigeon pose at the heated yoga studio near her Manhattan apartment in the West Village. She thought of how proud she had been when her now ex-boyfriend Connor had started going to classes with her, how satisfying it was to be one of those couples chatting before class, their mats next to each other, and how she would sometimes see other women and a few guys checking him out as he moved through the flows. Then she remembered she was at her grandfather's funeral, watching his eulogy get butchered.

Fred raised his head quickly, like he was a cartoon character whose alarm had just gone off. "Gerry and I met a very long time ago. Eulalia High. He was the best person in the world. His smile could light up a whole damned—sorry, Pastor—room. Everyone knew who he was. We built our construction business together, and there's no one better in the world to work beside every day. He loved music and was always dancing. He liked jokes." Fred was still slurring, but Ellen felt a small glimmer of hope that he could get this on track, that maybe the threat of complete disaster had passed.

But then he screamed, tears streaking down his face like streamers: "You all think he was my best friend! He wasn't my best friend, wasn't JUST my best friend. He was my Gerry. Mine. We were in love."

Between the nine still-functioning Williams hearts seated in that first pew, not a single one beat for a terrifying moment. They all wondered if they had heard Fred correctly, or if Fred really was so drunk that he was spewing nonsense. Only Carol Anne leaned forward, reaching for her weed pen before remembering where she was, completely intrigued, without an ounce of fear.

"He was," Fred said, pawing with huge swipes at his own face in a futile attempt to dry his tanned, wrinkly cheeks. The crying then transformed slowly, over a period of time that felt like one thousand years, into a chuckle, then into a roaring laugh. The whole church sat perfectly still, like they had been petrified, like *their* souls had also left their bodies.

"We weren't just friends. I mean, my God"—in between laughs—"and none of you knew. None of you had any idea." This was where he made arguably his biggest mistake, which was to look at Ellen and say, "Linda knew. I think you knew. Maybe you tried not to know. Linda knew. She probably told you, for all I know, who knows."

A wave of nausea passed over Red and his father, JJ, at the exact same time, though neither of them had the capacity to be aware of the state of anyone else's stomach.

By now, Pastor Tom had gotten his wits about him enough to know that it was time to intervene, and to do so quickly, decorum be damned (though he never would have used such language; well, not figuratively, anyway). He speed walked up to the pulpit and put an arm around Fred's waist.

"Yeah, I bet *you* especially don't want to hear this." The words were spilling out of Fred's mouth like oil as he leaned against the pastor the way a sorority pledge would on a sophomore. Pastor Tom jerked the microphone toward himself, still supporting Fred's weight, and began talking about how he knew Gerry, trying to tell the story of when he was new to the church and how kind Gerry had been to him, but it was difficult to hear over Fred leaning forward and shouting, "LOVERS!" into the microphone every few seconds through his returned sobs.

While all the Williamses by blood were too confused and stunned to do anything, Jennifer couldn't stand it anymore, and understood that it would have to be she who took action. She tossed her perfectly straight blonde hair over her shoulder, marched up to the pulpit, wedged herself beneath Fred's shoulder, and started to haul him down the stairs while

Pastor Tom halfheartedly and with lots of uncharacteristic "ums" talked about the year that Gerry built the manger for the Nativity scene.

Although every member of the family was too stunned to begin really considering what had just happened, Alice couldn't help but feel the beginning of a crack in her heart as she watched Fred's withered, drunk, and heavy hand trace the outline of her grandfather's coffin as Jennifer carried him to a pew. She was too sensitive to be able to keep Fred's tragedy at bay, no matter how consuming her own had felt just moments before.

Red felt like several hundred arrows had pinned him to the pew. His mind was a white-hot, blank slate, and even though doing so scared the shit out of him, curiosity overtook, and he turned to his left to sneak a peek at his father's and brother's reactions. Grant's big brown eyes were wide in confusion, which wasn't atypical. JJ's eyes were narrowed, flickering between his wife handling Fred and the preacher blabbering on. Red felt perverse for looking, like he was pulling back a curtain to watch his parents have sex or something.

Somehow, though no one there could have given an accurate play-by-play, the funeral ended. The Williams family robotically followed Pastor Tom and the pallbearers, struggling under the weight of the casket, down the aisle and out into the aggressive sunshine. They watched through tinted lenses as Gerry was lowered into the ground. They prayed over the grave, none of them able to focus on anything other than the fact that he might have been sleeping with their pseudo uncle.

By the time they got back to Ellen and Gerry's—well, now just Ellen's—house, there was nowhere to park, as cars covered every driveway on the street and every inch of curbside. The lawn was crawling with people whose plans earlier that day had been to attend a reception to celebrate the life of Gerry Williams, man about town. Now, like alcoholics at Communion, they were there to lap up one of the biggest scandals Eulalia had ever seen.

In their separate cars, not a Williams said a word, allowing the numbness they felt to spread throughout their bodies and across their family unit, unable to picture where they would go from here.

....

The cousins ended up crowded over a bowl of pimento cheese in Ellen's kitchen. As they entered the house, the guests clambered to get to Ellen and their parents first, under the veil of expressing their condolences but mainly to stuff their pockets with anecdotal evidence of how Gerry Williams's family was handling his posthumous outing. It seemed like everyone from Myrtle Lane, and even Eulalia itself, was in the house. Delia had beelined for the kitchen, and Grant, Red, and Alice had followed.

Alice looked back and forth between the pimento-cheese-topped crackers she had in each hand. She decided to pop the left into her mouth. "Well, that was fun," she said after swallowing.

Grant pulled a cracker through the bowl of cheese, piling on so much it was a miracle it didn't break. "Definitely the juiciest funeral I've ever been to, I'll say that."

Red looked around the crowded kitchen nervously. "Do y'all feel like everyone's staring?" Alice put her hand on her cousin's shoulder, which actually did calm Red's nerves a bit. He had always felt a special kinship with Alice, as they were the only members of the family to have inherited Gerry's red hair.

"Why did *Fred* do the eulogy?" Delia asked, as though not the day's revelation but the fact that it was revealed at all was the issue.

"None of us can be trusted, apparently," Grant said, tossing his head to flip the boyish peeking-under-the-helmet hair he no longer had. His overly gelled locks stayed exactly in place. "I tried. And I would have crushed it."

Red's eyes wandered through the wood-paneled kitchen and the entryway into the living room, and he felt an AED-level jolt in his chest when they snagged on a young man looking back in his direction. He sat at a card table set up for the occasion, sipping a glass of iced tea with Tina, the neighborhood gossip. Red felt his trademark flush creeping up his neck. The boy peered over his glass directly into Red's eyes, and Red quickly turned his attention back to the group.

"I don't know if *how* we found out is the thing I'm super worried about at the moment . . ." Alice said, looking around at her sister and both of her cousins. Delia's eyes suddenly widened, as if she were trying to signal to Alice, and Alice gave her younger sister a look of confusion. Alice gasped a little when she felt a tap on her shoulder.

She spun around and found herself looking right up into Peter Bell's brown eyes.

He swallowed, his Adam's apple bobbing down his neck. "Hey," he said.

She wanted to respond, knew, socially, that she should respond, but her throat suddenly felt so dry that she worried her neck would burst into flames should she try to speak. He went on, "I'm so sorry—"

He was cut off by Delia squealing as she ran around him to hug his sister, Rebecca. Peter and Rebecca Bell also grew up on Myrtle Lane, in a brick house down the street from Gerry and Ellen's. Peter was Alice's age, and Rebecca was Delia's, giving Alice and Delia the perfect built-in companions for every summer of their childhood and adolescence, in which the sisters would trade Atlanta's sweltering heat for Eulalia's. Grant and Red, Eulalia natives, grew up across the street from Gerry and Ellen, so they knew the Bells, too. Alice sidestepped, shoving Red forward a little, as though Red and Peter would be the two most excited to reunite. They dabbed each other up with all the awkwardness that comes with being family friends seven years apart in age.

Red stood aside, leaving Alice to face Peter again. They looked at each other.

Clocking this, Delia said, "Connor and I broke up," so loudly several people near them turned their heads. Grant and Red looked confused.

She tugged on the ill-advised, post-breakup bangs she'd recently had cut and flicked them out of her eyes. Rebecca put her arm around her childhood summer best friend and gave her a squeeze.

"I already told Peter," she said.

"I'm sorry to hear that, Delia," Peter said.

"Yeah, uh, I remember you met him last Christmas Eve, so I just wanted to save you the embarrassment of asking me how he is, only for me to have to awkwardly tell you that we broke up," Delia said. She hoped she wouldn't cry.

Peter looked to Alice for help, but she was looking around the room, at the ceiling, at her shoes, anywhere but at him.

"Yeah, thanks for letting me know," he said.

Delia nodded and shifted her weight from foot to foot. She slipped her sister a look and noticed the green tinges spiking up in Alice's cheeks. Alice started fanning herself, suddenly unbearably hot. "Um," Delia said. She returned Rebecca's squeeze. "People! Can we believe we're about to marry off the first of us in a week?"

"Are you okay, Alice?" Red asked.

"Yeah, yeah," Alice said, a bead of sweat running down her temple. "Rebecca, we can't wait for the big day! Sorry, I just gotta go to the . . ." And she turned quickly on her heel and practically sprinted down the shag-carpeted, family-photo-covered hall to the powder room, growing terrified of what would happen if she found it occupied. It was empty, and she breathed a sigh of relief as she slammed the door closed behind her, shaking the framed photo on the sink of herself at ten years old, but instantly feeling ten degrees cooler. She leaned back and closed her eyes. When she opened them back up to her reflection in the mirror, they immediately flickered downward to her stomach and hips. She turned to the side, looked back up into her eyes, and sighed.

Back at the pimento cheese, Red felt his nerves buzzing through his limbs. As the reassuring hand of his cousin had left him, the overwhelming sensation that everyone was staring at them returned. And he had never seen Alice behave so awkwardly in front of anyone before, much less Peter. It was like she had left a cloud of discomfort behind her, and it was moving over Red, bearing down and clinging to him. His breaths started to come shallower, a sure sign that anxiety was taking the driver's seat. He cleared his throat and muttered something; he hoped it was something along the lines of "Be right back," but he couldn't be sure. He padded down the crowded hallway, head down, dodging the mourners who would have loved nothing more than to stop him and engage him in conversation, and essentially dove into what had formerly been Carol Anne's childhood bedroom but was now the guest room.

Like most of the house, it was rather frilly, a lace throw across the four-poster bed, which was covered with crochet pillowcases. His eyes landed on the Bible resting on what little room was left on the bedside table considering all the framed family photos. He sat on the bed and leaned over, put his head in his hands, and took deep breaths, as he knew he was supposed to do when he got this way, which was less often now than in his youth, but not as infrequent as he would have liked. He twisted his head to the side and reached out, placed a freckled hand on the Bible.

It wasn't a meaningful family Bible; he was pretty sure he had never seen it before. But there was something about placing his hand on the stiff (which confirmed that it was just for show and not used) leather, pressing down, and feeling the resistance of the pages against his hand. His breaths deepened, and he felt himself returning to his body. He wasn't thinking of a specific verse, or even praying, really; he certainly wasn't at his most articulate. But something about the particular feel, the give of that particular book, managed to calm him.

Across the hall, feeling better and sucking in, Alice opened the bathroom door and, for the second time in five minutes, gasped to see Peter Bell. "Sorry!" he said, registering her shock, his eyes wide.

"It's fine," she said, exhaling. She was trying to superglue her abdomen to her spine and was proud she could get any words out. "How's . . . Texas?"

"Uh, fine," he said. "Listen, I want to make sure you're okay. I know how much Gerry—and especially after Fred's speech . . . I know you probably don't want to talk to me, but I just wanted to make sure you were okay." Peter swallowed, that brown Adam's apple bobbing again. He bounced on his feet a little, looking as nervous as he had when they were thirteen and he saw her in her grandparents' yard the morning after they kissed for the first time.

"I don't not want to talk to you, Peter," she said, unable to let him think that, even though her behavior up until this point had only indicated the opposite.

He nodded and looked into her eyes with such focus she physically felt the eye contact like it was, well, contact. "Look, I—"

"Oh, Alice, with that beautiful red hair!"

The tension between their gaze broke, and they simultaneously turned toward the familiar voice of Tina, another longtime resident of Myrtle Lane. Tina was older than even Gerry had been, and she had served as the neighborhood gossip all her life. She was wearing so much blue eye shadow Alice wondered if she had to buy a new container for every occasion.

"And, Peter, your height still shocks me every time. What a beautiful couple you two would still make." Peter shifted his weight to his other foot and forgot to breathe. Alice tried to smile and worried it looked like she was farting, which she was.

Peter's beauty was enough to make any couple he was half of worthy of Tina's ill-timed compliment. Alice stole a quick look up at his perfectly full and symmetrical eyebrows, raised in a wince over his bright brown eyes. He still had that bump on his nose from when he broke it the first time he drank in high school and walked into a door. Alice wondered if he still wore glasses, or was contacts-only these days. He was clean-shaven, which she knew from social media was rare for him. He probably liked looking older, considering that he had been late to puberty and, being the first Black youngster in the neighborhood, was called "precious" and "adorable" by all of Myrtle Lane's white ladies for far too long. It might have been well-intentioned, but the thought made Alice cringe.

"Your grandfather was just so proud of you," Tina said, gripping on to Alice's shoulder as though it were a handrail on a rainy day. "A real-life *author* in *New York City*—"

"Oh, Ms. Tina," Alice said, "that was all years ago, and no one read the book—"

"I read the book . . ." Peter mumbled. "I loved it—"

Alice felt her face turn a similar shade to her hair. There was no conversation topic Alice hated more than the book.

"What a funeral, huh," Tina said. "Honey, are you just . . . in shock?"

Or maybe there was a conversation topic Alice hated more. She opened her mouth to speak, but no words came out, as she had nothing to say. What *could* she say to a woman wishing to gossip about her dead grandfather's recently revealed gay sex life?

"Alice, will you show me that thing you were gonna show me at the . . . by the . . . the chicken salad? You said you would." Peter gulped. "You said you would show me the chicken salad?"

"Yes, yes," she said. She turned to Tina, shrugged, and said, "Men!"

Tina laughed, as though that comment meant something. Alice and Peter walked down the crowded hall, and Alice felt a bizarre yet completely familiar urge to lace her fingers through Peter's. She didn't.

After wolfing down more pimento cheese, Rebecca and Delia stepped outside into the Georgia heat. They sat on the stoop of Gerry and Ellen's porch, just as they had over the course of so many summers growing up. The two of them had gone from playing with Polly Pockets to spying on Peter and Alice's summer flirtations to comparing tampon brands and squealing through first-make-out stories. They still followed each other on social media, in an active way, actually pausing and thought-fully considering each other's posts, and felt warmth in their real hearts instead of just posting one in the comments. Now they went long stretches without seeing each other, but whenever they reunited, it was as if no time had passed at all.

"So," Rebecca said. "Do you want to talk about it?"

Delia sighed. "I don't know if I *want* to talk about it, but it feels like I'm never not talking about it."

Rebecca nodded. "Checks out."

"I think he may have cheated," Delia said.

Rebecca paused. "I'm truly sorry to ask this, but are we talking about Gerry or Connor?"

Delia barked out a dry laugh, then winced. "Jesus. Connor."

"Well," Rebecca said, pausing to choose her words carefully. "On the one hand, I could ask you why you think that. We could go forensic and try to figure it out. But on the other hand, I want to ask you how much that would change anything."

Delia huffed, blowing those damn bangs out of her eyes. "Of course it would change things." Rebecca squeezed Delia's shoulder and gave her a sympathetic look. There was a time for tough love and a time for the softer kind. Delia squeezed Rebecca's hand over her arm and swallowed with all of her might in an attempt to suck the tears that had welled in her eyes back into her body. "I'm gonna take a sec," she said, standing up. Rebecca nodded.

Around the corner, Delia leaned against the side of the house to avoid the people milling about the front yard. She couldn't go to the backyard, because thinking about all the hours Gerry and Ellen spent in their back garden would have been too upsetting. The brick was almost scalding against the back of her head, but the way the heat slowed everything down in that brain of hers felt good.

The constantly gnawing desire to call Connor was rearing its head higher than usual. She knew she shouldn't call him. There had been many a drunken night, a bad day at work, or moments she knew he'd find funny when she had walked herself down the mental road of why it would be acceptable to call, but ultimately had resisted every time. She had sent the occasional text, and his responses were so perfunctory they raised the threshold her pride would have to surmount in order to actually make a call.

But today was different. Her beloved grandfather was dead, and had also maybe lied to her for her entire life. Just like maybe Connor had lied to her, which made it all the more disgusting that she still longed to hear his voice. She huffed, making her bangs dance above her brown eyes. She unlocked her phone and went to her Favorites list in her contacts. He wasn't there, because she had removed him in a dash of bravery and rewarded herself after with an expensive skirt she didn't need. Remembering this, seeing proof that she had once taken this preventative measure, was enough to make her click the side of her phone, darkening the screen.

Here was the thing. Delia knew that if she called Connor, he would either answer or call back as soon as he could. Sure, they weren't in love anymore (or at least he wasn't in love with her), but they still loved each other, right? They had been together for four years; they *lived* together. Of course he still cared for her—deeply. And if she left some weepy voicemail on his phone, he would immediately be in touch in a real way, and that would be too much for Delia to handle.

But there were always the not-so-real ways. She turned her phone back on and went to the photos she had saved, the ones she had looked at tearily on her flight from LaGuardia to Atlanta, and again on the four-hour drive from Atlanta to Eulalia. There was Gerry smiling next to the horse a seven-year-old Delia straddled, grin almost as wide as the horse's flank. There was Delia at four, floaties and bucket hat on, swimming toward a waiting, laughing, pool-immersed Gerry. High school graduation, Gerry hugging Delia as she clutched her diploma. Gerry at Waffle House, Gerry with Alice on one side, Delia on the other, the last summer they had spent in Eulalia as kids, before Alice's senior year of high school.

She posted them on her Instagram story, knowing she would obsessively check the list of people who watched, hoping not only for Connor's handle to appear but also that it would be near the top of the list (someone had once told her that if someone was near the top of the list, it was because they visited her Instagram page often). God, how she hoped he was checking on her.

Delia looked up at the sky, at the brilliant blue that stretched so much wider over her head here than it did in New York. She was not religious, which she considered to be an intellectual attribute, but at that moment, it occurred to her that her grandfather was no longer on this earth, and according to most of the people in the house behind her, he was maybe . . . up there? Up in that gorgeous Hollywood-background blue sky. She suddenly felt watched. While she didn't *really* believe it (she lived in Manhattan, for fuck's sake, and ordered sushi to be delivered to her apartment at least once a week and raised her middle finger to rude people on the subway platform), a wariness crept in that Gerry saw what she was doing. And she did not want Gerry to see her making the day of his funeral about whether or not she should call her ex, regardless of how far off the rails the day had already gone.

Back inside, Rebecca peered through the mass of food-laden plates and black clothes. She pushed her glasses up—they kept sliding down her sweaty face.

"Well, well, if it isn't Miss Rebecca Bell."

She turned to face Grant. She hated that even though they were both grown adults, she couldn't quite shake the queasy feeling in her stomach that a cool older boy at Eulalia High was talking to her.

"Do they teach poetry on *The Bachelorette* now?" she asked.

"Hardy har," Grant said, absentmindedly flexing beneath his suit. "Play nice, remember it's a sad day for me."

Rebecca stopped herself mid–eye roll and squeezed Grant's shoulder.

The fact that it was rock-hard did not escape her notice, and the fact that it did not escape her notice did not escape Grant's.

"Med school's clearly treating you right," he said, giving her an unabashed up-down. This took more effort now that they were adults; growing up, she had always towered over him, even though he was a year older. She continued rolling her eyes, but she also self-consciously pushed her hair behind her shoulder. He had always loved when she let her hair naturally curl and wore it down, as she did now.

"Please don't make me slap you on the day of your grandfather's funeral."

"Ooh, don't talk dirty to me on the day of my grandfather's funeral, either."

"Jesus." Rebecca exhaled, and Grant stopped being the cool older guy at school and transformed back into the obnoxious neighbor she had known her whole life, the one who stole her Halloween candy every year and spent all of 2005 playing ding-dong-ditch on her. "Have you no shame? I'm getting married in a week."

Grant mimed stabbing his chest with a knife. "Just when I thought the day couldn't get sadder, you have to remind me of that." She smirked and took a sip of her iced tea, and Grant noticed the lip gloss stain left on her glass. "Does what's-his-face know your first kiss is invited to the wedding?"

"You know his name is Justin."

"Is *Justin* still a dweeb?"

Rebecca narrowed her eyes. "Hey, be nice to Delia this week," she said, changing the subject.

"Bell, I'm always nice."

"Mm-hmm. But seriously. She's really going through it. Although I gotta say, never liked the guy," she said. "Anyway, how are you holding up?"

Grant shrugged. "Fine. She may have been the Bachelorette, but it's not like she holds a candle to you."

From across the room, Jennifer noticed Rebecca talking to her older son and wondered where her fiancé was, while also clocking Alice taking deep breaths while Wilma patted her shoulder, and gossipy Tina slowly making her way from one group to another, the day's scandal painting a grin on her wrinkled face. She saw two ladies from Ellen's bridge club talking to the new widow, who stared blankly at them, her face drained of color. She also noticed how one of the card tables piled with food trembled when someone put their glass of iced tea down to grab a spoon and load up on some form of mushy casserole, and made a note to rectify that. As a (former) decorated and highly respected competitive cheer coach, Jennifer had an uncanny ability to look at a chaotic situation, parcel out every individual movement, and identify its shortcomings, all at the same time.

She narrowed her eyes and her heart rate quickened when she saw her husband, JJ, speaking to Stephanie, the associate producer of his radio show. She was young and had only been there for two years or so, getting the gig straight out of college and receiving no promotion since, even though JJ was always going on about how smart she was. Jennifer (rightfully) didn't think Stephanie would stand out in a crowd of women her own age as pretty, but only (annoyingly) because she didn't try. There was natural beauty there—clear skin, shiny hair, straight nose, big eyes, bigger bust—but her dirty-blonde hair was too long, her clothes baggy and outdated. Maybe her lack of effort only made her seem more attractive, Jennifer thought, irritated.

JJ nodded intently at whatever it was Stephanie said. Jennifer wondered what they were talking about, if it was work-related or dead-dad-related. She thought about how many more hours of the week JJ spent talking to Stephanie, or "Stephie," as he annoyingly called her, than he did talking to his own wife. She wondered if he thought about Stephanie when he was in their home across the street. JJ had been working late a lot recently, rushing in with his gym bag over his shoulder while Jennifer was halfway through a lonely dinner. Her jaw tightened like a corkscrew and bile rose up through her stomach at the thought that *Stephie* could be the thing keeping him.

She tossed her shiny, perfectly straight blonde hair over her shoulder and went to rearrange the plates so the table wouldn't collapse, feeling a small but noticeable relief that she could keep *something* upright that day.

Chapter 2

Eventually, everyone left. Even Tina, who staggered out dead last after asking every single attendee—even the ones openly weeping—if they had had any previous suspicions about Fred and Gerry. The Williams family usually gathered in the cramped, sunny family room that adjoined the kitchen, but today they spread themselves out in the formal living room, which was used only on special occasions. This day had certainly been special.

Empty glasses and dirty Styrofoam plates littered the card tables, and congealed casseroles were everywhere. The smell of cheese clung to the carpets. But Alice's mind was on all the Christmas mornings spent in this room with her grandparents, her mom, and her sister. The fake tree, hauled down from the attic, sprayed liberally by Gerry with pine-needle air freshener, was always in the corner by the window, and JJ and Jennifer would bring the boys and all their presents over from across the street. As a young child, Alice found it strange that Santa didn't wrap her and Delia's gifts, but did wrap Grant's and Red's. Not for long, though. Alice was one of those kids who found out about the

Santa thing pretty early, in a voicemail her dad left on the machine for Wilma. "Do the girls still believe in Santa?" he asked. Alice always thought his voice sounded sunny, like California had made it that way. "Let me know. Is a blank check fine again this year?" She played along for years, though, not telling her mother, Ellen, or Gerry that the jig was up, because she could tell how happy it made all the adults—even Carol Anne, the years she deigned to show up for the holidays.

The last one to take a seat in the living room was Jennifer, who came in from the bathroom, smoothing her black dress over her flat abs, and sitting on the couch arm next to Wilma instead of the open spot next to JJ. Red and Wilma were the only ones to notice.

JJ sat on the cream couch facing the other cream couch directly across from it. He sat beside Grant, the father-son pair spreading their legs and arms wide, like it was a competition to see who could take up more space. Red sat on the pink shag–carpeted floor because he didn't want to disturb Miss Sparkles, Ellen's shih tzu, who had fallen asleep on his leg. He petted her softly, knotting his fingers in her fluffy white fur. Miss Sparkles had been noticeably depressed ever since Gerry died. Gerry had been opposed to Miss Sparkles at first, and repeatedly told Ellen that if they were to get a dog, he wanted a "real dog." But one day he came home from work right before he was set to retire, and there Miss Sparkles was, yapping away, echoing his exact nightmare of what a dog that size would bring. They had been inseparable ever since.

Wilma, Jennifer, and Alice sat on the other couch. Both couches had benches so deep it was almost disrespectful to sink into them because you couldn't do so without getting practically supine. The only other option was to sit up straight or lean forward. Alice leaned back, hands folded over her stomach. Wilma leaned back, too, dead tired, while also sneaking frequent glances at Ellen. Wilma was almost always in a constant state of worry over her mother, and today had only electrified that worry. Jennifer sat up, her back straight as a ballerina's. Delia was in one of the worn printed armchairs, and so was Ellen, who already knew that someone would eventually have to help her out of it, given how exhausted she felt and how plush the chair was.

Carol Anne sat cross-legged and straight-backed on the floor, in what looked to her brother, JJ, like some kind of yoga thing (she just knew it was the most flattering position for her figure). She absentmindedly braided her almost waist-length, stringy hair. Her newest man, Robert, sat on the floor next to her, because he only felt comfortable doing what she did, though he couldn't have looked more uncomfortable, his freakishly long legs tucked under him at a bizarre angle. Everyone knew he was over ten years younger than Carol Anne, and Alice hurt her brain trying to do the mental math to figure out how close her potential newest uncle was to her in age. She gave up, realizing it was so close she didn't want to know the number.

Even though Carol Anne, Wilma, and even Jennifer thought the whole man-of-the-house thing was ridiculous, everyone waited for JJ to kick things off. Which he did, with a massive and wet throat-clearing.

"Well," he said, feeling extra pressure to establish some kind of authority given that they had all seen him cry earlier, at the visitation. He crossed his meaty arms over his small but noticeable gut. "That was bullshit."

"Dad," Red said, jerking his eyes in the direction of his grandmother, who did not like cursing. JJ had never allowed the boys to curse in front of her, not that Red had ever had the urge to, anyway.

"It was!" JJ said, looking individually at each family member as they all sat silently. He was actually quivering with anger, the overhead lights bouncing bizarrely off his buzz cut. "There's no way in hell what he said was true. And to have this day, his funeral, ruined by . . . with . . . lies! It's a damn shame. And we all need to get on the same page about this, remain a united front. That's what Daddy would have wanted."

"Well," Delia said, toying with her Cartier bracelet (a gift from Connor she was having trouble getting rid of), "it doesn't seem like we *knew* exactly what Grandpa Gere wanted, did we." It came out harshly, and for a moment the room was stunned to silence, and Delia immediately regretted saying it, especially in front of Ellen, whose eyes hadn't left the same spot of carpet since she first sat down. Delia didn't know if she'd meant it as a joke, or if she really was upset, but there the comment was, shot out of her own mouth.

"Jesus, Delia," Grant said.

"Your grandfather is barely in the ground, young lady," JJ said.

"Come on, JJ," Wilma said softly to her big brother. "There's no need for that."

"We could always have a séance," Carol Anne said. "If we really want to know what he wanted. I did one in *Now and Then.*"

"You were in *Now and Then?*" Alice asked quietly, fully aware that her aunt was not.

"A local performance, yes," Carol Anne said.

"Carol Anne," JJ said, feeling the almost ten-year age gap and unquantifiable personality gap he always felt when he was around his youngest sister. "Please, not now with your woo-woo shit."

"Won't Fred be at Rebecca's wedding next week?" Grant asked. The air felt charged with a million flying particles, and no one moved a muscle. "Okay . . ." Grant said, smushing himself as far as he could into the couch cushions. "Sorry. But I mean . . . just saying."

"I'll have a talk with Charlie Bell, see to it that he's not anymore," JJ said. "Not that I think the man will be showing his face around town anytime soon. The station was gonna give me the week off, but I think if I ditch the show for a week, it'll look like I'm hiding something. I'll go back in."

"Of course you will," Jennifer muttered. No one heard her.

"JJ," Carol Anne said, tipping her head forward in a *you're so silly* way, like he was her child and not her older brother. "What's the big deal? He was Daddy's best friend. He was Daddy's lover. It doesn't have to be negative."

JJ inhaled sharply and looked to the ceiling, as if he were asking God for help. But he only spoke to God in church or at his parents' dinner table, and both were performative. "It actually is pretty damn negative, Carol Anne. I'd say it's pretty fucking negative—"

"Dad," Red said again, quieter this time.

"—that Fred has lost his damn mind and lied to an entire congregation—"

"JJ," Jennifer said in a sharp, loud voice, her coach voice, petrifying everyone in the room. Her face was calm, expressionless, which made it all the scarier. JJ gulped, eyes wide as he looked at his wife. He looked both angry and scared, and if the whole situation weren't so fucked, Alice and Delia would have found it pretty funny. "How we respond to Fred as a family is up to one person and one person only, and that's Ellen."

Even though he knew to be afraid of Jennifer, and even though he agreed that the most important person to consider was his mother, JJ sure as shit did not like being spoken to by his wife like that. Especially in front of everyone else. He opened his mouth to say something, but her left eyebrow arched so immediately, into such a frighteningly perfect curve, that he snapped it shut real quick.

The collective gaze slowly made its way over to Ellen, but her eyes remained glued to the same spot on the carpet. She closed them and leaned back in her chair. "I need a drink," she said.

Now it was time for everyone's eyes (except Robert's, who had only just met her) to bug out of their heads. She might as well have said she needed a lobotomy, or a rocket ship, or a vibrator. While each of those requests would have been more unlikely than the last, they felt in the same realm of likelihood as Ellen requesting a drink.

None of the cousins had ever seen her drink, not once. They'd asked their parents about it before, and JJ could swear he remembered her drinking a margarita on a family trip to Florida, though Wilma disagreed. Wilma said Ellen had a glass of champagne at her wedding, though neither of them recalled her partaking in such celebrating at

JJ's wedding, nor at any of the weddings of Carol Anne's she'd attended, certainly. The cousins figured Ellen thought alcohol was sinful.

But after this day, what harm could a little more sin do?

"I'll have a bourbon," she said, to no one and all of them.

Alice, Red, Grant, and Delia all stood up at the same time, nearly falling over themselves for the honor of pouring their grandmother a drink.

....

The sun set, but the night air was still thick with heat, muffled by a blanket of stars. The cousins sat in the bed of JJ's F-150, the impracticality of which had been pointed out numerous times already by Delia, who simply refused to understand why anyone who only used his car to transport himself from work to home and sometimes the grocery store and more often the liquor store needed a gas-guzzling truck to do it. But it made an inarguably good hangout spot for the cousins, Alice sitting cross-legged, the boys and Delia with their legs sprawled out, leaning against the sides and occasionally tipping their heads up to check out the stars.

They were parked in a field used traditionally and almost exclusively as a haven for high schoolers to get drunk. Each cousin had spent many a night here, although not at the same time due to their age differences, except for Grant and Delia, who were only one year apart. Even JJ, Wilma, and Carol Anne had first imbibed with their schoolmates here back in the day; everyone would park their cars in a row and leave the headlights on to illuminate the field, lug out kegs and coolers filled with their parents' liquor and, on one particularly memorable night for Grant a generation later, three mason jars full of moonshine.

Rebecca and Peter had volunteered to come and pick them up once they were ready to go home so that each cousin could get good and properly drunk. Grant held up the bottle of Jose Cuervo he'd found beneath his childhood bed, which was barely visible in the darkness. "To Grandpa Gere," he said, taking a swig and handing the bottle to Delia, who sat to his right.

"The best there was," she said, swallowing a sip and passing the bottle over Alice's lap and into Red's hands. "Or . . . you know, so we thought."

"Whoa, whoa," Grant said. "I don't think so, missy. Alice, be a leader. Take a shot."

"Shut up, Grant," Delia said, looking at her knees instead of at her sister.

Grant threw his hands up. "What? I thought we came here to get drunk!"

"Um, yeah," Alice said. "See, the thing is, I can't really do that right now, and won't be able to for the next . . . few months."

They were all quiet for a moment. Grant looked confused, Red nervous.

Alice sighed. "I'm pregnant."

Red's jaw dropped into a big smile, joy for his cousin spreading in his chest. "Awesome!" he said, unsure what to do with his hands and the bottle of tequila in them. He had always liked babies, even as a young child. He hoped Alice's baby would have Gerry's red hair like they both did.

Grant nodded repeatedly like he was listening to a song with a particularly good beat. "Sick," he said, clapping his cousin on the shoulder.

"Could y'all really not tell?" Alice asked, allowing herself to do what she had been trying her damnedest not to do all day, which was to place a hand on her slightly bulging tummy.

"You know, I thought to myself, 'Maybe,'" Grant said, tapping his chin. "But sadly, making a comment about a pregnant lady who isn't actually pregnant is a mistake I've made in the past, and I wasn't really looking to repeat it."

Delia's face twisted as though she were smelling something unsavory imagining her cousin congratulating a nonpregnant woman. Alice gulped, remembering a time she had given up her seat on the subway to a woman who she thought was pregnant, only to have the woman ask her why she did that, shooting daggers with her eyes as Alice stammered helplessly over her words.

"So, sorry to ask, but is there, like . . . a father of this nugget? Or did you go shopping at a fancy sperm store?" Grant asked, bugging his eyes back and forth between Red and the tequila, signaling that the big news was no excuse to delay his shot.

"When are you due?" Red asked so that no one would have to deal with what Grant had asked as he unscrewed the cap on the Cuervo and eyed it suspiciously.

"December," Alice said.

"Okay, so you're in the second trimester," Red said. Grant raised his eyebrows at his younger brother. "What? All my coworkers at the ministry are married and having babies." Alice looked up to the stars, checking herself on the math and timing, as she always had to do when she thought about this. Numbers weren't her thing. She counted backwards, making sure she landed on March.

"Well, cheers to you," Red said, tipping the bottle back and opening his throat as much as he could, trying to get the liquid down without letting it burn him.

He passed the bottle to Grant, who took a swallow and said, "So does it suck not being able to drink?"

Alice sighed and tipped her head back. "Yes."

"Wait a second," Grant said. "If you're not drinking, should we tell Peter and Rebecca not to come pick us up?"

Delia looked at her knees again. Alice gulped. "I just . . . I'm not ready for everyone to know yet."

Grant narrowed his eyes at his cousin. "Hm. Anything to do with you not wanting your childhood sweetheart to know someone knocked you up?"

"Grant," Red said, shaking his head.

Alice sighed. "Something like that."

"How did Aunt Wilma take it?" Red asked. The question, like most things, made him nervous, even though he knew his aunt Wilma had entirely different reactions to breaks in traditional behavior than his father. He was always confused as to how his dad, Aunt Wilma, and Aunt Carol Anne could share flesh and blood, how they could've grown up in the same household and ended up with such different views on life.

Alice had told her mother four weeks earlier, after deciding to go through with the thing and have the baby. She called from her apartment in Prospect Heights, Brooklyn, staring out her window at the backyard only her superintendent had access to. It was the first warm day of the year, and her super sat in a lawn chair sunning himself next to his daughter, who was sprawled out on the grass looking at an iPad. Alice gulped, wondering if kids read books anymore. How was anyone supposed to raise a kid in this age of limitless information and technology?

The whole story just spilled out of Alice as soon as Wilma answered the phone. Alice couldn't quite put her finger on why she was so nervous—Wilma was never one to judge, and if there was ever a model for a woman raising kids without a partner, Wilma was it. Not that Wilma would have had a problem with Alice ending the pregnancy, either. And so Alice power walked her mother through the making of the appointment, her thought process, her sure knowledge that she wanted to have kids, her fear that she might not necessarily get another chance, the canceling of the appointment.

Wilma was quiet when Alice finally stopped speaking. Alice's heartbeat quickened even more. "Mom?" she said.

"Oh, honey," Wilma had said. "This is just wonderful." Her voice broke, and Alice realized her mother was crying, which was a rarity. The crying turned into quick, gasping sobs, and in a punctured way she managed to get out, "I'm. So. Happy."

Alice smiled at Red. "She took it great. She's excited, actually."

Grant nodded slowly, drumming absentmindedly on his flat tank-top-covered abs. "I could see that. So, are you really doing this whole"—he changed the absentminded drumming into motioning a fake bump—"thing by yourself?"

"Hey!" Delia said.

"What?" Grant asked.

"Alice can handle anything. It's not, like, a *crime* to be single, Grant," Delia said.

"Jeez, Delia, chill with the breakup sensitivity. At least you didn't get dumped on national television," Grant said.

"Don't act like you're upset about that," Delia shot back.

"Yeah, true, I can't really be upset with that edit!" Grant said, throwing up a hand for a high five that no one gave him. "Anyway, I'm up 120K follows on Insta, which will be good for the ole career." Grant was a trainer at a gym outside Atlanta, and he had been completely booked with personal training appointments ever since the season began to air.

"Wow, Grant, that's a lot!" Alice said.

Delia said, "It's not. Not for a finalist, at least."

"Top five isn't really a finalist, cuz, thanks for the reminder," Grant said, taking an ostentatious pull of the Cuervo, which had made its way back to him. But Grant couldn't convince any of them he was really upset. And yeah, he had enjoyed lounging by the pool all day and occasionally flirting with Lindsay, a nice girl, who, by the looks of social media these days, was now appearing on a lot of fan podcasts and attending music festivals that required little clothing after finding out that the man she ultimately chose had not one but two girlfriends back home.

When Grant got eliminated, he hadn't cried, which had been very important to him from the start. He told himself he would only consider shedding a tear if he made it to the final two, and even then, only if he felt like the competition was tight and he needed to demonstrate to Lindsay that she had really "knocked down his walls." But the truth was, it wasn't difficult for Grant to access tears. When JJ called the previous Tuesday night to inform him of Gerry's heart attack, he cried so hard that the next day the other trainers at the gym thought he'd had an allergic reaction.

When Grant left the mansion, he had hugged all the remaining contestants, and whispered (audibly, intentionally), "I'm rooting for you, man," to a guy named Jason. Jason and Grant did genuinely get along well, and Jason ended up making it to the final two, poising himself to become the next Bachelor, so Grant was thrilled to find his little well-wishing didn't get cut. He hoped he was at least a shoo-in for *Bachelor in Paradise*, or whatever other spin-off the network would inevitably cook up.

"You did get a good edit, Grant," Delia confirmed. "At least five of my friends want your number. Don't worry. I told them you're a douche."

"Show me pics and then I'll decide which ones you can put me in touch with after you retract that," Grant said. "But hey, I wish I knew you and Connor were done at that point. I totally would have trashed him on TV for you, Deel."

"Yeah, bummer, that would have made me seem really sane and over it," Delia replied, as if she were, in fact, feeling sane and over it.

"We were gonna go to a Preds game," Red said.

"What?" Grant said.

"Grandpa Gere promised to take me to a Preds game. The hockey team. In Nashville."

"When?" Grant said.

"We didn't have a date," Red said. "He just said he would because I've never been to a hockey game, obviously. And now . . . yeah." He tipped his biggest sip yet of tequila back into his mouth.

"Speaking of dates," Alice said, never one to shy away from a moment to lighten the mood. "Are you dating anyone special in Nashville, Red?"

Red was grateful for the dark, feeling his complexion morph into his hair color. The tequila caught in his throat, burning him in the exact way he had been careful to try to avoid. He coughed a bit onto his khaki shorts, then spit over the side of the truck.

Delia, Alice, and Grant all grinned. "Wow, must be someone *really* special, then!" Alice said.

"How hot is this chick?" Grant asked.

"Red, are you in love?" Delia asked, eyeing the bottle as it passed from Red to Grant.

"No, no," Red said, his legs twitching at the recent memory of trying a dating app for the first time. He had heard good things about YCHO ("You Come Here Often?") and had been texting back and forth with his match. But when he got to the bar and saw his date sitting there, he turned around and left and never said anything about it to anyone.

"Good," Delia replied, tousling her bangs. "Because love will fucking destroy you."

"I'm worried about Gram," Alice said, passing the tequila to Delia.

"Same," Red said. Alice's hand moved to her tiny bump; she was honestly more worried about telling Ellen she was pregnant out of wedlock than she was about her grandmother coping with the grief. And now the added shock.

"I mean, they were *goals*, you know?" Delia said. "Gram and Grandpa Gere. Between this and Connor, it's like, does real love even exist?"

"Those two relationships were pretty different, though . . ." Grant mumbled.

"And yeah, I mean, poor Gram. I still think Connor might have cheated, but to have it blasted in public like that?" Delia said. "Damn."

"I don't know, Deel," Alice said. "'Cheating' feels like a weird word here."

"There was that night he said he crashed at our friend Cody's place . . ."

"No," Alice said gently. "I meant a weird word for Grandpa Gere's situation."

"It's what it is, though, isn't it?" Delia said.

"It might not even be true. Fred was absolutely ham-boned," Grant said.

"Seems like quite a thing to make up just because you're drunk," Red murmured.

"I had only been worried about Connor cheating with a girl," Delia said. "Great. Now it feels like the possibilities are truly endless."

"So are you gonna make, like . . ." Grant said loudly above Red's coughing, which had started up again when he was reunited with the tequila. Grant passed him a disgustingly warm plastic water bottle. ". . . Everything about your breakup?"

"Grant!" Alice and Red said at the same time.

"What?"

Delia took the Cuervo out of Grant's hands and took a very long sip. "Most likely, Grant," she said. "Fucking deal with it."

They were quiet on the car ride home, after Alice and Delia hopped quickly into Rebecca's car. Peter guided JJ's truck along the bumpy dirt road before they hit Main Street. They were all silently and (except for Alice) drunkenly considering what they had lost, wondering about Fred. Red, who didn't drink much back in Nashville, had to ask Peter to pull over, and he spattered the dirt road with vomit. Getting back in the truck, he was humiliated, but said a silent prayer of thanks that he had at least made it out of the truck. Peter assured him it was no big deal, and Grant clapped him on the back, then ruffled his hair. The tenderness made them both quickly look out of their respective windows. Red rolled his down and leaned his head out, hoping the night air would cure him.

....

Carol Anne looked intently at her reflection in what had been Gerry's mirror, gathering her multitude of straw-colored hair on one side and

arching an eyebrow while she sucked in her soft stomach. Wilma sat on
the edge of the tub while Ellen brushed her teeth, avoiding Wilma's eye.
She spat and said, "Am I entertaining you?"

Wilma looked down and rubbed her left foot back and forth across
the smooth, heated tile. Ellen and Gerry had had their bathroom re-
done five years ago. There was a TV mounted on the wall above the
tub—Gerry had insisted on this for Ellen, even though she rolled her
eyes and told him over and over again that she would never use it. And
she never did, not once; she didn't even know where the remote was,
and it was too high for her to reach the buttons. The thought of her
father's sweet (and futile) gesture made Wilma's eyes fill.

Ellen returned her toothbrush to its holder and washed her hands.
Wilma was slightly amazed that the second glass of alcohol she had
ever seen her mother consume in her life didn't seem to affect her all
that much. "Just wanting to be in your company," she said, catching her
mother's eye in the mirror.

Ellen pulled her floss through her teeth slowly and didn't reply.

Wilma continued watching. It was only in recent years, as she had
felt herself starting to age, that she had really begun to appreciate how
beautiful Ellen was. Wilma crinkled her nose and scrunched up her forehead in the mirror every morning and every night, even though she
knew that was precisely what she was *not* supposed to do, noting with
disappointment how her lines seemed to grow deeper daily. Ellen's face
had some lines, but they were faded; her face was pleasantly softened by
age without ever seeming to fully sag from its once-youthful tautness.
Her blue eyes sparkled from her fresh-dough skin, and Wilma wondered
if she should buy Pond's.

Speaking of, Ellen rubbed some on her skin and tapped her cheeks,
turning away from the sink slowly. It felt like everything she did was
slow these days. She looked at her daughters, registered the concern in
Wilma's eyes that Ellen could swear had been there since the day Wilma
was born. Ellen was proud that Wilma had always been praised for

being so considerate of others. She went from being a toddler who always shared her snacks and held hands with kids whose steps were unsteady, to a high school student who volunteered to the point of obsession, to a woman who was always forcing friendships on her daughters with the kids in their class whose parents she knew had drinking problems, or marriage problems, or money problems.

Though Ellen wasn't one to raise a glass to divorce, she had been secretly relieved when Wilma and Trey split up. Because even though Wilma's caring nature made Ellen proud, there was always the nagging fear Ellen carried for Wilma all her life—the fear that Wilma would be taken advantage of. And Wilma dedicating her concerns to someone as self-involved, idiotic, and fake-tanned as Trey was the exact realization of that fear.

In recent years, as Wilma started making the four-hour drive from her home in Atlanta to her parents' place in Eulalia more frequently, it didn't escape her notice that Ellen would be slower to get from room to room or to unload the dishwasher. Wilma had felt her heart sink a few inches the previous Christmas when Ellen had served a store-bought cinnamon roll, explaining with a blush and a laugh that she had accidentally poured salt in her batter instead of sugar. Wilma could tell the difference between Ellen's listening face and her neutral smile when someone was telling a story she couldn't hear but didn't want to ask the speaker to repeat another time.

Ellen usually hated being watched this closely, but this night it felt good to have someone see her. Because the person who she would usually complain to—the person who would nod and say, "Just because we're getting older doesn't mean we're old yet!" and pat her hand and remind her that it was nice, something to be thankful for, to have a daughter who cared so much—was gone. And was also maybe not who she thought he was, but that was too unfathomable to really think about now.

Ellen started puttering her way to the bedroom, and her girls followed behind slowly. She sat on the edge of her bed, nightgown folding under her legs, and started to pull down the sheets on her side, turning away from the girls. She was tired, exhausted actually, from being in mourning, from being shocked, and from the anger she could already see waiting around the corner like a smiling Salvation Army Santa outside the grocery store at Christmastime.

"Daddy and I used to watch the sunrise together sometimes from the front porch," Carol Anne said, sitting on the edge of the bed.

"When were you getting up at sunrise?" Wilma asked.

"No, when I would come home," Carol Anne said, "from nights out in high school and community college."

Ellen just continued looking at her younger daughter, which was something she had had to train herself to do with Carol Anne. To not look away.

"I think I need to get up and say goodbye at sunrise tomorrow. So I'm gonna go to bed. Night, Mama," Carol Anne said, getting up and walking softly on the pink shag carpet to her mother's bedside and pecking her cheek, inhaling the Pond's. "I love you. And so did Daddy. Sex can really just be an expression of—"

"Good night, Annie," Wilma said. Carol Anne nodded and saw herself out. Wilma pulled one knee up on the bed and sucked her lips into her mouth, not sure what to say to the woman who had raised her, whose husband had just died and who'd just found out she was lied to by said husband, possibly for decades. Wilma tugged at her short hair, as though to make it longer, as Ellen had always wished it were.

"Mama," Wilma said, and Ellen looked away from her, picking a spot on the wall and staring at it, trying to ignore how the bourbon made her vision swim even though no one had been able to sense a difference. "Can I sleep with you tonight?"

After a moment, Ellen said, "Of course you can if you want to. But not if you feel sorry for me. I'll be fine."

"I want to," Wilma said, sliding under the covers into her father's spot, even though she hadn't changed into her pajamas or brushed her teeth or taken off the mascara she hardly ever wore. "Thank you."

....

An hour later, Wilma stumbled into the kitchen for a glass of water after waking up disoriented in her mother's bed, still in her black dress and makeup. Her short, dark hair, streaked with gray these days, was standing up at odd ends, and some mascara had dyed the skin under her eyes.

JJ, Jennifer, Carol Anne, and Robert were seated around the kitchen table. The dark, warped circular wooden table predated them all. It stood on one central leg with three uprights, so it never felt like there was a limit to how many chairs could fit around it. Carol Anne and Jennifer had glasses of wine in front of them, JJ a scotch. Robert sipped a glass of water. He was old enough to drink, of course, but something about his choice to abstain from alcohol made him seem even younger, and it wasn't doing him any favors. Everyone else seated at the table looked old—at least ten years older than they had that morning. Even Jennifer looked a little deflated—her blonde hair not as voluminous, and her skin a little saggy and sallow. She normally looked sun-kissed, fresh, like you could bounce a quarter off her.

JJ nodded to the empty chair across from him. "Did you take a little nap?" Carol Anne asked as Wilma sat down. JJ stood up silently and walked into the formal living room to the antique bar cart, which existed mostly just for show. He returned a moment later with a duplicate of the crystal rocks glass he drank from, two fingers of scotch in it. Wilma nodded and muttered, "Thanks," realizing that this would be far more relieving than the water she had come to get.

"She fall asleep?" JJ asked, reclaiming his chair.

"Yeah," Wilma said. "I guess having liquor for the first time in maybe your whole life will do that to you."

"Well, if there was ever a day," JJ said, shaking his head and taking a sip of his drink. No one had anything to say to that. The silence didn't make anyone uncomfortable except for Robert. "I always thought it was strange that two people could have a perfect marriage, and only one of their kids would end up in a normal marriage," JJ said, staring at his glass. He didn't mean to offend anyone with that statement; JJ spoke to speak more than he did to be heard.

"Well, it's statistically as 'normal' to be divorced as it is to be married," Wilma said, also looking into her glass. Robert jerked his head a little, worried that JJ's comment had upset Wilma, but it hadn't. Wilma understood that most things, including that comment, were not about her.

With JJ, it wasn't a question of love. He had loved both Wilma and Carol Anne from the moment they were born, a fact which further solidified his parents' theory that he was the most perfect boy in the world. Wilma was a nonfussy baby, a smart toddler, and a nice kid, and when she was really small, JJ liked to pretend she was his. While she was artsy and liberal enough to make him uncomfortable, he felt a love for her he would never feel for another woman again, a respect deeper than he could muster even for his own wife. In a town like Eulalia, wearing all black and looking at the world through a camera lens, casually quoting the Brontë sisters and wearing Pride buttons might have gotten you teased at best, hurt at worst. But Wilma never had to worry about bullies because it was common knowledge that messing with JJ Williams's kid sister was akin to a death wish.

Publicly, the same was true for Carol Anne, of course. No one would dare to mock her for her obsession with the drama club or the fact that she often wore sunglasses inside, because she was JJ Williams's sister. No one realized that JJ wouldn't have cared as much. No one noticed the flicker of pride that danced in his eyes when Wilma won first place in the Georgia Young Photographer's Contest, and its absence when Carol Anne was starring in *The Music Man*.

"I can't imagine wanting to be normal," Carol Anne said, tipping back her glass of pinot grigio.

"No one would have thought you did," JJ muttered. Jennifer kicked his leg under the table. Hearing him speak to his sister like that set something off in her that usually managed to stay in place.

"Your father seemed like an amazing man," Robert said, looking around the table and meaningfully tipping his head in everyone's individual direction.

"He was," JJ said. "Don't pay any mind to the lies you heard today."

"Thank you, Robert," Wilma said, choosing to skate over JJ's additional comment. "He was. I'm sure he would have loved to meet you." JJ audibly snorted and now it was Wilma's turn to kick JJ under the table.

"Hey, Wilma," JJ said, laughing and slurring those two words enough so that everyone at the table, even Robert, who had just met him, immediately understood that he was more than a little bit drunk. "Do you think Daddy could've told you all of Carol Anne's husbands' names in a row? Think he coulda picked 'em out of a lineup?"

A flicker of an almost-smile passed across Wilma's face—not out of cruelty, but out of genuine mirth. It was a funny thought, but she righted her face quickly.

"JJ," Jennifer said quietly, her bared teeth looking particularly sharp as she lifted her glass of pinot grigio to her mouth. JJ looked at her, and she saw his pain cut through his drunkenness, and Jennifer knew that she would allow him this one night to be a complete asshole. It had been difficult for Jennifer to bury her own father, and she hadn't even liked the man.

"Do . . ." Wilma trailed off, then regained her composure. "Do y'all think there was any truth to it? Or do you think Fred was just drunk and confused and said the wrong thing?" She asked the question of everyone but was looking at Jennifer, the only person at the table whose opinion she really trusted.

"Oh, honey," Carol Anne said, and Wilma instantly understood, not for the first time, how people could dislike her baby sister. "Come on."

"No way it's true. Daddy wasn't . . . I mean, he wasn't," JJ said, shaking his head at his rocks glass, unable to resist voicing an opinion even though everyone already knew where he stood on the matter. He liked to make things true for himself. Like when he first asked Jennifer out over thirty years ago and she wasn't that interested, but his unwillingness to back down, the fact that he kept showing up, ended up impressing her. It was no surprise to Jennifer that he would plant his flag in the denial camp and refuse to budge.

"JJ, you're not one of those men who can't say the word 'gay,' are you?" Carol Anne asked.

"'Course I can," JJ said, slurring still. JJ even had a gay friend. His former UGA football teammate and groomsman Matthew Framon came out to him three years after they graduated. Matthew won the Heisman Trophy and was a loyal, funny guy, and JJ had realized he didn't give a shit who Matthew slept with. "But Daddy wasn't gay. And Fred is senile. I love the man, he's like a second father to me. And not in that way, jeez," he said, shaking his head and grimacing at Carol Anne, as though she had said something, which she hadn't. "But he's been a little wonky ever since Linda died. And there's just no way . . . I mean, he didn't even really say anything."

"You mean other than when he said that he and Daddy were lovers and pointed at us, laughing, saying we had no idea," said Carol Anne, twisting her hair up into a bun and blinking rapidly, like she couldn't believe she had to explain this. JJ kept staring at his glass, as though acting like he hadn't heard Carol Anne would erase what she said. "I mean, I know from my time on the set of the Academy Award–nominated *This Time, Forever*—"

"I can't say I'm shocked," Jennifer said, rescuing everyone from hearing one of the many invented stories Carol Anne had teased out of her time as an extra on the set of a movie that ended up getting nominated for Best Picture seventeen years ago. Though it didn't feel like a rescue—everyone at the table looked at Jennifer in surprise, with an extra dash of drunken rage from JJ. She looked at him dead-on, in his half-closed eyes, and found something satisfying in contradicting him.

"Had you . . ." Wilma asked, training her eyes on her sister-in-law, ". . . sensed something?"

"Not necessarily," Jennifer said slowly. "But *something* was always there, I think. I never suspected anything before today, I'm just saying that I'm not shocked."

Carol Anne was nodding as though she and Jennifer were speaking a language none of the others could understand. "They always had such a powerful bond," Carol Anne said.

"Friendship is a powerful bond," JJ said, straightening up in the wicker chair, as if he could thin out the drunkenness. "It doesn't have to mean there was anything . . . more to it."

"Of course not," Wilma said, reaching across the table to pat JJ's hand. Jennifer shifted in her seat and stifled an eye roll.

"I just . . ." Jennifer continued, wanting to prove that she hadn't said it just to piss JJ off, which she hadn't (entirely). "There was this time years ago when Fred dropped your father off after work and I heard them laughing with each other. I was doing the dishes, so I saw them through the window, and I thought I'd go say hey. Something about the way that Gerry shut the passenger door behind him and looked back over his shoulder laughing, and the way that Fred was laughing, made me hesitate, and I didn't open the window and say hi. This was right when Grant had started dating, and I was training myself to let my kids be teenagers, telling myself that they didn't always need their mom so involved. Gerry smacked the door and Fred drove off, and Gerry stood there, looking after him and smiling. Something about the whole thing kept me from opening the window and saying hey to your daddy, even though I always said hey to your daddy if I saw him from the kitchen window. There was just . . . something about the two of them that made me feel like I should let them stay the two of them, if that makes any sense."

Everyone looked at her, and Wilma finally nodded. "So you're saying you always knew?" JJ asked, slurring the sentence.

"No, as I just said," Jennifer said, a vein in her forehead starting to bulge, "it didn't even cross my mind, really. I'm just saying that when Fred started . . . saying what he said, I remembered seeing that, and I didn't have a hard time believing it. Or as hard a time as everyone else seems to be having."

"I'm not having a hard time," JJ said, his voice rough like sandpaper. It was such a ridiculous statement. At the foundation of everything that was going on, his father, his hero, had just passed away. "It just ain't true. They were best friends. Fred is very old and he was drunk, for God's sake. You saw two friends laughing."

Jennifer didn't avert her gaze from her husband; she gave him a hard stare while he looked at his glass, fingering the bulbous edges.

"I just think it would benefit everyone to look at this for what it is: a learning opportunity. Humans aren't made to be sexually faithful to one person for their entire lives. Sexuality is a *spectrum*. Fred and Daddy loved each other, we all knew that. And it sounds like sometimes they expressed that sexually, and that's perfectly natural," Carol Anne said. Robert patted her hand, which was resting on the table, unable to avoid being supportive even though he, unlike Carol Anne, could feel how unwelcome her comment was. "When I was filming a sex scene once, or rather preparing myself mentally for if I ever did have to do one, I asked myself—"

"Has Fred seemed off at all lately?" Wilma asked in JJ and Jennifer's direction. No one in the family, even sweet Wilma, had a tough time cutting Carol Anne off. It was indisputably best for everyone. "I hadn't seen him since Christmas, and I barely spoke to him then."

JJ said, "Seems pretty off to me," while Jennifer said, "He's been fine." They looked at each other, then quickly looked away.

There was quiet for a moment before Wilma said, "Well, I'm gonna try not to dwell on it. That was one thing, and he lived a whole life. He was still our daddy, still the wonderful man we knew. Whatever else may have happened . . . may have happened. But that doesn't have to change the way we remember our relationships with him."

"Jesus, Wilma," JJ said. "Cheating is cheating. I ain't gonna just look away when I find out someone's done that. I'm not you."

Wilma's neck moved backwards, as if to keep his words from entering her ears. She shook her head in such a small movement it was almost imperceptible, then raised her glass to her lips and sipped.

"I thought you didn't believe it," Jennifer said to her husband. She could hear the blood in her ears and couldn't meet JJ's eye. She was too outraged and embarrassed, even though it was JJ's family anyway.

"Well, I'm gonna go to bed," Wilma said, pushing her chair back from the table and dumping the rest of her scotch in the sink before filling a fresh glass with water and padding softly past the table while her siblings sat in silence. "'Night."

⋯⋯⋯⋯⋯⋯

Hours later, at the same table, Alice sat in the dark, eating peanut butter out of the jar like it was soup. The kitchen suddenly flooded with light, and she froze, the spoon piled high with Jif halfway between her mouth and the jar. Ellen was equally startled. Their eyes widened in shock; then they both chuckled.

"Jeez louise," Ellen said. "You scared me." She filled up a glass of water and slowly made her way over to sit at the table next to her granddaughter.

"Sorry," Alice said. "Don't mind me. Just housing peanut butter in the dead of night alone in the dark."

"You didn't get enough food earlier?" Ellen asked, her worst nightmare being someone in her house going hungry.

"No, I did, I did, how could anyone not in this house right now? It's overflowing," Alice said. She stared into the jar of peanut butter and found herself tearing up, because despite all she had learned in her women's studies classes, despite what she herself wrote in her column for the world to see, despite the fact that she wrote a book about a woman who had sex and anyone who read the *New York Times* knew that, the thought of her pregnancy disappointing her grandmother was devastating.

"That's true," Ellen said. "And good thing, with how much food Grant can put away. And you and your sister."

"Hm, true," Alice said, shoving the spoon deeper into the peanut butter. "How are you doing, Gram? Today was a lot. I'm sorry you can't sleep."

"I suppose I'm fine as can be expected," Ellen said. Alice watched her grandmother primly fold her hands and hover them over the place mat. "How are you doing with it?" Ellen asked.

Alice sighed, wanting to respond exactly how her grandmother just did, even though the platitude had frustrated her. "I suppose the same, but it's hard."

Ellen nodded. "It is," she said.

"Seems like everyone in the neighborhood was here," Alice said. "It'd been a really long time since I saw some of those folks."

Ellen raised her eyebrows. "Yeah, it's nice for you grandkids to get to see Peter and Rebecca."

"Mm-hmm," Alice said, quickly shoving a towering spoonful of Jif into her mouth.

"Peter grew up into quite a fine young man, didn't he?" Ellen said, watching her granddaughter.

"Mm-hmm," Alice said again, trying to unstick the copious amount of peanut butter from the roof of her mouth. Ellen sat quietly. After a moment, Alice said, "Yeah, I saw him a few months ago in New York, actually. He was in town for a medical conference thing."

"Oh?" Ellen said. "Well, that's nice. Good to keep old friends close."

At this, Ellen took her eyes off her granddaughter and looked at her hands. Alice swallowed.

"I don't know what to make of what Fred said today," Alice said gingerly, reaching over and placing her hands on Ellen's. "But mostly I'm just so sad that he's gone. And I feel ridiculous, honestly, I'm thirty-two. Thirty-two-year-olds don't get to be this sad about a grandparent passing away. Sorry, no offense. But most of the people I know didn't have relationships with their grandparents like I had with Grandpa and like I have with you."

"It's true," Ellen said. "We've been lucky."

"We have been lucky," Alice said, sitting up straight and twisting the top back onto the Jif jar to close it. "Very lucky."

They both quietly stared into space, wondering privately if they really believed that.

Chapter 3

Wilma's left leg made a loud cracking noise when she hoisted herself up into the F-150, which she thought was a ridiculous car for her brother, a radio host, to have. The cracking noise made her laugh, though. "Did you hear that?" she asked JJ, as though they were children and she had just belched while they were watching TV.

"I'm not deaf, am I?" JJ said. Wilma shut the door and heard 97.7 The Jam, JJ's station, playing quietly on the stereo. She was surprised it wasn't louder, that JJ wasn't listening intently, monitoring it as if he ran the whole station and not just his afternoon show.

"I'm gettin' old. Maybe I should take a leaf out of Jennifer's book and work out more. Lord knows there's enough exercise classes in Atlanta," Wilma said. Jennifer was actually in an overpriced high-intensity exercise class at that very moment, at Eulalia's only workout studio. Jennifer and JJ both had been recently diagnosed with high blood pressure, which Jennifer happily took as an excuse to exercise

more. Less appealing to her were the meditation apps her doctor suggested she download.

"The woman is a machine," JJ said. Wilma felt relief in the silence
that followed; she had been anxious all morning, wondering if JJ remembered his cheating comment from the night before. There was also just
the new, more foundational anxiety of being around her brother now
that their father was gone. Wilma knew this was the hardest thing life
had thrown at JJ so far, and while Wilma herself was hurting, she wasn't
such a stranger to pain. She chided herself for thinking about this; she
had always resented the way her parents tiptoed around him, always
carefully navigated his feelings, preferences, moods, and whims. Now
here she was doing it, too.

"Listen," he said. "I'm sorry for what I said last night. About the
cheating thing."

"Oh, that's okay." Wilma shooed it away quickly.

There was another, less relieving moment of silence. "You know I'd
kill him if I could."

Wilma didn't know if he was talking about her ex-husband or Fred
or Gerry.

"Trey," he clarified. "You don't hear from him, do you?"

"Not anymore now that the girls are grown," Wilma said.

But did she *think* about him? Sure. It had been two decades plus since
the divorce, but Wilma was not a dater, didn't have anyone new to distract her. She had been persuaded to try Match.com but never actually
allowed any of the e-meeting or chatting there to lead to a real date. She
had allowed the occasional setup, but those usually went the same way:
some sad or angry (and often balding) man complaining about his ex-wife
as Wilma listened sympathetically over coffee. The only man who didn't
seem to hate his ex-wife was a widower, which was at least slightly more
interesting but significantly sadder. Wilma thought he seemed nice, but
he never called her. She figured he was embarrassed that he'd cried.

There were never second dates. The girls claimed that Allen, Wilma's New York–based agent, who sold a few of her photos and who she would grab a coffee with when she visited the girls in the city, flirted with her, but she thought he just had a friendly personality. She was wrong.

So, whenever Wilma's loneliness—which had been amplified and more frequent since she became an empty nester almost ten years ago—crept in, she only had one person she could attach her longing to, and that person was Trey, with whom she had fallen in love the moment she saw him at a poetry reading their freshman year of college. Trey, the "artist" (though it was never clear which medium he worked in), as handsome as a movie star, with a wandering eye to match. Trey, now the big-time Hollywood talent agent with a blue-check Instagram account that Wilma secretly stalked every now and again when she was a drink or two deep.

"Well, if he ever showed up around here," JJ said, "you know it wouldn't end well for him."

Wilma knew that it was problematic to be enamored with JJ's ridiculous show of masculinity, but she appreciated feeling protected.

"I know," she said, not taking the conversation any further, because she knew there was something solid in what JJ had said to her last night, and there was no need to get into all that now. Or ever.

"I was hoping we'd seen the last of this place for a while," Wilma said, even though she knew she'd be back for Ellen eventually. JJ grunted in agreement as he pulled into a parking space outside Mort & Sons Funeral Parlor. In everyone's rush to make the funeral happen, there hadn't been time to order a headstone. While no one in the family had particularly liked burying Gerry in an unmarked grave, they did what they had to do, and now it was time to mark his spot.

They walked into the foyer of the little house, immediately blasted by a stale air-conditioned gust. Wilma shuddered both from the cold and the reason for it. JJ led her down the hallway and into the back, where the offices were. His rather stupid-looking face looked even stupider when he was confronted with Bill's empty office. Bill, Mort's son, had been their guy from the moment Gerry was pronounced dead, and JJ also knew him from Little League baseball, where he had been Red and Grant's umpire.

A man with thick, dark hair and practically golden skin poked his head out of the office next door. He looked to be a little younger than Wilma and JJ and was wearing a tucked-in button-down shirt and khakis.

He said, "Hi, are y'all the Williamses? I'm Derek Saab. 'Saab' spelled like the car. No relation, though. Unfortunately." He smiled and went on: "I was out last week and Bill called in sick today, but y'all are here for the headstone, right? I can gladly walk y'all through that."

JJ narrowed his eyes. He knew picking out his father's headstone put him in a vulnerable position, and any hint of vulnerability, however slight, made him defensive. Plus, having grown up in a town as small as Eulalia and lived there all his life, he was always irked to have to speak to people he didn't know.

"Come on in," Derek said, stepping into his office.

Wilma followed immediately, JJ dragging his feet behind like a toddler. They sat, and Wilma noticed a photo of two young girls on Derek's desk while also clocking the absence of a wedding ring on his finger. She and JJ sat down in the two thin-cushioned chairs that faced his desk.

"I'm Derek," he repeated, standing up again and shaking both of their hands before sitting back down and leaning forward, looking them square in the eye. "I graduated from Eulalia High, Carol Anne's year. I worked the lights for the drama club, so she was always nice to me."

He paused, and Wilma chuckled. JJ's glare was so intense that Derek quickly looked away. He continued: "And I'm so sorry for your loss."

He paused again, but neither of them thanked him. Manners were the furthest thing from JJ's mind, and Wilma was too taken aback to speak; she had momentarily forgotten why they were there. Derek kept right on, though: "I remember when we were real young, middle school age, and Tracy Kitman, girl in our class, remember? She had a coed dance party and a bunch of the parents chaperoned, including your parents. I remember your daddy seemed like he was having the time of his life, more fun than any of us kids. He was trying to dance with your mama, making everybody laugh. She was having none of it, by the way, and shining a flashlight on all the kids who were dancing too close." He chuckled at the memory, and Wilma smiled. "Good man, your daddy was."

"Thank you," Wilma said, and Derek smiled at her. He had crow's feet, had clearly spent a lot of time in the sun. Wilma accidentally pictured him in a tank top. He slapped a gigantic binder resting on his desk, and she jumped at the loud *whack* his hand made on the leather cover.

"Oops, sorry," Derek said, also looking surprised by the sound. "Here are some options. We'll need to decide shape, size, font, what we want the text to say." He pushed the binder in their direction, and JJ pulled it closer, turning it so it faced him and flipping through it. After a minute, he remembered he wasn't the only person there and pushed the binder closer to the center of the desk so that Wilma could look, too.

"We've been seeing a lot of the rectangular cut in recent years," Derek said, pointing to some photos with his ringless hand. "As opposed to the more traditional rounded top you see around, you know, Halloween." He smiled.

"Is that s'posed to be a joke?" JJ asked, his mouth a thin, flesh-colored line. "About our father's headstone?"

"No," Derek said, the smile sliding off his face like a magnet down a refrigerator door. "Wasn't a joke at all. Just trying to . . . evoke an image."

"Thank you," Wilma said forcefully, cutting her eyes over to JJ, hoping he would read from her terse tone that the fact that they were tasked with this was not Derek's fault. "How long have you been doing this?" she asked in a lighter tone, genuinely curious.

JJ flipped through the pages of the binder with his stiff left pointer finger while he stared at the same spot on the top of each page, not really looking at any of them while Derek the funeral director struck up a chat with his sister.

"Few years," he said. "I'm from here, like I said, then I lived in Macon for a while, and I sold insurance there. It's been just over five years, actually." He tapped a five-year chip sitting on his desk, which Wilma recognized from a documentary she'd shot two years ago. It was from Alcoholics Anonymous.

"Great," she said. "And what made you pick . . . ?" She gestured around the office, unsure how to phrase "the business of death."

He smiled; he got this question a lot. "I know it's a little unusual. I suppose most people think about people who work at a funeral home as, I don't know, a creepy old lady or a man with a pitchfork stickin' out of his head, or something. But when I moved back here to be closer to my parents five years ago, I needed a job, and we've always known Bill and his family. And you know what?"

Wilma leaned forward, then immediately blushed, wondering if she looked overeager, if he could tell that she was staring at the golden flecks in his brown eyes between the lovely crow's feet. "What?" she asked, betraying herself even further.

"I love it," he said, throwing his hands up. "It's the most rewarding job I've ever had, and I think it has to be one of the most rewarding jobs that exists. It's really meaningful to be there for someone when they lose a loved one."

Wilma nodded and cast her eyes down, realizing she now fell into that category: the kind of person who had lost a parent, an anchor.

"Plus," he said, the corners of his mouth creeping up his face, "job security's pretty good. People ain't gonna stop dyin', far as I know."

Wilma smiled and exhaled. "No, doesn't seem that way."

"And Bill said you live in Atlanta, right—"

"I like the rectangle," JJ said in too loud a voice to be normal. He didn't really know what he liked, but he needed the small talk to end immediately. It might as well have been Miss Sparkles yapping at the mailman for how it grated on his ears.

Wilma leaned over and nodded. "I do think it's more dignified," she said.

"Great, and have you thought about the inscription?"

They had, and had written it together, deciding to keep it simple: "Gerald H. Williams, 1935–2019, Loving Husband, Father, and Grandfather."

Delia had suggested to Wilma and Alice that morning that they amend it to "Loving Husband, Father, Grandfather, and Adulterer." Alice had smacked her arm but chuckled. Wilma did not.

....

Alice tried to fan herself with her hand as she walked Miss Sparkles down Myrtle Lane toward what they all called "Miss Sparkles's turn-around stop sign." She quickly realized that not only was this ineffective, but she looked ridiculous doing it, like some sort of Scarlett O'Hara wannabe (and she did *not* wanna be Scarlett O'Hara). She had offered to take Miss Sparkles, who did not want to go on this walk and protested by moving at a snail's pace through the thick humidity, to think over the submissions she had just sifted through for her advice column.

She preferred to work from home on Mondays, even back in New York. It helped her concentrate as she clicked through the advice column submission emails, and she always took a walk after reading them to see which ones stuck, which writers-in she actually cared about helping, which ones she actually felt like she could. Her apartment in Brooklyn was near Prospect Park, so she usually mulled the submissions over there, even on snowy days, which she longed for in this heat.

This Monday, one particular submission nagged at her conscience. "Suspicious" had written in with concerns, and circumstantial evidence, that her boyfriend was cheating on her. The solution to this person's problem was clear to Alice (confront him), and she knew she could turn around a decent column quickly and be done with the thing, but between Delia's constant speculation and the Gerry situation, the thought of exploring more infidelity accusations made her feel very, very tired.

There was a work-related submission about a boss acting like a best friend that could spark something. Alice was relieved that this week there was nothing that pulled on her heart strings enough to make her write back to someone directly, offering advice, good vibes, or support, which her bleeding heart sometimes made her do even when there was no potential for the column. In her mind's eye, she tried to focus in on this inappropriate-boss behavior issue, and was successful enough that she didn't notice she was approaching the Bells' house, or Peter mowing the lawn, or Peter *stopping* mowing the lawn when he saw her.

She did notice Miss Sparkles start pulling in Peter's direction as he approached. She looked up at him walking toward her, how his Eulalia High Basketball T-shirt was soaked through with sweat, how his dark, lean arm muscles practically glowed in the heat. He bent down to pet Miss Sparkles, who was jumping up and basically frothing at the mouth to be touched by him.

"Whore," Alice muttered.

"Hey," Peter said, looking up at Alice as he scratched behind Miss Sparkles's ear. The dog wiggled her butt in pleasure.

"Hi," Alice said. "Christ, Miss Sparkles, be a lady."

Peter laughed, which made Alice smile. It had always been easy for her to make Peter laugh. When Alice was a kid spending her summers in Eulalia, she would bring Mad Libs, and she would have Peter cracking up for hours. There was one time, when they were ten, that he even peed his pants (though he would never admit it).

He wiped some sweat off his forehead with his wrist. "How are the Williamses holding up?" he asked.

"Hm," Alice said, looking like she was considering the question when she was really asking herself if she had put deodorant on before embarking on this walk. "You know, I wouldn't say we're thriving."

Peter nodded. "I know you know this, regardless of whatever . . . yesterday was, but Gerry was one of the best people I've ever known. He really . . ." He trailed off for a moment, and Alice wondered what would happen if he cried. She certainly wouldn't survive that. "He was such a role model to me. God, it just sucks when someone dies, because not only are they dead, but everything that I can say about it is so cheesy and has been said a million times. I guess it doesn't feel like there are words good enough for Gerry."

Alice looked away because this sentiment, coming from him, was too much. She swallowed the knot in her throat and said, looking at Miss Sparkles to avoid looking at him, "You know he loved you. Like you were one of his own."

Out of the corner of her eye, Alice saw Peter nod. "Well," he said, clearing his throat and bouncing on his feet a little. "I'd hug you, but I'm pretty gross."

Even though it was scorching hot out, and Alice could guarantee she was in a grosser state than Peter was, she would have loved a hug from him. Then she remembered herself. She started backing away toward home even though they hadn't reached the stop sign yet, much to Miss Sparkles's relief. "I'll see you around, I guess," she said.

"Al, watch out for the—" But it was too late. Alice was on her ass. Miss Sparkles was unconcerned but sat down in solidarity (and exhaustion). Alice's hands immediately flew to her pelvis, even though she had fallen backwards. She was momentarily pleased with herself for this maternal instinct, which was immediately replaced with terror that she had done something to the fetus, and humiliation that she had fallen down in front of Peter. He lurched forward, extending one of his large hands, but Alice hurried to get up so she wouldn't need it. It wasn't that she necessarily *wanted* to go out of her way to refuse it, but she did.

Upright, she realized what had happened. The roots of a nearby magnolia tree had extended and risen, causing a rise and crack in the pavement, and she had tripped over it.

"Those damn magnolias," she said, trying to choke out a laugh even though her backside, and pride, stung. Peter opened his mouth to say something, looking concerned, but she spun around and walked away as fast as she could, Miss Sparkles following unwillingly behind.

....

"So, what do you think the rules are when it comes to your ex and a death in their family?"

Grant sighed and looked out the driver's window, his right wrist draped lazily over the steering wheel. "I'm famously not much of a 'rules' guy, Deel."

"Well, obviously I don't mean, like, *you* you," Delia said, whipping her head around when the gallon of milk they had just bought rolled over with a thud in the back seat. It was whole milk, as Ellen had requested, even though Ellen drank her coffee black and Delia hadn't consumed milk from a cow in five years. "I just mean generally, like if you find out your ex lost someone in their family, is it fine to reach out? Normal, even? Expected? Like the right thing to do?"

"Sure," Grant said, reaching over and turning up the stereo volume. A country song was playing on the radio:

I saw her from my truck
Felt like dumb luck
Dancin' in that bikini top
And you know I just couldn't stop

Delia rolled her eyes. "WHAT is this garba—" Grant drowned her out by turning the volume up as high as it would go, the chorus crashing through his truck's painfully bass-heavy speaker.

And I looked and she looked and we kissed and we took every
*   chance*
Like the Lord said, Here, have this dance,
And we fell and we tangled and we married and we even grew old
And best of all, the beer was cold

Delia rolled her eyes as Grant tapped on the steering wheel, trying to
nod his head along with the rhythm, but it was too fast. She opened Instagram to see if Connor had replied to her story of Gerry, not even
realizing what she was doing, what she was hoping for, until her throat
constricted with disappointment to find only a meme Alice had sent and
nothing else. She checked the list of people who had viewed the story
and there it was, his handle. He had seen it and said nothing. She
huffed her bangs out of her eyes and flipped her phone upside down.
She looked over to Grant, eager to pull something apart.

The song had looped back around to the chorus. Grant began to
sing along, "*And I boinked and she boinked and we boinked and we took
every boink like the Lord said, HERE, HAVE THIS BOINK!*" Delia's face
scrunched in disgust.

"Are you serious?!" she yelled over the music.

Grant screamed louder: "*AND WE BOINKED AND WE BOINKED
AND WE BOINKED AND WE EVEN BOINKED AND BEST OF ALL
WE BOINKED!*" Delia reached forward to lower the volume of the mu-
sic while Grant dissolved in a puddle of laughter.

"My God," she said, shaking her head at him.

"Come on!" he said, between laughs. "'Boink' is a hilarious word. I
do this whenever I'm down. 'Don't Stop Boinkin'' is a favorite." Delia
stared at him. Grant shook his head, said, "Your loss," and turned the
music back up just in time for the chorus. "*AND WE BOINKED AND
WE BOINKED—*" He looked at Delia and waved his hand, motioning
for her to give it a try.

She started quietly at first, just mouthing the words to appease him, to prove that there wasn't a stick up her ass. Or that the stick that was definitely up her ass had at least a bit of flexibility to it. "*And we boinked and we boinked . . .*" she murmured. She was horrified to feel a smile creeping up her face, to hear a laugh escape her throat. "Boink" was such a ridiculous word.

Grant nodded with exaggeration, like she was a toddler taking her first steps. Also like a toddler, she took the encouragement and began screaming even louder than Grant: "*AND BEST OF ALL WE BOINKED!*"

By the time they pulled into the driveway, Grant was smacking his steering wheel because simply laughing didn't do the moment justice. Delia clutched her stomach, tears streaming down her face.

....

Red walked down Myrtle Lane, hands shoved in his basketball shorts, shoulders hunched. His parents always hated when he stood or walked that way, and it was basically the one cause for discipline JJ and Jennifer ever had for their younger son. He became angry at himself halfway down the street when he realized he should have brought Miss Sparkles and relieved Ellen of the task of taking her out.

Like his cousin with her advice columns, Red always took walks when he had a sermon to plan, and he was leading his youth ministry YouthLyfe's next meeting. Maybe there was something from this week that he could draw on, a thread that he could pull from all this post-funeral mess and distill into something meaningful. And if he could share it with his kids, maybe that would make it all okay.

The YouthLyfe staff referred to all their attendees as "kids," even though the kids would have hated that, seeing as how they were teen-agers and felt nothing like kids and everything like the adults they

weren't. Most of Red's kids were outgoing, popular even, more interested in YouthLyfe for the social aspect than for the Jesus aspect.

There hadn't been a YouthLyfe chapter in Eulalia when Red was in
high school, and he was glad for that. It would have intimidated him
too much, shy kid that he was. Red hopped on the Jesus train during
freshman year of high school when he got involved in the Fellowship of
Christian Athletes program, which some of the older boys on his cross-
country team encouraged. Red didn't love being around other people;
he could feel their expectations on him like a weight, and that expec-
tation was often to be entertaining and loudmouthed, like his (locally)
famous grandfather, father, and older brother. Unlike them, Red often
found that he didn't quite know what to say to people.

At FCA, people were just happy he was there at all. The leaders, all
seniors, didn't need Red to be loud or funny or smooth; they just needed
bodies in the multipurpose room on Wednesday afternoons. The leaders, three boys and three girls, all seemed so self-assured to Red. They
seemed to have something glowing within them, keeping them warm
from the inside, sparing them the pressure to search for validation in the
wrong places (or what they thought were the wrong places).

He soon realized that the glowing thing in them was their relationship with Jesus. And Jesus! Like nearly everyone in Eulalia, it was a
given that Red identified as a Christian, but it wasn't until FCA that he
really started to understand (or feel like he understood, anyway) what
the love of Jesus really meant. He and his loved ones were saved from
death; all the nightmares that jolted him awake in the middle of the
night, the car crashes that would kill his family, the diseases that would
come for Ellen and Gerry, weren't things he *really* had to worry about.
And he was loved, flawlessly. This was a force of love that didn't hinge
on how good at sports he was, how high his grades were, how funny he
was, or whether or not he had a girlfriend. Red always felt Jennifer's
love, and knew he didn't have to fit into any kind of mold to earn it.
But with FCA, Red really started to understand that while God was the

ultimate father, He wasn't *his* father. Love from a figure like that, a figure that wasn't JJ, filled all the dark holes in Red with a brilliant light.

And there was Stanley. Stanley was a junior when Red was a freshman, and he also ran cross-country. He was the one who encouraged Red to start coming to FCA in the first place. He and Red ran at a similar pace, so they spent countless summer morning training sessions and afternoon practices side by side, matching step for step, running too hard to talk but somehow bonding all the same. While Red wouldn't have described Stanley as outgoing, he never hesitated to reach out to Red—congratulating Red after a good race, inviting him to FCA, giving Red rides to school, practice, and meets.

Stanley had this girlfriend, Grace. They weren't together anymore, but everyone in Eulalia assumed they would be yet another high-school-sweetheart story gone right. Stanley had gone to UGA, Grace to Vanderbilt, and they broke up after first semester. In Red's first few weeks at Vanderbilt, Grace took Red to lunch. But without Stanley, Red found he didn't really know what to say to her. He never wanted to go to lunch with her again, but he appreciated the gesture all the same.

Stanley had married a Georgia girl right after graduation, which Red knew only from Instagram. When Stanley had gone away to college after being what Red would have called a legendary FCA leader his senior year, he promised to keep in touch. Red called him a few times on his way home from cross-country practice, newly licensed but with no one to ride with. Stanley rarely answered, and when he did, he could only ever talk for a few minutes or would send Red a quick text saying sorry he missed him, he was at his new college ministry, or his fraternity chapter meeting, or on a run with friends. On Instagram, Red could see that Stanley was living a vibrant college life: sorority date nights with beautiful girls and midnight (sober) visits to Waffle House and unlimited bowls of cereal in the dining hall. Stanley had moved on, was too busy for Red, and so Red stopped trying.

But Red still had God, and while Stanley's moving on had stung,

God made him untouchable. Not just from Stanley, but also from the constant, lurking feeling that he was disappointing his dad; from his lack of interest in dating, which he knew his family found strange; from the times when his heart would race and his chest would squeeze even though nothing was wrong. The closest human love Red could compare it to was the love he knew Gerry had for him and the family, how Gerry was always pleased just to be around him. He seemed to take delight in all of them, in a way that felt pure. Or so Red had thought.

Maybe Red's sermon should center on human heroes and the idea of idolatry, and how easy it is to idolize people, who are flawed, and place them before God, who is perfect. And how this will inevitably disappoint. And confuse.

He kicked fallen magnolia leaves out of his way as he walked. Even though it was summertime, leaves still covered his neighbor's yard and the sidewalk because magnolia leaves fall all year. This particular tree was in Ms. Tina's yard, and she absolutely and loudly despised it. Magnolia trees had been popping up around the neighborhood at random since before Red was even born. Some miscreant had the audacity to surreptitiously plant the sometimes problem-causing trees without the blessing of the neighborhood association, and it put the whole neighborhood in a tizzy. It was the kind of small-town drama Red told people about in Nashville to make them laugh, to put them at ease.

Maybe there was a sermon somewhere in there. Some metaphor about how the leaves fall all year, and how God's love never stops, no matter what. He bent down and picked up a leaf, squatting and looking at it. He was racking his brain for a verse when a voice made him jump up and out of his sweaty skin.

"Well, hello, Gerald." Red had no idea how he hadn't noticed the tall blond boy he'd clocked at the funeral reception standing right in front of him, sipping a smoothie and pulling his wireless headphones out of his ears. He peered at Red over his oversized sunglasses.

Red felt a flush creeping up his neck that was unrelated to the day's heat. "Um, hey," he croaked out with a voice crack, as though his flush had penetrated his skin and reached his vocal cords. He cleared his throat, tried to return to himself. "Most people call me Red."

"I know who you are," the boy said. He grinned mischievously, and Red wondered if it was physically possible to die of embarrassment. The boy softened his wicked grin into a kinder smile.

"Brady. My parents moved onto the street a few years ago when I started at UGA," he said, sticking out his hand. He gave a strong shake, which surprised Red, given Brady's higher-pitched voice. Then Red remembered that wasn't the proper way to think about these things. "So great to finally meet JJ and Jennifer's sweet boy. You're taller in real life than in photos." He smiled again, which caused Red's blush to finally reach his face.

Red gulped, but Brady didn't say anything else. "Good to meet you, too, man," Red said, shoving his hands and the magnolia leaf in his pockets.

"Your mom is a cheer icon," Brady said. He leaned in conspiratorially. "By the way, I'm home for the next few weeks, just a few doors down. I know y'all are staying in town through Rebecca Bell's wedding, so I'm around if you ever want to . . . hang out." Then he *winked* at Red, which nearly sent him into cardiac arrest. He rubbed the back of his neck, willing the color to be anything other than one resembling a fire truck.

"Oh," Red said, laughing a little even though Brady hadn't made a joke. He cleared his throat and started nervously crunching the magnolia leaf in his pocket. "Listen, I know that . . . but I haven't—"

Brady held up his pointer finger as if he were about to wiggle it at Red, then drew it back to his lips and mimed zipping them shut. Red breathed a sigh of relief, and the muscles in his armpits jumped, as though his brain had instructed his arms to reach out and hug Brady (which would have been insane).

"Well, I'm off," Brady said. "I'll leave you to your . . . leaf." He walked past Red down the street, and Red stood there, feeling like an idiot. He turned around, and just as he did, so did Brady. Brady gave a little wave, and Red turned back around quickly. He dropped the leaf, straightened his shoulders, and started speed walking down the street, wishing he were wearing his running shoes so he could just take off.

⋯⋯⋯⋯⋯⋯

Alice was lying on her back, hiding—or trying to, anyway—behind one of the cream couches in Ellen's living room when the sound of someone saying her name cut through the podcast in her headphones. Her eyes flew open and a man stood at her feet. She blinked and Peter Bell swam into focus.

"Are you okay?" he asked, bending down a little.

"Yes." She pulled her headphones out of her ears and wondered if her ratty old "Life is Good" T-shirt was loose enough to hide the bump Grant had made her worry was noticeable. "I was listening to a podcast."

"Oh," he said. "Cool."

Alice nodded, forcing herself to inhale and exhale while her legs itched to carry her away. It wasn't lost on her that this was the second time in twenty-four hours that she was speaking to Peter from the ground. "What are you doing here?" she asked.

"Sorry, I know—"

"No, I didn't mean, like, WHAT ARE YOU DOING HERE?" Alice adopted a deep, thunderous voice, and it made Peter jump. She cleared her throat. "I just meant like . . . what are you . . . doing here?"

"Yeah, no, got it," he said. He nodded toward the corner of the living room. "Those are my parents' card tables, and they figured y'all would want them out of your hair." He straightened up and walked over to one of the two tables and began breaking it down.

"You didn't have to rush back to your Texan patients?" Alice asked.

"The hospital is letting me stay for the week since I was already going to be here for Rebecca's wedding," Peter said as he kicked a leg in on the collapsible table. "But thank you for piling onto the guilt." He smiled, and she smiled back.

"Make sure to thank Rebecca and your parents for the wedding timing. It's a joy for our family to be trapped together for a week," Alice said as she stood up and walked toward him. Peter smirked and opened his mouth to respond, but Alice just shook her head. "I'm kidding. Here, let me help." She knocked a fist against the table leg, trying to bend it. Grant poked his head from the kitchen into the living room doorframe.

"Hey!" he said, jogging over to Alice and hip-checking her out of the way. "No heavy lifting for you, missy." Alice felt heat creep up her neck and into her face, but Peter, now bent over a different leg, didn't seem to notice Grant's comment. She breathed a sigh of relief. "You need help getting these down the street?" Grant asked Peter as he flipped over the table.

"I got it," Peter said. He gripped each of the card tables' handles, and Alice stared at his hands. He had always had huge hands, even as a kid. Gerry always joked that he was like a puppy with big paws, and one day he would grow into them. Peter had, in fact, grown very tall, but his hands still felt disproportionately large. Alice pictured how small a stethoscope would look in them, how safe his cancer-ridden patients must feel under them.

"I'll walk you out," Alice said, and Grant bounded into the kitchen. She opened the door for Peter, and he waddled out awkwardly into the heat with the tables. He turned around once he was outside and Alice leaned against the doorframe.

He exhaled. "Look," he said. "I have no reason to think you would want to, but would you want to have dinner with me tonight? I—"

Grant squeezed past Alice in the front doorway, his tank top smelling so strongly of sweat that Alice leaned her head back and grimaced.

"Later!" he called as he jogged across the front yard, flipping his hair and interrupting Peter. Before making it to the street, he turned back around.

"Oh, wait, Al," he said. Peter twisted his neck to see him, too. "You know I sometimes sub in and teach a prenatal yoga class at the gym, right? I can totally lead you and the little one through some flows. Just let me know!"

He grinned, patted his stomach, and jogged into his yard, disappearing into his parents' house.

Alice's heart stopped beating and she felt bile rise in her throat. It took Peter an eternity to twist his neck back around to Alice. He looked at her face, and she could only imagine what it must look like. His eyes flitted down to her stomach and back up again.

"Um," he said. Alice opened her mouth to speak, then shut it quickly, no words rising up for release. She opened it again, still nothing came out, so again she closed it. The whole routine made her look like a fish. "You're pregnant?" he asked.

She opened and closed her mouth a third time, then nodded, swallowing in an attempt to push the bile down. He shook his head and scratched the back of it at the same time, which made it look a little like he was trying to rip his head off. Or keep it on.

"Is it . . . I mean, I have to ask. Is it mine?" His eyes were the size of saucers.

She rested her hand on her bump and hoped the way her heart was pounding against her chest wasn't a problem for the baby. She looked at her toes. "Do you want it to be yours?"

Peter sputtered, shocked by the question. It was a big question, especially considering they had been out of touch for years until he texted her in March that he was in New York for a conference, would she like to have a drink? She felt cruel that she had asked it, so she said, "Yeah. Yours."

Peter doubled over, hands on his knees, like he used to do in the summer when they were kids racing up and down Myrtle Lane. It always made Alice feel better to know that even though he always won, he clearly had to try hard to do it. Looking back, she liked that he hadn't let her win.

She searched frantically for something to say, her thoughts bouncing around in her brain like Ping-Pong balls, but nothing clear emerged.

He said, "Holy shit, Alice." He stood up straight, and both of the tables, which had been resting against his legs, fell over. He jumped up a little, shocked by the sound they made hitting the ground. The quickness of the movement, and how spastic it was, made Alice burst into laughter, but she quickly covered her mouth to stifle it. There could not have possibly been a more inappropriate time to laugh.

He looked into her eyes, eyes he'd known his whole life. He saw her right hand covering her laughing mouth, while the left one waved back and forth in front of her and she sputtered, "Sorry, I'm sorry." She meant sorry for laughing in his face after delivering life-changing news, but she also meant sorry for the way this life-changing news was being delivered. And he understood that.

Peter began to laugh, too. He leaned his head back and really laughed, like she just said the funniest joke he had ever heard. They laughed and laughed, maybe for one minute or maybe for three hours.

"Alice!" someone called from inside the house.

"One sec," she called back between gasps.

"I need you!" Carol Anne said. "You promised you'd run lines with me!"

Peter wiped his eyes and caught his breath. Alice felt bashful. "So, uh, yeah, I can do dinner tonight."

Peter nodded, the smile slipping from his face. "Good. It seems we have some things to discuss." But he barely got the sentence out because the giggles came soaring back to him. Alice started laughing again, too, and pressed the door closed, trying, unsuccessfully, to make herself stop.

Chapter 4

Across Myrtle Lane, Jennifer inhaled, like the meditation app her doctor had suggested she download instructed her to do. She knew JJ should do the same, but she also knew that offering the suggestion would only make him more frustrated. His head swiveled from his phone to the mounted TV and back, and his neck grew redder by the second.

Grant and Red sat on the couch, watching their father try to connect his phone to the Bluetooth TV speakers and witnessing his mounting anger as he failed. Either of them could have offered to use their own phone or take a look at JJ's, or could have suggested he make sure his phone wasn't already connected to his wireless printer, which of course it was. Either could have stood up and made sure the TV soundbar was on, asked Jennifer to make sure her phone wasn't already connected to the speaker. But they both sat on their hands, frozen except for their eyes, which looked everywhere but at each other. Or, worse, their parents.

Red actually *wanted* to do something to help, feeling that with every passing moment it was getting harder and harder for him to swallow, and like his heart was lost inside of his own chest. But stronger than the anxiety was the fear of his father's reaction to his trying to help, that he would be pressing a finger on the bruise technology always gave JJ's ego. So he just prayed that the damn thing would connect and they could get on with it. Grant hated the tension his father caused, as he lived by a strict motto of "Good vibes only." But like his younger brother, he knew the only thing that could worsen the vibes would be someone trying to help JJ, and that was not a line of fire Grant was ever trying to be in.

"I can try connecting my phone," Red finally offered, unable to stand the tension any longer. JJ's neck became so red he looked like he belonged to a different species, and the temperature in the room instantly dropped ten degrees.

Jennifer rolled her eyes, sighed, and went to peer over JJ's shoulder. "You're already connected to the printer, JJ," she said harshly. "You have to disconnect from that first, and then connect to the speaker."

JJ jerked his phone away from his wife's eyeline. "Okay, smarty-pants," he said, then swallowed hard when disconnecting from the printer worked. Red visibly relaxed on the couch.

"All right, Mom," Grant said, standing up. "Time to throw it back to your choreo days."

"Oh, please, Grant," Jennifer said, smirking. JJ tapped on his phone to access the song he had paid $1.99 for on iTunes because he didn't understand streaming. That ever-familiar guitar opening started to play so loudly the whole family jumped. Grant started nodding his head and shimmying, riffing on an air guitar. Red felt the urge to laugh.

"*Hey, where did we go . . .*"

"You don't have to play it yet!" Jennifer shouted over the music. JJ paused the song. "We don't even know the moves." She scrolled through her phone to find the video she had saved last week, trying not to roll her eyes as she did so. She still thought a flash mob with their close Eulalia friends at Rebecca's wedding was a stupid idea.

And if Jennifer thought it was a stupid idea, JJ thought it positively unhinged. He hated dancing, especially the idea of doing some kind of *performance*. He figured the worst gift he could give Rebecca would be forcing her and all of her wedding guests to watch him do some corny arm movements to an American classic. His hands grew clammy and he suddenly felt very hot. And Jennifer cutting in with her bossiness certainly didn't help.

"Why don't we all watch the video first?" Grant suggested, getting up to stand by his mother's side while she searched through her texts with Deborah Bell to find the YouTube link. Red flanked her other side, and JJ peered over Jennifer's shoulder. A gangly white couple stood on a porch in a split screen so that viewers could have a front and back view.

"Right hand sweep, right hand sweep, left hand sweep, left hand sweep," the man's monotonous voice bleated through Jennifer's iPhone speaker. Grant and Red laughed quietly.

"Christ, he is not messin' around, huh?" JJ asked, starting to smile, unlike the couple in the video, who wore looks of extreme concentration. Well, at least the man did; all that was still visible of the woman was her backside.

As if the man in the video heard JJ, he continued in his dead voice, with a completely straight face, "Don't forget to have fun with it," while he punched to the left, then right, then left, then right with his fists. The boys burst out laughing, and even Jennifer couldn't help but quietly crack up.

"Maybe we try to do it along with the video first, then try it with the song," Jennifer said once the instructions ended and they had all gotten it together after laughing. The man breaking into a shimmy at the end had really killed them. She played the video again, and they all reluctantly started moving their arms along with the couple.

Jennifer felt silly doing these movements in her trendy, recently re-done living room. She also couldn't help but roll her eyes at how juvenile the choreography was. Maybe this would be cute on the wedding day with everyone doing it, but she felt she was almost insulting her past self by participating in such an asinine routine. Grant looked to Jennifer's iPhone, propped up on the glass coffee table, with real concentration, while Red felt so embarrassed he was practically having an out-of-body experience. JJ barely moved his arms, and his legs felt itchy with his desire to be anywhere else, doing anything else. Though no one except Jennifer even kind of had it down, Grant, for fear of becoming bored, said, "Let's try it with the music. Hit it, Dad."

JJ pressed Play on his phone, but the song wouldn't start. He groaned and mashed the Play button again. Nothing happened.

"Do you have the song downloaded?" Jennifer asked, hand on hip, trying not to roll her eyes.

"Jesus, Jenn," he said stiffly. "You just deal with it, then!" He slammed the phone down on the coffee table in Jennifer's direction.

Grant cleared his throat. "Whoa, whoa," he said gently, his fear of tense situations briefly overcoming his chronic fear of his father. Casting his mind for something to say, he clapped his hands and said, "We can do this. I know this wasn't a thing when y'all were getting married, but this is, like, my fifth mid-wedding-reception flash mob. Don't tell me y'all will be this on edge about dancing whenever I finally find someone to marry."

Jennifer stiffened. Her throat felt like a javelin at the thought of herself and JJ at Grant's wedding, whenever that might be. An unwelcome memory popped up, and she blinked, as though that would erase the reel of her own wedding that was now playing in her head.

Throughout Jennifer's childhood, her father came and went like their home was a resort, a place you visited but didn't stay long-term. When she was little, Jennifer assumed based on a movie she saw that her father was a pilot, and that when he was away it was because he was flying planes, transporting people all over the world in the sky. As an adolescent, she realized she didn't actually know what in the hell he was doing, and she was in her late teens when she answered a phone call not meant for her, and discovered she and her mother were not the only family he had.

That was when she stopped speaking to her father. The half-assedness of it all bothered her more than she could stand, and she concluded she would rather just not deal with him. He was not invited to her wedding, a fact that was somehow not conveyed to the DJ she and JJ hired for the reception.

"Aaaaaaaall right, folks," the sunglasses-wearing man (indoors, at night) crooned into the mic. "Please gather round for the father-daughter dance." Everyone froze, and the room's chatter instantly sank to silence. But there was no quiet for Jennifer; in fact, there was a deafening roar in her suddenly burning ears. JJ turned to her in his white tux and blinked, squeezed her hand, but she couldn't move.

She felt a tap on her shoulder and spun, looked directly into Gerry's eyes. He smiled, and to this day, she could see the crinkly skin around them like he was in the room, right in front of her. Gerry took Jennifer's hand out of JJ's, led her to the dance floor, and they swayed in the middle of it, like two palm trees in an ocean breeze.

Jennifer didn't cry when JJ proposed, or when she saw herself in her wedding dress, or when she walked herself down the aisle. She was clear-eyed and full-throated when they said their vows, exchanged rings, and kissed for the first time as man and wife. But then, when she was swaying with Gerry, leaning practically her full weight on him, all broken nerves, the tears slid out of her eyes like they had someplace to be. Gerry could feel her body quaking with the sobs. Jennifer looked so wrecked she would forever push away the photos from that part of her wedding night. She didn't remember the song, wasn't even aware of it at the time, but she remembered how it picked up tempo and Gerry spun her out and started dancing that little jig he always danced and she laughed and did it, too, and their guests spilled onto the dance floor and JJ enveloped her in a hug.

"Mom?" Grant asked, jolting Jennifer back to the present. "When do we come in again?"

They heard a knock at the door. Jennifer turned to answer it, trying to pull her shoulders down, away from her ears. The memory of her wedding had tensed her up. She opened the door and the tension snapped right back as she looked into the young face of JJ's associate producer. *Stephie*.

There was a quick, sour, sick moment when Jennifer expected the girl to widen her eyes in shock, for her words to trip over themselves as she realized JJ's wife was home, that she was supposed to come to the back door, or on a different day, or whatever. But she did no such thing. She just smiled and said brightly, "Hi, Jennifer!"

Jennifer's eyes narrowed and she could feel her neck vein beginning to bulge. "Stephanie," she said, the corners of her lips quickly turning up in a terrifying and fast smile before immediately settling back down into a frown. "What are you—"

"Stephie!" JJ said, pulling the door open wider, standing behind his wife, who turned to see him genuinely smiling like his father hadn't just died and been publicly disgraced by his lover. "Everything good?"

"Yep," she said, pulling a stack of papers out of her bag. "Buck said he's been emailing you the reports, but I know you like them printed, so I figured I'd drop them off."

"Aw, Stephie, that's—"

"Pretty out of your way, isn't it?" Jennifer asked, crossing her arms over her chest.

"Jennifer . . ." JJ started to say.

"Not really!" Stephanie said, shaking her head emphatically. She smiled. "It's a small town."

"Big-city girl," JJ said, and she laughed familiarly, this clearly some repartee they shared. Jennifer walked away like she had been called elsewhere, though the house was silent. She stood at the front window and watched her husband escort Stephanie to her little sedan, parked unevenly against the curb like she was a fucking idiot. JJ used lots of hand gestures when he spoke to her, at one point mimicked throwing a football. Jennifer felt hungover, nauseated.

"Everything okay, Mom?" Jennifer jumped at her younger son's voice.

"Yeah, yeah," she said, turning from the window and heading upstairs, though she had nothing to do up there.

Red looked out the window and scratched the back of his head. He realized his dad probably wouldn't consent to practicing the flash mob again, at least not in front of all of them. Red thought this was a shame. Surprisingly, something about dancing with his family made him feel more settled than he had in a long time.

....

Alice and Delia were thirty-two and twenty-seven now, but they felt exactly as they had at seventeen and twelve, Alice sitting at her grandmother's vanity putting on what was still a minimal and rare amount of makeup, Delia lying on her grandparents' floral bedspread, chin in her hands, watching her older sister get ready for a date. With the same guy.

"When was the last time you two went on a date?" Delia asked.

"Does the time we got catch-up drinks because he was staying in the city for a conference and he accidentally knocked me up count?" Alice asked.

"Did he pay?" Delia asked.

Alice thought. "Yes."

"It was a date."

"Is that how you tell these days?" Alice asked.

"Well, I haven't exactly *dated* in, you know, four years. But yeah, I think so. Going dutch is what you do with your friends. I'm not saying the guy has to pay, but one person treating another person is what makes it feel like a date. It's romantic."

Connor paid for his first date with Delia, when they got Moscow mules at a tiny bar in the West Village. He had teased her for her Southern accent, and she loved the way his face lit up when he talked about his mom (Delia didn't know at the time she was a stiff Connecticut WASP with whom she would never get along). She texted Alice on the way home and said, "He's the one." The memory made Delia's eyes feel like they weighed one thousand pounds.

"Okay, then by that standard, fourteen weeks ago was the last time we went on a date."

"Before that."

"Um," Alice said. "I mean, the summer before my senior year of high school, I guess."

"So, fifteen years ago?" Delia said.

"I guess. Wow."

Alice stood and pulled a light gray, short-sleeved, extremely billowy shirt over her head and looked at herself in the mirror. "You can't be serious," said Delia, who couldn't imagine experiencing an increase in boob size and hiding it under all that fabric.

"I mean, it's not like I haven't been on *a* date in fifteen years, just not one with this particular gentleman, jeez. I'm not Mom."

"But she might be hotter than you if that's what you're planning on wearing!" Delia said.

"My only other option is the shirt I wore on the plane or the dress I'm wearing to Rebecca's wedding. What should I do, raid Gram's closet?" Alice said.

"I mean, maybe," Delia said.

"I don't know if you're aware," Alice said, "but the rapid weight gain associated with, you know, growing a child inside of you doesn't exactly a hot date make. I don't know how to be sexy right now!" She sat back down at Ellen's vanity with a huff.

Delia stood up and walked over to her sister, stroked her shoulder. "Would you say you ever really knew how to look sexy, though?" she asked.

Alice laughed and started yanking a brush through her red hair with a vengeance. She hadn't let it get this long in years, and Delia noticed how pretty and thick and shiny it was. She had heard pregnancy changed a woman's hair, and it seemed that Alice's gorgeous hair would just get more gorgeous, even if Alice considered being a redhead a curse.

"No, Delia, I wouldn't," Alice said. "Would you like to help or just criticize?"

"Let me see what I brought," Delia said. She jogged upstairs, rifled through her suitcase, and realized she had the perfect option. Delia was a good packer and a generous sharer of clothes, had been all her life. She loved being the benevolent girl who always had *just the thing* to perfect a friend's outfit.

She swirled into her grandmother's room holding the summer dress that had magically appeared in her mailbox weeks ago (if ordering something after drinking too much wine to remember doing so could be considered magic). It was light blue, with fluttery sleeves and a low neckline, gathering under the bust and hanging down past the knee with a loose fit. "Prairie chic," Delia said.

Alice pulled it on and looked at herself in the mirror, while Delia stood behind and poked her head out from Alice's left side. "Yeah," Delia said. "You're welcome." This had been happening for as long as Delia could pick out clothes for her sister—she would choose something for Alice, or even let Alice borrow something of hers once they were the same size, and the glamour Alice felt or the ease or the combination of the two would make her promise herself that she was going to get better at finding clothes that were the right fit for her, that she actually liked and would be excited to wear, instead of just picking things out based on whether they were comfortable and/or on sale. But then, whenever she got the urge to go shopping just for the hell of it, she became exhausted almost immediately upon entering the store, and would tell herself her clothes were fine and head home.

"Do you think Connor cheated?" Delia asked.

Alice's brows furrowed in the mirror as she looked into her sister's reflection. "You know I don't think he did, Deel," she said. "He's not that kind of guy."

And he wasn't. Connor actually *liked* for Delia to always know where he was. Before things started to deteriorate between them, he called her nearly every time he was in transit, going from the office to drinks with a client, from drinks to a quick stop at Duane Reade, even though he was minutes away from seeing her at their apartment at that point. He would keep her on the line sometimes even when he was checking out, and she acted like it drove her crazy, even though it never did. Tears stung her eyes when she thought about how much she would like to hear him interacting with a cashier now. Anger quickly flushed out the tears when it occurred to her he might be making those calls now, but to someone else.

The doorbell pinged through the house, and Alice and Delia both looked up in alarm and gasped. Then they both laughed at the absurdity of it. Maybe no time had passed at all, and this was Alice and Peter's first date, and they were fourteen and Delia was so enamored by the very idea of a date she could barely stand it. Everyone else was across the street, and Alice felt the same relief she felt those summers when Gerry and Ellen would be out, and no one would have to pass her off to Peter. She opened the door, and there he stood, holding *flowers*, for God's sake, looking somehow the same as he always had, and for a second, Alice allowed herself to feel that she was simply a girl going to spend a summer night with a boy she liked.

"Hey," he said, smiling.

"Hey."

"And hey," Peter said, nodding toward Alice's stomach, breaking the teen spell.

"Did you just say hey to the fetus?" Alice said.

"Yeah, I . . . Sorry," Peter said.

"Don't keep her out too late!" Delia said, poking her head into the doorframe. "Wouldn't want anything unchristian to happen."

"Wouldn't dream of it," Peter said.

From the backyard, Ellen heard the doorbell ring, and was relieved she didn't have to answer it. The flat, fenced-in backyard wasn't much except for her and Gerry's garden, tucked away in the western corner next to the shed Gerry had built himself. She stood there, looking at what they had planted: the shrub roses, the hydrangeas, the squash, the tomatoes. She had waited all day to come out here, wanting to check on her flowers and get out of the stuffy house but rightfully fearing the heat. If Gerry were here, he never would have missed the doorbell ringing, would have bounded to the front porch like a golden retriever.

But Gerry wasn't here, and Ellen didn't much feel like talking to anyone. She looked at the hydrangea bush and tutted, shaking her head. She thought it looked . . . fine? Gerry was the one with the green thumb. They had tended this garden together for as long as they had lived in the house, over fifty years. Ellen assumed she had picked up enough from watching him to be able to come out here, check on things, and do the appropriate work that needed to be done. But she stood still, realizing all she ever really did back here was follow Gerry's lead, take his directions.

She sighed and slid her gardening gloves off, wiped some sweat off her forehead even though this was supposed to be the coolest part of the day. Magic hour. She saw the hydrangeas, the rosebush, could see a green tomato looking sizable on the vine and a squash that seemed ready to her, but was it really? Linda and Fred had always gardened together, too. Linda was brilliant in a garden; her mother had been a florist. Ellen wondered if Fred felt this helpless when Linda passed. Surely he couldn't have, because when Linda passed, Fred still had Gerry. He wasn't alone like she was now, looking at a garden she'd thought she understood, realizing she didn't know the first thing about it.

....

Across the street, Red and Grant stopped their game of one-on-one basketball to wave as Peter drove off with Alice. Inside, JJ, Carol Anne, Wilma, and Robert sat around JJ and Jennifer's living room. A baseball game was muted on the TV, but this didn't stop JJ's eyes from constantly wandering over to it, then quickly flitting back to his siblings.

"I'd be glad to stay here for a while with Mama," Wilma was saying. "It shouldn't be hard for me to set up my monitor in the basement, and I can edit down there. I'll obviously need to go to Atlanta for shoots, but I can probably do most of my work from here."

JJ nodded. "I can check in on her every day, multiple times a day, if we need," he said. "Although I'm sure that'll drive her crazy."

"Well, it sounds like I'm not really needed around here, anyway, then," Carol Anne said from behind her dripping Korean face mask. "Of course, I'd love to be here as much as possible to support Mama and everything, but a lot of my auditions are so last-minute, it could really hurt my career to be unable to pop by a casting director's office at a moment's notice."

"You also have school in the fall," Robert said gently.

Carol Anne nodded and waved her hand. "Yeah, that, too." She didn't like to be reminded of her day job as a middle school drama teacher, even though it was how she had met Robert, who taught math.

Wilma double-blinked, then looked over at JJ, who was already looking at her, shaking his head. She shrugged and smiled toothlessly, unsurprised that Carol Anne wouldn't be helpful moving forward. No one said anything for a moment, and Jennifer came into the room, hair in a bun, baby blue workout outfit on, on the way to the kitchen.

"Going to work out, Jennifer?" Wilma asked.

"Sure am," Jennifer said from the kitchen as she filled up her water bottle.

"I really only thrive in workout-class settings," said Carol Anne, whose physique did not suggest she worked out often. "Good for you for finding the motivation to just hit the gym and lead yourself."

"A new workout studio opened up on Mable," Jennifer said. "They have high-intensity classes and everything, that's what I'm going to now. I really recommend it."

"Yeah, if you're trying to light your money on fire," JJ said, turning to his sisters. "It costs about an arm and a leg for one of those classes."

"Well, good thing it's not your money, huh, JJ," Jennifer said. It was meant to be muttered under her breath, but they all heard her loudly and clearly. JJ twitched in his armchair and said nothing in response.

"Speaking of money," Carol Anne said, jumping a little as Jennifer slammed the door on her way out, "and bear in mind, I of course hate to ask this. But it's going to have to come up at some point."

"Annie," Wilma said warningly.

Carol Anne paid her no mind. "What do we think the situation is going to be with Daddy's will?"

"Annie," Wilma said again, more sternly, in the voice she used on the girls when they were little and would try to sneak cookies or watch shows they knew they weren't supposed to.

"I'm just wondering!" Carol Anne said, throwing her hands up on either side of her caftan-clad shoulders. "He was such a saver, Daddy was. There's gotta be a lot, and I'm just wondering about the . . . process. Don't act like it hasn't even crossed your mind."

"Shouldn't you believe that you, I don't know, already have every-thing you need or some sort of spiritual bullshit?" JJ asked.

"Well, of course I believe that everything I need is already within me. I believe that for you, as well," she said, nodding benevolently toward her big brother. "But I'm also wondering if we're about to get a lot of money."

"It's all going to Mama," Wilma said.

JJ turned to her, quickly enough that some Triscuit crumbs fell off his T-shirt. "How do you know that?"

"I'm the witness on their will," she said. "I signed it a few years back. It's all going to Mama, and there are some bonds for the kids. That's it until . . . That's it for now."

JJ's eyes narrowed in suspicion. "How come I'm not the witness? Hell, I've been right across the street for thirty years."

Wilma shrugged and looked at the floor.

Carol Anne sighed dramatically (as if she ever did anything that *wasn't* dramatic) and slumped back in her armchair. Robert patted her knee. "Well . . ." She paused for an ostentatious pull of her weed pen. "It may not be as much as we think it is, anyway," she said as she exhaled.

"What makes you say that?" JJ asked in an exasperated sigh, waving his arm around even though there was no smoke.

"People who keep secret lovers are probably spending money on them. A lifelong secret lover? That's *lots* of cash. And who knows if Fred was even the only one," Carol Anne said, matter-of-fact.

JJ shot up from his chair and let out something like a yelp. He started pacing around the room and shaking his head back and forth quickly, like a wet dog. "JESUS, Carol Anne!" he said.

Now it was Carol Anne's turn to double-blink. "What?" she said, looking to Wilma.

Wilma shook her head at her sister. "Not necessary, Annie," she said.

"I wasn't trying to say something necessary!" Carol Anne said. "I'm just saying something that might be true! I'm sorry that's so difficult for the both of you." And with that, she stood up and stormed out of the house, slamming the newly painted door so hard behind her it shook in its frame. Robert still sat on the couch, looking uncomfortable. They all sat in silence for a moment.

"Rebecca Bell's wedding should be fun," Robert said nervously. "I love weddings, always cry." He swallowed. "I'll go check on her." He unfolded his long legs and slipped out of the house.

"What a piece of fucking work," JJ said when he was gone.

"Him or her?"

"Her. Well, I guess him, too. I don't know."

"I don't think Daddy would have been hemorrhaging money on Fred or anybody else. He's not . . . He wasn't stupid." Wilma swallowed a lump in her throat. "He was always real good with—"

"Oh, come on, Wilma!" JJ said, stopping his pacing and boring his eyes into his favorite sister. "Anybody else? There wasn't anybody else! There wasn't even Fred in . . . in that way! Christ!"

Wilma sat quietly for a moment. "Don't you think Fred would have corrected himself by now if he hadn't meant it?"

"He called the house this morning."

"Oh," Wilma said. "Did you talk to him?"

"No."

"Did anyone?"

"Yes. Jennifer. Apparently he apologized for ruining the eulogy," JJ said, turning and staring out the window.

"So, not to take it back," Wilma said quietly.

"Wilma," JJ said warningly, in a voice not unlike the one she had only just used on Carol Anne. "Don't."

She sighed, though not loudly enough for JJ to hear. She didn't have the energy to fight him on this, and didn't really see the point in it anyway. How much could forgiving someone matter if they were already gone?

....

"Do you take all your baby mamas to Mellow Mushroom?" Alice asked as she slid into a booth, sucking in as though her tummy couldn't fit behind the table, even though it easily did.

"It was this or Mama June's, and a buffet just felt . . . not classy enough for the occasion," Peter said.

When Peter was in New York City for an oncology conference three months earlier, they sipped martinis at a hotel bar in the Flatiron District. Alice was nervous to see him—their postadolescent interactions consisted only of their families' annual Christmas Eve gathering. It also didn't help that she hadn't been on a date in over a year, even though she kept telling herself this wasn't a date. Just old friends catching up. Sitting across from him at a Mellow Mushroom in Eulalia, Georgia, felt far more natural, and Alice found she wasn't nervous at all. They had frequented the lightly psychedelic-themed pizza joint when they were teenagers, and it had barely changed, though Peter, wearing contact lenses and a button-down, certainly had (not that she ever minded his glasses and superhero T-shirts).

"I found something," Peter said.

"I feel like when you're a cancer doctor, you can't just say that to people."

Peter laughed, which Alice loved. She wondered how long they could keep acting like this before they had to be grown-ups and discuss what needed to be discussed. He pulled an envelope folded in half out of his pocket and slid it across the table. It was addressed to him, and Wilma's Atlanta address was scribbled in the top-left corner. She peeked into the already-opened envelope and pulled out a piece of paper—clearly torn out of a notebook, not loose-leaf; the frayed edge was worn. There was a penciled curlicue line covered in daisies snaking up the margin, Alice's go-to middle and high school doodle. Every now and then, when she was on a call or supposed to be jotting down ideas for her column, she caught herself drawing it. The letter was dated October 1, 2004. It read:

Dear Peter,

I'm writing this to you from math class, which you know I freaking HATE. I have a much nicer teacher this year than the one I complained to you about all summer, the one with the sweating problem. I feel bad now that I complained about him so much for two reasons. The first is that he's a nice guy, and just because he sweats a lot and I suck at math doesn't mean that I should have free rein to spend an entire season (summer) talking shit about him. He was always patient with me asking so many questions, even though it still annoyed me that if he had just explained it better the first time, I wouldn't have had to ask.

The second reason I feel bad is because I feel like I should not have wasted a single second that I got to spend with you complaining about math. I mean, jeez. I always know when I'm with you that I'm having fun, and it's rare to have fun like that with a guy. In those moments with you, I didn't think I was taking anything for granted. But now that I'm sitting here trying (sort of) to understand calculus, I wish I had spent every moment with you being 100 percent glad that I was. But I guess that would have been kinda weird.

How is student training going with the football team? I'm so happy for you that you got picked to do that. I knew you would, even though I have no idea how Eulalia High works. Uncle JJ can't wait for Grant to try out for the team next year, and that's about all I know. And I'm even happy for you despite the fact that this means you can't drive to Atlanta to go to Homecoming with me. It's okay, though, a group of us are going without guys and I think it'll be really fun to just have a night with the girls. But I wish I could share it with you.

I'll IM you when I get home, probably. I just wanted to write you this letter because I'm bored. And I think it's fun to get mail. But mostly because I miss you.

Love, Alice

Alice put her head in her hands, reading aloud, "'. . . trying (sort of) to understand calculus.' Jesus. I clearly wasn't trying AT ALL. No wonder that was the only C I ever got."

She finished the rest of the letter in silence, cringing at her writing. The mention of IM made her chuckle, and she remembered how Christopher Smythe, the asshat she sat next to in that class, had tried to read every letter she wrote to Peter when she was supposed to be taking notes. He once referred to Peter as her "imaginary boyfriend," and she hated then and she hated now how much she stammered when she tried to defend herself. It was weak, and she knew that it made him look right. It also made it all the more confusing when he drunkenly professed his love for her at Senior Beach Week after graduation.

"I found it today in my closet—they're all in a box together, actually, so there's more if you want to read them," Peter said. Alice knew exactly which box in her childhood closet held the letters and cards and notes Peter had sent her. She cringed realizing that their entire correspondence could be resurrected. She wondered if he'd happened upon the letters, or if he went looking for them.

"Only if there's one where I share what actually happened at homecoming. I'm on the edge of my seat now," Alice said.

"Always the writer," Peter said. "Even then."

"Oh, God," Alice said, wishing more strongly than she had in the last fourteen weeks that she could have a drink. She disliked talking about her writing, especially with people who knew nothing about it. And no, she didn't consider someone reading it to mean they really *knew* anything about it. And Peter probably didn't even read her work.

"Speaking of your writing," Peter said, "I don't think I've ever told you how much I loved your piece on Michelle Branch."

Alice almost spit out the sip of water she had been pretending was vodka. "What?"

"I LOVED YOUR PIECE ON MICHELLE BRANCH," he repeated.

"You read that?"

"Of course," Peter said, furrowing his eyebrows in a way that Alice would have found comical were she not so horrified at the idea of Peter reading her stuff. "I read all your work." Alice blinked. Surely he didn't mean *all* of her work. She wrote an advice column weekly, and regularly contributed to staff roundups for the online magazine. The Michelle Branch piece was a deep cut. Not even Delia or Wilma read *all* of her work. She was fairly certain not even her editor did.

Peter's eyebrows slowly unfurled and he shifted in his seat. "Is that weird?" he asked. "I mean, I don't read it in, like, a stalker way. But it's not every day that your ex-girlfriend is a famous writer. I mean, we were kids, sorry if it's weird to be like 'my ex-girlfriend, la la la.' What I mean is that the only other published writers that I know have been published in medical journals, and that's just . . . not the same thing. And I told you at the Christmas party a few years ago how much I loved your book—"

"Let's not talk about the book," Alice said. Alice never wanted to talk about the book. The fucking book.

"Right, right, I knew you hated talking about the book and I guess you still do and I'll respect that, even though I don't really see why, because it's so genius. And even the *New York Times*—"

"Peter."

"Fine, fine. I just like your writing, okay? I'm a fan. Sue me!"

Alice loved her job, but talking about writing made her feel ill, which was part of why she had needed to get the hell out of the community she found herself in during the publication of the fucking book. Her disdain for the whole thing came into sharp focus at her book party, when seemingly every conversation she had about her book went the same way. Alice's book was a novel about a young twenty-something who moves from a small town in Georgia to New York City to pursue her dream of becoming an actress ("Not from Atlanta! And not a writer!" Alice would repeatedly chime to confirm it was not about her) and is forced to reckon with how damaging a lot of her Christian, Southern upbringing was to her, particularly with regards to sexuality. Its title was *As the Belle Rolls*, and there was a joint on the cover. To Alice, it felt like every chat at that party went from sparkling compliments to a condescending skewering of the South from people who had never spent time there.

She didn't say much back to these editors and publicists and assistants and random hangers-on, unsure of how a person was supposed to act at a book party, even though it was her own, even though it was at the Strand (a bookstore she practically lived in), and even though she knew everyone was jealous of the stellar *New York Times* review she had gotten. For a debut, at age twenty-seven! What they didn't know was how many strings her agent had pulled to even get an advanced copy on the reviewer's desk (not even Alice knew they were sleeping together), and what they couldn't know then was that the book would go on to sell approximately four copies.

But of course, it would be a lie to say she wasn't flattered, and she felt pleasure snaking out of her chest and up her neck at the thought of Peter reading, and enjoying, what she wrote. "Well," Alice said, unsure of what more to say, landing bravely on "I won't sue you."

"Good," he said.

Alice stared at her menu, only pretending to read it because the words might as well have been in a different language. Anxiety began to seep into her skin like steam. Was she supposed to ask Peter how his succulent was, because they had joked about it on what was, according to Delia, their most recent date? Or was she supposed to just ask him if he wanted to co-parent this baby, if he had debt, what his view was on religion with regards to raising a child? Should she tell him she had been wanting to leave New York for a while, and this felt like the right time, but she didn't know where to go? Or was it okay to keep it light-hearted in the name of reacquainting herself with the *father of her baby*?

He said, "How's the attempt at being a vegetarian going? I'm wondering what my chances with getting away with some pepperonis are here."

She said, "I'm not ready to get married."

Peter's jaw dropped, and he let out an unnaturally loud guffaw, which embarrassed both of them. Not that Alice could really be more embarrassed, considering what she had just said.

"Oh, God," she said. "I'm sorry. I don't know where that came from."

"I really meant pepperoni . . . That wasn't, like, a coded proposal," Peter said, laughing a little, even though nothing about what she said had been particularly funny.

"No, no, of course," she said. "I don't even, like, not want . . . I don't know what I want. I wasn't planning on saying that. I didn't even know that I was thinking that. That was a weird thing to say because of course that's not what you're thinking. Well, I don't know what you're thinking. You probably don't even know what you're thinking, I mean, you've known about this for, what, six hours?" She was sweating, and her words were picking up speed. "It's just, like, I know how old-fashioned people here are, but I'm not ready to get married, even though I'm pregnant and everyone around here thinks I'm one thousand years old."

"You're thirty-two . . ."

"I know, Peter, I know I'm thirty-two! In New York, I'm practically considered a child!" She took a sip of water, and it felt very cold in her throat. "Sorry."

"You don't have to marry me, Alice," Peter said. "No one's gonna make you do that."

Alice nodded. "Cool," she said.

He maintained eye contact and nodded slowly, like she was a kid who fell down and he was trying to convince her that she wasn't hurt, just scared. To Alice's surprise, it kind of worked. She took another sip of her water.

"I don't know exactly what I'm supposed to say here," he said. "I've never quite been in this situation before." Now it was Alice's turn to nod. "But I am—"

"You don't have to say anything now," Alice said in a rush. He opened his mouth to protest and her nodding morphed into an almost violent headshake. He shut his mouth.

"Okay," he said. "But—"

"Twenty-four hours. You deserve at least twenty-four hours. It's a lot to process."

....

JJ fidgeted in the chair, his thick football thighs bouncing off each other. Jennifer watched from her perch on the arm of the chair, disgusted. When she first met JJ, when he was interviewing her after she and the competitive cheer squad she coached won another national title, she was attracted to his solidity. He was stocky, didn't jump around on his feet or fidget with his hands, and his gaze held steady, too. He seemed sturdy, like a landing pad; she was used to even the most solid-seeming dudes squirming in her presence, a competitive woman who knew her way around a gym and didn't take any shit.

Maybe it was a grief thing, the fidgeting; maybe getting plunged into this new, fatherless life was making him anxious. Or maybe it was the nerves, she thought to herself, the sick guilt he was feeling from the affair he was carrying on with *Stephie*. Not that she had any concrete evidence of this, but the thought made her shoulders tighten in anger.

They were in the Bennetts' living room for the neighborhood association meeting. JJ and Jennifer were always neighborly, especially considering JJ had grown up on Myrtle Lane. This neighborhood was as much a part of his identity as his fingerprint. But they had only started attending the meetings in the last few years, when Jennifer had gotten her real estate license. These meetings were a good hub for gossip about whose house would be next on the market, and it was also just helpful for her to be informed of the goings-on of the neighborhood, since most of the homes she sold were in it.

They had friends on the street, so it wasn't like JJ actually hated the meetings, but that didn't stop him from pretending to hate the meetings and making a big stink whenever it was time to go to one. Like with church or shopping, because Jennifer was the one demanding they go, he felt he had a right to grumble about it.

The whole family was pretty sure Gerry was the only one who actually *enjoyed* the meetings. He held no official role in the neighborhood association, but since he was the longest-attending member of the neighborhood and one of the most popular, most decisions were made with consideration for his opinion. There were the official ones, like when there was a vote to request a taller street sign marking Myrtle Lane so that kids would stop stealing it, many people voted no just because Gerry did (he couldn't help but love a little hell-raising). And there were the unofficial ones, like when Charlie and Deborah Bell, with a two-year-old Peter, first moved onto the street thirty years earlier, and were the first Black family to do so. When they walked into their first neighborhood association meeting, there was a palpable awkwardness until Gerry welcomed them with his trademark enthusiasm, and any uncertainty in the air vanished.

JJ felt like his stomach had instantly hollowed out upon remembering that Gerry wouldn't be at the meeting. Still in a post-funeral haze, he didn't feel like the full weight of Gerry's death had settled on him yet. He had thought picking out the headstone would make it a little more real, but the whole thing had been too irritating for the emotion to find a place to grip in him. This, the neighborhood association meeting, of all things, knowing there would be no Gerry to crack jokes and stay later than everyone else socializing, activated JJ's pain.

Ellen had opted to skip the meeting, which JJ understood. But JJ didn't feel like he had a choice in going when he imagined what the neighbors would think if he didn't show. He had nothing to hide, nothing to be ashamed of, as far as he was concerned, and he wouldn't have anyone thinking otherwise.

Jennifer suspected his willingness to come was to appease her, to distract her from his affair. She wondered if she could get away with sitting somewhere else, so bothersome was JJ's fidgeting, and JJ generally, to her. But then Tom Bennett stood up in front of his fireplace and cleared his throat, and the twangy chatter died down.

"Not much on the agenda tonight," he began, as he began every meeting. "But I do want to mention that I received an email about the magnolia problem from the head of the Dixie Neighborhood Association. There's a new one that popped up about a month ago on Carter."

Some people chuckled. Bob Jett actually threw his head back and hooted. Some sighed; some grumbled. Charlie and Deborah Bell groaned; they were days away from throwing a wedding and did not have time for this. Mrs. Shirston rolled her eyes like she had never been more bored, while gossipy Tina raised her painted-on eyebrows and perked up. After the week she had had with Gerry's funeral, no one would have expected her to give a rat's ass about the magnolia problem. But she wasn't picky.

JJ raised his hands and slapped them down on his bouncing thighs, completely exasperated. It made Jennifer want to scream. The neighborhood association had been complaining about the "magnolia problem" for years, for what felt like almost as long as Jennifer had lived in the neighborhood. Sometimes it was once a year; sometimes there would be a sneak attack where a bunch would crop up in a single week. The rub was that some mystery person liked to plant magnolia trees, ranging from tiny baby trees to teen saplings, randomly and across town, but the pattern showed them cropping up mostly in their neighborhood and near it. Not that there was far to go in Eulalia, anyway.

This might not sound unpleasant. Trees are objectively good—until they get to be huge and fall on your house, and with magnolia trees in particular, there was the issue of the nut litter, and for Tom Bennett's youngest child, a crippling allergy, though no one in their neighborhood had ever heard of anyone being allergic to magnolia trees and everyone assumed (rightly) Tom just wanted something to blame for his child's asthma. Gerry always thought the magnolia problem was hilarious, and would laugh loudly whenever the subject was raised at this meeting. He referred to the issue as "Magnolia P.I."

It all bored Jennifer. Nature, like most things, made her impatient, and she didn't understand why everyone got so worked up about some trees that would only *maybe* become a problem after most of the people in that room were dead. She needed to know who was putting what on the market and when, whose renovation was going well and whose wasn't. Her brain was too packed to make room for a big tree with long branches, thick, shiny leaves, and the occasional gorgeous bloom. Who cared?

"Happy?" JJ said in a low voice through gritted teeth up into Jennifer's ear, even though she hadn't even forced him there that night. Jennifer might have been annoyed before, but she skyrocketed to irate immediately.

"I need to know this shit," she said, also through gritted teeth, "so I can keep bringing home the bacon, sweetie."

JJ's buzzed head twitched like a fly was on him. Bringing up the fact that for the last two years Jennifer had made more money than JJ was the lowest blow she could have dealt, and that was precisely why she dealt it.

....

Several houses down, in Ellen's kitchen, Delia and Wilma went back and forth trying to decide which of the many dropped-off-from-friends Tupperware dinners they should heat up. Ellen wasn't hungry, which was unfortunate considering the volume of food in her house. She hadn't been hungry since Gerry's heart attack. Tonight, the thought of eating didn't actively disgust her, though, which felt like progress.

She had sat at the kitchen table for a while, after she came in from staring helplessly at her garden in the twilight. But as Wilma and Delia argued about Tina's lasagna, Ellen could feel how often Wilma's widened eyes would wander over to her, give her a scan. Like she was an

X-ray that could see emotional damage. Ellen didn't much feel like being examined, so she wandered out of the kitchen, padded her bare feet over the shag carpet, down the hall past her bedroom, and into the laundry room.

Ellen had always loved the laundry room, partially because she held the conviction that nothing smelled better than laundry detergent, and partially because no one else ever went in there. It was just a big closet, basically, a tiny room slapped onto the side of the house, with a small window facing the trees and bushes that separated their property from the Sandells' next door. When either the washer or the dryer was going, the sound overtook the room, bouncing off the tile floor and reverberating between the light blue walls, so that she couldn't hear anything in the house. No kids calling her name, no Gerry asking what was for dinner, no telephone ringing.

She sighed as she shut the door behind her, thankful she had unnecessarily put some towels in the wash earlier just for something to do, so the sound enveloped her, and for a small moment, everything else fell away. It was just the whoosh of the machine in her ears, the air-conditioning on her sweaty blouse and chinos, the cool of the tile under her feet. But the moment ended quickly. As much as she had craved solitude, it hit her like a gust of wind that after a few days, her visitors would go back to their lives, and solitude would be her only option.

The realization made her torso feel completely empty. She put her wrinkly hand around the doorknob to stop feeling like she was going to float away, to remind herself that she was grounded, here, on the tile. She swallowed. She didn't know if this grief was something she could face alone.

....

The next morning, Red went for a run. Despite having grown up running in the Eulalia summer heat, he had never gotten used to feeling the rivers of sweat snake down his legs as they hit the pavement. He guessed he could fill a baby pool, at least.

He picked up speed at the end, started sprinting when JJ and Jennifer's mailbox came into view, then slowed down when he passed it as if it were a finish line. He knew from his years of cross-country that he was supposed to stand up straight and raise his hands above his head to avoid his abs cramping up, but he ignored this knowledge and bent over, hands on his knees, panting. Even though he ran almost daily to help alleviate his anxiety, he had forgotten how much more taxing it was to move through that thick South Georgia air.

"Hi, Red."

He shot right up, the pain in his cramped abs provoking a sharp intake of breath. Sweat blurred his vision, but he blinked the moisture away to see Brady standing in front of him, pushing those same oversized sunglasses up on his head, wrist weights strapped on his arms, not looking sweaty at all. Even though Red knew it would appear indistinguishable from the flush the run had brought to his face, he could feel a different kind of blush creeping up his neck.

"Hey, Brady," he said. "Brady, right?" he added in a futile attempt to appear nonchalant.

"Yeah," Brady said, raising an eyebrow, as if they hadn't talked on this very street merely a few days earlier.

"What are you . . . ?" Red started to ask, not sure where he was planning on going with this sentence. "Um. What brings you to . . . the street today?"

"I live on it," Brady said, narrowing his eyes and smiling, but mercifully not calling Red out on the fact that they had already previously discussed this. "Well, my parents do anyway, two houses back." He jerked his head back and to the left side of Myrtle.

"Cool," Red said, feeling like too much of a jackass to explain that he meant to ask Brady what brought him out on this walk, not why he was on Myrtle Lane. He wiped the salty sweat from his mouth. Brady continued looking at him. "Do you, uh, like it?"

"I don't really know it," Brady said. "My parents moved here when I was a sophomore at Georgia. I grew up in Vidalia, so I've only been here on breaks and stuff."

"Ah," Red said.

"Enough about me. *Jennifer* tells me you live in Nashville?" Brady said, emphasizing the fact that Jennifer told him, that this was not information he would have found any other way. "And you work for a church or something?"

"A youth ministry," Red said. "YouthLyfe."

"Ah, yes, I'm familiar," Brady said, a smile stretching across his face. "'Lyfe' with a *y* so I'm to understand that it's, like, *hip*, right?"

Red chuckled, but also thought he might die of embarrassment. "It's a pretty dumb name, can't argue with you there."

"There was a chapter at my high school. It was a fun social scene for a while, but then someone gave a talk on the evils of homosexuality, you know, the Georgia of it all," Brady said. "So I saw myself out."

"Oh," Red said, bending down to tie his already-tied shoelace. "I'm sorry for that. That wouldn't happen at our chapter," he said to his shoe.

"Would it not?" Brady asked, cocking an eyebrow.

Red looked up at him and blushed. He stood up. "No, the organization as a whole has gotten a lot more . . . open-minded in the last couple years about that stuff."

"I'm sure it has," Brady said, looking Red up and down.

"Um," Red said, casting his mind for something to say. "Are you gonna be in Eulalia all summer?"

"God, no," Brady said. "Only a few more weeks. I'm moving to New York July first."

"Whoa, New York," said Red, who immediately wondered how

Brady interpreted such a vague statement, because not even Red knew
what he meant by it. "Cool."

"Definitely a lot cooler than here," Brady said. "No offense."

"None taken," Red said. "Well. I better go."

And before Brady could say anything else, Red spun around quickly
and speed walked into the house, not bothering to say hello to Jennifer,
who was doing squats in front of *Million Dollar Listing*. He bolted right
to the bathroom and locked the door. The sweat on him had chilled,
but he turned the shower on before he undressed, running it as cold as
it could go.

Chapter 5

When Wilma walked into Ellen's kitchen, Carol Anne was sitting at the table, writing in a journal. "Where's Robert?" Wilma asked.

"He's on a run or something," Carol Anne said. She went back to journaling and said, "By the way, I consulted my horoscope, and I think it would be best for you to take my new headshots later this week." Wilma sighed quietly; she should have known at some point Carol Anne would demand new headshots.

"Sounds good," she said, knowing there was no way out of it (not that Wilma was particularly prone to trying to weasel her way out of anything helpful).

Wilma started to walk out of the room, when Carol Anne said, "Oh, I received a lovely Facebook message from Derek Saab about Daddy. He said he enjoyed meeting you."

"He did?" Wilma asked, halting her step. Her brow furrowed. This was certainly a surprise.

"Yes," Carol Anne said. Her pen kept moving, and Wilma wondered how she could journal and hold a conversation at the same time, how Carol Anne could even see the page clearly, considering the dark paneled wood of the kitchen and the fact that all the lights were off. She craned her neck a little to take a peek at Carol Anne's notebook. She was just drawing concentric circles all over the page. "We ended up having a little chat and thought it could be fun if we all went to dinner, like a little double date or something. We're going tomorrow."

Wilma's jaw dropped, but she snapped it back into place as quickly as she could. A spark of annoyance lit up in her chest. "Well. Were you going to . . . ask me if I wanted to do this, or . . . ?"

Carol Anne didn't look up from her journal. "It'll be fun!"

"Okay, but you didn't think it may make me feel a little, I don't know, strange to go on a date with Daddy's . . . funeral director?"

Carol Anne cocked her head to the side in her trademark look of confusion, although Wilma had come to suspect that Carol Anne wasn't actually confused that often; it was closer to a curiosity as to how everyone couldn't see things just as she did.

"He wasn't Daddy's funeral director," she said. "And I don't see the problem. He's always had a beautiful spirit and, judging by his Facebook photos, a smokin'-hot bod. I could sense a good energy from him. And it would actually be really good for you to go on a date. Delia told me you never go on dates. You're not required to be lonely, you know."

Wilma blinked and suddenly felt very small. She cast her eyes about the dark-paneled kitchen, and they landed on the framed needlepoint mounted above the doorway that read, "When I Count My Blessings, I Count You Twice."

"I'm not lonely," she said.

Carol Anne went back to her circles. "Gino's tomorrow night at seven," she said, dropping her pen, picking up her phone, and looking at her eyebrows in the front-facing camera.

Wilma opened her mouth to say something, then realized it would be pointless. She exited the kitchen, beneath the needlepoint, while Carol Anne called after her, "Don't worry! We'll find you something to wear!"

....

Later, at the same table, Delia closed her work laptop as soon as her grandmother sat down in a wicker chair next to her.

"When did you start wearing glasses, honey?" Ellen asked as she entered the kitchen and found her granddaughter there, squinting at her laptop and sitting at what looked to be an uncomfortable angle to avoid the slant of hot afternoon light that fell across the doily-covered table.

Delia straightened up, instinctively raising her hand to touch the bottom frame of the left lens. "I don't, really. They're blue-light glasses, they help protect my eyes from my screen."

Ellen smiled. "Know what would protect them best?" she asked.

"Hm?" Delia asked, knowing full well what was coming next. But Ellen was one of the only people for whom Delia was willing to scale back her know-it-all tendencies.

"Not looking at so many screens."

"Very true," Delia said. "But gotta pay the bills somehow." She bit her lip to avoid complaining about how she was in her third month of being responsible for her apartment's total rent instead of just half, one of the many costs of her breakup. Ellen hadn't been a huge fan of Delia living in sin and, truth be told, she hadn't been a huge fan of Connor, either. Two years earlier, he had planned to spend Christmas with the family, but canceled last minute because he felt too guilty and anxious to miss Christmas with his own family, which Delia understood. He felt that he'd more than made up for it the next year, but Ellen wasn't one to make a place setting for someone and then forget about it when it went unused.

"Work is okay with you taking the week off?" Ellen asked.

"I can do enough remotely that I can make it work, and it's not like it made sense to go back to New York, just to turn right back around for the wedding." Delia paused, realizing that Rebecca's wedding would mark her first unused plus-one in years. She cleared her throat and continued, "I just want to stay on top of it right now even though I'm out. Someone above me is leaving soon and I want to get promoted."

"Oh, that's great, sweetie, I know you'll get picked," Ellen said, even though she hardly understood Delia's job, much less the intricacies and politics of her office. Delia did digital marketing for a startup called PanTEE, an underwear company. PanTEE's goal was to revolutionize women's underwear. The company claimed to eliminate the often-necessary choice between comfort and sexiness, and Delia was responsible for plastering their slogan, "A T-shirt for your nethers," on as much of the internet as she could. She felt good about her chances for the promotion, especially considering the success of her brainchild, the "PanTEE Grabs Back" campaign. It also helped that she had worked harder than she ever had post-breakup, as the job provided something to focus on outside of Connor memories and wine and the lies of the romantic comedies she spitefully watched nightly.

"Thanks, Gram," Delia said. "We'll see. How are you holding up?"

"Oh, fine," Ellen said, bending down to adjust her slippers, not without difficulty, Delia noticed.

She bent down and said, "Here, let me help you."

"No, no, I got it," Ellen said, repositioning the slipper and sitting back up, taking a deep breath as though she had exercised. "I think it's time for some new ones. I've about worn these out."

"Where do you get them?" Delia asked.

"Belk," Ellen said. "I know just the ones I like and I'll be so sad when they stop makin' 'em. Your grandfather would pick them up for me on his way home from work when I needed a new pair. And men aren't really good at that kind of thing, usually. But you know how he always paid attention to clothes and shoes. Sometimes it was nice. Sometimes

I just didn't want to be commented on." She chuckled, but looked without focus somewhere above Delia's head.

Delia wondered if Ellen was about to draw a connection between what she just said and the fact that her husband had been sleeping with a man, but Ellen didn't say anything else. She was thinking about the fact that Gerry would never pick up her shoes on his way home from work again. She wouldn't have guessed that this would feel anything more than inconvenient, but the realization had totally enveloped her. Stolen her breath.

"Well, I'd be happy to go to Belk for you, or I bet we can find them online, and then they can get delivered right to your door," Delia said.

"Oh, I don't know about all that," Ellen said, returning to the moment.

"I think you would like online shopping, Gram, seriously. It's easy. I order stuff to my apartment all the time."

"You do?" Ellen asked. Delia nodded. Ellen said, "But the more you leave the house, the more you have a chance of meeting men, like at the grocery store."

Delia laughed; she couldn't help it. "And how does one meet men at the grocery store, Gram?"

"I had a friend when I was young named Sissy. I wonder what happened to Sissy. Anyway, she went on a date with a man she really liked, I think she had met him at a party. And they had a great time and everything, but then he didn't call her. She was real anxious about it but then some other man asked her out and she started seeing this other man. One night, she was gonna cook supper for him, so she went to the grocery store. She was putting all the things you put in a cart when you're making dinner for a man, you know, two steaks, two potatoes, so on. And who should she run into but that first man who never called. They chatted for a bit, and she said she could see him peekin' into her cart, seeing clearly that she was going to be cooking dinner for another man. Well, I guess he didn't like that because he called her the next day. They ended up getting married," Ellen said, laughing. "Although I don't know what became of them. She was kind of fast, but I liked her."

Delia leaned in while Ellen was speaking, relishing her grandmother's storytelling. It was always Gerry who was the talker, Ellen the quiet one. Delia had long admired how her grandparents balanced each other out, how one pushed where the other pulled in perfect harmony. Clearly, things had not been perfect, but now Delia smiled seeing Ellen smile, and wondered if Ellen would share more, now that there was more space in the house. But then, as she so often did in those days, Delia darkened. She said in a flat, dead voice, "So you're saying I shouldn't use Amazon because I might trick a man I run into at a store into falling in love with me?"

Ellen clucked and shook her head. "No. You don't need to trick anybody. Although . . . it did work for Sissy."

"Good for Sissy," Delia said, smiling again with her mouth but not with her eyes, letting her greasy bangs fall over them. "I'll keep her in mind."

"You'll have to get back out there sometime, sweetie, if you really think it's over with that young man," Ellen said. Delia cringed at Ellen calling Connor that, like she hadn't met him several times over the span of four years. Maybe Ellen had already forgotten him. Considering that he had said nothing after seeing the news about Gerry, it was as if Delia could physically feel him evaporating out of her life. She hadn't expected anything to hurt worse than when he actually walked out the door, but this slow fade did.

"I don't know," Delia said. "It feels kind of soon. Between you and me, I don't think I'm quite over him just yet."

"Oh, really," Ellen said, nodding as though this was news. She reached out and patted her granddaughter's hand. "That's okay, sweetie."

"That's interesting that your friend thought she was done with that guy, but she ended up marrying him," Delia said, drumming her gelled nails over her laptop.

Ellen frowned. "Well, they had been on one date and he hadn't called her in a little bit. He hadn't done anything really bad. And then"—Ellen looked right into Delia's brown eyes—"*he* called *her*. She didn't go cha-sin' him. It's not like she was reaching for a man who was reaching in the opposite direction."

Delia swallowed a knot in her throat and felt the Williams blush—very uncharacteristic for her—making its way up her neck.

"Can I ask?" Delia said after a moment, flipping her hand upside down so it held her grandmother's. "After, I mean, the time you've had the last few days, I wouldn't have necessarily guessed that you would be encouraging me to go out and meet men."

Ellen pulled her hand from Delia's and rested it on the table. She sighed. "Well," she said, looking over Delia's head and out the window into the backyard, "I hadn't thought about it like that. But look at what I have." She nodded toward Delia, squeezing her hand. "I have you and your cousins and Alice and your mom and Carol Anne and JJ. There's a lot to be thankful for," she said, frowning. Delia nodded and Ellen continued, "I know that you young women are doing things differently and you have different options than I did. If you don't care about men, and *that's*"—she nodded to the closed laptop—"the thing that matters to you right now, that's okay. But I guess what I'm trying to say is, no matter what happens, and I've seen some things happen to some people, no one that I know has ever regretted starting a family."

"Including you?" Delia asked, even though she knew the answer.

Ellen tutted and playfully smacked her hand. "*Especially* me."

Delia swallowed a new, tight knot in her throat, pecked her grand-mother on the head, and went off to take a shower. Ellen continued to sit at the kitchen table, staring out the window into the backyard, wondering if she had just lied to her granddaughter.

Chapter 6

JJ woke up angry. Even if he hadn't already decided to go back to work, he would have violently thrown on his work clothes (khaki pants and a University of Georgia collared shirt), slammed both his front door and the door to his precious F-150, and stomped the gas pedal as though he were trying to kill a rodent, anyway. He felt like the walls—not only of his house but also of his childhood home across the street—were closing in on him.

He usually liked having the boys home; it felt natural to him to see them around the house, to throw a head nod their way or grunt a "good morning." He was no good on the phone. Plus, it was a nice distraction for him and Jennifer, and their presence was like a vacuum for some of their tension.

But now he felt like everyone in his family was a vessel of thoughts and feelings about what Fred said at the funeral. He was paranoid that each of them had some desire buzzing just below the surface to talk about it, and talking about it was the absolute last thing JJ wanted to do. There was certainly no respite across the street, what with the concerned eyes of Wilma and the cloud hanging over Ellen. Of course Carol Anne didn't seem too worried about any of it, but that was also offensive to JJ, partially because everything that Carol Anne did was offensive to JJ.

And then, of course, there was Jennifer's attitude and last night's comment at the neighborhood association meeting. He didn't know when she had gotten so angry, but he was pretty sure it had to do with her getting so into her work.

Going to the station would help. He was in charge there, and while he felt like he was mostly friendly, he knew that everyone there was a little bit scared of him, too, and would likely avoid eye contact. That would be good. They were in the midst of the NBA Finals, and the NASCAR All-Star Race, and he'd slap on his headphones and talk about them. He'd go over paperwork, look through his emails, bounce his rubber band ball, unable to hear anything outside of his office over the roar of the air-conditioning.

He had just started to relax when his strings were pulled uncomfortably tight yet again by a small black bug flying around his car. It knocked into the side of his face like it had some kind of personal problem with him, and JJ growled like a caged animal. He swatted it away, but less than a minute later he saw it crawling up the driver-side window. He smacked the glass but was a millisecond too slow, and it buzzed behind him.

Now would have been the time for JJ to take some of the deep breaths he and Jennifer had read online would lower their high blood pressure, but stopping to breathe was not JJ's thing. He knew what the bug was: a carpet beetle. Though he had scoffed at the magnolia problem the night before, this was a rare instance in which JJ understood the annoyance: magnolia trees attracted beetles that also loved carpet. Gerry had always had a carpet beetle issue in his truck, as he parked near a mystery magnolia at work.

Larvae in his carpet were the absolute last thing JJ needed. He cursed the fact that Red had driven his car in from Nashville, and Grant from Atlanta, forcing JJ to park down the street under a magnolia tree. He kept his car clean, but if there was some kind of infestation . . . well, while JJ never would have used the term "mental breakdown," it's safe to say his beloved F-150 crawling with baby beetles would have undone him.

He whipped into his VIP parking space and shoved the door open, practically spilling out of the truck like the ton of angry bricks he was. He growled yet again as the beetle flew out, and he slammed the door to lock it out. He stalked around the side of the truck to open the passenger-side door, then made his way around, opening every door to lean over and inspect the carpets, pulling them out of the car and flapping them over the asphalt.

There was nothing. It was just the one beetle. No real damage had been done, but instead of feeling relief, the anger that had entered JJ's bloodstream continued to course through him like a drug. Somehow, the thought that he wouldn't be able to tell Gerry about this close call permeated his anger, and he felt his father's absence like it had settled into his very body. It was enough to make him stop dead in his tracks a few feet from the front door.

Horrifyingly, he felt a lump forming in his throat, and he shook his head as if he could shake it out. He caught his reflection in the glass door, gave his third growl of the morning, and pushed through into the office entryway, the AC blasting him like a hose that could wash away everything.

....

Alice and Ellen were flipping through photo albums when Peter called. Seeing his name on her phone screen thickened the perfume of nostalgia Alice felt looking at the old photographs. She bit her lip and quickly flipped the page upon seeing a photo of Fred and Gerry, wearing cowboy hats, arms around each other at a horse ring. They were both smiling big and looked to be around forty. There was a photo of Fred and Gerry leaning against Gerry's old truck on the next page, which she also flipped quickly. She brought her phone to her ear.

"It's been twenty-four hours," Peter said. "I'll pick you up in five."

"Where are we going?"

"You'll see." And he hung up.

Outside, Grant flicked his wrist, sending raindrops of sweat and his basketball soaring. It bounced off the rim and he dropped his head back, dreading the short jog to get it. It was too hot for outdoor exercise, but for Grant it was something of a relief compared to the frigidity of his parents' tension.

That morning, he and Jennifer had been downing protein shakes and scrolling through their phones side by side in a peaceful silence when JJ walked into the kitchen and said, "You know those things will kill you."

Grant raised his eyebrows as he watched his mother's knuckles go white, clutching her phone, like something out of a horror film. He cleared his throat. "Nah, I think I beat the whole cell-phones-give-you-brain-tumors thing with my AirPods. Phone's never close to the noggin."

JJ narrowed his eyes. "Not the phone." He dipped his head sharply toward the thick cream-colored sludge in Grant's Eulalia High Football stadium cup. "Those. Saw it on the news."

Grant grinned and shook his head. "I'll make you one before your next workout. Trust me, you will be whistling a different tune. This has upped my game at the gym, like, astronomically."

"Oh, I didn't realize you were drinking it *for work*," JJ said sarcastically. Grant shifted in his seat, face-planting into his father's insult but desperate to avoid conflict.

"Hey!" Jennifer said. "What are you, mad that our son does what he loves for a living instead of watching other people do it, sitting on his ass and talking about it?" Just like that, Jennifer felt the vow she made herself during her morning meditation—to be nice to her husband on account of his grief—dissolve.

JJ's previously narrowed eyes widened so quickly it would have been comical had the air not been sucked out of the room. Before he could respond, Grant said, "Mmkay, see y'all later," rushed out of the kitchen, grabbed the basketball from the hall closet, and found himself here, shooting hoops in the unforgiving heat, continuing even after JJ went to work.

Grant had always loved basketball, though he wasn't as naturally gifted on the court as he was on the football field, mostly due to his stocky build. JJ loved that his son was a lineman, the exact mirror of what he had been in high school and college. But Grant didn't get the same joy from the sport that his father clearly had. He much preferred basketball; it was less overwhelming, and the games themselves were shorter, allowing him to get to the after-party quicker. Plus, he liked the group of basketball guys more; they weren't so *serious* about it all.

But his talent for football was still undeniable, and he happened to have been on arguably the best team Eulalia High had seen since his father's years, which had been arguably the best team since Fred and Gerry were in high school. Grant knew this because the night of the state championship game his senior year, JJ gave him a coin so rusted and old Grant thought it was a piece of hardened soil at first, but it was no such thing. It had been Fred's lucky penny, though anything marking it as a penny had been rubbed off by Fred, who was given the penny by *his* father. JJ didn't remember why Fred's father found it lucky, or where he got it in the first place, but he did know that Fred had hidden it in the lining of his left cleat for his state championship game his senior year of Eulalia High, and they won, with Fred scoring the game-winning touchdown. Linda was head cheerleader, and it was that night that she decided she would marry Fred, though she never told him that.

Fred passed it on to JJ before his senior-year state championship game, when everyone knew that while Eulalia had a perfect record, it would take a miracle to beat Tuckson High, whose players all looked like they were in their mid-thirties. Fred had stopped by the house on his morning bike ride that game day and waited in the driveway until JJ pulled his first truck out to go to school. Fred explained the penny's lore and JJ, honored that a Eulalia High football legend would bestow such a gift upon him (even though he was basically JJ's second father), sealed it in his cleat. And they won, with JJ scoring the game-winning touchdown.

So, JJ knocked softly on Grant's door the night before *Grant's* senior-year state championship game, which was bizarre, because JJ wasn't much of a knocker, and certainly not a soft one. Grant was in bed, innocently (thankfully) flipping through a *Sports Illustrated*, hands where JJ could see 'em, when JJ somberly walked in and sat slowly on Grant's desk chair. Grant's first thought was that he was in trouble—JJ had found his stash of booze, heard about his failed chem test, or discovered that Grant had snuck out the night before for a blow job from Cindy Truett.

But it was the coin, and unlike most things, Grant took the responsibility for it seriously. He wanted to make JJ proud, and Fred, too, the Eulalia High football legend. He took the coin, slipped it under the insert on his left cleat, and theatrically lost the championship.

Losing didn't bother Grant the way it seemed to bother everyone else. It took more than a football game to keep Grant down for long, full of helium as he was. What bothered him was that the loss froze his house into a tundra; JJ couldn't even look at him. JJ had scored his game-winning touchdown on a turnover; he and Grant both played defense. Did he really expect lightning to strike the same place twice?

Was it Grant's best game? No. Was it one of his worst? Actually, yes. But not for lack of trying, and he wasn't alone—the whole team seemed to be off that night. People were upset about it enough at school, the air too thick with disappointment for Grant's lighthearted jokes and charm with the ladies to travel down the hall. And for home to be no reprieve, well, it bummed Grant out. He started eating dinner most nights at Gerry and Ellen's across the street. Gerry and Ellen were delighted to have him, and JJ inwardly nodded and approved of the new habit; he felt it made sense that Grant was too ashamed to eat dinner with his father after such a whopping disappointment, after everything (meaning, the old penny) JJ had given him. That iciness just wasn't Grant's vibe. In contrast, Gerry and Ellen had stopped caring about the game on their drive home from the stadium that chilly November night.

After one of those dinners, when Ellen was washing the plates (though Gerry and Grant had pretty much cleaned theirs spotless, only chicken bones remaining), Grant said, leaning back in his chair, "Ugh." (He was a teenager at the time.) "I so do not want to go home."

"Now, why's that?" Gerry asked, studying the toothpick he had just plucked from between his lips.

"Dad is, like, giving me the *hard* cold shoulder. He can't even look at me since the game."

Gerry nodded slowly. "That right?" he asked. Grant nodded. Ellen kept washing the dishes.

"I mean, it's like, I know that it's a bummer that we lost," Grant said. "But what am I supposed to do, spend the rest of my senior year being all depressed about it? Basketball season starts in a week, which I like more anyway. I just can't understand why he's so bummed out."

"Men always need something to be upset about," Ellen said into the running sink. No one heard her.

"Your father loves his sports," Gerry said. "Gets real emotional about 'em. Always been that way. I s'pose that's part of why he's so good at his job. But you and me, we ain't like that. We bounce back. And you listen here, that's a good thing."

"Yeah, I guess," Grant said.

"Why don't we go for a drive?" Gerry said. "Get some ice cream?" Grant smiled, never too old to find dessert exciting, one of his and Gerry's similarities.

The sun was setting when they bumped along in Gerry's truck to the Cream Dream, which was just a trailer in a parking lot. They sat on a bench and ate chocolate cones in silence, occasionally laughing at some young girls doing a little dance routine for their parents on the bench next to theirs. They drove back to the house, Grant went home, and that was that.

Grant shook his head when he realized the moisture obscuring his basketball shot was not sweat, but tears brought on by the memory of eating ice cream with his grandfather, the wallop of the fact that it would never happen again. He wiggled his shoulders as if to shake this realization out of himself, then lazily chased the ball as it rolled down the driveway. He saw a woman running down the street as he brought the ball back up to his chest, and his eyes scanned her sneakers, her toned legs, the part of her midriff revealed by her shirt riding up, and, finally, her face. Grant and Rebecca Bell locked eyes. She slowed down and pulled her headphones out.

"Hey, Bell," he said. "Out for a little afternoon jog?"

"I mean, yeah, but why do you have to make it sound . . . creepy?" she asked, trying to catch her breath. Grant shrugged and grinned.

"Keepin' it tight for the wedding," he said. "Respect. Though let it be known, I'd marry you even if you had to be carted down the aisle by a forklift."

Across the street, Alice waited on the porch steps for Peter to pick her up, even though it was approximately one million degrees out, two million with humidity. She raised her hand to wave to Rebecca, who was too busy chatting with Grant to notice. Alice's legs bounced up and down on the step with nervous energy, as the weight of today's conversation plunked itself down in her head. She was embarrassed to realize that she also felt slightly giddy and sugar-drunk at the thought of this boy picking her up from the porch, just like he used to on summer days like this one. But she wasn't a teenager; she was thirty-two. And the film that had settled on her life, the residue that being a real person in the real world for thirty-two years will bring, made it impossible for her to feel excited without the added self-judgment. Also, her stomach felt tight and not in a good way, and she had been on the cusp of a burp for the last two hours.

Peter rolled up in his mom's Lexus, which was at least fifteen years old. Alice recognized it because it was the site where she saw Peter's penis for the first time, or any penis outside of a health textbook. This only amplified her complicated mood. He tilted his head forward and down to peek at her through the rolled-down, passenger-side window.

"Hey," he said. "Anyone's hand I need to come in and shake?"

"Well," Alice said, "if you mean that in the patriarchal sense, which you do, my father is not in there, as he never really is anywhere near me, and my grandfather isn't in there because he's dead." She didn't get up from her seat.

Peter pursed his lips and nodded thoughtfully. "Sweet," he said. "So are you getting in or what?"

Alice smiled and, with what she feared was a noticeable amount of effort, leaned forward and lifted herself up to walk to Peter's car. The air-conditioning hit her skin immediately, and it might have felt better than Peter knocking her up did. She opened her mouth to say so, then remembered she had sprung a lot on him in the last twenty-four hours. The least she could do was avoid comparing his lovemaking abilities to the HVAC situation of his mom's Lexus.

"Nice ride," she went with instead.

"Yeah. Good times in here," he said, reaching over and squeezing her knee before putting his hand back on the steering wheel and peeling back into the road, moving at approximately five miles an hour. It was such a small gesture, the knee squeeze. But it made her feel wanted and safe, and out of nowhere she felt herself actively holding back tears. It really was a bitch to be pregnant and grieving at the same time. Of course, it was also possible that Peter simply had that effect on her.

"Why are you being sketchy about where we're going?" Alice asked, wondering when Peter had purchased the designer Wayfarer sunglasses he was wearing. Had he picked them out himself? Or had a girlfriend? Did he balk at the price, holding his breath and pushing down nausea as he shelled out two hundred bucks for an admittedly flattering and handsome piece of plastic and glass? Or did he hand over his credit card without a second thought, paying it off in full that month with autopay?

"Don't say it like that," he said. "It's a surprise, yeesh, I'm not kidnappin' ya. Although . . . I'm surprised it's a surprise." Alice furrowed her eyebrows. "Just thought you woulda figured it out by now."

They had turned onto the main road, but he peeled off on a dirt road, and Alice's eyebrows unfurrowed, and the corners of her mouth crept up. "Ah" was all she said.

When Peter parked the car, they got out and entered the woods without saying a word, the river birch trees in the woods shielding them from the oppressive afternoon sun. Soon enough—though not as soon as memory would have had her believe—Alice and Peter emerged from the last of the brush and into a clearing. Everyone called it the swimming hole, and Gerry had referred to it as a river, but it was really just a creek, muddy but pleasantly babbling. Deep enough to swim in, even to jump in. Alice looked to her left and, sure enough, a rope swing still hung from the same magnolia branch that reached over the water, but it looked brand-new. The bright yellow of it shocked her, although she knew it would have been blatantly hazardous if kids were still swinging off the same one she and Peter had used almost two decades ago.

The dirt on the creek's ledge looked dustier and drier than she remembered, and the magnolia tree seemed smaller. She wondered if it was even fun to swing into the water; it seemed so anticlimactic from where she stood now. Neither of them spoke. Peter bent down and started untying the laces of Alice's sneakers, and she let him. She braced her left toes on the back of her right heel, yanking her swollen ankle out of her shoe and then doing the same thing on the other side while Peter untied his low-top Vans and slid them off. The fact that he wasn't wearing socks momentarily disgusted her, but that quickly disappeared when he, still bent down, reached over and held her pale ankle and tried to peel off her damp yellowed sock.

"Oh, Peter, don't," she said. "I have famously sweaty feet. You'll pass out."

"I'm a doctor, Alice," he said. "I've seen worse. And smelled worse. And you don't have to remind me of your sweaty feet. I remember them."

"Well, that's . . ." Alice paused, genuinely unsure what it was. "Mortifying."

"It's really not." He walked away from her and lightly jumped off the little ledge and into the water so he was knee-deep.

"Is the sand rocky today?" she asked.

"Smooth as butter."

She walked over and stepped down slowly into the water, letting a sigh of relief escape at how good it felt. It was the perfect amount of cool, and the gentle pull of the water flowing downstream was like a balm.

"You know it's very triggering that you brought me here," she said, smiling at the water she made murky by kicking at the sand around her feet. He looked over at her, and the quickness with which he snapped his neck in her direction made her look up at him. He looked completely horrified, like she had just told him she was pregnant with a dragon. Which was actually how she had expected him to look at her when he found out she was pregnant with a human.

"I'm kidding," she said, her round face stretching itself wide in a smile. He deflated with relief, lightly shoving her shoulder. "Careful," she said, putting her hand on her slightly swollen abdomen. "Precious cargo."

"Yeah," he said. She liked that he brought her to what had been their spot. Like something out of *The Notebook*, Peter, Alice, the cousins, and basically every youth in town at some point—or most likely several points—over a Eulalia summer made their way over to the swimming hole, usually bringing a cooler filled with beer, or a joint for the edgier kids.

But it felt like just theirs. There had been a few precious days when Alice and Peter had been able to swing off the rope swing, paddle around, eat Minute Maid frozen lemonade, and float on inflatable tubes without anyone else around. Sometimes, they would bring books and lie on towels, only going in the water when they got overheated, which happened quickly and frequently. They were often distracted from their books anyway, horny teens in love that they were.

One day when they were seventeen, the summer before their senior year, they were floating on separate tubes. Alice had her face tipped up to the sun, her red hair, which had been very long that summer, drifting in the water. She was practically asleep when Peter said, "I think we should have sex."

Alice snapped her head up like a wasp had stung her sunburned stomach. It wasn't like this sentiment was a surprise to her—they came close enough to sex every time they hooked up, which was pretty much daily. But neither of them had said anything about it, and she had sort of thought it would just happen. She didn't realize it would be a whole . . . conversation.

"Um," she said. "Like right now?"

Peter laughed a laugh that wasn't his, clearly relieving more tension than usual after having worked up the nerve to make such a bold state-ment. "I meant just, like, whenever," he said.

"Oh," Alice said. She knew she was supposed to hesitate and be un-sure. She knew she was supposed to cry to her mom about it, maybe, or talk to her best friend on the phone, perhaps journal. She knew she was supposed to really think critically about this huge decision that she had been made to believe would change her life forever, before finding the perfect outfit and wearing the perfect panties that were somehow girly and womanly at the same time. She knew she was supposed to say no at first, and wait for Peter to ask again, to throw a rock at her bedroom window, which she would open and climb through so she could shimmy down the side of the house and leap breathlessly into his arms. She knew she was supposed to kiss him and say, solemnly yet somehow also with excitement, "I'm ready." Then she would give him her virginity and he would give her his, and they would each treasure it forever, and would remain in love forever, because that was how that worked.

But Alice had already known what she wanted. "For sure," she said. "Groovy."

They decided to go back to the swimming hole that night, even though she usually preferred the field when the sun was down. Something about it just felt right. She didn't want to be outside by the actual creek, in case someone else came upon them, so they laid down in the back seat of his mom's Lexus, and laid a towel down, as well, because she knew from her friends that it was likely she would bleed. He had a condom he had purchased with shaking hands at a pharmacy two towns over, for fear that he would run into someone he knew. Which was a completely legitimate fear in a town as small as Eulalia.

When it finally came time for entry ("finally" meaning about two and a half minutes into making out), Alice knew she had to relax. And nothing was less relaxing to Alice than knowing that she should relax. He tried to push himself into her, but it was like a walrus trying to get through a peephole. Neither of them was sure he was even in the right place, let alone approaching from the proper angle and with the correct amount of pressure.

She tried to help guide him in, going off instinct. At one point, they both felt a sliver of relief and spike of excitement when it seemed like he was going to break in, ecstatic that he had at least found the right spot. She pulled on his back, trying to bring him into her body, but neither he nor she would budge down there. At first, he was apologizing repeatedly, and she was shh-ing him softly and telling him it was okay. "I'm sorry," she finally said.

"Let's stop."

"No, no," she said, hoisting her legs up further, hoping that would help, even though she felt the scratchiness of the towel digging into her sunburned back. "We can do it." He pushed again, softly, but nothing happened. He added a little more strength to it, and she yelped out in pain.

"Oh, God, Alice, I'm sorry, I'm sorry," he said, pulling himself up onto his knees and kissing her cheeks, resting on his elbows.

"No, it's okay, it's okay," Alice said, though she felt the tears coming. "I figured it would hurt. We just have to get through it the first time, then it'll be good."

He lifted his head up, looking into the brown eyes she had told him she wished were blue but he thought were just fine. More than fine, actually. She looked back up at him and a tear escaped. He wiped it away, his brows knitting together, and his eyes seemed to Alice like they were growing larger in the dark every second with concern. And with love; that was there, too.

"I can't hurt you, Al," he said.

Alice had been naked with Peter many times by then, but she had never felt it more than she did in that moment. She had never felt safer, either.

"Okay," she said, relieved. All of her earlier resolve that she wanted this to happen and wanted it to happen as soon as possible had disappeared.

He leaned back down and planted his lips on her forehead, holding them there for a long time, pressing his palms into the sides of her head while tears slid down her cheeks. She wasn't quite sure why. "I love you, okay?" he whispered.

She nodded almost imperceptibly so that he would feel it but not have to move his lips or his hands, because she wanted them to stay there. "I know," she said, because she did. "I love you, too."

"So," Peter said, jolting her back to the present, to her swollen feet and ankles in the water, to Peter shoving his hands in his pockets. "I've

had my twenty-four hours." He looked up, right at her, and she wished
she had brought sunglasses.

"Yeah," Alice said. "And I understand if you want more time. You
can take as much time as you need."

"Why didn't you tell me before?" It occurred to Alice how insane
it was that there was no anger, not even an ounce of annoyance in his
voice as he asked this. She took a step closer to him and saw his brown
eyes, opened wider than usual.

"Well," she said, "I found out, like, six weeks ago or whatever. And
then it took me a sec to figure out what I was going to do. At first, I was
like, okay, well, obviously I'm just gonna nip this in the bud, but I've
been wanting to make a change and it just felt like this could be the
thing that got me off my ass and *made* me change my life. And I know
I want kids, and it's not like I have unlimited time and a 100 percent
guarantee that I'll get another chance. So I decided to keep it." Peter
nodded, and Alice appreciated that he was letting her work her way to
the answer. "So then, I knew I needed to tell you. And you had texted
me and everything and that was nice and I'm sorry I didn't respond.
But I didn't know how to just call you and tell you this, and I knew I
would be seeing you at your sister's wedding, so I procrastinated, basically. Obviously, I wish Grant hadn't blown it, but I was going to tell
you this week. Plus, they say you're not supposed to tell people until
twelve weeks, anyway, and I'm only a little past that."

"I don't think that rule applies to the father, but I hear you," Peter
said, nodding and looking solemn. Alice turned and moved toward the
ledge, sitting on it and keeping her legs in the water. Peter did the same,
his knees comically higher than hers. They were quiet for a moment.

"Well, I want you to know that I'm in. I realize that I don't know
what I mean by that at this point. I don't know if you would want me to
move for you or what you want this to look like. But you should know
that I'm in for whatever's best for this kid. *In* in, like I want to be as

involved as you'll let me be." Peter exhaled, having said that all very quickly.

Alice's stomach knotted. Not in a bad way, but it was like her body was snapping her in as close to the moment as she could get because it knew that she needed to know this was real. This was happening. She was having a conversation with the father of her baby about raising that baby. This was her life she was discussing, and . . . *its* future life.

Alice exhaled, too. "Okay," she said quietly, trying to force back all the questions that had been bouncing around her brain like tennis balls every time she had considered telling him. Questions like: Would you move for this? Should I move to Austin? Can we split costs, like, fifty-fifty? How much do we need to keep each other updated on our own lives if we aren't going to be together? She looked at Peter and burst into laughter, which was not very nice, because he looked absolutely terrified, his face almost totally drained of color. "I'm sorry, I'm sorry," she said, catching her breath. "You just looked so afraid."

"Well, yeah, because I just told you I'm in for raising a kid with you and you just said, 'Okay,' and looked bummed out," he said, splashing her. She splashed him back, but much harder, and he actually got wet.

"No! I'm sorry," she said, laughing again. He was laughing now, too. They calmed down and she said, "Thank you for saying that. I'm glad to hear it. Obviously, I don't know shit. So I have a lot to figure out."

"*We* have a lot to figure out. Or I have a lot of support to give while you figure it out, I don't know."

"Cool," Alice said. "Shit," she added.

Peter reached across Alice's back and pulled her in for a hug. She was sweating so much that she didn't even realize she wanted his arms around her until they were.

They didn't try to have sex again the summer they were seventeen. Their first time, and their last time for a long time, was in her freshman-year dorm room at Northwestern. It still hurt, but they powered through.

They cried when they parted ways, even though Alice had a crush on a guy in her Intro to Poetry class, and even though she hadn't really thought about Peter since she had come to campus.

Only when she passed a magnolia tree on her way to the dining hall, with one branch that stretched particularly far, did she think of him.

....

They stood, staring at it, sweat the only thing dripping from their faces because it was too hot for tears. The sun weighed on them like armor. JJ bent down on a knee to get a good look, to make sure Derek hadn't messed anything up, perversely hoping he had because of how irksome he found the guy. Robert stood behind everyone respectfully, not blocking any of the family, who crowded around it.

It looked just like all the other headstones in the graveyard except that it stood out for its shininess and newness. Alice thought it looked a little garish, and Delia found herself wondering how a headstone company marketed itself. Wilma imagined her body in this plot one day, and she wondered where she'd go, if there was a designated spot for a partner she wouldn't have. Jennifer thought about Gerry lying here, all alone, and despite the heat, a tear pricked at her eyes behind her Miu Miu sunglasses.

Carol Anne looked bored, because she was, and Ellen wiped some sweat off her forehead with a Kleenex. The heat made her feel like she was wrapped in bubble wrap; she couldn't feel a thing.

"It looks . . . good," Red said to no one in particular.

JJ nodded and muttered, "Thanks," and Jennifer rolled her eyes, drying her tears immediately. He hadn't made the damn headstone; there was no need for him to take credit for it. She didn't see why they all had to come out here and look at the thing together. There had been enough pomp and circumstance around this death, and she had shit to do.

"I can recite a poem I memorized for an audition," Carol Anne said.
"Please don't," JJ said.

Grant approached the headstone and slid his hand across the top.
He didn't say anything, and Ellen watched him. It felt like her heart had
become very small and was shrinking up against her spine. Something
about the way her grandson's hand lingered on the top shattered her,
but she remained standing and said nothing.

They drove home to Myrtle, and they all went to Ellen's house and
spread themselves into the kitchen and adjoining family room, except
Jennifer, who claimed she had too much work to do to "sit around."
Ellen put on a pot of coffee, even though the thought of drinking a hot
beverage made the rest of them want to join Gerry in the ground. But
Ellen was never not in the mood for a cup of coffee.

She pressed the Brew button and opened the refrigerator to pour
cream into a little ceramic mug, even though she drank her coffee black
and absolutely no one else wanted any. She turned back around and saw
that the coffee had not begun to brew, so she pressed the button again,
harder this time. It didn't light up the way that it was supposed to.

The third time it was hardly a press and more of a jab, so forceful the
whole coffee maker jumped back and clinked into the supersized jar of
sugar behind it. Still, the light didn't turn on. She thought of another
light, of the sun gleaming on the headstone as Grant ran his hand over
the top, and the words "Loving Husband, Father" leapt out at her in her
memory, blinding her further, so she didn't even see the not-working
coffeepot. Loving husband.

Lying husband was more like it. He was a lying husband. He lied to
her; he lied to the kids and the grandkids, the grandkids who stood in
front of his headstone holding back tears, running their young hands
over it like he was magic and some of it might rub off on them, too. The
anger Ellen had seen approaching flowed through her now like lava.
She had been humiliated in front of practically everyone she knew. She
was a fool. She panicked, feeling suddenly like she was floating, like

everything around her was a dream, swirling, leaving her with nothing to hold on to.

She got her hands around the lifeless coffeepot and yanked it so that it flew off the counter and crashed to the floor. On its way down, she noticed the cord flying after it like an underweight water-skier. It hadn't been plugged in to the wall. Her anger melted into humiliation quickly, then turned back into anger when she realized how sick she was of feeling humiliated. She didn't yap her mouth the way other people did to avoid feeling this exact way, intentionally kept her nose out of other people's business and kept her opinions to herself. How had her whole marriage dissolved into one humiliating moment, completely beyond her control? Her mortification grew when she realized her whole family was staring at her, all shock and alarm.

JJ and Grant stood quickly when they heard the crash, ready to be valiant on Ellen's behalf, only to realize she was the perpetrator, not the victim. No one breathed until she inhaled so that she could say, "It wouldn't turn on."

Ellen was raised to leave things nicer than she found them, but she turned her back on the shattered, aromatic mess on the floor and walked quietly past her gaping family members. She walked through the formal living room, down the hallway, and into her bedroom, the door to which she closed quietly, after pausing so that Miss Sparkles could scamper in first.

She sat on the bed, raised her hands, reeking of coffee, to her face, and cried.

Chapter 7

The dolls in what had been JJ's childhood bedroom had never not creeped Alice out, even when she was a child and that was the kind of thing she was supposed to enjoy. Ellen had waited until JJ not only finished college but moved across the street as a newlywed to throw out the University of Georgia and Atlanta Falcons football posters, the navy blue duvet cover, and, to her dismay, a stack of *Playboy* magazines beneath the bed. She had Gerry paint the walls pink, covered the bed in tiny throw pillows fringed with lace, and placed two terrifying porcelain Victorian dolls on the lime-green-and-white-striped window seat.

It was the room that Delia and Alice always stayed in when Ellen and Gerry were hosting lots of guests, and the room Alice stayed in the summers when she and Delia would come. Delia always opted for Carol Anne's childhood bedroom herself. She found its four-poster bed intoxicatingly classy.

Alice, lying on her side for an afternoon rest, felt like the dolls were watching her, so she got herself up and turned them to face the wall.

Delia, who was scrolling through Instagram, back against the headboard next to Alice, snorted. "Loser," she said to her older sister.

"You can't shame me," Alice said. "They are undeniably scary."

There was a soft knock at the door and Wilma slowly pushed it open, popping her head in. "Mind if I come in?"

"Of course," Alice said, sitting up a little. Wilma went and sat on the window seat, automatically turning the dolls back around to face in their proper direction. "No!" Alice said, taking in a sharp breath.

Wilma chuckled. "Okay," she said, turning them back. "You're a grown woman, soon to be a mother, but okay."

"I don't know what kind of mother I'm going to be, but I can commit to being one that will not buy creepy dolls for my kid," Alice said.

Delia sighed. "I wish you would find out the sex. I know gender is a construct, but I'd like to know."

"Okay," Alice said. "Sure. This is about you, after all." Delia gently nudged her.

"I'm worried about Mama," Wilma said, studying her cuticles.

"Are you ever not?" Delia asked. Now it was Alice's turn to gently nudge Delia.

Wilma raised her eyebrows. "Have you ever seen her throw an appliance?"

Delia thought. "Only thing I've ever seen her throw is shade toward Tina."

Alice snorted. "True," she said. "I don't know, Mom. I'm actually kind of relieved she blew off some steam. I mean, my God, the woman is going *through* it, and she always keeps everything so damn bottled up."

"I guess," Wilma said. "But I don't think I should go to that dinner tonight. I think I should just stay here and keep an eye on her."

"Nice try, Mom," Delia said sternly. "But don't."

Wilma double-blinked. "What?" she asked innocently.

"You're going to this dinner," Delia said. "If you need me to list the reasons, I will: You should take the chance to have fun and be distracted from all this craziness. You deserve to have a man be nice to you and buy you some freaking spaghetti. Gram is going through what Gram is going through, regardless of your activities tonight. If anything, she probably wants to be alone."

"Plus, I'll be here tonight," Alice said.

Wilma sighed. "Maybe that could be a good time for you two to talk." She looked at Alice pointedly.

Alice winced. "Woof," she said.

"You never know. It might make her happy," Delia said, frowning and rolling her eyes as she typed "SO THRILLED FOR YOU TWO!" on a photo of a blonde woman holding out a fat engagement ring toward the camera while her cheek was kissed by a man wearing a vest.

Alice cut her eyes at her younger sister. "Would you be excited to tell Gram that you were pregnant out of wedlock?"

"I might be more excited to tell her that than to have her believe what she currently believes about me, which is that I'm destined to be an old maid."

"She does not think that," Alice said, rolling her eyes.

"Do you think she thinks that of me?" Wilma asked her younger daughter, raising her eyebrows, driving her point home.

Delia sighed and rolled her eyes. "Okay, obviously not, sor-ry for trying to make you feel better, Alice. And, Mom, of course no one thinks that about you, but just saying . . ." Adopting an overly sassy voice and tossing her hair, she finished with, "Good thing you have a date tonight, mmkay?" The three of them laughed, then were quiet for a moment. Somewhere inside, Wilma knew her daughter was right, and she wondered privately why she wasn't more excited for her date.

Alice's eyes filled with tears. "I keep catching myself in this moment where I'm worrying about Gram, and then telling myself that it'll be okay because Grandpa Gere will lift her spirits. And then I remember that's the whole problem." She said it quietly and tried to swallow the knot in her throat.

"I know what you mean," Delia said. "I keep wondering where he is. And then I remember that he's gone. And then I remember that I'm mad at him."

"I'm just sad," Alice said, a tear rolling out of her eye and into her ear canal.

"Well, you're a better person than me," Delia said.

"You're both good people," Wilma said. "This is a complicated situation. It's okay to have complicated feelings about it."

Delia sighed. "Yeah, complications are okay. Like the complicated long-distance relationship you're going to have with Death Derek."

Wilma and Alice both laughed. "Did you just come up with that?" Alice asked.

"Yep," Delia said.

"I don't like it," Wilma said.

"You don't have to like the nickname, just the *man*," Delia said in an exaggerated tone, wiggling her eyebrows suggestively, which made all three of them laugh again. And in that moment, just the singular snapshot, everything felt okay.

....

It was still light out as Red made his way down Myrtle Lane later that day. Miss Sparkles, his excuse for going on a walk, strutted in front of him, her hips swaying to and fro like a runway model's. His headphones remained in his pocket, and the heat was roaring in his ears like ocean waves. He looked up at the hanging Spanish moss and prayed that Ellen would find a way to heal. When they reached the stop sign at the end of the street, Miss Sparkles automatically halted, ready to turn around and head back home to the air-conditioning, to Ellen, to her post at the front door should Gerry finally come home.

But Red kept going, tugging gently on the leash so Miss Sparkles would follow. She actually huffed like a teenager, but followed him, expanding the arc of her swaying hips to indicate even more sass. They walked and walked, until it was just Red walking and carrying Miss Sparkles, who gave up after a mile and a half.

Without his family to lead him, it took Red longer than he thought it would to find the headstone. It was magic hour by then, and the roaring heat in Red's ears simmered down. The crickets were beginning their nightly song. He lowered Miss Sparkles onto the grass, and she sniffed at the stone and the ground all around it. She lifted her head into the air suddenly, and started barking as ferociously as if she saw the mailman, which was as ferocious as barking got for her.

Miss Sparkles stopped barking and let out a few whines, finally quieting and lying down, making as much body contact as possible with the headstone. Red sank into a seated, cross-legged position, like he was in elementary school preparing for a game of duck-duck-goose. He always hated that game, hated the anxiety of not being picked, and the anxiety of having to spring into action if he was. Then the image of him sitting on his dead grandfather's body entered his brain, and he jumped up as if he had, in fact, been picked in a game of duck-duck-goose. He resettled so he was catty-corner to the headstone.

Red knew that if he were in a movie, now would be the time to start speaking to the headstone, to tell his grandfather all that he had previously been unable to say, the truth about who he was. He opened his mouth, then immediately closed it, too self-conscious to say anything out loud. Did his grandfather already know? He racked his brain trying to think of a time when Gerry asked him about his dating life, as he always asked Grant if there were any cute gals around, or teased Alice and Delia about chasing boys away with a shotgun. Had he made comments like that to Red that he just couldn't remember, or had there never been any comments like that at all? And if not, was it because he thought Red was shy and wanted to respect that, or was it because he knew? And did he know because he understood, really understood?

Anger bubbled, popped, and spit in Red like the cheese on top of one of Ellen's casseroles in the oven. His breath grew heavier, and he felt hot tears behind his eyeballs. Red understood that Gerry couldn't have told anyone; there was no canvas for that, no space, particularly when he was young, he could imagine. But he was mad at Gerry for keeping the secret, for never brushing his hand across Red's life to make a clearing for his grandson. Red carried his shame around with him like a suctioned-on knapsack, like a parasite that weighed three tons. A lethargy settled in Red, pulling him down toward the earth, toward the grave, toward Gerry, like he had become exhausted by Gerry's secret, by how long Gerry had kept it. Red was already worn down enough by his own. But his anger still glowed. Was this his fate? To just carry it around, to shut down the part of himself that everyone else seemed to service constantly? Delia, crying about her ex; Alice, starting a family with Peter; Grant, with all his . . . conquests. Would Red ever get that, any of that?

He felt his soul jump out of his skin and skyrocket upward when he heard someone behind him clear their throat. "Sorry," Fred said as Red turned around, clutching his chest like he had been stabbed. Fred's bike leaned against his hip, his helmet straps dangling past his tanned, leathery chin. "I didn't mean to disturb you."

Red looked up—really up, as Fred was still very tall—and became so embarrassed he wished he could physically turn inward, crawl inside of himself, and disappear. Miss Sparkles remained unruffled. Red scrambled to his feet, his whole body numb. He heard himself say, "Sorry, Mr. Fred, I . . ." but there was nowhere for him to take that sentence.

"Now, what have you got to be sorry for?" Fred asked.

Red shook his head and inhaled. "I dunno, sorry. Er. Yeah." He looked up at Fred, whose eyes trailed over to the headstone. He bent down, and Miss Sparkles bounded over to him, standing on her hind legs and licking his hands. She presented him with her hindquarters for a scratch, a symbol of joy and trust in Miss Sparkles's language. Fred obliged. "She's excited to see you," Red said dumbly.

"Well, she wasn't at the funeral, was she," Fred said. Red stiffened, feeling his trusty trademark blush creeping up his neck. Fred straightened up, and Miss Sparkles sat down right in between his feet. They both looked at Red. "I'm sorry about the funeral, Red," Fred said. "S'why I don't usually . . . imbibe."

"Oh," Red said, "it's . . . it's okay," because politeness and the need to erase any awkwardness from a situation covered everything Red was feeling like a blanket of snow.

"Naw, it ain't," Fred said. Red shrugged. They stood there and looked at the ground. "How's Ellen?" Fred asked. Red shrugged again, looking upward as though the response he should give would be written in the sky. It wasn't, so he said nothing. Feeling was returning to Red's body, particularly in his heart, which he could feel splintering down the middle in a jagged line.

Red picked up Miss Sparkles's leash and gave it a light tug, and she loyally made her way back to him. He bent down to scoop her up, knowing she had reached her limit on steps walked for the day, and knowing that he did not want to risk the mortification of having to tug even harder on the leash to yank her away from Fred, should she decide that was whose company she preferred.

"Well, see ya," Red said, wishing that Fred wasn't there so he could nod or give some sort of acknowledgment to the grave without feeling pathetic. He made it a few steps, then looked back over his shoulder as Fred said: "Gerry once told me of all his grandchildren he admired you most because you were the most like Ellen and the least like him." Red felt his eyebrows furrow. Fred continued, "Please don't take offense, I do think you're like Gerry in some ways, you know, kind and thoughtful-like. I just wanted you to know that he, you know . . ." Fred stroked his thumb along the handlebars, and it struck Red as something a nervous middle schooler might do. "He saw you. And he loved you."

Red's throat felt like it was the size of a tennis ball. He nodded, barely, for fear that the tennis ball would burst, and he turned, carrying his white fluffball through the cemetery and back toward home, night falling around them like a veil.

....

"I don't know what this says about me and I don't think I want to know," Delia said. "But I'm excited to go out."

"I think it says that just because you're mad trampled by a breakup and the death of your grandfather and the news that he cheated on our grandmother with a man you trusted doesn't mean you can't have a good time," Grant said, not looking up from his phone as Delia applied a layer of lipstick in the hallway mirror. "And I think that's a good thing."

"Hm, thanks, Grant," Delia said. "Okay. How do I look?"

She was wearing cut-off jean shorts and a red tank top that looked like a bandana, her hair down but with a braid in the side, which successfully kept those damn bangs out of her face.

"Great," he said, still not looking up from his phone.

"Okay, good," she said. "Oh my God, remember that summer when they suddenly started checking IDs and that guy caught Alice passing hers back to me?"

Grant laughed. "Yeah, what was it he said again?"

"He said, 'For the love of all things good, lady, if you're gonna do it, at least try to be subtle.'" Delia laughed at her own deep fake accent. They were going to Ricky's, Eulalia's nicest bar. It was a shithole, and also their only option. They had to occupy the night somehow.

"Rebecca's meeting us out," Delia said.

Grant raised his eyebrows repeatedly and suggestively, and flexed beneath his much-too-tight T-shirt. Delia glared at him, jaw dropping. "She's about to get married!" she said. "Don't get any ideas."

"You don't own me."

"Yeah, I would have asked for a refund on that one a long time ago."

"Well, that's very mean," he said.

"Y'all about ready?" Wilma asked, coming down the hall. She had agreed to drive them to the bar, grateful for an excuse to get out of the house and therefore a headshot strategy session with Carol Anne or, worse, threats of a predinner makeover from her.

"Aunt Wils, do you seriously think Gram is cool with us going out tonight? After today?" Grant asked once they were in the car and it was too late for anyone to change their minds. "My parents said it was fine as long as it was fine with her, but I don't know if I really believe her when she said it was fine."

"I really think it's fine, Grant," Wilma said. "I think she's looking forward to some peace and quiet in the house, honestly. And Alice will be there." Wilma said it to convince herself as much as to convince him.

"Yeah, I thought so, too," Grant said, turning and looking out the window into the evening light. Wilma was touched by his double-checking with her.

"What are you wearing tonight, Mom?" Delia asked.

Wilma looked down at her black, sleeveless, cotton, painfully plain shift dress. "I was thinking this."

Delia winced. "Oh, cute," she said, looking out the window, sacrificing her eagerness to makeover for the sake of her mother's self-confidence. Wilma furrowed her eyebrows, then remembered she didn't even particularly want to go on this date in the first place, and if Death Derek had a problem with her outfit, he wasn't a man worth spending time with anyway.

Wilma returned to an empty house, and concern immediately engulfed her. She hurried across the street to Jennifer's, where she found Ellen, Carol Anne, Robert, Jennifer, and Alice on the back porch.

"Mama, I didn't know you were coming over here," Wilma said, voice tense as she slid the glass door open to join them.

Ellen sighed and said wearily, "I didn't know I had to make an announcement to go across the street." Wilma tried not to stare as she noticed her mother's puffy eyes.

"I didn't mean . . . Anyway," Wilma said, "what's everyone up to?" She looked around the group, and her eyes snagged on those of her older daughter, who looked a little green. Wilma tried (and mostly succeeded) to keep her face passive; Alice should be out of the woods on morning sickness by now. Wilma had certainly had rough first trimesters with both girls, but by fourteen weeks all was settled.

Wilma had been more shocked by the news that Alice would be having a baby, less so by the fact that she had gotten pregnant in the first place. Things happen; Wilma understood that. She was mostly thrilled for her daughter (and herself—a grandchild!). Wilma loved being a mom and couldn't wait to watch Alice experience it. She thought Alice would be a great mother: she was patient but could be silly, listened well, had always been consistent and open-minded. But there was another part of her that was scared for Alice to do this alone. Not that she ever thought Peter would be uninvolved, but Wilma had always felt like she was raising the girls by herself, even before she and Trey officially split, and while she loved the special bond she, Alice, and Delia had, it wasn't something she would have wished for her daughters.

Alice wasn't feeling or looking sick directly because of her pregnancy, but because she knew that her mother was right, and it was past time to *tell* everyone about it, especially now that Peter was "in." Fear of Ellen's reaction was the reason for Alice's pink complexion turning green. She knew intellectually that she had nothing to be ashamed of; she was a grown woman who chose to have sex, and she could do what she wanted with her body. And it's not like anyone in the family thought she was a virgin: the protagonist of her book had sex with a stranger, more than once! The Thanksgiving after it was published had certainly not been Alice's favorite.

Should Alice have been more careful, more insistent that Peter wear a condom instead of getting swept up in the romance of the evening?

Sure, but it's not like that was just on her. And she found it ironic, the idea that she would be ashamed to tell someone who clearly would have been outwardly far more horrified by an abortion, but would probably inwardly wonder why a single woman like her hadn't secretly had one, therefore sidestepping the public shame of having a baby out of wedlock.

But despite this knowledge in Alice's head, her gut kept checking her, because different as they might have been ideologically, the last thing she wanted to do was disappoint her grandmother. Her eagerness to please her, and her lifelong admiration for Ellen, was too baked in to avoid this.

As for the rest of them, their opinion of her was fairly immaterial to Alice. But she was hesitant to tell them for the simple reason that she knew that as soon as she did, she would become the center of attention, and that was not something she was sure she could handle, although she did have a sneaking suspicion that Ellen would be pleased to pass that particular mantle off.

"Oh, we're just shooting the breeze," Carol Anne said airily. "I was just regaling everyone with the story of how uncomfortable it was when one of my student's parents recognized me from a local production of—"

Alice took a breath and tried to conjure up how she felt at the creek earlier that day. "I'm pregnant," she spit out. Robert gasped, and then there was a very sharp moment of silence.

Carol Anne broke it with an aside to Robert, "And everyone in this family seems to think *I'm* the one who can't get enough attention . . ."

Robert, who had been staring at Alice with shining eyes, gently nudged Carol Anne, who was rolling *her* eyes, while Ellen, Jennifer, and Wilma all stared at Alice. Wilma quickly took a side glance at her mother; she thought Ellen would understand why she hadn't told anyone, would understand that Wilma had to respect that this was Alice's news. But she gulped all the same, trying to steel herself for the judgment she worried Ellen would pass.

Jennifer blinked. "On purpose?" she asked.

Robert giggled, then immediately tried to disguise it with a cough. Ellen just continued staring, though her eyes narrowed at the question.

"Uh . . ." Alice said, unsure of how to answer. Now that she knew that Peter, widely admired by the family, would be this kid's father in both genetics and life, she had the opportunity to spin this. She could draw on their old friendship and romance, make it seem like they both knew time was running out and so she asked a favor of a good man, one with fantastic DNA. Surely that would go down more easily.

But it wasn't the truth. And lying wasn't something that came naturally to Alice.

The light was beginning to fade, and there was the faint sound of the crickets' song. The air hummed under the weight of the humidity. Alice braved a look at Ellen, and their eyes met.

"She doesn't have to answer that," Ellen said. Wilma could swear she heard a rare tremor in her mother's voice.

Jennifer gave Ellen a side-eyed glance. Sure, Jennifer could respect someone's privacy, but weren't they supposed to be a family here?

"No, it's okay," Alice said, sighing and readjusting in her rocking chair. "Not on purpose, per se, but I feel very comfortable calling it a happy accident."

Jennifer and, in spite of herself, Carol Anne smiled. The tears in Robert's eyes spilled over, and he wiped them away while mumbling apologies. Jennifer clapped her hands together, then stood up and bent over her niece, enveloping her in a hug.

"Oh, congratulations, honey," she said, silently thanking the universe that JJ wasn't there to shame Alice and, on a pettier note, glad that she would know before he did.

"Thanks," Alice said, mortified to feel her eyes filling up.

"How far along are you?" Carol Anne said, unsubtly staring at Alice's stomach.

"Fourteen weeks," Alice said.

Ellen nodded slowly. "Hm" was all she said.

"May we ask how this has come to be?" Carol Anne said.

Alice blinked. "Are you asking me how babies are made?"

Carol Anne giggled softly while glaring. "No, I mean, is there going to be a man in our lives we should know about moving forward?"

Alice wished she had waited for a time when Delia was around to make this announcement. She would have loved to make eye contact with her younger sister now, clocking how quickly Carol Anne had made this about her—who would be in her life now. Luckily, Wilma was there to catch Alice's eye. Mother and daughter had to look away from each other quickly to keep from laughing.

Alice thought for a moment. She wasn't sure if Peter had told his family yet, and knowing this town, that news could spread quickly. She didn't want to risk his family hearing about this from someone other than their son. "There won't be anyone new, no," she settled on. Jennifer nodded curtly.

"Well," Ellen said. The family turned to look at her, all buzzing with nerves. "A great-grandchild." She shook her head slowly, in judgment or awe, the family didn't know. But slowly, a smile started to spread across her face. She actually giggled a little, in spite of herself. "I can't believe it. This is just wonderful."

No one knew what to do. Alice felt like her throat might explode; there was no hope for keeping her tears in now. She tried to wipe them away before they could fully fall, and she tried to clear her throat with a little laugh, which made her sound like she had internal plumbing problems, or like she was a donkey. She knew she was nervous, but she didn't realize until now just how worried she had been—not only that Ellen would react badly to the news itself, but that Alice would have picked the wrong way to tell her, or waited too late to tell her, or that she would have wanted to be told alone.

"Really?" she asked her grandmother. "You're not . . . You're okay with this?"

"Well," Ellen said, adopting a sterner expression. "It's not necessarily how I might have pictured it. But this is exciting." She looked around. "I can't wait for you to tell—" And then she stopped because she remembered.

"Who?" Carol Anne asked. Robert looked away. Wilma's eyes filled, and Jennifer studied the floor. Alice felt like her chest had been pierced open. She wished she could tell Gerry, too. His adoration for babies had been endless; he never would have batted an eye about where it came from as soon as he knew the child was going to exist. And once he did find out where it came from . . . Alice could hear in her head the jokes Gerry would make about how huge her child's hands would be. She felt that week's now-familiar crack in her heart pierce her further.

They heard the doorbell pinging from inside the house, rescuing everyone from having to make the moment even more awkward (which seemed basically impossible at that point) by explaining to Carol Anne. Jennifer stood to answer it.

"Well, I think I'm gonna head on home. I'm not in the mood for company," Ellen said, standing up slowly. Wilma lunged forward, offering a hand to help her out of her chair, which Ellen swatted away with narrowed eyes.

·······················

Gino's was one of those South Georgia restaurants that called itself Italian but also had fried shrimp and hush puppies on the menu, which was printed in Comic Sans font and had remained unchanged for the last thirty years, when it opened to much fanfare. But for all the judgmental eyebrow-raises Wilma, Delia, and Alice gave it, it was still one of the nicest restaurants in Eulalia and it was impossible to ignore how good the spaghetti was.

Derek picked Robert, Carol Anne, and Wilma up from Ellen's house, and Carol Anne immediately got into the front passenger seat. This was a little mystifying to Wilma, as she was pretty sure she was supposed to be the one on a date with Derek, and she found herself praying that she wasn't getting herself into some sort of insane date-switch situation she assumed (correctly) Carol Anne enjoyed. Robert seemed a little confused, too, which made Wilma feel better.

Derek had made a reservation, which Wilma found gentlemanly. They sat down and she regarded the familiar menu, suddenly feeling like a teenager: wondering if ordering the spaghetti would be childish, worrying that it would be too messy. Even though every life choice she had ever made had led to a decidedly un-Ellen-like existence, Wilma had never been able to shake Ellen's voice from the back of her mind. And Ellen would certainly discourage her from ordering spaghetti on a date.

"Wait, what are the vegan options here?" Carol Anne asked, tossing her braid over her shoulder. Derek laughed, then stopped abruptly when he realized she was being absolutely serious.

"Annie, the menu hasn't changed in thirty years," Wilma said, even though she was inwardly wondering how Carol Anne could possibly consider herself a vegan—she had been chowing down on fried chicken and cheesy, eggy casseroles all week with the rest of the family.

"Not sure how good the vegan options here would be, anyway," Derek said. "Carol Anne, remember when a group of us came here right when it opened when we were all visiting home from college?"

"No," Carol Anne said.

"Oh," he said, nodding, keeping a smile on his face. He was wearing a crisp white button-down rolled up at the sleeves. He leaned back in the booth, and Wilma caught an overwhelming scent of cologne. Her face automatically scrunched up, but she smoothed her expression over fast. Openly grimacing was certainly not a polite way to behave on a date. He tried again: "So, Carol Anne, you said you're an actress? That sounds exciting!"

"You know, it really is," she said, nodding. "Exciting, anxiety-inducing, heartbreaking. It's a very tough industry," she said to the man who worked at a funeral home. He nodded politely. "But sometimes it's just the best—there's nothing like being on set."

"I'll bet," Derek said. "I actually took my girls out to LA a few years ago, and we did the Warner Brothers studio tour. It was really neat. What kind of sets have you been on?"

"I've also done the tour, so all of those," Carol Anne said. "And I'm not sure if you've heard of the film *This Time, Forever*, but I was actually in that." The fact that she was an extra was always excluded.

"Wow!" Derek said, while Wilma sipped her water and wondered when they would be able to order drinks with alcohol. "I don't know much about movies, but didn't that win a bunch of Oscars?"

"It didn't so much win Oscars as get nominated for a bunch, yeah," Carol Anne said with faux modesty. "But that's basically the same thing. All that awards stuff is so *political*, anyway. For me, it's about the art."

"Wow, an actress who doesn't want an Oscar! That sounds—"

"That's not what I said," Carol Anne hissed, looking around Gino's as though it were teeming with Academy members.

"Oh, I'm sorry," Derek said, smiling, but his eyebrows were knitted in confusion. "Wow, I'll have to rent that one of these days, unless it's on Netflix or something, which I just love. It seems like there are so many new shows every day. Hopefully that means you're getting a lot of work! Wilma, have you been watching anything—"

"You know, you would think so, but it's just really competitive, and as I'm sure you've read, the industry is just *so biased* against women. I can't just act like Wilma, you know, and not care about how I look. I mean, even Trey, Wilma's ex, could hardly get me an audition, and he's a big high-powered, well-connected talent agent. Or so he claims, anyway," Carol Anne said, rolling her eyes.

Wilma felt like *her* eyes might pop fully out of her head. Why was Carol Anne bringing up her ex-husband on the first date she had been on in, well, she didn't even know how long? And this didn't even touch the comment on Wilma's appearance. Wilma had even blown her short

hair dry and come very close to applying mascara. She wanted desperately to cast out a lifeline to rescue the table from this conversational
hitch, but her mind was blank.

"Oh," Derek said, glancing at Wilma, who smiled helplessly and,
though she didn't realize it, sadly. It was the sad smile she always got
when Trey came up in conversation, and would be the one she wore
when Gerry came up from now on, too. A smile with visible traces of
loss in it. Nodding to Robert, Derek saved everyone by saying, "And
what is it you do?"

"I'm a math teacher," he said. "For seventh grade. It's how I met
Carol Anne, actually." Derek smiled, looking from Robert to Carol
Anne, eager to hear how a glamorous Hollywood actress met a seventh
grade math teacher.

Carol Anne cleared her throat and lowered her eyes while raising
her eyebrows. "I also teach middle school drama. It's important to give
back to the community," she said. Wilma suppressed an eye roll.

"Oooh," Derek said, shimmying his shoulders a bit. "Teacher romance! Do the kids know?" While Carol Anne and Robert (but mostly
Carol Anne) told Derek all about how the kids suspected, but they
wouldn't confirm, Wilma snuck a peek at Derek's profile. His dark hair
had enough silver in it to undoubtedly qualify as salt and pepper, just
like hers. He had a strong jawline, a bump in his nose, and big brown
eyes whose brightness somehow hadn't dimmed with age. He was undeniably handsome. Wilma had always had a weakness for blue eyes on
a man, feeling that the lightness of the color suggested a vulnerability.
Trey had blue eyes, but the last time she saw him (at Delia's college
graduation), she had been too distracted by how immobile all the Botox
had rendered his face to notice them.

Hearing Carol Anne say her name snapped her out of her reverie.
"I'm sorry, what?" she asked, feeling like she had been plunged in cold
water.

"I was just saying that I'm glad you went to pick out the headstone because you two got to meet"—she smiled at Wilma and Derek—"but I just didn't think it made a lot of sense for *me* to go help pick out the headstone, because I don't find it all that important." Wilma double-blinked, her go-to reaction when something shocked her. Carol Anne always received more double blinks than anyone. "You know," Carol Anne continued, as she didn't need a response from Wilma, or anyone, anyway, "because I think the spirit has moved on, and the body is really just a vessel. So, a headstone, to me, is just an expensive marker over, you know, a bag of bones."

"A bag of bones," Wilma repeated slowly, under her breath, upset on her own behalf, her dead father's behalf, and Derek's behalf, as Carol Anne basically took a shit all over his livelihood. Carol Anne, who, when asked about her job, would wax poetic about *This Time, Forever* when she didn't appear in even the background of a single shot. And Wilma would know, because she and Gerry had painstakingly paused it frame by frame once to be sure. Gerry did this out of pride that his daughter was in a big movie; Wilma just wanted to have her suspicions confirmed.

"Well, I gotta say, Carol Anne, I'm glad not everybody sees it that way, because otherwise I think I'd be out of a job," Derek said with a smile.

"Are the women you date typically disturbed by your work?" Carol Anne asked.

"Annie!" Wilma said, horrified. Carol Anne raised her hands by her shoulders, confused. Robert sipped his water. Derek laughed.

"It's not the sexiest thing, I'll admit," he said. "But I was telling Wilma just the other day about why I actually really like it. But either way, gotta pay the bills somehow."

Thankfully, finally, a zitty teenage waitress with a stressfully tight ponytail came to take their drink orders. Wilma and Carol Anne ordered glasses of wine, Robert a beer. Derek shook his head politely and the waitress left. There was a pause, which Derek filled with "I'm sober," even though no one had asked or was planning on asking.

"That's great," Robert offered, leaning forward.

"It is," Wilma agreed.

"Sober-sober or Cali-sober?" Carol Anne asked.

"I don't know what Cali-sober is, so I'm gonna guess sober-sober," Derek said.

"Cali-sober is when you use marijuana but don't drink alcohol. I tried it, but it wasn't for me."

"Yeah, definitely sober-sober," Derek said. "You know what they say. Give me an inch, and I'll drain my bank account, flip a car, and wake up in a bed full of prostitutes." He chuckled uncomfortably, then widened his eyes and shook his head upon realizing the height of that particular overshare. Wilma looked into her lap, uncomfortable but appreciative of his honesty. People who didn't know their own flaws (present company included) made Wilma feel embarrassed.

"Fascinating," Carol Anne said. "Is that why you moved back to Eulalia?"

Wilma's instinct was to admonish with another "Annie!" but she also wanted to know the answer, so she settled with just shooting Carol Anne one of her best mom looks. She didn't notice.

"Kinda, yeah," he said. "It was a . . . big problem, and a big part of why my marriage didn't work, and why my ex-wife didn't want me around the girls—rightfully, I'll add. I needed to get on the straight and narrow and really stay there, and give my wife some space, prove that I was serious, you know. So, yeah, came back home, ran into Billy at the Winn-Dixie, next thing I know, I'm a funeral director!"

"Good for you," Wilma said. "I think that's great. It really does seem like such a fascinating job."

"It definitely ain't boring," Derek said, launching into a tale involving old Mrs. Ashbury's will, which instructed that she be buried with her cat, but no one could remember where the cat's—apparently frozen—carcass was. Wilma had to jerk her head backwards a few times, so wild were his hand motions. But it was nice: his inability to be smooth freed her of feeling like she had to be, too. So much so that she ordered the spaghetti without thinking twice.

Even though Carol Anne had ridden shotgun on the way to Gino's, Wilma got it for the ride home, mostly because Robert unsubtly grabbed Carol Anne's hand and effectively yanked her into the back seat with him. He did the same thing in reverse when Derek pulled up to Ellen's curb, leaving Wilma and Derek alone in the car. "Thanks for the ride!" he called over his shoulder while Carol Anne limped to the house, whining that Robert had made her twist her ankle.

Being alone in the car with Derek made Wilma feel like she was seventeen, even though teen Wilma had only ever really been alone with a boy she liked in a car one time, and she wasn't sure she liked Derek, anyway. The boy was Eric Butler, JJ's best friend, because JJ had to get out of the car and puke his guts out on the side of the road when she had gone to pick them up from the end-of-football-season party. She had a crush on Eric for the entirety of her youth, but even the barrier of the car door wasn't enough to override the vibe killer that was her brother projectile vomiting. Not that she would have made a move anyway.

But she knew enough about the world to know that typically, for a seventeen-year-old in this position, the charge in the car came from the anticipation of a kiss, and she knew that she wouldn't be kissing Derek that night. She thought he was handsome and interesting, but as often happened when she was on some kind of date, it was as though a steel door had slid up over a room in her heart. Plus, she didn't want to get any closer to that cologne.

"Thanks for dinner," she said. The waitress had presumptuously brought two checks, one covering Carol Anne and Robert, which Carol Anne immediately and unceremoniously shoved in Robert's direction, and one for Wilma and Derek, which he picked up, despite Wilma's objections, with a classic: "Your money's no good here."

"And thanks for the headstone," Wilma said, immediately wondering why in the world she said it.

"Oh—sure," Derek said, his neck twitching a little in surprise. "No problem."

She smiled without showing her teeth and turned to the door, grabbing the handle.

"Would you want to walk my dog with me sometime soon? While you're still in town?" he asked.

She turned back around to face him, impressed and thankful for the idea of a date so practical it didn't even sound like a date at all.

"Sure," she said. He smiled, showing all his teeth. They were so white they glowed almost unnaturally brightly in the dark. It was almost disconcerting, which Wilma chided herself for thinking on her walk from the car to the front door. There was no reason why she should complain about a nice man smiling at her.

....

Ricky's was just as loud and smelly and cavernous as Delia remembered. Rebecca, still in her scrubs, got there only a few minutes after them, opening with "I had to inspect Coach Lommer's ball sack today at work. And he was one sack of eight. Let's get drunk."

"I can think of a ninth—"

"Grant, why don't you get us drinks instead of finishing that sentence? I'll get the next round, thanks," Delia said.

Grant scampered to the bar, and Rebecca started telling Delia about her urology rotation for med school, the horrors of which she felt grossly underprepared for, despite the fact that her fiancé, Justin, had completed the same rotation a year earlier.

"He didn't warn you?" Delia asked, laughing.

"No!" Rebecca said, also laughing. "He's too sweet to complain. Like, about anything. Ever."

"Aw!" Delia said. "That's good, though. Right?"

"Yeah." Rebecca nodded. Delia tried not to think about the fact that if she and Connor were seated at a wobbly table at a restaurant, he would talk about it for hours. Grant came back with a tequila shot and a Bud Light for each of them. They clinked glasses, Rebecca and Grant knocking their tequila back like water, while Delia embarrassingly sputtered and choked on hers like a teenager, like the teenager she had once been in that very bar.

"So, how droopy were Lommer's balls?" Grant asked. "Like, could he play croquet without a stick?"

Delia rolled her eyes and was surprised when Rebecca burst out laughing. She quickly tried to act like she hadn't, which escaped neither Delia nor Grant's notice.

"Speaking of, where *is* Justin?" Delia asked pointedly. "It's wedding week!"

Rebecca stopped laughing and took a sip of her beer. "He doesn't get to town until tomorrow. Residency, man."

"And you think you'll get Atlanta for residency, too? They pay attention if you're, like, *married*, right?"

"Yeah, that's partially why we're going ahead and—"

A group of boys in khakis and fraternity T-shirts (though their college days were clearly behind them, with the burgeoning beer guts of their fathers to prove it) burst into Ricky's and immediately engulfed Grant. He was high-fiving them all, throwing his head back and hooting at the verbal abuse they doled out for his performance on *The Bachelorette*. Delia recognized one of the guys, the only relatively gutless one. Logan Whitt was always hanging around JJ and Jennifer's house in the summers Delia spent with Gerry and Ellen. Delia always referred to him internally as her "summer crush." While his hairline wasn't exactly *pre*-ceding, he still looked pretty good.

"Well, if it isn't little Miss Delia," he said, wrapping his arm around her shoulders and pulling her in for a side squeeze. His remembering her caused a pleasant tingling sensation to radiate in her limbs. She realized how long it had been since she had flirted with someone, or had a crush on someone, and the radiating dulled. But then he said, "You sure did grow up nice," and the tingle came back, so pronounced not even her own negativity could squash it.

"Hi, Logan," she said.

"Was real sorry to hear about your grandfather," he said. "He was some of the best of this town. I was at the funeral, but couldn't make it to the reception. I had to go back to work."

"And what is it you do?"

"I help manage my family's forestry service. For us, money *does* grow on trees, babe."

"Ah," Delia said. "Nice." She waited for him to ask her what she did, but he didn't.

"Hey, Delia," Grant called from across the circle. "Remember how these guys were in a band, the Hard Gents?"

"Sure," Delia said, recalling the time that she went with Grant to hear them play in a garage when she was a rising sophomore. They made loud noise for about ten minutes, then sat around and drank Keystone Lights all afternoon. Delia had nursed one the whole time they sat in that garage; she didn't know yet that she liked beer and certainly had never had alcohol in the daytime before.

"They're still together," Grant said. "They're playin' tonight!"

"Great!" Delia said. She turned to Logan. "What instrument do you play?"

He strummed an air guitar and rocked his head back and forth. "Drums," he said.

When they took the stage, Rebecca, Grant, and Delia stood together and whooped and hollered like groupies.

"Hi," the lead singer—Brett, Delia believed his name was—said through the curtain of dirty hair hanging over his face. "We're the Hard Gents and we're gonna play some music for y'all tonight."

The band began to play, and neither Grant nor Delia nor Rebecca recognized the song, if you could even call it that. They hadn't improved much since that summer long ago; it seemed like every member of the Hard Gents was just shoving out his own individual wall of noise.

Grant, Rebecca, and Delia tried to sway and dance, though there wasn't really a beat or tempo to follow, and the stickiness of the floor made it difficult to pick up their feet. "More drinks?" Grant called.

"Please," Delia said.

More tequila shots. Maybe it was that the band just needed to warm up, or maybe it was the alcohol (it was definitely the alcohol), but by the third song the Hard Gents were starting to sound pretty good. The fourth song was even recognizable as a song, though that might have been because they played "Sweet Home Alabama," made apparent by all twenty of Ricky's patrons singing—well, screaming—along.

Soon, the Ricky's crowd started to thicken and old buddies from Eulalia High kept pulling Grant away, but like a tide, he always came back to Delia and Rebecca. Delia's eyes were glued to Logan as he played the drums, catching how the dim spotlight overhead reflected off his forearms. He didn't take his eyes off his drum set, clearly using all his concentration. But once, in between songs, when he reached down, pulled up his beer, and took a sip, Delia caught his eye and he winked at her. She smiled back, taking a sip of her beer, as well. It might have been nonverbal, but it was flirting, and at this point, flirting was a personal victory for Delia.

The Hard Gents capped off their set with "Wagon Wheel," the lyrics to which Delia and Rebecca screamed at the top of their lungs, heads bent back toward the ceiling while they spun each other around in circles. Delia liked being in a big bar with space to move, feeling momentarily relieved not to be crammed into some precious, misshapen little Manhattan bar sipping an eighteen-dollar cocktail. She was so content she didn't even mind when Grant cut in and stole Rebecca away from her for a few spins.

"Need another drink?" Logan asked Delia as he stepped down from the stage.

Delia needed another drink like she needed a sharp stick in the eye, but she batted her eyes and, like the good down-home Southern girl she was playing that night, said, "I'd love a Bud Light."

Logan nodded and went off to the bar, and Delia watched him lean over the scratched wood to order their drinks and decided to ignore the massive sweat stains under his arms. She waited patiently for her drink, and nodded her head and swayed a little, as actual music was now streaming from the ancient speakers.

She was too distracted to notice Grant twist his fingers around Rebecca's, or notice him gently tug her hand and walk outside of Ricky's. Rebecca pulled her hand back and looked after him for a moment, then looked around. She hurried outside.

She found him leaning against the side of Ricky's, looking up. The sky felt heavy, threatening rain.

"Hey, Bell," he said lazily as she leaned next to him, billowing her shirt in and out in an effort to cool off.

"What, were people sneaking pics of the now-famous Grant Williams on their phones?" she asked.

"Nah," he said. They were quiet for a minute.

"Can I ask you something?" she asked.

"Anything, Bell."

"Why did you go on the show?" She looked over at him. "Just for more Instagram followers, more clients? Or did you really think you could find love?"

"The desk girl at the gym is one of my best buddies at work. She put me up for it. I know that sounds like an excuse, but it's true. And then I actually got an interview, and then . . . I don't know." He shrugged and laughed. "It seemed kinda fun. So I did it."

Rebecca exhaled in a little laugh. "Jesus," she said.

"What?" he asked, still looking up at the stars.

"That's just," she said. "I don't know. If you were anyone else, I wouldn't believe you. I would think there had to be some deeper reason, but for you, I genuinely believe that it seemed fun, so you just did it."

He furrowed his eyebrows and stopped looking at the sky, looked right down into her eyes. "I can be deep, Bell."

The wood of the wall felt scratchy on her bare arm. She looked up at her neighbor, at the man who was once a boy whose name was in the center of hand-drawn hearts all over her childhood diary, and she suddenly didn't feel like a woman days away from marriage, months away from becoming a doctor. She felt sparkly and juvenile and like the whole world was open before her, endless with possibilities of who she could become.

"I'm sure," she said quietly. Her heart rate quickened; she had meant for it to sound lighthearted, teasing and flirty, but the words somehow snagged on his eyes looking into hers and felt weighted, sentimental.

The way she was leaning on the wall, looking up at him, was too much for Grant. Without considering it for even the briefest of moments, he leaned down to kiss her.

Rebecca's heart skipped a beat, and for a second she believed that this would happen. His face coming toward hers felt natural and radical at the same time, and the wonder of it caught her breath. Then she focused in on his puckered lips headed straight for hers and she remembered herself.

"Jesus, Grant," she said quietly, shaking her head and stepping away from him.

He put his hands up, questioningly. "What?" he said.

"What?!" she said. "*What* is that I'm getting married in three days! You can't just go around kissing people who are getting married in three days!"

"Oh, come on," he said, tilting his head to the sky before slumping against the wall of the bar again. "We were just having a moment. And you're not people, Bell."

"Having a moment?" Rebecca looked to the stars now, shaking her head. She let out a sharp laugh. "God."

Grant shrugged. "Could be good to get out of your system before the big day. A last hurrah, if you will." He leaned his head back into his hands against the wall, turned to look at her, and winked as he did so. Nothing could have been more frustrating to Rebecca than the fact that he looked damn good doing that.

"You can't just do whatever you want, whenever you want, Grant. Just because something 'sounds fun' isn't always a good enough reason to do it. At some point, you have to be a fucking adult." Her voice rose as she said this.

Grant blinked, that maddening grin still on his face. He chuckled and shrugged. "I don't know about that, Bell. Things have worked out pretty good for me so far."

"Oh, yeah?" she asked. "Don't you think that's what your grandpa did? Whatever he wanted? And how did that work out for Ellen?"

The grin fell off his face, and Rebecca was mortified to see his eyes fill with tears. Moisture immediately rushed to hers, too, and she realized her lips were numb, a telltale sign that she was drunk. Grant cleared his throat.

"I'm sorry, I didn't mean that the way it came out," Rebecca said. "I've . . . I'm drunk."

He raised his hand to silence her and waved her words away, like they were no big deal. "S'all good, Bell," he said. "I think I'm gonna . . ." And he headed back inside.

"A city gal who remembers her roots, I love it!" Logan yelled over the music as he handed Delia her Bud Light. She held it up in a cheers motion, and he clinked his glass against hers. Suddenly, the music slowed down, some man crooning about how good his wife looked without makeup on. Logan leaned forward and offered out a hand in an over-the-top gentlemanly manner. "May I have this dance?" he asked. Delia laughed and took his hand, and he pulled her in, and they continued swaying, but more slowly and facing each other.

"You really like it up there in New York?" he asked her.

She nodded, smiling at him, wondering if it was acceptable to lay her head against his chest, like she and Connor used to do after dinner sometimes when they first moved in together. She quickly tried to shove the thought of Connor out of her mind.

"Lotta libs up there," Logan said, grinning.

"Please don't," Delia said, not finding the energy to finish saying, "Please don't say something that will turn me off immediately."

He chuckled and said, "Okay." Then he said, "You always were such a little firecracker," and he slid his hand down her back, over the pocket of her jean shorts, and squeezed her ass cheek so hard the pain overrode the alcohol in her dulled system and she yelped.

"What the hell, man?" she said, twisting away from him.

He shrugged and threw his hands up in a *don't shoot* motion. "What?" he said.

She knew she was too drunk to really be the quick, sparking firecracker he had just claimed she was, and no insults to him or defenses of herself were coming to her slowed, Bud Light–slicked brain, so she turned on her heel and stormed off to the bathroom, humiliated to feel tears pricking the corners of her eyes.

While the thought of Connor seemed to always be humming in the back of her mind, for the first time since almost calling him after the funeral, she felt the stabbing, immediate, consuming pain of missing him, of wishing that he were her boyfriend, right there with her. It was the kind of missing she only let herself do when she knew she would be seeing or speaking to him again. She pulled out her phone and went to his contact information.

She looked at her screen, at the picture she had chosen as his caller ID icon in her phone. They had been at a friend's birthday party all afternoon, drinking heavily on a boat docked off the West Side. People had started making plans to go to a nearby Italian restaurant for dinner; it looked like rain was coming. But Connor and Delia looked at each other and mouthed "Sushi?" at the same time, trying to hide their satisfied smiles that they had managed to find a person who understood them so completely, who wanted the exact same thing at the exact same time all the time. They went home and ordered an obscene amount of sushi, and Delia had taken a photo of Connor sitting on the couch, their bounty laid out on the coffee table in front of him. He was smiling, his mouth wide open, as though he were going to attack the table full of food with his face.

She wanted to hear his voice. It actually felt like she needed to hear his voice or something really bad would happen. She swatted at her cheeks; some of the tears had fallen. She thought about Gerry, and again had the eerie feeling that he was able to see what she was doing, was shaking his head and lamenting her low self-esteem. "What's a beaut like you doin' actin' like this," he'd say.

But Gerry was gone, and even though she knew she wasn't really, she felt that she was alone. No one could offer her the support that Connor could; only their love could unlock the comfort she truly needed. Or so her drunk mind had her believe.

She caught her makeup-smudged eye in the mirror just as she pressed her phone to her face. She turned away and huffed, making those damn bangs, which had fallen out of her carefully constructed braid, defy gravity for a brief moment. The phone rang three times, then went to voicemail. Sober Delia would have immediately understood that this meant Connor had rejected her call, and she would have hung up, debated sending a text apologizing for the pocket dial. But she was not sober Delia.

"Hey, it's Connor, leave a message." She felt her heart crack for how young his voice sounded.

"Hey," Delia said, her voice wet and broken. "I know this is out of the blue because we haven't been talking, but I wanted to say that Grandpa Gere died. And I mean, you know that because you saw my Instagram story already. I know that's not, like, chill to talk about, but fuck it, it's true, why act like it's not. I know you're not my boyfriend, and it's not your job to, like, care about this. But it feels weird that we haven't

talked at all. Like how could you not . . . but I know you're . . . whatever. Miss you and also fuck you." She hung up and inhaled sharply.
Now *that* was done.

She turned, marched to the mirror, and wiped away the makeup that
the tears had smudged under her eyes. She took a long pull of her Bud
Light, a deep breath, and emerged back into Ricky's, a phoenix from the
ashes.

⋯⋯⋯⋯⋯

"What are you doing here?" Red asked Brady when he walked into his
kitchen and found the guy sitting at the table. Theatrically, an ear-
splitting clap of thunder shook the house right after Red finished the
question. This was lucky for Red, as it distracted Jennifer, who sat at the
table with Brady, from the opportunity to berate him for being rude to
their guest. "I mean, it's great to see you again so soon! Just surprised, is
all," he tried to save himself.

"My parents went to go see my grandpa today in Vidalia, and I came
home from the Liquor Barn and realized I had forgotten my key so . . .
I'm locked out," Brady said, looking amused.

"Wow, you really must be new around here if you're lockin' your door
when you leave the house," Red said, and smiled. Brady smiled back.

"Well, I'm selfishly glad for it," Jennifer said, nodding to the glasses
of white wine in front of her and Brady. "I'm the only wine drinker here
usually. It's nice to have a drinking buddy." They touched their glasses,
and Brady winked.

There were decks of cards between them. "Wanna play with us?
We're about to start a new game. I've never played this and I'm *loving*
it," Brady said.

"Double solitaire, babe," Jennifer told Red, "but we can easily make
it triple."

"Uh . . ." Red said, feeling like he should find a way out even though he wanted to stay and play cards with his mom and this intriguing boy. He squared his shoulders and said, "Sure."

Jennifer pushed a deck of Snoopy playing cards that were as old as Red was in his direction as he sat down. Brady took another sip of his wine, and tipped the glass in Red's direction, silently asking if he wanted some, as though Red were in his house and not the other way around. Red shook his head and looked away, the force of Brady a little too bright for him.

"Where were you?" Jennifer asked.

"I was . . ." Red started, not sure how to finish his sentence. He worried that declaring he was at the graveyard would bring about unwanted attention, and he didn't want anyone near his reasons for wanting to go. "Out." Brady kept his eyes on the cards in Jennifer's hands as she shuffled and redistributed the decks, but Red could not miss his cocked eyebrow at his choice of words. Jennifer shrugged; she wasn't going to force her twenty-five-year-old son to tell his mother where he had been. She pushed another deck of cards, with racehorses on them, to Brady.

The trio began silently setting up their solitaire games. "Ready, set, go!" Jennifer said, frowning, eyes glued to her cards, and they began furiously playing against themselves, until Jennifer got the game started by slapping an ace of hearts in the middle, which Brady followed with a two of hearts almost immediately.

"Really getting the hang of this, Brady," Jennifer said, biting her lower lip, perfectly waxed eyebrows knitting together in concentration. She slapped another ace between them. The game continued, Jennifer and Brady slapping cards down in the middle at a pace much faster than Red, who hadn't played the game in at least a year. He finally found a five of spades to add to the pile, and as he went to slap it down, Brady did the same.

Their hands landed on the stack of spades at the same time. The shock and competitive nature of each caused them to keep their hands pinned to the table, and it wasn't until they both quickly drew breath in at the same time and looked at each other that Red realized their fingers were touching. Jennifer slapped a card on a nearby pile with alarming force, but for a small second, they stayed completely still, neither of them looking away. Brady grinned at him, and Red felt his stomach drop through his backside and figured it had probably splattered all over the kitchen floor.

Not looking up from her own game of solitaire, Jennifer said, "Do I need to step in and referee here, or can you boys work it out?"

Red watched Brady as he smiled and shifted his eyes toward Jennifer and back to Red, giving him that grin again. "No need," he said.

After two rounds of Jennifer winning handily, they decided to take a break. Cards resting on the table, Jennifer asked Brady where he would be living in New York (the Upper East Side, with his paternal grandmother's sister, until he could find a place of his own), if he was excited (yes), and did he know the best places to shop in that neighborhood (no) because she'd be glad to send him a list (yes, please).

Brady's phone dinged with a text. He read it and bit his lip, raised his eyebrows.

"Everything okay, hon?" Jennifer asked.

"Yeah," Brady said. "My parents are gonna spend the night in Vidalia because of the storm."

"They should," Jennifer said, turning to look out the kitchen window and into the slanted rain. "Of course, you should spend the night here." Red gulped.

JJ hurried through the door, shaking his wet head like a dog. Jennifer couldn't help but scrunch her face up in disgust.

"Where were you, Dad?" Red asked, grateful for something to say that wasn't addressing Brady. Jennifer silently thanked him; she wanted to know the same thing but didn't want to have to ask.

"Worked late, then went to the gym."

Jennifer had to envision sandbags hanging from each pupil to keep herself from rolling her eyes. She didn't look away from JJ, even though the sight of him dripping all over her newly redone floors made her hair stand on end. He looked at her, then looked away quickly, guiltily, she thought. He did have his gym bag, though. Nice touch.

"Oh, hey, Bradley," JJ said.

"It's Brady," Jennifer said.

"That's okay," Brady said. "Hi, Mr. Williams. Jennifer has been kind enough to let me hang out here while I'm locked out of my parents' house."

"Oh, where are your parents off to?" JJ asked.

"Vidalia, visiting my grandpa."

"You didn't want to go?" JJ said, throwing his dripping rain jacket and bag over a kitchen island stool that cost more than the rent of Jennifer's first apartment. She felt like her head might explode. Red tried to ignore the slump in his dad's shoulders as he asked this. He knew JJ was thinking about the fact that his sons would never be able to see their grandfather again.

"I'm sort of persona non grata where he's concerned," Brady said, smiling, which Red thought was brave. "He doesn't love my . . . vibe."

"Ah," JJ said, blinking and looking like he didn't know what to do with his hands.

"How could anyone not love your vibe, Brady?" Jennifer said, recovering herself and everyone else. "New York will be lucky to have you. Delia and Alice will have to take you out to lunch or dinner or something."

"New York, huh?" JJ said as he pulled a beer out of the fridge. "You like crowds? Lots of crowds up in New York."

"I didn't mind the crowds when I interned there last summer, so I think I'll be okay," Brady said.

"Lots of strange people in those crowds, too," JJ said, leaning his hip on the counter and taking a long sip of his Miller Lite. Red felt every hair on the back of his neck stand up individually, and suddenly could not believe how bright the kitchen was. The overhead lighting, and the way it bounced off the white marble, was completely overwhelming.

He tried desperately to think of something he could say to change the direction of the conversation.

"What does *that* mean?" Jennifer asked.

"Well, you know," JJ said, shrugging. "It's New York." His eyes landed on Jennifer as he stifled a belch, and he saw how narrow her eyes were, like lasers pointing right at the center of his forehead. "Oh!" he said. "I didn't mean, like . . ." He twisted his left wrist and moved the left hand, the one not holding a beer, around in a figure eight, making eye contact with Brady and then casting his eyes up to the ceiling. Everyone knew what he meant by that.

"Totally know what you meant, Mr. Williams," Brady said, meeting JJ's eye and leaning forward like they were old friends. He was used to assuring well-enough-intentioned folks that he didn't interpret their homophobic statements as, well, homophobic.

Red's skin felt very hot and his innards felt very cold during this exchange. "I think I'm gonna go to bed," he said, overwhelmed by his need to avoid the rest of the interaction.

Jennifer turned to Brady. "You can stay in Red's room. He still has his childhood twin beds in there, so you won't have to share." Red felt like his intestines had snaked around inside of his stomach, tangled themselves together, and pulled. Hard.

"Oh, I don't want to put Red out," Brady said, waving his hands in front of his chest. "I'm happy to sleep on the couch or wherever."

"Oh, please, Red doesn't mind," Jennifer said, standing up and shoving the decks of cards into the credenza she'd bought herself at her favorite antiques market in Atlanta the year before.

Red opened his mouth as he felt everyone in the room turn to him, no doubt in their minds that he would say, "Of course, man, it's no problem." But there *was* a problem. Red felt as though his throat had become a ball of wet sandpaper, and he was flabbergasted by the thought that an elaborate prank was being pulled on him. Then he had the even stranger thought that maybe he was in a crazy porn scenario, which

Red understood from his peers was actually not so strange a thought to have. But to Red it was completely bizarre, as he had tried to watch porn exactly one time.

It was a Thursday night, and he had just led a Bible study for Vanderbilt students. They had talked about their duty to help those less fortunate, a decidedly unsexy topic, or so one would think. But his first "date" was approaching (the date that never was), and while he didn't really expect the date to go anywhere, he liked to be prepared. He understood sex conceptually. He knew that he wanted to have it, but he just had so many *questions*. He figured it was time to watch something properly, on Pornhub like a real man, instead of frantically looking through wiki-Hows with disturbing illustrations when he was lying in bed half drunk. Selecting a video had taken him almost half an hour. The home page alone was enough to set his head spinning—not with arousal, but with a fear-nausea combo. Every thumbnail looked so . . . visceral.

In a panic, he typed "instructional" into the search bar, completely horrified by the suggestions cropping up as he typed the word. Dicks, balls, and anuses inundated his vision, and he peered at the screen with only one eye kind of half-open, skin turning green beneath the light of his laptop screen. He felt filthy. He tried to remember if he had even had to click anything asking his age, which of course any kid could lie about, but how was that legal?

He understood the internet as much as anyone—he was no techie, but he had used it all his life. Still, it shocked him that all he had to do was type in one word and suddenly a parade, a complete deluge, of men's genitalia was before him. He clicked on something that had "twink" in the title, but when the boy said something about being only fourteen, he snapped his laptop closed instantly. The boy's partner (was that the right term to use here?), a man with a penis so large it would have been comical had it not scared Red so much, moaned so loudly and for so long that the sound escaped from the laptop even after the screen had closed on the keyboard.

Red had panted and shaken his head, like he could knock the images right out. The moaning stopped, and it occurred to him that maybe shutting the laptop so suddenly had somehow frozen his computer, which was brand-new and had been a gift from his parents, and he certainly couldn't afford to buy a new laptop off his student-ministry salary, for Christ's sake, so if the terrifying and evil and hopefully unrealistic porn had broken his computer, he would have to get it fixed, and then the guy at the Apple store (or girl!—"Women in tech!" Delia would have said) would know that he had been watching porn. Not just porn, but gay porn! And that would be how he came out—that would be the first and only other person to know the truth about Red. Well, other than God.

Hence, it was very strange that Red had the sudden thought that his kitchen was a porn set. And by the way, his computer did not break, because, as it turns out, porn does not actually automatically make a computer implode.

They all stared at Red, and Jennifer's eyebrows had traveled so far up her head they were practically a headband, even though Red was pretty sure it hadn't been that long a silence. "Uh, yeah, sure," his sandpaper throat somehow managed to croak out.

"There are extra toothbrushes in one of your bathroom drawers, Red," Jennifer said. "Brady, holler if you need anything else." She got up and grabbed her keys.

"Where are you going?" JJ asked, shutting the sliding cabinet that housed their garbage and recycling bins after depositing his empty Miller Lite bottle. JJ preferred the bottle to the can. He said only trailer trash drank beer from a can in their own home.

"I'm going to run an errand," Jennifer said, marching over to the cabinet and yanking it open. A huff blew through her nose as she reached in, pulled JJ's beer bottle out of the garbage, and slammed it in the recycling. JJ cocked his head and widened his eyes in mystification; he realized his mistake, but where was her anger coming from?

He shook his head and remembered that she had just said she was leaving. "What kind of errand are you running at this time of night? In the rain?"

"I'm just gonna go check on them across the street." JJ looked at her like she had just spoken in Portuguese (JJ didn't speak Portuguese).

"Why do you need your keys?" he asked.

The vein on Jennifer's neck that always bulged when she was about to blow a fuse was as engorged as the penises that scared Red on Pornhub, but JJ didn't notice. The boys had learned to Fear the Vein, but JJ never had, which was why, even after all these years, Jennifer's outbursts still shocked him, while Red and Grant had properly anticipated them since they were in the single digits. She spun on her heel, spit out "Just in case" through bared teeth, and shut the door behind her. JJ watched as she crossed the street and marched through the rain like a soldier into his parents' house.

Alice's and Ellen's heads jerked up in alarm at the sound of Jennifer slamming the front door behind her. Miss Sparkles leapt up, ready to defend her homestead, but sank back down when Jennifer stalked into the kitchen. From the kitchen table, Alice's and Ellen's eyes widened at Jennifer's dripping hair, at the anger radiating off her in waves. She looked like some kind of creature that had just escaped from the sea.

"Hello, Jennifer," Ellen said.

"Hi," Jennifer said, brushing some rainwater off her shoulder. She looked at the pulled pork, corn bread, and baked beans that sat on the plates in front of them. "The Bennetts send over Porky Pig?"

"Sure did," Ellen said.

"Yeah, they sent that when JJ had his hip surgery," Jennifer said, trying not to visibly shudder at the memory of having to nurse JJ after his surgery three years prior. She got the in-sickness-and-in-health thing in theory, but that whole situation sure had been a test. It's not like Jennifer minded extra work; it was more that JJ hated being helpless like that. It made him mean, which pissed Jennifer off. He should have been grateful for her waiting on him hand and foot, or at least acted like he was even if he wasn't.

"Would you like to sit down?" Ellen asked.

"Oh, sure," Jennifer said, loudly dragging a wicker chair out and plunking herself down in it. She folded her hands on the table, and Alice couldn't help but stare at her aunt. Everything about her was so tense. Jennifer stared at the warp in the wooden table and Alice cast a glance over to Ellen, who was also looking at Jennifer as she chewed on a piece of corn bread that might as well have been cardboard to her.

"Everything okay?" Ellen asked her daughter-in-law.

Jennifer's eyes shot up. She blinked. "Yes," she said. She cleared her throat and tried to relax a little into her chair, as if she could squelch the anger out of herself. She only looked more on edge. Aware of this, Jennifer cast her mind for something to say to draw the attention away from herself. "Alice, how was your first trimester?"

Alice grimaced and looked at her grandmother again. "We were just talking about that as you came in," she said. "It was pretty rough. Rough enough that I shouldn't have been so surprised when I found out why I was feeling like shi—why I was feeling so bad every day. Then again, they do call it morning sickness, and it's not like it was just in the morning."

"Hear, hear," Jennifer said, trying to focus on the sickness part and not the surprise part, even though she was overwhelmingly curious.

They sat there, with only the sound of the rain lashing against the window over the kitchen sink. It would have been peaceful, were the energy of the room not made so insane by Jennifer and Alice constantly side-glancing at Ellen, wondering if Ellen's previous joy was subsiding and disappointment was setting in. Naturally, the ever-present need to lighten a situation reared its head.

Looking between the two of them, Alice said, "You two can keep a secret, right?" Ellen looked blankly at her. Jennifer nodded. "Peter Bell is the father."

Jennifer's jaw dropped. Shock, then immediate joy, melted her lingering anger. She started to smile, and laughter overcame her. "No! Way!" she said in between laughs.

Alice felt the color rising in her cheeks, which was unsurprising. She was, however, surprised by the bloom of pride she felt in her chest. She realized she didn't just want to tell them because she thought it would make them happy, would make Ellen feel better about the father being someone Alice had known for a long time, or would just distract them from the mess that was their current lives. She wanted to say it because she was really fucking happy about it. She was excited about this, and she was relieved that she was excited about it.

"How did this even . . . Well, of course we don't have to get into that," Jennifer said.

"The conference," Ellen said to her plate full of food.

"Hm?" Jennifer asked, leaning in.

Ellen looked up at Alice. "You said he was there for a conference a while back, and you saw him."

Alice nodded, her blush darkening at the thought of her grand-mother playing Sherlock Holmes with her sex life. Ellen looked back at her plate. Fear cropped up in Alice. Was she wrong in thinking that her grandparents loved Peter? Oh, God, could this be a race thing? Was Ellen hoping it would be someone else? Who the hell was she even hoping it would be?

Jennifer was looking at Ellen expectantly, too, trying to read her mother-in-law, a task that had always been difficult for Jennifer, even though it rarely was with other people. It was one of the qualities that imbued Jennifer with so much respect for Ellen. But now she just wanted to know what she was thinking.

"Yeah. And he's, like," Alice said, trying (and failing) not to pin all of her hopes on her grandmother's reaction to this news, "*in*. It wasn't planned, but we're both excited, and I've talked it over with him, and we're going to work out some way for us to do this together. I won't lie, there's no, like, romantic commitment here right now.

Maybe . . . Anyway. But we're going to do this whole kid-raising thing together." She took a shallow breath and glanced at Jennifer, who met her niece's gaze and smiled. She lightly shrugged her shoulders at Ellen.

The truth was, Ellen didn't know what to say. She felt like the breath had been stolen right out of her lungs and all of her organs were pressing in on each other in a tight Ziploc bag. She was momentarily too overwhelmed to make sense of this feeling, to make sense of the speechlessness that had come over her upon learning her granddaughter was having a baby with a boy who had turned into a man right before her eyes, a person she had thought highly of throughout his entire life. There was joy, with some relief mixed in, too, that Alice would have this, a loving family. With a man that she could trust. It comforted Ellen that this wasn't going to be Wilma's fate repeated.

Confusingly, there was also an overwhelming sadness. The feeling trickled up through Ellen's esophagus and formed thoughts, and she slowly realized that capping the joy was a lethally sharp stab of grief. As happy as this news made Ellen, Gerry would have been truly beside himself with excitement. If he hadn't already had the heart attack, this might have caused it, so intense would have been his reaction. Gerry adored Peter like he was one of their own, and now, in a way, he really would be. She wanted to share this moment with him so badly she felt she might get on her hands and knees, search the house, just in case his ghost lingered.

But she knew there was no ghost. Gerry was gone. Forever. And for the first time since the funeral, she felt like she knew exactly what she wanted, and it was simple. She wanted to tell Jennifer and Alice this. They were family, and she should be able to express how badly she missed him to them. But the nagging knowledge that she had broken down earlier in front of them was getting in the way. She had already shown a weakness, and while she couldn't undo the coffeepot incident, she could make it singular.

Strangely, even though her outburst felt close enough to dictate her behavior, the afternoon's overwhelming anger had ebbed, almost completely. It was like the sadness of Gerry's absence had expanded enough inside of her to push it out. She didn't quite know how to make sense of this, but she did know that she could no longer allow her granddaughter to sit in this place of uncertainty on her feelings about the pregnancy. She could feel Alice's expectant and nervous eyes on her. She tried to clear her throat but couldn't. She took what felt to Alice and Jennifer like the longest sip of water in human history.

She cleared her throat again, successfully this time. "That's wonderful, sweetie," she said. Alice felt tentative relief and relaxed into her chair just a bit, keeping her eyes trained on her grandmother. Alice saw that there was no trace of joy in her grandmother's face. Ellen continued, "I'm sorry, I'm just overwhelmed by . . . but that is the most wonderful news you possibly could have told me. I mean that."

Alice reached across the table and put her hand on her grandmother's. She nodded, understanding, because she felt it, too. "I get it," she said. She moved her other hand over, reaching for Jennifer, who reached out for her niece. Alice flipped both of her pinkies up at them. "Absolutely no telling that part yet," she said.

Jennifer smiled and hooked her pinky with Alice's. Ellen stared at Alice's pinky in confusion. "What am I supposed to do with this?" she asked. Alice and Jennifer smiled.

An hour later, Jennifer locked Ellen's door with her spare, darted across the street, and circled around to the back porch instead of going inside. She sat, dripping, in a rocking chair and looked out at her backyard, at the rain pelting the grass and sliding off the magnolia leaves. She tried to focus on the sound of the storm instead of the feelings whirling inside of her: an embarrassing envy of her niece, of the hope she got to feel, of the potential in something so new and unbroken. This misery that she felt in her marriage, was this how it would always be?

Inside, Brady had followed Red down the white carpeted hall into the boys' bathroom, which was nestled in between Grant's and Red's bedrooms. Red had never really thought about how strange it was to have a bathroom with three entrances until now. He realized he didn't think he had ever seen another one like it, with all doors lockable from the inside, which had caused some real issues in their adolescence. Red always locked Grant's door and forgot to unlock it, which resulted in Grant running through Red's room to get to the toilet, often shouting "Fuck you, firecrotch!" or "Who jerks off in a toilet, dammit!" on the way.

Red found the package of new toothbrushes in his drawer, ripped one open, and handed it to Brady, who leaned on the bathroom door-frame, watching him. Red blushed and washed his hands for something to do.

"Red?" Brady said. Red looked over, right into Brady's bright blue eyes. Spiky anxiety pinched him all over his body. Here it was, Red thought, the moment that Brady would say something, would directly ask Red why he was lying to his family. Brady batted his eyes and said, "Where do you keep your toothpaste?"

Glee flickered in his eyes, and the skin around them crinkled as he smiled. Red immediately understood that Brady was messing with him, which made him feel more exposed than ever, but somehow less anxious. This was a shock, as the two feelings usually had a direct correlation.

Red opened his medicine cabinet and handed the toothpaste to Brady. He suddenly didn't know if he was supposed to also brush his teeth now or wait for Brady to finish. How intimate was brushing your teeth next to someone? Too intimate? Or would it be weird for him to walk into his bedroom and then wait until Brady was done and then go back into his bathroom and brush his teeth alone?

Brady nodded to the uncapped toothpaste in his hand and gestured toward Red. "Would the gentleman like some?" he asked.

Red chuckled at the joke, mostly out of relief and gratitude that Brady had made the decision for him. He lifted his toothbrush out of the white tile holder next to his faucet and held it out like a child to Brady, who squirted the thick white paste onto the brush. Red blushed.

They brushed their teeth, and Brady followed Red into his bedroom with the twin beds that had been there since Red graduated from his crib, JJ and Jennifer anticipating a higher number of sleepovers than Red would ever have. In school, Red was social, but at the end of the day, he always preferred to be in his own room alone, removed from all the pressure he found in other people.

"Do you need clothes to sleep in?" Red asked, in a muscle-memory effort to be polite.

"I don't know, Red, do I?" Brady said, raising one eyebrow and putting his hands on his hips in a faux-seductive stance. Red sat on his bed and put his elbows on his knees, grimacing.

"Okay, listen," he said. "Obviously, we've . . . You've . . . Well, you've obviously seen me."

"Yeah, Red, you're, like, never not walking or running down the street."

"No, on . . ."

Brady's eyebrow traveled further up his forehead, and he offered no assistance, clearly entertained.

Red inhaled and he sputtered. He cleared his throat. He felt the back of his neck grow hot as a stove, and he finally managed to spit out, "I know you saw me on YCHO."

Brady nodded, pushing his mouth to one side of his face in a vain attempt to hide his grin. He tapped his pointer finger to his chin and looked to the ceiling. "Hm," he said. "I don't recall seeing a Red on YCHO, the dating app, an app where anyone who came across my profile would be a boy looking for the profiles of other boys. But you know, I saw a *Gerald* who looked remarkably like you . . ."

"'Red' is a nickname," Red said. "I felt like . . . I don't know, there wasn't space on the profile-maker thing to write, 'My name is Gerald, but everyone calls me Red.'"

"Uh-huh," Brady said, standing over him with his hands on his hips.

Red looked up at him, having genuinely no idea what this cute boy was thinking. "What?" he finally asked.

"Sure it has nothing to do with you wanting some kind of, I don't know, false identity to hide behind?" Brady asked.

Red felt the blush crawling up to his ears, but he didn't look away from Brady, figuring that would appear weak. "That . . . mighta had something to do with it," he said. He honestly hadn't thought about it that way before, but there was no denying it.

Brady dropped his eyebrow and his hands from his hips. He sat on the bed next to Red, which pureed Red's insides.

"Babe, do you want to talk about it? I know it's hard." Brady dropped his tongue-in-cheek, saucy attitude quickly, and while it was a bit jarring, Red felt his almost dangerously tensed body slacken a bit. He put his forehead in his hands, and Brady tentatively put a hand on his shoulder. He didn't move it in circles or anything comforting like that, for which Red was grateful.

"I mean," Red said, "can I ask . . . how was it for you?"

"How was what?"

"How was . . . telling people and stuff."

"How was coming out, you mean," Brady said gently.

"Yeah."

"It was . . ." Brady said, sighing. "You know. Complicated. When I was growing up, it felt like I had this huge secret, but looking back, it's laughable how obvious it was. And I mean, my mom always knew. I think my dad always knew, but that was, like . . . like he knew, I think, deep down, but didn't want to deal with it until he absolutely had to. My sister was the first person I told, and she said she had been waiting for it. Well, she was the first person I ever said 'I'm gay' to, but I had already gotten up to some mischief." He winked at Red. "And she was happy for me—she's older and was living in New York at the time. I figured I should tell my parents in person, but I didn't want to tell them without her, you know, buffer vibes. It all actually went pretty well, like on the surface, but I think she and my dad must have had some conversations I don't know about. Used her daddy's-girl power for good."

"So, like," Red said, "you just sat them down and were like . . . 'This is me'?"

"Pretty much. I told them the Saturday after Thanksgiving my sophomore year of college. I had barely been eating and was so nervous and my mom was so worried about me because I'm obviously her favorite person on the damn planet. I had thought about telling just my mom first, but I figured that would make it even harder to face my dad, like he would respect it less, like it would be a pussy move. Which it would've been, I guess. My mom immediately was like, 'Oh, honey, we support you, of course, thank you for telling us,' yada yada yada. My dad didn't say anything for a really long time. He just, like, nodded and grunted at what my mom was saying, and then afterwards he hugged me for what felt like an insane amount of time because we, like, don't do that.

"And it's kind of weird because, like, my dad and I never talk about it. He's never asked me if I'm seeing anyone, he's never made any kind of comment about any of it. And sometimes that kind of sucks, like, I'll be honest, but at the time I was so relieved he wasn't mad and outright, like, mean about it or whatever. But I know it's hard for him, and I know he does his best. I get annoyed because sometimes some of the other gay guys I knew at college were from these, like, progressive families, and they thought it was so fucked up that my dad didn't make more of an effort. But I'm like, him even just being okay with it to the degree that he is is enough for me, which is FUBT."

"Fubbed?"

"Fucked up but true," Brady said.

"Oh." They sat in silence for a moment. "So were you, like . . . glad that you did it?"

Brady laughed. "Sorry," he immediately said, putting a hand over his mouth. "I don't mean to be an asshole. But yeah, I'm glad I came out to

my family, Red. You kind of like . . . have to do that to have a relationship with them."

"Yeah," Red said, staring at the opposite wall and not moving.

"Does anyone else know?"

Red shook his head, not counting the guy he stood up on the date
that never was.

"Hm," Brady said. "It might be good for you to say it."

"To say it?" Red asked. "To say what?"

"To say the words 'I'm gay,' Red," Brady said. "Practice it. Manifest.
It may not feel like such a big deal once you just call it what it is. Also,
own who you are. People are clearly obsessed with you, and this is a part
of the you that they all love so much. The people who love you want
every part, even this one, maybe even *especially* this one, trust me. And
if your family were actually homophobic, they wouldn't be so cool to
me. And you know it."

Red gave a tight nod, also knowing that Brady knew that being publicly tolerant of gay people was different from being comfortable having
a gay kid. Red felt like having a gay kid could be seismic for JJ, which
was ironic, because he didn't feel particularly significant to his father,
or anyone really.

"You can do it," Brady said, giving Red's shoulder a squeeze. Red had
not lost awareness of Brady's hand for even a second, even though up
until this point Brady had not done anything extra to make that presence known. Red inhaled. He let the air out. He looked at his hands,
stretching his fingers wide, noticing how lined his palms were. Had they
always been this lined?

He knew he needed to just say it. The person he was saying it to
already knew, for fuck's sake. But the words jammed in his throat because saying it out loud would finally vanquish any possibility that it
was maybe not true. Then again, Red already knew the truth. He took
a shallow inhale, and he said (not whispering, though the temptation
was there), "I'm gay."

Brady clamped his hand down on Red's shoulder, loosened it, and moved it to Red's other shoulder to pull him into an embrace. The movement reminded Red of that jokey pickup line guys used to do in middle school: "If you were a pirate, would you keep your parrot on this shoulder or *this* shoulder?" A sneaky way to put your arm around someone. He drew a shaky breath, feeling rattled, but also not really knowing how he felt. He felt fine, he guessed? That wasn't *so* bad.

But any emotional reaction Red could have had to admitting aloud for the first time that he was gay was very quickly overshadowed by the stress he felt that Brady, a cute boy, was in his childhood bedroom with him, and he had his arms around him. Any slackness his body had allowed was instantly removed by the thought that something could happen that night, even in that moment, between him and Brady.

The thought was exciting. He was attracted to Brady, and realized that twenty-five years was a very long time to go without kissing anyone he really wanted to kiss. Red knew what he wanted, but there was also the fear. There were the jittery fears that Red knew were normal before a first anything, the jittery fears he felt he should have experienced over a decade ago. And Brady had *actual experience*. Oh, God, did Brady pity him? It was certainly possible.

And of course, there was this: even though Red had just said it, and saying it had been terrifying, kissing a boy was a whole different beast. It was really just follow-through, but it felt like saying it was reaching the peak of a mountain Red had hiked, and anything happening with Brady was jumping off it, arms flailing, legs running on nothing, plummeting.

He swallowed a lump in his throat that he knew wasn't tears but couldn't identify. Mustering every ounce of courage he had, pulling it from every joint, sucking it out of his toenails, scraping it out of his spine, he looked into Brady's eyes. The courage and the fear collided in a bolt of connection when Brady looked right back, and each of their pupils seemed to swallow the other's.

"Oh, sweetie," Brady said, shaking his head gently. "That won't be happening now."

Red jumped back like he was the flame and Brady was the hot iron poker. "Right," he said, not because he needed to affirm anything, but because that was the word that happened to launch itself out of Red's mouth, open with humiliation. He looked at his knees, somehow still safe in the space Brady had put him in, the one where he was being honest. "Yeah. Sorry."

"Oh my God," Brady said. "Red, let's not get into the, like, apology business. You have nothing to apologize for! I just have a little boundary where I don't hook up with guys who aren't, like, *out* out. *Believe me*, it's not that I don't want to, and I'm sorry not to be more fun." (Red didn't know whether or not to believe this, but that didn't change the fact that relief unfolded in his abdomen and an electron of pleasure sent itself down his spine at the thought.) "You just don't graduate from Georgia unscathed from that kind of thing, especially when you're me, not to brag, someone who's friends with all the sorority girls, and then I get invited on all the date nights, and there's always that closeted SAE or whatever who sees his chance, and next thing I know, I'm completely in love with someone who thinks camo is a color and will have a wife and kids who will sleep every night blissfully unaware of the fact that Dad is in the living room jerking it to *Call Me by Your Name*. Know what I mean?"

Red shook his head, not because he didn't understand exactly what Brady was talking about, but because this guy made him chuckle in the same way that the college students he worked with did—even though Red was barely older, they spoke in a way that made little to no sense to him, but he seemed to get it all the same.

"Red?"

"Yeah?"

"I do need pajamas, though." Red laughed out loud and so did Brady. The moment was broken, but it wasn't unpleasant. When Red stood

IF WE'RE BEING HONEST   171

up to get a T-shirt and shorts from the dresser Jennifer had painted for
him when he was a kid, with basketballs and baseballs and footballs
stenciled all over it, Brady stood up, too, and, considering their height
difference, easily slipped his arms under Red's and pulled him close. Red
placed his arms over Brady's shoulders with caution.

"Prouda you, big guy," Brady said.

"Thanks," Red said as Brady clapped him on the back like they were on
the same basketball team, praying before a game, which made Red laugh.
He tossed a Eulalia High Baseball T-shirt and some basketball shorts to
Brady, who caught them. Red busied himself with getting in bed, wrapping himself in his sheets, and looking at his phone while Brady changed.

Brady got into his bed, too, and they lay there, their symmetry perfect.

"Good night, Red," Brady said.

" 'Night, Brady," Red said, rolling over onto his side and facing the
wall. Because even though the lights were off, he didn't want Brady to see
him smiling into his pillow.

Chapter 8

Ellen wasn't a morning person, never had been. She preferred to stay up late, to earn the quiet after a long day. She could never fall asleep early, anyway. Gerry also liked to stay up late, but he liked waking up early, too, and somehow rarely seemed tired. It was like there weren't enough hours in the day for his energy to fully expand, and he seemed to wake up earlier and earlier as he got older, like he sensed he was running out of time. Ellen, on the other hand, found getting out of bed even more difficult with each passing year, her back aching, her bones creaking and joints popping as she eased herself out of their California king, her brain beeping to life more slowly than the ancient twenty-pound computer she used to send e-cards.

But Ellen had been waking up early since Gerry died, her eyes flying open and her heart jumping as though she had been startled awake, even though, for the first time in sixty years, there was no one in the bed to have disturbed her. This, combined with her family constantly eyeing her with concern, made Ellen marathon-level exhausted by early afternoon, but it was also convenient, because Miss Sparkles was used to being walked first thing in the morning. Gerry said she liked to march out into the day with the sun.

Miss Sparkles was equal parts stimulated by and wary of all the houseguests, the sounds they made throughout the house very different from the soft pattering of her parents she was used to. But still, she could not be distracted from the fact that her Gerry was gone. She had been peering through the Coke-glass pane by the front door all day every day, and looked up eagerly every time the door opened, returning her head to her paws in disappointment when Gerry didn't come thundering into the house calling her name.

As Ellen took what felt like a long time to straighten up after clipping the pink leash onto Miss Sparkles's pink collar, she wondered if Miss Sparkles remembered Gerry's death, if she knew at the time that Gerry had passed and just forgotten, or hadn't even realized in the moment what was going on. Like most folks from rural Southern towns, Ellen had been (correctly) raised to believe that animals had a sixth sense, could understand more than humans gave them credit for and just plain more than humans period. When Gerry crashed to the floor of the vet's office, Ellen thought that Miss Sparkles knew, by the way that she was barking frantically, her fluffy white fur raised on her back, that something was very, unchangeably wrong.

In the hospital waiting room, Miss Sparkles had burrowed into Ellen's lap, pressing all her warmth and aliveness into the center of Ellen. Ellen thought that maybe Miss Sparkles was digging for comfort, cuddling so close as to become one with the only human she knew she had left. It didn't occur to Ellen that maybe Miss Sparkles wanted to comfort *her*. She thought maybe she should bring the dog to the grave, and maybe Miss Sparkles would be able to sense that Gerry's body was there, underground, his stilled hands never to pet her again. She quickly dismissed the depressing idea, also because she realized she was being one of those people she disapproved of: the kind of person who took their shih tzu much too seriously.

Miss Sparkles was the first dog Ellen and Gerry had gotten since their kids went to college. Once they became empty nesters, they had enjoyed going on trips with Linda and Fred so much that dealing with a dog just seemed like an extra hassle. The foursome had cruised around Italy, lounged at a resort in the Dominican Republic, taken another cruise to Alaska, and—Ellen's favorite—traveled to Paris. She found the general unfriendliness there completely jarring and utterly delightful.

Then Linda died, and the trips stopped, even though Ellen didn't want them to. She mentioned to Gerry exactly two times that they should plan something: Once, when they were eating pork chops for dinner, Ellen said that she had always wanted to go to Greece, and the two of them weren't getting any younger. Gerry said it was a good idea, but when she finally brought it up again after no planning from Gerry, who loved to research and plan trips, he said he just didn't think it made any sense and was uncharacteristically ornery about the whole thing, so Ellen never mentioned it again.

Hence, the dog. Gerry had wanted what he called a proper dog, like what he had growing up and what they had raised the kids with: a golden retriever (Milly), a border collie (Max), or a Labrador (Rascal). But when a litter of tiny white fluffballs was dropped off at their local vet's and they saw the picture in the paper, they ended up with Miss Sparkles, who was not necessarily a proper dog, but was a dog and was undeniably proper.

She held her head high as she marched down Myrtle Lane, her short tail twitching in what could only be described as a sashay. She swished over to the tree on their corner, one of the mystery magnolias the neighborhood association was always getting so worked up over. Miss Sparkles sniffed at the trunk, which was thicker than Ellen remembered it. It was growing. Ellen disagreed with the neighborhood association; she thought it was lovely to see a tree grow that would one day be big and mighty, where children, maybe even her grandchildren's children, would climb and swing from the branches.

Miss Sparkles lost interest and made her way back to Ellen. Ellen knew she loved Miss Sparkles because of the way she delighted in her. Ellen was tickled by Miss Sparkles's little sneezes and how she sometimes looked like she was smiling. She liked feeling her warm body against her leg when she went to sleep at night. She knew Gerry loved Miss Sparkles because Gerry had told Miss Sparkles about four hundred times a day how much he loved her, how she was the prettiest girl in the world, how she was Gerry's special girl. She knew that Miss Sparkles loved them both, never taking her eyes off either one of them if she could help it. Ellen wondered why. Surely Miss Sparkles sensed that she depended on them for survival. She saw who grabbed a leash and took her outside when her bladder was full, who filled her water and food bowls, and who brushed her tangles out. But she seemed to love everyone who came through the door, and no one else was doing any of that stuff.

But she loved Ellen and Gerry best, and it felt outsized compared to what they did for her, didn't feel earned. JJ had once told Ellen that Miss Sparkles's brain was the size of a walnut, and while Ellen didn't necessarily believe that, she did have the suspicion that Miss Sparkles did not love them for any cognitive reason at all. Maybe Miss Sparkles had picked up love that someone else had dropped, and was using that supply on everyone around her. Or of course, Ellen thought, it could be the love of God. The wholeness of it, the perfection of it, the sheer force of the love of Miss Sparkles did, in fact, feel closer to something that would come from the Lord than the cracked stuff that came from the humans Ellen had known, at least.

Ellen sighed as Miss Sparkles squatted over some tall ivy, blissfully relieving herself, and Ellen of the task of picking up her waste. Maybe it wasn't so complicated, she thought. Maybe Miss Sparkles loved her simply because she did.

Alice took a sharp intake of breath when the loose wire on Gerry's key chain dug into her palm. She hadn't realized she had been squeezing the keys so hard. She looked back up. He appeared so much smaller than he did when she was a kid, when she'd stare every summer Sunday at the blood trickling down from the crown of thorns, at the blackened part of the palm where the nails were driven. It wasn't that she thought he looked *good*, necessarily, but she thought to herself how undeniably flattering this position was for Jesus, flexed muscles and all. Crucifixion worked for him.

It was the middle of the day, and she hadn't planned to stop here on the way home from the dollar store where she had gone to buy the Aqua Net hairspray Ellen insisted she would need for Rebecca's wedding. But she saw the chapel peeking up as she crawled down the road, and before she knew it, here she was, at First Baptist.

Sweat coated her. She couldn't remember the last time she had been in a church that wasn't for a wedding or Gerry's funeral. Not only did Jesus look smaller now, but she felt smaller, too. Maybe it was that she had never been in the church alone, but she felt like an ant in an empty football stadium. Except maybe that football stadium was located some-where on Mars because she had the sensation that she had disappeared, that no one could find her there. Not because no one would expect her to be there, which was true, but because she had the feeling that if any-one were to drive down the road where the church was, they wouldn't even be able to see it. Like upon her entry, it had swallowed itself.

Alice scoffed, looking at the statue, and the sound echoed. The wars fought for this dude; the number of people who had been killed, hurt, or made to feel worse about themselves, all in his name. The world was the way that it was directly because of the myth represented here, and most of the world was shitty.

Of course, Alice supposed, plenty of people thought that all the good-ness in the world was because of this guy, too. Or his dad. She thought about her kid. What would she say to her child when they asked her about death? Christian parents had a real easy out with the whole heaven thing. And what would her child even sound like when they spoke to her? Would they even ask her questions like that, or would they be too dumb to think about them? Or would they be smart, smarter than Alice? What if the kid asked her a question, caught her in a bad mood, and she snapped, and it was a really important question, and she scarred the kid for life with her sharp response? What if she moved somewhere and had a car and left the kid in the car on a hot day and they died and then she had to not only lose her child but be on the news for it?

And what about all the things she couldn't control? What if she did everything right, what if she never lost patience, answered questions well, never left her kid in the car, but then they got cancer? Or were struck by lightning? Or hit by a drunk driver? Or choked on their own vomit in college? And there was the fact that her child would be Black. How was she, a white lady, supposed to prepare her kid for the racist world? How could she teach her kid about life experiences she hadn't personally had? And though she chided herself for the selfishness of this, she worried that her child would resent her, would wish for a mother who could understand, could *really* understand.

How did anyone do this?

"Um," Alice said, her voice bouncing around the empty pews and off the stained glass. "How . . ." She bounced on her feet and turned around to make sure she was still alone. "I'm not sure if this is idiotic, actually I'm pretty sure it is, I mean, unless saying that hurts my ask? My ask is that, uh, for help? Please help me do this. And please protect him or her. Or them! Because gender isn't, like . . . Anyway, I know I've had it pretty good, so I'd rather not pay for that with this kid, if at all possible."

She looked at Jesus. He didn't reply. She waited. Suddenly, she heard a high-pitched whine and jumped, her heart going completely still. It took a second for her to realize it was the sound of her own fart. She bent over and caught her breath. She straightened up, turned around, and laughed hysterically the whole way down the aisle.

....

Delia was lying in her shared room with Alice, under the watchful eyes of Ellen's creepy Victorian dolls, stewing in her own self-hatred. She checked her phone yet again. Nothing from Connor. She couldn't believe that after months of almost-calls, after countless considerations overshadowed by self-protection, she had finally broken down. What *really* killed her was that the impetus was some random jerk from Eulalia.

She opened the phone app, and Connor's contact immediately popped up, fresh from last night's call. She felt a stabbing in her gut seeing that photo of him with the sushi, feeling the sunburn from the chink in her armor. It was ten a.m. on a weekday; there was no way he hadn't heard the voicemail at this point. She cast her mind for some excuse as to why he wouldn't have been in touch, and her heart sank as she came up with nothing.

She couldn't do this anymore. She was so tired; she was so hungover. The constant checking of her phone, being on edge all the time that he might have direct messaged her, that he might have texted her, and the constant disappointment to find that he hadn't, her mind's never-ending whirring, conjecturing all the tech issues that could have interfered with their reuniting over the airwaves. She caught her finger hovering over the Call button in an act of muscle memory, and she almost vomited.

Delia moved her finger two inches to the left, though it felt like it had to travel two miles. She didn't take a minute to pause, consider, or breathe. She just pressed the Block button. She was done. She also deleted her Instagram app for good measure. She cast her phone to the side, took a deep breath, and started moving slowly down the stairs to get some damn coffee.

"*The first boink is the deepest, try to boink again,*" Delia sang slowly and deeply to herself until she heard a knock at the front door. She opened it and looked down automatically to the doorstep, expecting yet another casserole. Her eyes were slow adjusting to the light, which felt like a direct assault considering her post-Ricky's hangover. Instead of a tinfoil-covered dish, she saw feet. She traced the person up, looked into his face, snapped out of her hangover real fast, and said, "Oh, shit."

Fred rocked on his heels and tapped the bike helmet he held at his hip. "Hello, Delia," he said.

Delia's instinct was to say, "I don't think so," and end any possibility that he could interact with any member of her family, for his sake as much as theirs. But she couldn't actually bring herself to slam the door in an elderly man's face. So they just stood there and looked at each other.

"Well, I assume you're not here to see me," Delia said, putting her hand on her hip.

"Is she home?"

"Is who home?"

Fred sighed. Delia had always been difficult. "Is your grandmother home?"

"My grandmother?" Delia cocked her head like a puppy. "Ellen? Ellen Williams? Best friend of your late wife? Wife of your late best friend? Woman who was disgraced publicly? By you?"

"Please, Delia."

"She's here. Whether or not she wants to talk to you? Different story. Hang on a sec." Delia did shut the door in his face now, although more gently than she felt her level of frustration warranted. She marched into the kitchen, where Ellen was sitting at the table with Carol Anne and Wilma, drinking coffee.

"Gram?" Delia said, and her rage immediately evaporated upon realizing her grandmother was about to be in a vulnerable position. "Um. Fred's here to see you. He's at the front door. I'd be MORE than happy to send him on his way, but . . . yeah."

Wilma's eyes widened and Carol Anne nodded her head sagely, as though she had summoned him there herself. "Here to make amends," she said. "Could be really beautiful, Mama."

Ellen tapped her acrylic nail against the side of her iced tea glass and sighed. "I don't want to see him." She didn't look at Wilma or Carol Anne, so she didn't see Carol Anne's face contort in confusion or Wilma's eyebrows travel so far up her forehead they nearly touched her hairline.

"Are you sure, Mama?" Wilma asked cautiously.

"Yes, she's sure," Delia snapped. She nodded in Ellen's direction. "Right on, Gram. I'll tell him to get lost."

"Well, there's no need to be rude," Ellen called after her, as Delia had immediately headed back for the front door.

Fred looked up expectantly when Delia reopened the door, and his face fell a little upon seeing her again and not Ellen. This annoyed Delia, even though she had done nothing to make him happy to see her. She thought about lying. "She's not here right now" almost came out of her mouth, but Delia wasn't about to let the general manners of her surroundings infect her. She was a New Yorker now.

"She doesn't feel up to seeing you," she said.

He nodded. "Okay. I'm sure you've had a lot of people comin' by. Must be exhaustin'."

"Uh, yeah," Delia said. "I don't really think oversocialization is the issue here. I think it's more you and your little coffin-side confession."

She crossed her arms, even though her self-patrolling bitch radar was going berserk, and the thought of any of her gay friends seeing her in this moment made her feel slightly ill. But this wasn't about civil rights to Delia; this was about betrayal.

He looked down and nodded, pressing his bicycle helmet closer to his side. "I'm sorry, Delia. We—I—never wanted to hurt anybody."

"Yeah, well." She couldn't think of anything else to say. She didn't want to admit that he had hurt her, and he hadn't really. Gerry had. And Gerry hadn't really, even. Connor did. But Delia was too hungover to be that honest with herself.

IF WE'RE BEING HONEST

Fred inhaled and opened his mouth like he was about to say something else, and Delia braced herself. But he just turned around and walked toward his bike, leaning neatly against the mailbox. She closed the door softly, leaving her hands on the wood, and instinctively wondered what Connor was doing. Then she tried not to think.

....

"Sounds sick, can I join?" Grant asked upon learning Carol Anne was leading all the girls in a yoga class. She had been teaching yoga ever since she saw a "Now Hiring" sign on the door of a yoga studio back in Los Angeles that she had heard was frequented by lots of agents and producers. The class was to take place in Ellen's backyard, next to the garden, which they all agreed would be lovely, even though it would be a naturally heated yoga class in the hundred-degree weather.

"It's girls only," Delia said in a half-fake, all-haughty tone.

"I thought gender was a construct," Grant said, pleased with himself.

"We'll be surrounding ourselves with purely feminine, yin energy today, Grant," Carol Anne said. She tipped her head—on top of which all her hair was piled in a gigantic mound—toward him.

"Boo!" Grant said.

"You have a lot of feminine energy within you," Carol Anne said, placing a hand on Grant's shoulder and closing her eyes. "But just combined with the masculine—"

"Yeah, I'm out, thanks," Grant said, turning on his heel and making a show of bouncing his basketball on the grass, which didn't really work. "Later!" he called over his shoulder as he did a spin that was supposed to show his athletic prowess but really only reinforced Carol Anne's point about his feminine energy.

Jennifer, who was wearing a bright pink tank-top-and-leggings set, twisted her hair into a pristine bun that sat right on top of her head. "I need to burn some calories," she said.

"It's really not about burning calories, Jennifer," Carol Anne said. "It's about the marriage of breath and movement."

Jennifer had a proper yoga mat, while the rest of them had to use beach towels dug up from Ellen's basement. Carol Anne had asked Ellen to join; yoga was something she had been pressuring Ellen to try for years. "I don't do that pretzel stuff," Ellen always said, despite Carol Anne's arguments, and today was no exception.

Carol Anne had insisted on using the only towel unspotted by bleach stains. Everyone lined up and faced her, and she smiled benevolently upon them. "Let's begin our practice today by setting an intention. Maybe it's just to be present, to focus solely on your breath. Any intention is acceptable and welcome. My intention is to focus on myself, to try and distance myself from the burdens of others, which I take on too easily as an empath. I can be strong on the mat, but I don't have to be strong for everyone, all the time." She rolled her eyes at herself and smiled. "Would anyone else like to share their intention?"

"My intention is to keep it tight without getting injured so that I can post a photo of myself from the wedding that will be so bomb Connor will cry," Delia said, planning to redownload Instagram for Rebecca's big day.

"Thank you for sharing, Delia," Carol Anne said, dipping her prayer-position hands and head in Delia's direction. "But how about we set an intention that has to do with the present—the here and now—not about what this practice could do for our bodies in the future."

"I thought any intention was welcome and accepted," Delia muttered into her padded sports bra.

"Alice," Carol Anne said, "I'd imagine your intention is to connect with your inner sanctuary, the home for your unborn child?"

"Sure, great," Alice said, swatting a mosquito swarming around her head.

"Although I of course can't dictate what anyone's intention is," Carol Anne said. "For instance, I'd like to tell Wilma that her intention should be to focus on the present and allow herself some enjoyment for once, and I would love to encourage Jennifer to set her intention to keeping her brain space within the four corners of her mat, to focus solely on her breath, so that some of that anger she's marching around with might melt away. But I can't do that because everyone must set their own, individual intention." She kept her eyes closed for this whole speech.

"Mmkay, Annie," Wilma said. Jennifer just gritted her teeth and pretended she hadn't heard.

"Connor and I used to go to this great heated yoga class near our apartment," Delia said. "At first, it was like I made him go, but then it got to a point where he started to go even if I couldn't. I guess—"

"Thank you, Delia," Carol Anne said. "Let's drop to our knees and begin in child's pose."

Carol Anne began to lead them through flows, and it was so suffocatingly hot that not even Jennifer could appreciate how many calories she was burning. She only broke once, when she fell out of toppling tree pose and muttered, "Fuck," which caused Carol Anne to make the whole class pause and om, to "reset the energy," although she did not make them do that when her phone rang from inside the house, which she sprinted to answer just in case it was her agent (who was really an "ambitious" agent's assistant), only to return muttering, "Fucking spam."

Alice whispered to Wilma halfway through, was she sure this was okay for the baby? To which Wilma replied, "You'll know if it's wrong. Drink water." The heat blurred Delia's thoughts so much that she really didn't think about Connor at all until the end, when she remembered how he would sometimes hold her hand in corpse pose. Her sweat smelled like Bud Light.

"Allow your body to release the tension it's been holding. Allow the spirit and the body to meet," Carol Anne said while she lay down in final shavasana, one hand on her chest and the other on her belly.

As Jennifer lay in corpse pose, she felt completely spent. It was probably heat exhaustion, and something about the fact that she hadn't moved her body so smoothly or peacefully (excluding the toppling tree, well, toppling) in she didn't even know how long. As she lay there, under the shade of a magnolia tree but still baking in the heat, she saw the crags in her heart with perfect clarity. For the first time since she started suspecting JJ of cheating, her eyes weren't darting around looking for evidence, and she wasn't violently shoving the thought of it down so she could do what needed to get done. On her mat, with her palms upward, sweating profusely, she realized that she was devastated, and she felt like indulging in an activity that only occurred to her about once every five years. She cried.

On a raggedy beach towel five feet away, dizzy from the heat, Wilma missed her father. A voice inside her head, as clear as though it were coming from the headphones the girls had gotten her for Christmas, said, "You will never see him again." Even though she had already buried him, she truly considered for the first time that she would never hear his voice again, never dance around the kitchen with him, faking reluctance. That was all done now, and she was alone. Wilma began to quietly weep, too.

Alice was tired; she was so tired. She tried to relax her jaw, as Carol Anne instructed. She was going to have a *baby*. She had the thought that in a few months, if she wanted to do something like take a yoga class, she would have to arrange for a babysitter. Although that sounded inconvenient, it was a change, and change was a relieving thought. She was finally getting what she wanted: something she didn't already know. Tension released itself from her eyes and tears leaked out, mixing with the sweat on her face and in her hairline.

Delia wondered if Connor had taken any yoga classes recently, if he had tried to get in touch with her. She didn't know which was scarier: Connor not trying to reach her, or Connor trying to call or text and realizing she had made communicating a non-option. So she cried, too.

"What the hell?" Grant said as he approached the group, unable to stay away. "Is everyone crying?"

Delia, Alice, Jennifer, and Wilma all sat up slowly, gingerly, blinking and looking around at the others, embarrassed, hesitant, and hopeful to believe that they weren't the only one crying. They all caught each other wiping their eyes, and Delia was the first to laugh. Then Alice began to laugh, and so did Wilma, and even though Jennifer could still feel the cracks in her heart, she couldn't help but laugh, too. They were all too tired and too hot not to.

....

There was no real reason why Alice should have been surprised when Peter called her and invited her over to his house for a happy hour/appetizer get-together. Charlie and Deborah Bell were about to be the grandparents, Rebecca and Justin the aunt and uncle, to the nectarine-sized almost-person swimming around in her uterus. And there was *certainly* no reason why she should have meeting-the-parents jitters considering she had known these people for as long as she could remember being alive, and considering that she and Peter weren't dating or anything anyway. But the nerves were still there, even though Peter had told her they basically exploded with joy upon hearing the news.

It was less of a reflection on the Bells and more of a reflection on how Alice anticipated Eulalia folks to behave, but she was suspicious that the delight they felt upon finding out that Peter would be a father wouldn't automatically be extended to her. She was a woman who had had sex, unprotected sex, no less, with someone she wasn't dating, and even though Peter, their son, was equally as culpable as she, that wasn't a fact Alice suspected always computed to folks in Eulalia.

So it was with slightly shaking hands and shallow breath that she knocked on the Bells' door. It swung open to Peter, who had a collared shirt and a big smile on. He stepped forward and enveloped her in a hug, and her nervousness shrank to nothing between his arms. They hugged for longer than was normal, until Alice stepped back. Peter put his hands on her shoulders. "Hey, you!" he said.

"Hi." She smiled, and they looked at each other, and she didn't know what she was supposed to feel, but she knew that she felt good. Peter's hands fell away from her shoulders as he was hip-checked by Rebecca, who also pulled Alice in close, though their similar heights made the hug significantly less engulfing.

"Alice!" she said, squeezing her, then stepping back and giving Alice's stomach an unsubtle glance. "Congratulations! I couldn't be happier for you two."

Alice wished she had a stress ball, even though she had never used a stress ball in her life. Having something to squeeze just sounded nice. It made sense that Rebecca would be happy for both of them, and that was what you said to an expectant mother and father. But did she mean that she was happy for them separately or together? And if she meant together, how *together* did she mean? Had Peter said something to imply he wanted a certain kind of *togetherness*?

The question itself was less disturbing to Alice than the hope she felt bubbling around in her chest thinking about it. When Peter reached for the check the night they got drinks in New York, it was like the image of his oversized hands grabbing that leather black book had burned itself on her brain. Her heart had stopped beating and she felt short of breath, as in one complete crash she realized how badly she wanted him that night. And then there was the whole not-being-able-to-stop-thinking-about-him thing afterwards, even before she found out she was pregnant.

Surely, she told herself at the time, that had to be more of a reflection of her loneliness, and less of a reflection of any kind of actual feeling worth examination. Peter had been her first love, the boy (almost literally) next door, and she was at a point in her life when she was painfully aware that things had not all turned out exactly as she had planned. It was only natural that after a sparkling night with someone kind, an old friend, she would catch herself acting like she was half in love with him, right? But it didn't have to indicate anything real.

Even though, if she were really being honest with herself, nothing had ever felt as solid, as real, as Peter Bell.

Rebecca stood aside so that her fiancé, Justin, who had gotten to Eulalia that day, could step in for his hug. He was about to be a real part of the family, after all. "Alice, congratulations!" he said warmly, patting her on the back in a friendly way, which was appropriate considering he had met her twice.

"Same to you, Justin!" she said. "And my congratulations to you is more heartfelt because you did your thing on purpose."

Justin blinked and made a weird grimace, not knowing if he was supposed to laugh at that or be horrified by it. Alice realized her mistake, and turned her head quickly to Peter, who snorted and smiled at the floor.

Rebecca rolled her eyes. "Oh, please," she said. "And honestly, can't thank you enough for stealing my thunder. This wedding has made my parents absolutely obsessive, and a happy distraction is the best possible thing that could have happened right now."

As if on cue, all five feet two inches of Deborah Bell practically skipped into the bright entryway, wrapping her arms around Alice's waist and pressing her head into Alice's chest. She stepped away, leaving a tearstain on Alice's shirt. She wiped at her eyes and laughed, looking up at Alice, only for them to fill again. "Oh, honey," she said. "What can I even say."

"I'm hungry!" a thunderous voice called from the kitchen. Thank God for Charlie Bell.

Deborah spun around and yelled back into the house, "This is a MOMENT, Charlie!"

"We can't have a moment if I die of starvation!" he called back immediately.

"Oh my goodness, Lord, give me strength," Deborah muttered as she grabbed Alice's hand and led her through the Bells' family room, which, with its bright upholstery and family-photo-covered gallery wall, had not changed since she and Peter were in high school. Charlie stood by the kitchen island, which held a cheese board and several filled cocktail glasses on it, as well as a big pitcher of iced tea. He had his hands behind his back, presumably in an effort of self-control.

He took them out from behind his back and spread his arms wide, seeing Alice. "Hey there, mama!" his voice boomed. He covered the distance between them in two strides with his absurdly long legs, and put his arm around Alice, giving a classic dad/teacher hug. She barely reached his armpit.

"Hi, Dr. Bell," she said.

"Alice Williams," he said, voice stern. "If there was ever a time to start calling me Charlie."

As she looked around the bright kitchen, with the big window and the breakfast nook, the framed cross-stitch that said, "The Heart of the Home," and the leash hanging from a hook (even though the Bells' dog had died years earlier), Alice's nerves fled. She had been in this home dozens, or more likely hundreds, of times. She had known these people all her life, and she was just as at home here as she was at Gerry and Ellen's.

"What can we get you?" Deborah asked. "I was reading about drinks without alcohol in 'em all afternoon. Have you heard that people call them 'mocktails'? I thought that was cute."

Alice smiled. "I have heard that before. Water should do it, thanks."

Peter went to fill a glass with ice, and Alice reached for the mozzarella, noting that every cheese on the board was safe for pregnant women. This was to be expected, considering that the Bells were all doctors, but she was touched nonetheless. "That's our Alice," Charlie said. "Always hungry."

"Especially now," Alice said. She took a seat, the guest seat, at the breakfast table, where the Bells had always eaten all their meals.

"Oh, honey, we can go to the dining room," Deborah said.

"Why?" Rebecca asked, taking her seat at the table. "It's Alice. She's part of the family."

Alice had to look away as she felt a blush rising and a smile spreading so violently it embarrassed her, which only made the blush more pronounced. "Um," she said, clearing her throat. "Sorry, Justin, is this your spot now?"

Justin smiled and sat on Rebecca's side, squeezed close to her on the bench even though there was barely room for the two of them. He shook his head and put his arm around Rebecca. "Nah," he said. Giving his bride a little shake, he added, "I like to keep her close."

Rebecca rolled her eyes and muttered, "You're a freak," but Alice saw the exact same fight not to smile too hard that had just come for her come for Rebecca. Alice had first met Justin two and a half years ago at the Williams and Bell families' traditional Christmas Eve gathering, and she and Delia had both gushed into the night in their shared creepy-doll-occupied room over how moony Justin clearly was for their friend. The kid had stars in his eyes, was absolutely overtaken. They had been dating for around six months at that point, and Delia had said, "I remember when Connor used to look at me like that," wistfully, though she said she wasn't actually wistful for a thing. She liked that she had gotten past any kind of honeymoon phase, that at that point she and Connor were clearly in it for the long haul (or so she thought).

Then there was the Christmas Rebecca spent with Justin's family, and this past year, the one when she got a ring. At the time, Alice had noted with a kind of sadness for her younger sister, even though Connor and Delia hadn't yet broken up, how the stars in Justin's eyes hadn't gone away, that it wasn't some honeymoon phase after all.

Peter took his seat across from Alice, placing the cheese board with Alice's glass of ice water balanced on top. Their eyes met, and he moved the water to the side and spun the board around, so the mozzarella was closest to her.

....

Ellen stood in her closet in just her slacks and a bra. She had never understood people who liked to be anything less than fully clothed even when they were alone. Linda once told Ellen, giggling maniacally, that when Fred was away, she liked to walk around the house naked, and one time she even forgot to draw the blinds and was pretty sure her little neighbor, walking his brand-new puppy, saw her. Ellen hadn't even bothered to fake a laugh, she was so horrified and confused, which only made Linda laugh harder. Gerry had probably walked around naked when she wasn't in the house. It occurred to her that maybe Fred had done that, too, *with* Gerry, and she shook her head, imagining the thought flying out of her brain, through her ear, and landing on the carpet, scuttling under her shoe rack.

It was Thursday, which meant bridge club. It would be her first solo outing since Gerry died. She felt it was impolite to leave the house when she had company, but she felt more strongly that if she didn't get out of her house, and out of the concerned gazes of her family members, she might die. But she didn't know which blouse to wear—the yellow one or the blue one with polka dots. They were practically identical, and she knew that it didn't really matter how she looked; she had been playing bridge with these women for going on twenty years. She was too tired to choose, and she thought to herself for the millionth time that she had too many clothes. But Gerry was always encouraging her to go shopping, and liked to go with her; he was the only man she knew who enjoyed shopping with his wife. Her friends were always jealous of that.

He liked to watch her try on different outfits, and would "ooh" and "aah" in the Belk dressing room, and he would say to any poor soul who happened to find themselves in there, "Don't I have just about the prettiest wife in the world?" Ellen hated when he did that. She didn't mind having a husband who thought she was pretty, but why did he have to talk about it in front of other people? She would roll her eyes and snap at him to stop, shoving down whatever feelings of pride and pleasure would inevitably rise.

"Wear the yellow one!" he would have said without giving any reason, were he there with her. And because she didn't really care, she would have. She was so tired that even the thought of Gerry suggesting she wear the yellow one felt reason enough to slide it off the hanger and pull it over her head.

The bridge club always used the same little meeting room at the country club, had had it reserved for Thursday evenings at five for at least a decade. They used to rotate hosting in one of their homes, then thought, to hell with the extra cleaning and tiptoeing around a husband. Though none of them phrased it quite like that.

When Ellen arrived, Greta and Mildred looked at her with concern, as though she had fallen into her chair or taken a ridiculous amount of time lowering herself down, which she hadn't. Tina, as usual, was running late. "Evening, ladies," she said.

"Hi, Ellen," Greta said as Mildred reached across the table and squeezed Ellen's hand. Ellen surprised herself with the urge to smack it away, but sat still, relaxing when Mildred let go. "How ya doin'?" Greta asked gently.

"You know, fine as can be expected, I reckon," she said. "How are y'all?"

"Oh, we're fine, we're fine," Mildred said.

"Speak for yourself," Greta said. "Earlier today that woman called—" And Greta launched into a story, as she did almost every week, about her daughter-in-law. She always referred to her as "that woman," even though her son had married her twenty-four years ago.

"Sorry I'm late!" Tina called as she made her way to their table, reaching immediately for a deck of cards. They all murmured that it was fine. But Ellen didn't think it was fine; she rarely thought Tina's behavior was fine. Thankfully, they all quietly began to play, and the silence warmed Ellen's soul like it was Miss Sparkles curled on her lap. The *shh* of the passing cards, the occasional thwack on the table. Ellen was so thankful to have something other than Gerry occupy her mind, not even Mildred's loud mouth-breathing could bother her. The other ladies were focused on the game, too. The lack of prying eyes on her, of questions, of senseless chatter in a bad attempt at distraction felt like a high from a particularly good drug. Not that she would know.

Naturally, Tina ruined it. "Ellen, how are you doin'?" she asked.

"Oh, fine," Ellen said, dropping a four of hearts on a pile of spades. Hearts was always the trump suit for this club.

Tina huffed and shook her head. "You're a stronger woman than me," she said. Ellen, Greta, and Mildred said nothing, but unfortunately, Tina didn't require encouragement. "Any word from Fred?"

Mildred stiffened, and Greta snuck a look at Ellen, whose face didn't change. "Nope," she said. She technically had heard no words from Fred when he stopped by the house, and she certainly wasn't about to mention his visit to Tina. She might as well announce it into a megaphone to the whole town.

"Mm-mm-mm," Tina said, shaking her head again. "You know, *a lot* of people don't think it's true. They think Fred was just drunk or confused, and that Gerry would never have run around on you, no matter what kinda . . . urges he may have had."

"Gerry was certainly not the adulterin' kind," Greta said. "I've always told Michael, if you treated me half as nice as Gerald Williams treats Ellen, I'd be happy as a pig in mud." She nodded encouragingly at Ellen, who said nothing, because what was there to say?

"Speaking of Michael, I meant to tell you that Winn-Dixie just got in the biggest, most beautiful watermelons I've ever seen," Mildred said to Greta. "I will never forget that barbecue where he ate so much watermelon I thought, this man will grow a watermelon inside him!" Ellen wanted to reach across the table and hug Mildred for this change of subject, a strong departure from her earlier urge to smack her hand away.

"Perfect, I'm going to the store tomorrow," Greta said.

"Have you been to the store, Ellen? Are you worried about bumping into Fred when you're out and about?" Tina asked.

Ellen took a sip of her water. "I've got more food 'n my house than I know what to do with," she said, not allowing herself to hope that this would be enough to satisfy Tina.

And she was right not to. "What do you think you'll say to him when you do see him? You'll have to see him eventually. Maybe even at Rebecca Bell's wedding, I reckon. Don't you just wanna give him a piece of your mind?"

Not even Mildred could resist looking at Ellen expectantly. "I haven't really thought about it," Ellen said.

"Whew, that's all I'd be thinkin' about. I'd have a lot to say in confession on Sunday, I'll tell you that," Greta said, adding quickly, "Not that I think there's truth to it. I don't. Fred's always been a little off to me. But to behave so badly at my husband's funeral, that's what I'd be ragin' about."

"Well, we won't know if there's truth to it until Ellen talks to Fred, right, Ellen? Unless . . . well, did you already suspect anything with those two?" Tina asked Ellen as she took a sip of her water, like she was asking her what she thought of the weather or last night's episode of *Dancing with the Stars*.

A drowsiness came over Ellen, like she had taken a sleeping pill before arriving and it was just now hitting her, which she was pretty sure she hadn't done. This conversation was exhausting her. The ten years since Linda passed slipped out of Ellen's mind, and she wished Linda would jump in and tell the ladies to back off, because Linda was never afraid to speak up, and had told Tina to shut up several times. Then she remembered that Linda was gone, and so was Gerry. There was no one left to defend her.

"Tina," Ellen said, slowly rising to her feet and pressing her hands on the table to steady herself, "my husband of sixty years is dead. I don't have to put up with your nonsense, or anyone else's, and I won't." She picked up her purse and nodded at Mildred.

And for the first time in bridge club history, she left early.

Chapter 9

Jennifer sat in her bright home office trying to find an appealing way to describe a house that was so small it was practically unlivable. "Cozy" felt like a ridiculous word in this heat. It made her think about the tiny shotgun house she lived in with her college friend Vivian when she first started coaching cheerleading. She wondered how Viv was doing. It had been two years since she finally divorced her husband, Tyler, and Jennifer found herself picturing Viv's post-divorce life. She was probably thriving.

JJ and Tyler had always gotten along well, and had become close friends when Jennifer and JJ first started dating long-distance. According to social media, Tyler had gotten remarried last year, to a woman fifteen years younger than him with comically huge implants. Jennifer wondered what JJ would do if she divorced him. She was confident he would get fat. She was the one who made sure they ate healthy, and felt he only spent as much time at the gym as he did because she worked out a lot and he was competitive. Well, back when she believed he was really going to the gym.

But *Stephie* would probably find him attractive even if he grew huge, despite the fact that she was more than two decades his junior, because that was how being a divorced man worked. But he would be miserable without Jennifer, she thought to herself with glee. JJ had no idea how much shit she did for him; he fancied himself independent, but was actually just a stocky baby with an unflattering buzz cut. She ran his life, even when she had a full-time job and made more money than him. And what was his value again? What was his excuse for being in a bad mood, or not being able to go to the grocery store, or forgetting to pick up the vase Jennifer had custom-made for Ellen for Mother's Day?

And she never lied to him. She never lied to anyone, opting for a stony silence instead of a white lie when the situation called for it, which people often found terrifying. Lying, especially for someone else's benefit, was a form of accepting bullshit, and Jennifer did not do that. If she did, she wouldn't have the national cheer titles she had under her belt, and she would earn a bad reputation as a real estate agent if she let people buy homes she knew had mold or wouldn't get the approval they wanted for their dream landscaping.

Who the hell was JJ to lie? Lying was easy, so of course he did the easy thing, the lazy thing, because he was entitled. A big brat. Jennifer felt like steam was rushing out of her ears, sitting in her velvet (custom-upholstered) desk chair thinking about this. He had built his entire career on being a mediocre member of a national-championship-winning college football team, and "built" was a generous term. He just landed his radio job out of college, then floated right on up the ranks by running his mouth about his hobby all damn day. People let him do whatever he wanted. And she was one of them, she thought, vibrating with anger, her computer screen swimming in front of her. She wasn't crying; the rage was just blurring her vision. Allowing him to lie to her was the same thing as accepting bullshit, the same thing as lying. She wasn't going to be complicit anymore. She was going to catch him.

She blinked fiercely until her computer monitor swam into focus in front of her. She went to 97.7 The Jam's website, as they no longer had a radio in the house, much to JJ's chagrin. The old stereo they had had since their wedding didn't look good when Jennifer redecorated a year ago, so she tossed it, because they could listen on their computers or phones, and she found no reason to be sentimental about it. It was 4:30, just when the show should be wrapping up.

She clicked the big Tune In button on the website's home screen. Her husband's voice began blasting out of her speaker with such immediacy she jumped a little in her chair. He was cracking up. "All right now," he said, his laughter subsiding. Jennifer scowled at the slightly exaggerated Southern accent, the gregariousness he somehow inserted into his radio voice. "That's all for today. Be sure to tune in tomorrow for our recap of Game Four of the NBA Finals. As always, I'm your host, JJ Williams, and it's time for me to go home, kiss my wife, and have a cold beer. I hope the same for you."

She actually groaned. She could not believe there was ever a time in her life when she had found that sign-off charming. But because of the official sign-off, she knew he wouldn't be pitching in to cover rush hour. By all accounts, he should be wrapping up for the day so that he could leave at 5:30.

Come 5:30, Jennifer found herself sitting in her car, in the farthest parking spot she could find that still allowed a decent view of the radio station entrance. At 5:31, she shook her head in disbelief that she was now the kind of woman who stalked her own husband. But she didn't want to confront him without a leg to stand on, and it was past time for confrontation. He walked out at 5:36, Stephanie nowhere in sight. Maybe they met up later, somewhere else, possibly her place, to keep their colleagues in the dark. He climbed up into that ridiculous truck and pulled out of his spot.

"People are gonna think you're overcompensating for a small member when they see you in that thing," Jennifer had said to JJ when he proudly drove the souped-up F-150 home five years ago. Nowadays, a comment like that would spark a huge fight between the two of them, but things were different then. He laughed and pulled her close and said, "Well, you know that's not true," grabbing a handful of her ass as she smacked his shoulder but laughed. Now she was thankful for the size of the truck as it meant she could conceal her Mercedes behind two or three cars without losing sight of him. He turned onto Main Street, past a young magnolia tree that had been planted several years ago, one of the mystery magnolias.

She held her breath as Jackson Street approached, where he would turn if he was really going to the gym. Ahead of him, the light turned yellow. Jennifer cursed under her breath; of course one of Eulalia's only stoplights would thwart her. Sure enough, the Toyota Camry in front of her crawled to a stop right before the light turned red, and Jennifer hit her steering wheel in frustration. But she kept her eyes trained on the F-150. It went straight past the Jackson turn, and a wave of nausea roiled in her stomach. The road and the F-150 curved, and JJ rounded out of her sight.

She stared through her windshield, seeing and feeling nothing. She jumped when she heard a honk behind her; she hadn't noticed the light change to green. This brought her back into her body, and a pristine bullet of rage shot right through her. Her hands shook on the wheel as she drove through the intersection, wondering what in the hell she was going to do next.

....

Alice could feel magic hour coming on as she sat with Peter on a blanket in the field typically used for getting drunk, just like they used to, a continuation of that week's apparent theme of nostalgia. It was all too comforting for her to find it contrived. They were leaning back on their elbows side by side with their legs stretched out, digesting all the cheese they had consumed at the Bells' house, when Alice bolted upright suddenly, wincing with a cramp.

"Are you okay?" Peter asked, sitting up, too, worry spreading across his face.

Alice inhaled. "Yep," she said. "Just . . . pregnant."

"Is it kicking?" Peter asked, his worry turning to curiosity.

"No, no," Alice said. "That's not a thing yet. Jeez, is the doctor thing just a lie you use to get women into bed with you?"

Peter laughed, tipping his head back a little as he did so. "Not that kind of doctor, although I did complete an OB-GYN rotation. So, you're right, I should know better."

"Can I ask you something?" Alice said. He nodded. "Did you decide to become an oncologist because of your grandparents? And if not, then how did you make that decision?"

"Okay, Miss Journalist," he said, smiling despite the weight of the question, and despite the fact that "journalist" was a generous term for the type of writing she did. All four of Peter's grandparents had died, too young, of cancer. Both of Peter's parents had already lost a parent by the time they met, and by the summer that Peter and Alice were seventeen, he only had his maternal grandfather left. "It's definitely part of it." Alice looked at him, wondering if he still suffered from the anxiety he had then, that his parents would get cancer and die, too. "I wanted to, and I want to, make sense of it, as much as anyone can. Or, I can't make sense of their deaths, that's a little . . . beyond me. But it feels productive to try to make sense of the disease. Makes me feel like less of a bystander to my own life, I suppose, were that to happen to my parents or someone else I loved."

Alice nodded, tracing his knuckles. She hadn't really decided to touch him; it just happened. "Are your days at work really sad?"

"It's not like a carnival all the time," he said, watching her finger on his hand. "There are good days and bad days. Like with all things, I guess."

"Not like with all things," Alice said. "A bad day for me is, like, my editor didn't like my piece or I don't like any of the questions submitted to the column and the trains are messed up and the line at the grocery store is long. A bad day for you is . . ."

"Being unable to stop someone from dying of cancer, yeah," he said, chuckling. After a moment, he said, "You help people, too, Alice, you know you do."

Alice scoffed. "Jesus, Peter, not like you."

"Not in exactly the same way, no. But you do. You help people. In an emotional and possibly more meaningful way. Doctors aren't the only people whose profession is to help people. And I know you don't like to talk about it, but don't you think that your book helped people, too?"

"Peter."

"No, seriously, like, your book was so insightful and good and probably made so many people feel less alone. And made them laugh, and inspired them. You took your skills and made something good from them. I take my skills and try to make good things happen, too. It's different in the day-to-day, but it's really no different big-picture."

"Agree to disagree, Peter," Alice said. "But how do you, like, deal with it. When your patients . . . when your patients pass away, how do you deal with it?"

Peter thought. "Sometimes it's harder than other times. There's always more work to be done, and that helps. Don't know how healthy that is, but. Yeah."

"Yeah," Alice said. They sat in silence for a moment. "If I've learned anything in the last few days, it's that I don't think anyone really knows how to deal with death."

"Well, yeah," Peter said. "And how are you holding up, Al?"

"I don't know," Alice said. "I mean. Of course, I'm sad. And when I think about him lying to my grandma, I guess there's anger there. But mostly, it just kind of . . . breaks my heart for him. The thought of him living his life closeted, you know? But also, it's like, he spent sixty-plus years with Gram. Built a whole family with her, and the thing is, I know he really did love us all so much. I know that. I obviously don't *really* know, but I kind of feel like he wouldn't have had it any other way. I don't feel regretted. I just hope that my grandma knows how much he loved us. And her. I wonder if she knew, also, I mean *that's* been going through my mind. But I don't know if any of that even matters, because the only thing we even know for sure is that he's gone."

Alice choked a little on the last word. Peter covered her hand and she continued. "But anyway, back to *me*." She wiped a little moisture from her eyes as she finished. "I've mostly just been thinking about me. And . . . this thing," she said, pointing to her stomach. "And . . . that thing," she said, pointing to Peter. "Like, thinking about how we're gonna . . ." She searched for the right way to phrase it. "Do this."

"I love you, Alice," Peter said, ripping from her brain an image she was conjuring of Venmo-requesting Peter for diapers from a different time zone. She didn't breathe, but that didn't matter because time had stopped. "I think you know that. I've always loved you, and I've never stopped loving you. I wouldn't know how to stop loving you, even if I wanted to. You are so tangled in here"—he patted his heart—"that there's just . . . there's no version of events where I don't love you all my life. I don't know what that will look like with this, and I didn't know what it could look like even before all this. But I've always known that, and I felt like I really knew that after seeing you in New York. I like my life and everything, and when we're apart, it's not like I'm unhappy. But it's been true since we were kids that when I'm back with you, I'm just like, 'Oh, right. This was the missing thing.' And everything is just better. Full color, full light."

Alice blinked rapidly, hoping the moisture forming in her eyes would somehow evaporate right into the air. He was looking at his hand holding hers, and then he looked up at her, and she was so taken aback by

the truth of what he said that she couldn't speak. She wasn't wrong
without him, but she suspected that being with him was as right as she
could ever be.

She felt the imbalance of it, but all she managed to say back was,
"Same."

....

"I don't understand why you can't shoot this from a more flattering angle!" Carol Anne called down to Wilma on the ground.

Wilma sighed and looked behind her, at Robert, for help. But he
only shrugged his shoulders, a task made more difficult by Wilma's heavy
camera bag slung over his shoulder. Wilma looked back up at Carol
Anne, who sat several branches up in the mystery magnolia planted
by Miss Sparkles's turn-around stop sign. She adjusted her seat, which
looked uncomfortable, affording Wilma a full-frontal view of the nether
regions of her younger sister, who had, of course, forgone underwear.

"I'm sorry it didn't occur to me to arrange to rent an apple picker
right before my father's funeral," Wilma called up through the branches.
"Annie, we're running out of time. Maybe you should just come down."

The blinding brightness of the Eulalia summer days meant that the
only times it made sense for Wilma to take Carol Anne's new headshots
were either dawn or dusk. Dawn was a non-option for Carol Anne, so
she had spent that evening perfecting her makeup and donning a summer dress with an optional caftan. They had no choice but to set out as
the sun was starting to sink, and the clock was ticking.

"I want my photo to be in nature!" Carol Anne moaned, looking
up through the web of branches, heavy with white blooms, up into the
blue-but-darkening sky. "I don't understand why that's difficult to understand. Are you just in a bad mood because Derek hasn't reached
out?"

Wilma willed herself to take a deep breath. She was in a bad mood, but not because of Derek. It was because Gerry's absence was becoming all too real. Maybe it was finally hitting her now that there was nothing left to do except for wait for Rebecca's wedding. No funeral to plan or discuss the ramifications of, no headstone to pick out, no date to go on. Maybe it was even the yoga. And contrary to Carol Anne's conjecture, Derek *had* texted her, at first to find a time to walk his dog, but then just to see how her day was going. She hadn't had much to say about her day, and he ended up asking her what she had eaten for lunch, which she found irritating. She then became irritated at herself—shouldn't she be glad to hear from a nice man after a date?

"He did reach out, Carol Anne," Wilma said. "I'm just . . . I guess I'm just not in the best place right now."

Carol Anne sniffed. "I can tell," she pouted. "And be careful, because Derek may be able to tell, too." Wilma waited for Carol Anne to realize that maybe Wilma was in a foul mood because their father had just died, not because she feared a date had gone wrong. Carol Anne said nothing.

"Carol Anne." Wilma put on her best pseudo-patient mom voice. "We still have some daylight left. I cannot climb this tree to take this headshot from your eye level, so why don't you go ahead and climb down, and we can take these out in Mama and Daddy's garden."

Carol Anne let out some cross between a groan and a scream, followed by a deep yogic breath and an om. "I already told you, Wilma. I need to have a headshot that *stands out*. Posing in front of some random bush just feels basic."

Even though Gerry wouldn't have been insulted by Carol Anne referring to his garden this way, Wilma felt a stab of anger that her sister would so flippantly degrade something their father cherished. Suddenly, as if she had no control over it, her hand flew to her eyes, her camera dropping by her side, dangling from its shoulder strap. For the second time that day, it all seemed to swallow her: The fact that Gerry was gone. He wasn't here to talk Carol Anne down (figuratively from her ego, literally from this tree), wasn't there to hear Wilma's complaints about how disastrous this shoot was going. He wasn't anywhere.

"Did you look directly into the sun?" Carol Anne asked, dropping not ungracefully from the lowest branch down beside her older sister. Wilma removed her hand from her eyes and hoped there were no visible tears. "Or did you just look at me too long?" Carol Anne asked (jokingly, Wilma hoped), swishing the skirt of her maxi dress in a way that made Wilma's sadness morph scary quick into annoyance.

Carol Anne didn't notice. She sauntered over to Robert and threw her arms around his neck. He wrapped his arms around her back and kissed her on the cheek. She stepped back. He said, "You looked great up there, babe." Wilma snapped a quick photo of them almost reflexively, then gritted her teeth so that she wouldn't puke.

Delia had always found hydrangeas to be tacky, and for a wedding, she thought they were downright hideous. But she kept her mouth shut as she arranged them in vases tied with white and baby blue ribbons, happy for a distraction from the phone she had now guaranteed would show nothing from Connor. She had scurried down the street to help the Bells with the flower arrangements for the wedding reception as soon as Rebecca texted that Peter and Alice had gone out on their own. There was plenty of wine and cheese left over from Alice's visit, and besides, Rebecca wanted Delia to have any chance she could to get to know Justin a bit more before the big day.

Deborah and Charlie, positively giddy from Alice's visit and all the baby talk, were upstairs in the attic, rooting around to see what, if any, baby clothes they had saved. Rebecca, Delia, and Justin could hear the occasional *thunk* of plastic bins being taken down, the skid of unused furniture being pushed across the attic floor.

Delia eyed Justin as she bent a wire around a hydrangea stem. He

looked like a stereotypical medical school student: skinny, glasses, probably ran long-distance but wasn't much for contact sports growing up.
"So, are you going to be pursuing surgery, or is this just your style?" Delia
asked as Justin leaned over a stem, furrowing his brow in concentration
as he made a painstaking effort to cut it to the exact length of the stems
next to it.

He looked up, tongue sticking slightly out of his mouth. He met
Delia's eye and laughed. "Nah," he said. "Internal medicine for me. But
I do plan on treating this task with the seriousness I would a life in my
hands."

Rebecca rolled her eyes but smiled. Untying a bow on a vase to redo
it, she said, "You're such a loser, babe."

He nudged her, still sitting closely on the bench next to her. Leaning
closer to Delia, he said, "I want to do right by Bridezilla."

"Oh, you're referring to yourself in the third person now?" Rebecca
asked, tilting her head and drawing her eye away from her new, but still
unraveling, bow.

Justin laughed. "What, now?" Delia asked, admitting to the third-
wheeldom she had felt from the moment she walked into the house.

Shaking her head, Rebecca said, "Come on, Deel, you know I couldn't
care less about this shit. What!" she said when Justin faux gasped hearing
her refer to the details of their nuptials in such a way. She continued, "If
it were up to me, we'd just go down to city hall and get 'er done."

"Oh, hush," Justin said. "You know you're having fun." Rebecca raised
her eyebrows, and Justin widened his eyes in exaggerated fear, which
made Rebecca laugh. "Okay, you know we'll treasure the pictures."

"Ah, so *Justin* is our bridezilla," Delia said.

"I'm not a bridezilla, nor am I a groomzilla," Justin said, while Rebecca made exaggerated eyes at Delia behind Justin's shoulder, indicat-
ing the opposite. "I just know—"

"Here we go," Rebecca murmured, though she was smiling.

"Shh," Delia said to her friend. "I want to hear this."

"Finally, someone who's interested in my spiel," Justin said. "I just know it'll mean a lot to our families, and we've worked hard for the last few years and I think we deserve a big party."

"Hear, hear," Delia said, though her post-Ricky's hangover had left her more than a little scarred, and the thought of drinking (especially considering what alcohol had made her do) was rather scary.

"But mostly," Justin said, turning to Rebecca, who stiffened and clearly fought a smile, "I do want to have a big wedding because I would like to declare in front of everyone I care about, and everyone that you care about, and who cares about *you*, that I love you, and promise to be with you forever. And there should be flowers, and there should be a fluffy dress, and there should be dancing and merriment. Because it's a big damn deal."

While Rebecca rolled her eyes, but lost her fight with the smile, Delia was mortified to find herself shoving down a knot in her throat with all her might. Delia had always loved weddings, and she felt that Justin wonderfully articulated why she did. She had always struggled to justify her fondness for weddings to Connor, but Justin made it sound so simple.

Connor hated weddings. "It's the kind of thing that should be private," he would say. He felt that making that kind of promise was as intimate as it got, and you might as well just bone your significant other in front of your friends and family if you wanted to have a big wedding. Delia would laugh at this joke at first, especially when the idea of their ever getting married was far-fetched. But as time went on, as their shared calendar became more and more filled with weddings, as they moved in together, as it seemed like they were getting so intertwined in each other's lives that their future wedding was no longer a far-fetched idea but a likely possibility, perhaps even an inevitability, Delia would find herself unable to laugh, and uncharacteristically at a loss for words, when Connor would complain about wedding after wedding.

This didn't change the fact that Delia felt a sharp sadness that seemed to permeate her stomach lining at the thought of going to a wedding without Connor. Not only was this an adjustment, but also, despite Connor's private reservations about weddings, he was a great date. Good dancer, smooth small-talker, and he looked damn good in a tux. There were some weddings when he was so on his A-game that he even managed to convince Delia that maybe he didn't actually hate them.

"I told you my dress isn't fluffy," Rebecca said.

Justin clapped his hands over his ears dramatically. "No spoiling!"

"I'm not spoiling," Rebecca said, pulling them down and holding his hands in hers. "I just don't want you to be disappointed."

Delia was looking at them as though they were a couple she was watching on TV, so intently and unabashedly was she staring at them as they stared into each other's faces. Justin smirked, but there was nothing snarky about it. Rebecca smiled, but she also looked serious. He said, "Impossible."

....

"It's still one of my favorite albums, and I'm not embarrassed to admit that, and I'm not sorry," Peter said, slowly driving the Lexus down the dirt road covered with snaky tree roots the dark concealed, making for quite a bumpy ride. "Play our song. I'll beg. I'll stop this car and get on my hands and knees and beg, Alice," Peter said, fake pleading, both of them giddy and high, postcoital.

Alice thumbed through Usher's 2004 hit album, *Confessions*, which they had played on repeat, nonstop, that whole summer with all the cousins. Alice and Peter would laugh at Delia, a mere child, singing about the pain of impregnating a side chick. She scrolled down trying to get to their song, willing to indulge in the cheesiness, too sparkly on the inside not to.

They hit a particularly rough bump, which lurched her forward and made her lose control of the phone in her hands. It was Peter's phone, and it dinged with a text as it fell. Righting herself in her seat and looking back at the screen to play the song they were both itching to hear, she realized she had accidentally opened the message. It was from a Samantha, and the screen was filled entirely with blue bubbles, so Alice could tell this *Samantha* had been blowing Peter up, with no response from him. She knew better than to look, and she tossed the phone away from her like it had suddenly become one thousand degrees. But she still caught a glimpse of some phrases, like "ghost me" and "four months" and "thought you were different." As the phone sailed away from her and onto the floor of the passenger side, she could have sworn she caught the word "love," and she suddenly felt nauseated. She put her hands up, *don't shoot* style, and looked up at the folded mirror hanging from the ceiling, loose with age. Peter looked over at her and said, "Sorry, you okay?" before looking back to the road illuminated only by the headlights.

"Um," she said, anger twisting up her abdomen and into her throat, shame and disgust extending out toward her fingertips. "Samantha?" she said, pointing to the phone on the floor, which Peter saw as he turned his head from the road to check on her again.

For a brief second, for the smallest moment, Peter looked confused. Alice could tell that it was genuine because he didn't even bother to look at her. The center of his mouth pushed up, the corners pushed down, and his eyebrows furrowed together, scrunching his face as he looked at the road ahead of him, not trying to gauge any kind of reaction she might be having, not rushing to explain himself, not smiling and saying Samantha was a coworker or his barber. He was so unconcerned he just kept driving.

Then realization hit. He looked at her, pale as though she had just seen a ghost, and at his phone on the floor. He stopped the car so that he could fully turn in his seat, focusing all his attention on her. "Samantha is a woman I was seeing," he said, the words tumbling out of his mouth like teeth in a bad dream. He took a breath and reached for her hands, which stayed stiffly by her shoulders. He pulled, and she jerked back, folding them in her lap and looking at the road ahead. "It was very casual," he said slowly. "I mentioned her when I saw you in New York! We had been on a date, maybe two at that point. My friend from work set me up with her. We've seen each other occasionally over the last few months, but I wasn't committed to her or anything. I couldn't, not after New York with you. And I felt gross about it all because I could tell she really liked me but never asked for more than I was giving her, which wasn't much because I was trying to figure out how much it mattered that I was in love with you."

Alice looked at her hands, folded in her lap over her stomach, which was only slightly bulging in reality, but felt like a foreign, protruding padding to her. She looked out the passenger-side window to the dark woods surrounding her, wishing she were anywhere but there. For the first time in a very, very long time, she longed for her moldy Brooklyn apartment, far away from everyone. "Oh, God," she said, panic rising in her throat like bile.

"Alice," Peter said, "you have to listen to me. I haven't said anything to her since I've been back here. And it wasn't serious. I meant everything I said to you. I know it's bad that I haven't officially told her I'm not into it. I'm going to, I just didn't know what to say to her. I—"

"So, what?" Alice said, snapping her neck back to Peter, eyes blazing with a maelstrom of emotions that she couldn't and wouldn't parcel out to identify. "So you're just, like, ignoring the shit out of this probably really nice girl who clearly likes you a lot, maybe even loves you, and then you'll, what, figure out what to do with her once we've figured our shit out?"

"No, no, that's not what I meant—"

"That is so unfair to her, Peter. I'd have thought better of you. You've been seeing her for months? I mean, how can anything that you just said back there to me be true if you've been seeing someone for months?"

"Alice, come on, don't do that. You said back there that you felt the same way and I know that you've seen other people over the years—"

"Not right after seeing you. I couldn't have seen someone else right after I saw you."

"How was I supposed to know that, Alice? You didn't call me, you didn't even respond to my texts. I texted you *repeatedly*, I made an ass out of myself. I thought you regretted sleeping with me. How was I supposed to know anything?" Peter's voice was getting louder and his hands were practically flailing, so wild were his gestures. Desperation coated his body like Saran wrap. "So, yeah, I kept dating this girl who really liked me, who, you're right, is really nice. And I'm sorry if in three days I haven't perfectly figured out how to handle the fact that I'm gonna be a dad soon."

"It's too much, I get it," Alice said, feeling the tears coming, and swallowing with all the force she had in her to keep them at bay. "I can't expect you to give up your life for this. And I don't. It's fine. I should have . . . I should have, like, known better, I guess." She crossed her arms and looked down at them, then up into Peter's sad face.

"What does that mean?"

"I can't just, like, expect you to give up your life because we had un-protected sex once. I mean, if the roles were reversed, I wouldn't want to give my life up because of that."

Alice didn't have time to regret saying this because she already hated the words as they were coming out of her mouth. It was like someone pulled a shade down in Peter's eyes; they suddenly seemed to change color. He nodded a very small nod and turned back to face the road. He gripped the steering wheel tightly, then loosened his grip and sighed, looking down into his lap. He wiped his hands over his face, as if he could wipe her words off him.

"Okay, Alice," he said quietly. "I don't consider starting a family with you, whatever that family may look like, to be 'giving up my life.' When I found out you were pregnant, I felt . . ." He exhaled in an unhappy laugh. "I felt like I was starting my life, actually."

IF WE'RE BEING HONEST

He shifted the car into drive, and they continued along the dirt road, painfully slowly. Alice could feel guilt bubbling in her body like acid. They didn't speak for the rest of the ride. She didn't know how or what to feel, and it made her want to rip all her hair out. She didn't know what she was supposed to do, how to be a mother, where she was supposed to live, what her powerful emotional reaction to seeing those texts meant, if she was supposed to apologize or if she was completely right. They made it back to Ellen's house and she unbuckled her seat belt.

"Al, are you okay?" he asked, reaching across the car to put a hand on her cheek, which she rejected by jerking her head toward the passenger door. She opened it and got out.

"The fuck if I know," she said, closing the door behind her and going to the house. As she walked up the pathway to the front door, her ears were pricked for the sound of him driving away.

But the sound never came.

Chapter 10

Even though Wilma felt a little guilty for thinking it, she was thankful there was no Carol Anne to awkwardly fight for shotgun as she lowered herself into Derek's Toyota Camry at the unsexy hour of eight a.m. A gigantic brown dog was laid out on the back seat, and Wilma was greeted by its smell before its lazy eye rolled in her direction, its tongue lolling about. She thought it looked a little dead.

"Good morning!" Derek said with an enthusiasm that did not fit the early hour. He nodded toward two to-go coffees sitting in his cup-holder as he pulled out of Ellen's driveway. "I brought you a coffee. I don't know how you take it, so I grabbed a bunch of all that crazy sweet stuff and that's in the bag by your feet there." He nodded to a brown paper bag on the passenger-side floor. "My sweet tooth extends to my coffee, so no judgment if you need to add enough sugar to send a diabetic right to me." Wilma smiled, a little confused. "Because I'm a funeral director," he clarified.

"Right, ha," Wilma said, laughing. "Thanks, that's really *sweet* of you." A slow smile crept up her face, the silly little joke helping to penetrate her self-consciousness.

"Good one!"

He drove her to the creek, parking north of the rope swing, where there was a worn dirt walking path. The morning was misty and, of course, sweltering, but not yet unbearably so.

"I like it out here," he said as they exited the car and he opened the back seat to clip a leash on the big, smelly dog. "Zeus does, too."

"Zeus?" Wilma asked. Guilt flooded her for judging the dog when he rolled himself out of the car and she saw that one of his front legs was missing, forcing him to hop along instead of properly walk. It was such a goofy gait for a dog his size that she immediately loved him. She bent down, though she didn't have to go far, to give his head a pat.

She took a sip of her coffee and gagged. "Yeah, it's from the Exxon. Not great," Derek said. They walked along the water. "So," he said, "not to go all intense death guy on you, but are you doing okay with everything?"

The question surprised Wilma, and she realized no one had really asked her that. Her muscle memory of manners, ever present, forced "I'm fine, thank you for asking" to her lips, but she swallowed it down, thinking about how rough yesterday had been for her. Instead, she said, honestly, "I don't think I really know."

Derek nodded as he walked alongside her, Zeus hobbling up ahead. "I think that's normal at this point. It's usually a little bit after the funeral that it hits people, when all the logistics have been handled."

"Yeah," she said. "Well, I'm not sure if you heard what happened at the funeral, but that's been pretty distracting from the actual grief, too, I think. The speculation."

"Well, I don't think there's anyone between here and Babylon that hasn't heard about what happened at the funeral," Derek said.

He didn't press her on it, but Wilma said, after a minute, "At first, I didn't want to dwell on it. I thought, whether or not it was true, it didn't have to change anything for me. But I keep thinking about it, and I think it is true. And so, I think my next step will be, okay, how does this fit into the grief part?"

Derek was quiet for a moment. "Are you angry with him?" he asked.

Wilma inhaled, considering. "Yes. But more on my mother's behalf than my own. Not that I'm selfless or anything, but as a parent, you have your secrets. I think you have a right to your own life outside of your kids. But it's a different set of obligations with your spouse. I know this one is more complicated than most cases, but I know being cheated on, and I hate it for her." It was like Derek had cast a line and Wilma had swallowed it, and he was reeling the words right out of her mouth. She never decided to say them, and she couldn't remember the last time she had spoken so openly about something so personal with anyone. She shook her head and said, "I'm sorry. I don't mean to put this on you."

"I asked you how you were doing and you answered," Derek said. "It's great you're being honest about it. Not airing it out, that'll only feed your resentment. That's the AA line of thinking, anyway."

Zeus decided that moment was an excellent time to take a shit, and it broke Wilma's heart how his front leg shook with the effort to balance while he took care of business. Derek scooped up the rather huge turd in a bag, tied it off, and held it up. "Pretty romantic, huh?" he asked, jokingly swinging it in her direction.

"Oh, Lord!" Wilma said, catching a whiff of the feces and jerking her head back violently. She tried to fix what she knew was her disgusted facial expression. It had been a long time since she had been around someone who made a poop joke. "Do you make sure he does that in front of all your dates?" she asked, in an attempt to get them back on track.

"What, you mean like a test?" Derek said, laughing. "Not a bad idea, honestly. But I don't date enough to have good data for you on that." They passed a lone trash can and Derek tossed the bag in, and squirted Purell on his hands from a key chain that dangled on the leash handle. The cleanliness of that, the preparation, was simply erotic for Wilma, and she felt some of her previous disgust dissipate. "I don't get out there much," he said.

"Me, neither," she said. They were quiet for a moment, and Wilma wondered if she was supposed to say something else, to divulge more about her romantic life, or total lack thereof. She hoped not. Derek reached over with his newly sanitized hand and closed his fingers over hers. She squirmed a little so their fingers were intertwined, then immediately realized how sweaty her hand was. It had been a long time since she had held hands with someone, and she had forgotten that it wasn't very comfortable.

....

Grant and Ellen both jumped when Ellen padded into the kitchen to make the morning's first cup of coffee and Grant, sweaty and sunburned, was standing at the sink washing his hands. Their outfits were in stark contrast: he was in a once-white, now-yellow tank top and basketball shorts, while she was in a nightgown, housecoat, and fuzzy slippers, as though it were the dead of winter.

"Grant!" Ellen said, her hand over her heart. "You almost gave me a heart attack!"

"Sorry, sorry, Gram," he said, grimacing at her word choice. "Sorry."

"Don't be, I'm glad to see you. You're up early."

"Yeah, can't really sleep in these days. I cleaned your gutters. And then I noticed the hummingbird feeder was empty, so I refilled that. I'm gonna get out the pressure washer later and deal with your deck," he said as Ellen turned the coffee maker on (successfully this time). She always filled it the night before.

She sat down at the kitchen table and said, "Why, how sweet. Thank you, Grant."

"Happy to help, Gram," he said.

"Will you stay a minute and visit? Have some coffee."

"I'll definitely stay and visit, but no coffee for me," Grant said. "I'm overheated as it is." He took his time getting himself a glass of ice water so that the coffee could finish percolating. "How do you take it again, Gram?"

"Oh," Ellen said, head snapping around at the sound of his voice, like she'd forgotten he was there. She had been staring at the kitchen table, wondering why it looked different. Had someone shined it? "Black, please. What a treat to get to have coffee with my grandson."

Grant poured her coffee and sat down at the table. They smiled at each other. "How are you doing, Gram?" Grant asked.

Ellen looked into her coffee, then back up at Grant. "Well," she said, "I suspect I don't know." Grant nodded. "I'm sad. And the sadness is stronger than anything else."

Grant leaned back in his chair and hoped that he could pass the tears gathering in his eyes off as sweat should they fall. "Me, too," he said.

"You know," she said, "I know I'm not supposed to say this kind of thing. I love all of you so much, but you're my favorite grandchild."

"Gram!" Grant said, shocked that Ellen would say something like that at all, and doubly shocked that it could be true.

"Don't tell," she said.

"They wouldn't believe me, anyway." He paused, then asked, "Why?"

"I think you're the most like your grandfather. You've got lightness of heart and you make people laugh, but I know that you're thoughtful. I know that you're considerate. Generous. Braver, maybe," she said, eyes trailing down to the table. "I know your daddy fancies that you're just like him, but you look outward more than he does. More like your grandfather does. Did."

Grant nodded and patted her hand resting on the table, not sure what to make of that. "I love you," he said, because it was all he could think to say. And: "Thank you."

Ellen realized what it was about the table that was different. There was no flower-filled vase on it. JJ and Jennifer had gotten her a lovely vase last Mother's Day, but even before that, Gerry had always kept a vase of flowers on the table. Either cut from the garden, or from the supermarket if there were no blooms in the backyard.

"I love you, honey," she said, sipping her coffee. They sat for a moment, and Ellen turned to look out into the backyard. Two hummingbirds circled the bird feeder before landing and beginning to drink.

....

"Is it possible that I'm experiencing a two-day hangover?" Delia asked, elbows on the table at Waffle House, putting her head in her hands. Alice, who sat next to her, patted her back, happy to have the attention off her. She hadn't told any of them, even Delia, about last night's fight with Peter. "Never get old," Delia said to Red.

"You're like two years older than me," he said.

"If anything will heal you," Grant said, waving his hand over the bounty of hash browns, waffles, scrambled eggs, and biscuits between them, "it will be this."

"Wait, where did you and Rebecca get off to when we were at Ricky's?" Delia asked, tucking into her smothered and covered hash browns.

"What do you mean?" Grant said as he drowned his waffle in syrup.

"Exactly what I said," Delia said. "You two were both missing for a while, right after that asshole groped me. Where had you been?"

Grant shrugged. "Outside."

"Doing what?"

"Talking."

"Grant, I swear to God. She's about to get *married*."

"Yes, Delia, I'm aware."

"Good, you better be," Delia said. Grant shrugged, so she narrowed her eyes at Red, eager to zero in on a new target. He was looking at his phone under the table. "What's up with you, Red, texting your mystery lover over there?"

Red snapped his head up and locked his phone, where he had, in fact, been trying to compose a message to Brady. He told himself he just wanted to thank Brady for listening and for being a literal shoulder to lean on the other night. This was true, but he also just wanted to talk to him.

"Mm-hmm," he said. He took a sip of his sweet tea, and the sugar immediately made his teeth ring.

"Red, why won't you just tell us who you're dating?" Alice asked gently. "We won't judge you or anything. Or do any internet stalking if you don't want us to."

"It's okay if she's not hot," Grant said knowingly.

"Um, that's not it," Red said, shaking his head, part of him wishing, per usual, that the subject of his love life had not been brought up and part of him, shockingly, glad that it had. He knew he wouldn't come clean unprompted.

"Good," Grant said. "You know how vicious Mom can be."

"Right," Red said, his heart leaping up to his throat. "Well. There's not a mystery lover, not *really*. But I do think there's something I should say."

This piqued everyone's interest, and Grant, Delia, and Alice all raised their eyebrows and sat up a bit straighter in the booth.

Red took a deep breath. "You might have, I don't know, guessed it by now," he said, taking another breath. "I'm . . ." And then another breath, and a pause that felt like an eternity to the rest of them. Red's heart refused to beat and threatened to burst with the stress of it. "Gay."

Grant blinked. Alice and Delia smiled, Alice exhaling and Delia clapping her hands. "Red," Alice said, placing her hand over her heart, then thinking better of it and reaching across the table to give his shoulder a squeeze while he turned the color of a tomato, "thank you so much for telling us. I'm so proud of you."

"Red, that's AMAZING!" Delia said. "Amazing. I'm sure that wasn't easy and I'm so glad you told us. You'll notice I hadn't gendered ANY-

THING when talking about your mystery lover, I'll add." Alice side-kicked her sister's foot without ceasing her beam at Red.

"Thanks, y'all," Red said, feeling Grant's eyes on him but also feeling his bravery drain. He didn't twist in the booth, couldn't look at Grant directly. But Grant reached an arm over and pulled Red in for a hug, which wasn't super easy for two grown men crammed into a Waffle House booth to do. He crushed Red's shoulder blades into the top of his abdomen and cradled Red's head against his chest like he was a newborn.

"Little brother," he said, "that's tight." Red awkwardly patted Grant's strong arm, unable to speak because, as sweet as the gesture was, he was cutting off Red's air circulation. He patted a little harder, their old symbol for when Grant had him in a headlock and it was getting dangerous. "Oh, my bad," he said as Red straightened up and coughed.

He waved his hands and smiled at his older brother. "No, that's okay," he said, and when their smiles met, their eyes immediately filled with tears, and they looked away from each other very quickly. Discussing sexual orientation was one thing; seeing each other cry was another.

"So, are you, like," Grant asked, reaching for his water and taking a performative gulp and belch, "hooking up with any hot dudes right now?"

Red shook his head, while Delia and Alice continued smiling at him as though he had just won a Nobel Prize. He pulled his glass of sweet tea toward him, but his teeth started ringing preemptively, so he pushed it away again. He looked up. "But there is someone . . ."

....

Alice, Grant, Delia, and Red were sitting around Ellen's kitchen table, which had to be the most frequented, least lonely table in existence. After Waffle House, Grant and Red didn't want to go home yet, so the four of them went to Ellen's, who they figured was hiding in the laundry room. They clutched their full stomachs, and Alice took trip after trip to the bathroom.

Delia sat next to Red, and they looked at her phone together.

"What about him?" Delia asked.

"He's okay," Red said.

"Him?"

"I don't think so."

"Ooh, what about this guy?"

"Yeah, he's really cute," Red said, the flush creeping up his neck.

"Okay, I can work with that," Delia said.

"Hey," Grant said. "What about Herbert Grove?"

"What about him?" Red asked.

"He was in my grade, and he came out when we were all in college. I feel like he's got something going on," Grant said.

"Where does he live?" Red asked.

"I don't know," Grant said.

"Grant," Delia said in her most condescending tone, the one that made everyone in the family's hair stand on end. "You can't suggest men for Red *just* because they're also gay."

"I just said I feel like he's got a little something going on! He's like six foot—"

"Hello, children," Carol Anne said as she waltzed into the kitchen, slinging her purse on the kitchen table, Robert trailing behind her.

"Hi," he said, with an awkward little wave.

"Where's Mom?" Delia asked, narrowing her eyes at her aunt. She'd thought they were finishing headshots this morning.

"She had a little dog-walk date this morning," Carol Anne said with a smile as she opened the fridge and pulled out a cube of cheddar from a leftover cheese platter. Robert opened his mouth to point out that cheese was not vegan, then closed it.

"Nice," Grant said, grinning.

Delia scoffed, offended. "Why didn't she tell us!"

"Hey, she's a grown woman with a right to her secrets," Alice said. "We don't all have to tell everyone everything all the time, anyway. Probably best not to," she added grumpily, more to herself than everyone else, who ignored her anyway.

They all straightened up and tried to look casual when they heard the front door close and Wilma's soft footsteps nearing the kitchen. She walked in, and everyone turned to look at her. She stared back.

"What?" she asked, knowing a blush was rising in her cheeks.

"Mom!" Delia said. "Don't 'what' us. How was your dog date?"

Wilma opened her mouth, but Carol Anne cut her off. "Had to be great," she said. "You should have seen them at dinner the other night. They completely hit it off, and Derek is an absolute gem. Totally hot, funny, and nice." She reopened the fridge for another piece of cheese. "You're welcome," she said to her older sister, winking.

"That's hype, Aunt Wils," Grant said.

"Well, I don't know," Wilma said, playing with her leather bracelet so that her hands would have something to do. "I'm not sure if—"

"He's an alcoholic, well, you know, the sober kind, which I actually think is an attribute. I've dated *a lot* of guys in AA, and I think they're given a remarkable number of tools to keep in their emotional toolboxes," Carol Anne said. Robert looked to the ceiling and exhaled. "I even go to meetings from time to time."

"You do?" Wilma asked, double-blinking.

"You never know when you'll meet the agent, scout, or casting director who will change your life, Wilma," Carol Anne said. "Or when I'll need to play a convincing addict." She took a long pull from her weed pen. Wilma sighed, while the cousins tried to stifle their laughter. "Anyway, Wilma, I'm glad you had fun, although I'll say, I hope you were more relaxed this morning. The other night you came off as a little, well, stiff. I feel like you barely said anything at all."

This was cause for a quadruple-blink. Wilma stammered, anger tingling in her abdomen. She huffed and said, "Do you not know that cheese is an animal by-product, or did you just feel like saying you were vegan for attention?"

Carol Anne froze, the fingers holding the cheese cube pausing in midair. Delia's jaw dropped; Alice guffawed, then tried to hide it in a fake cough; Grant snorted; and Red's neck turned the color of a Christmas bow. Robert turned to a cupboard and pulled down a glass so no one could see that he was smiling. Before she could allow the guilt to sink in, Wilma spun on her heel and left her stunned family members behind in the kitchen. Carol Anne, realizing she had been out-diva-ed, threw the cube of cheese on the counter and stalked out of the house, slamming the door behind her.

Grant let out a long sigh. Delia's eyes flickered over to Robert, who was filling up his glass with iced tea from the fridge. "Robert?" she asked.

"I know, don't worry," he said, smiling. "I'm gonna go make sure she's okay."

"Oh, that's not what I was going to say, like, at all," Delia said. "If you don't mind my asking, how do you . . . put up with that?"

"Delia," Alice said under her breath, giving her sister Wilma's classic mom look. *Wow,* Delia thought to herself, *she really is ready to have a kid.*

Robert took a long sip of his tea and leaned against the sink. The cousins all looked at him. He thought, and after a moment said, "I know myself. I live a very quiet life that's objectively boring. It was fine before I met Carol Anne. I didn't know I was bored. But she sort of woke me up. She makes me feel alive, I guess. I know that's a cliché, and I get that most people don't really know what to do with her. I know that I sure don't, but that's almost the fun of it. She keeps me on my toes."

"That's nice—" Red said.

"Okay," Delia said, cutting her cousin off. "But is there any part of you that ever, I don't know, thinks about being with someone maybe a little more . . . *stable?*" Alice raised her eyebrows, understanding Delia's post-breakup phase of forensically trying to understand other people's relationships. Then she looked at Robert, curious to know the answer herself.

"I know what you mean," Robert said. "But anyone who's more"—using air quotes, he continued—"'stable' isn't her. And no one has lit up my life like she has. At this point, the worst thing that I can imagine is the boredom of a life without her." And with that, Robert tipped his head and calmly left the cousins sitting at the table. Delia watched him go without replying, because she didn't have anything to say to that.

....

An hour later, the Williams family spread themselves out in Ellen's kitchen and small family room. Ellen had insisted everyone eat lunch at her house, in part because she had to make headway on the food that was still being dropped off at her house, and she also preferred when the whole family was together. The company helped with the loneliness, and when everyone was together, it was inevitable that *someone* in the group would assume the spotlight, therefore keeping it off Ellen.

Ellen sat in her seat at the table after Jennifer and Wilma insisted they could heat up the leftover lasagna and squash casserole and uncover the seven-layer salad without her help. Red, Delia, and Alice sat at the table with her, Delia wondering how she could possibly put another meal away post–Waffle House, Alice marveling at the fact that she was hungry. JJ, also at the table, leaned back obnoxiously in his chair, while Carol Anne studied his face next to him.

"Friendly reminder to relax your jaw," she said, patting his forearm. He scowled, and so did Jennifer as she pulled the lasagna out of the oven. Why were they always doting on him? And, she thought, how frustrating that JJ would scurry home in the middle of the workday just because his mother had asked, while Jennifer couldn't even get him to come home on time once the day was over. Not that she particularly wanted him around, anyway.

"Can I help with that?" Robert asked Jennifer as she removed her oven mitt and placed it on the counter.

"No."

"Okay," he said, nodding. The landline rang.

"Got it! Retro." Grant called on his way back to the kitchen from the bathroom. He picked up the once-white, now-yellow phone off its cradle nailed to the wall. "Hello, Williams residence. Grant speaking. Big Pete! What's up!"

The color drained from Alice's face, and she slid down in her chair. Jennifer, Wilma, and Ellen tried not to look at her, while Delia smiled at Alice, then immediately frowned upon seeing her sister's face. Alice tried not to grip the table and scream. The landline? He had been texting her all morning, and had called her cell phone, too. But apparently, her stonewalling made Peter fully regress to 2003. She cleared her throat and turned to Grant. She said in a low voice, "Do not tell him I'm here."

Grant rotated the phone so the mouthpiece was behind his neck and gave Alice an exaggerated look of confusion. He shrugged his shoulders. Alice shook her head violently.

"Uh, yeah, sorry," Grant said back into the phone, while rolling his eyes at his cousin. "She's not here right now. She's actually . . ." Now it was Alice's turn to bug her eyes out at her cousin. Grant didn't need to account for Alice's location. Delia's eyes flickered back and forth between them at an alarming rate. "She has a gnarly stomach virus. Both-ends kind of thing, totally unable to come to the phone. Yeah, not good." Alice threw her hands up in angst, then put her head in her hands in defeat. As if thinking she was sick was going to calm Peter down. Grant continued, "Oh, yeah, it's fine, she called her doctor, who said this doesn't have anything to do with . . . yeah. Okay. I'll tell her." He hung up, and it couldn't have been fifteen seconds before Alice's phone pinged with a text from Peter: "You're sick? Please talk to me."

She sighed and turned her phone over. "Thanks a lot, Grant."

He shrugged. "You didn't give me a lot to work with." He hopped up on the counter and started scooping the still-too-hot lasagna onto a plate, took a bite and immediately made a face, leapt off the counter, and started hopping around as his mouth seared.

"Calm down," JJ said.

At this, just the sound of her husband's voice, Jennifer slammed shut the drawer she was placing the oven mitt into. Everyone jumped and looked at her. She blinked.

Grant finally swallowed. "Anyway," Grant said, eager to take the attention off whatever was going on with his parents. "What the hell, Alice?"

"Grant," Red said, casting an eye at Ellen.

"We're sitting down to lunch, I can talk to him later," Alice mumbled. Ellen looked at her granddaughter.

"The Bells could probably help with this food," Grant said. "Should I call him back and invite them over?"

"No," Alice said quickly enough that Delia gave her a full-on *what is going on* glance.

"Are you sure, Alice?" Wilma asked tentatively, trying to get as much of a read as she could on whatever it was that was going on here.

"Oh my God," Alice said, her temper flaring up again, not unlike it did last night. She slammed a fist down on the kitchen table, making everyone at the table jump. "I don't want to see Peter right now. I don't want to talk to Peter right now. Just because he knocked me up doesn't mean I have to stop everything and just, like, fly into his arms or whatever. I mean, *Jesus*."

Silence fell into the room like an anvil. Delia and Wilma looked at each other; Carol Anne's eyes narrowed, trying to work this one out in her head. Ellen looked at the table, at that damn spot where the flowers should be. Everyone else stared, fairly open-mouthed, at Alice.

Wilma broke it. "All right, so should we—"

"PETER is the FATHER?" Grant asked, a smile spreading over his face. "Holy SHIT!"

"Grant," Red said again, shifting in his seat.

"That's AWESOME!" Grant declared. "That's, like, the best thing I've ever heard. That's some serious rom-com shit—"

"Grant!" Red said, the blush that had been traveling up his neck fully taking over his face.

"I'm gonna go for a drive," Alice said, standing and grabbing her mom's keys out of the porcelain bowl on the credenza and marching out of the room.

Delia started to stand. Ellen reached out a hand. "Seems like she wants to be by herself, right now, honey," she said.

The Williamses left in the kitchen all shifted in their seats. Red tried to take some deep breaths to calm his heart rate down. Grant was looking at all of them, eyes bugging out of his head, wondering how no one else was freaking out here.

"Alice is pregnant?" JJ asked.

....

Without ever really deciding to, like her rage was the one in control of Wilma's Prius, Alice drove to the creek. She swallowed hard, her rage level spiking upon seeing cars parked off the entrance, making it clear some high schoolers had beat her there to ruin her solitude. The fact that she had once been one of those very high schoolers was not relevant at the moment, and she screamed so many curse words Ellen surely would have had a conniption.

If only she hadn't already done the desperate-pregnant-lady-prays-in-church thing. She had no desire to go to the field in broad daylight, and was in no state to run any kind of errand, even though it would have been nice to turn this outing into a productive one.

She pulled into the Zaxby's parking lot, essentially the only place in Eulalia left to go. It would have been nice to sit at the bar in Ricky's, but seeing other people drink while she couldn't would have been anything but helpful. Through her anger, she somehow reminded herself that it was wasteful to sit in the lot with the car running, but it was too hot for her to lose AC. She should just go in, she thought to herself, even though she had consumed a considerable amount of food merely hours before. Fried chicken didn't sound unappealing.

But she was too tired to move. The sun, her fury—it was wearing her out. Before coming to Eulalia, she had fully come to terms (or at least told herself she had) with doing this whole have-a-baby thing on her own. She didn't tell Peter *hoping* that he would have the reaction that he did, didn't do anything to encourage his response. She felt like Peter had gotten up on a podium, made this huge declaration, then walked away, only for her to realize he wasn't wearing any pants. He wasn't really ready for everything he had claimed to be ready for, and she shouldn't have believed him so easily.

She rested her head against the headrest and let out a long moan. If Peter had just handled the news of his impending fatherhood like her own father eventually did, with the "is a blank check fine again this year?" attitude, all would have been fine. If her father, Trey, hadn't started out ignoring all of his career ambitions, hadn't attempted to deepen his sea level to appear anything other than the shallow man he was, he wouldn't have broken Wilma's heart, wouldn't have left Alice without a father figure in Atlanta. And what of her father figure in Eulalia? What if Gerry hadn't ignored what Alice believed was his true identity? Ellen's (and the family's) heart wouldn't be broken as it was now. Of course, they wouldn't exist, either, but that was beside the point.

They all could have done with a dose of reality, and she took a breath, and told herself she was glad she was getting that dose of reality now. She'd be better for it. It was time to jump back on the train she had launched herself on when she canceled that doctor's appointment: she could do this, and she could do it alone.

Chapter 11

Jesus Christ, if I have to wrap another casserole, I'm gonna—"

But the world will never know what Delia would have done had she had to wrap another casserole. She started the sentence as she opened the front door, but she didn't finish. A man stood on the steps, pale in the face with nerves, a look Delia had rarely seen on him before. He puffed his chest and took a breath as if to say something profound, but opened his mouth, said nothing at all, and deflated with an exhale.

"Connor?" Delia asked, as though it were plausible that the man she had loved for four years and shared an apartment with for the previous two was maybe *not* standing there. As if the guy whose shaving schedule she knew by heart, the guy who always wiggled their apartment door-knob too much to the left, the guy whose mother preferred tulips on Mother's Day and peonies on her birthday, could have been anyone else standing on the stoop of her grandmother's home.

"Deel," he said, his eyes filling as he reached for her, as the moment that she had pictured on a loop for the past three months proceeded to actually happen. Her muscle memory of him instructed her to reach out, to wrap her arms around his back, to lean her head on his chest and tell him not to ever leave her again.

Instead, she slammed the door in his face.

She pressed her back to the closed door, sliding down it à la Diane Keaton in a Nancy Meyers movie, except Delia was wearing an old, smelly Eulalia High T-shirt instead of something cozy and adorable. She pressed her forehead into her hands, feeling herself go paler than she had ever let herself get, even before discovering St. Tropez in-shower self-tanner. The shock of him, and the need to protect herself, numbed her entire body.

Grant came bounding around the corner, excited at the prospect of more fattening food being left at the door while also coaching himself through the rounds of lifts he would have to do at the gym to burn it off. More fodder for his Instagram, anyway, he reckoned. "Oh, shit," he said. "Is it Ms. Cassidy's meat surprise?"

"Con . . . Con . . ." she muttered.

Grant squatted and punched the air while he visualized himself at the gym later. "Was it Jimmy asking if he could borrow Miss Sparkles? Grandpa Gere was too nice to that kid."

Like a flash of lightning, Delia leapt to her feet and grabbed both of Grant's hands by the wrists. "Listen, fuckwit," she whisper-shouted. "That was Connor at the door. As in *Connor* Connor. And before you say something insulting, no, this is not a period hallucination or what-ever. This is genuinely the moment in the movie where the heroine's former lover comes knocking on the door out of fucking nowhere to, like, profess his love."

"Uh, what?" Grant said.

"Shhhh," Delia immediately shushed him. "He can probably hear you."

He wondered if Delia was seeing things. With both of his wrists held hostage, he peered through the Coke glass on either side of the door, and could tell by the height of the coiffed hair, business-casual attire, and stance that it was certainly not someone from Eulalia.

"ALIIIIIICE," Grant called uselessly into the house.

"He'll hear you!" Delia whispered, manic. "What do I do?"

Grant looked into Delia's panic-filled eyes, and a pool of familial love welled up inside of his smushed beer can of a heart. He yanked his wrists, from which Delia clung like a puppet, to the side, and she went flying dramatically, hampered by her own efforts to always appear as though she were sub-one-hundred pounds, into the dining room. Grant opened the door and propped his elbow on the doorframe, leaning against his forehead as though he couldn't stand to be bothered in this heat, which was partially true.

"Hello?" he asked slowly and lazily, in an attempt to appear smooth and unruffled.

Connor had been gazing at the street helplessly, trying to decide whether or not he should call Delia, or try the house across the street, where he was pretty sure her aunt and uncle lived. He turned quickly to the door. "Uh, hi," he said, slumping a little upon seeing Grant. "Sorry about *The Bachelorette*." He offered a fist for a potential dab, or fist bump should the recipient feel more comfortable.

"Her loss, dude," Grant said, casting his mind for ways to make his cousin look cool. "And I could still get the call for *Bachelor in Paradise* any day now. Anyway, the funeral was a few days ago, and was pretty much invite-only, so . . ."

"No, of course," Connor said, so earnestly, like such a wuss, it kind of broke Grant's heart. "I'm just here to see Delia. And I'm so sorry about your grandfather. He was such a great guy, always put family first."

"Mm-hmm," Grant said, straightening up a little and subconsciously flexing. Connor didn't know what to say, and Grant enjoyed watching the guy who'd shattered his cousin's heart—however annoying he found her most of the time—squirm.

"So, like I said, I'm here to see Delia . . . ?" Connor said finally, the condescension buzzing in his tone, as if Grant had been blocking him because he didn't understand what was going on.

"Maybe she's here. Maybe she's not. But I doubt she wants to see you, bro," Grant said, pushing his cheek out with his tongue as though he were bored.

"Well, she left me this voicemail—"

At this, Delia, brushing herself off from being shoved into the dining room, had no choice but to woman up and poke her head around the corner. She smoothed her hair down and hoped to God she didn't look as bad as she imagined (she did).

"Connor?" she asked. "Oh my God . . . hey."

"Uh, hey," he said. "I think you just slammed the door in my—"

"Big ole gaping—" Grant began, before Delia silenced him by hip-checking him out of the way.

"Sorry about that," Delia said. "But also . . . what?" She made a point to noticeably tilt her head and take a look at the very small, but existent, carry-on suitcase resting against his leg.

"You got bangs," he said. Delia blinked and he smiled. "Anyway, hi, Deel."

Delia's heart catapulted right out of her chest. Hearing him say her name like that made her soften like the Velveeta she had seen Ellen push around a pan the night before. She felt called, called to a home she had built for herself. She felt the months of wishing he would call, of feeling the empty space in their bed next to her, of staring at the blankness on her home screen that typically showed a text from him saying (in the earlier times) that he missed her, was thinking of her, wanted to know what she wanted to eat that night, what type of air freshener she liked best to cover his nasty day-after-drinking shits or (in the later times) that he would be home late, and had she gotten a chance to pay the power bill yet? She felt meeting him at that ridiculous SantaCon pregame in her friends from high school's friend from college's apartment, and hearing him say "Delia" as he shook her hand and raised an eyebrow, having never heard the name before, how his mouth formed around her name like an expensive glove on a hand in a department store. She felt the way he cried when his childhood dog, Sadie, died, and she had held him and whispered to him that Sadie would always love him, and she felt the weight of their last hug, the one where he had rolled that final suitcase down the hall, tipped the brim of his Mets cap in her direction, not allowing himself to touch her, and then heard the sound of the handle on the tile of their hallway floor as he dropped his suitcase and sprinted back to her, wrapping himself around her and pressing his lips to the top of her head because he was scared to leave her, and she clutched him like he was a buoy.

It took everything in her to stop herself from clutching him now, but she did. "What the hell are you doing here?" she asked.

"I just . . ." he said, and took a breath, squared his shoulders, and started saying the words he had carefully mapped out on the plane ride down. "I was concerned because I stopped hearing from you after you left that voicemail, even though I've tried to be in touch several times. I reached out to Miranda and Grace, and no one will reply to me. I know how much your grandpa meant to you, and so I wanted to make sure you were okay."

Delia blinked. "You wanted to make sure I was okay . . ." she said, trailing off, unsure of how or when original words would come to her.

"Yes. And I was feeling particularly guilty because of how much I haven't been in touch over the past few months. I hope you know that our breakup was really tough for me, too." His voice was starting to falter, sounding less like he was in the middle of a presentation. Because no matter how many times you practice saying something in your head when you're on a plane, there's really no way to prepare for being presented with the person you loved most, who loved you best, for four years (well, maybe more like three if only the good parts count), whose heart you broke, which breaks your heart, too. "And I just hated the thought of you being down here, stuck—I know you don't like Eulalia—and being devastated over your grandpa and I just . . . I didn't want to be the asshole ex anymore."

"You didn't want to be the asshole ex anymore . . ." Delia said, because apparently it was still not yet time for original words to appear in her brain.

"I know you blocked me. I know you're probably really angry at me. But can I come inside?"

"Um," Delia said, drawing in breath. "I . . . I guess?" Those were the best and only words that ended up arriving. She turned away, leaving the door open, and Connor followed her through the foyer, through the dining room, and into the kitchen.

Ellen was standing by the sink, washing a casserole dish she would have to return to Mildred. She turned around at the sound of people coming in, and her brow furrowed upon seeing Connor. It took her a moment to place him; he hadn't made much of an impression. She frowned when she realized who he was.

"Hi, Mrs. Williams," Connor said, closing the space between them and giving Ellen a light hug she didn't want. "I'm so sorry for your loss." He stepped back and she looked up into his face.

"Thank you" was all she could think to say. She looked past him to her granddaughter, asking a silent question. Delia couldn't look her grandmother in the face. "Well. I guess I better . . ." And with that, she left the room, lightly squeezing Delia's shoulder on the way out. Delia felt the touch radiate in her stomach.

Connor and Delia stood there. Delia rocked back on her heels, and Connor chuckled. "You nervous, Deel?" he asked. Delia fought a smile, because apparently even though this man had ripped her heart out of her chest, taken a gigantic shit on it, and stomped it with the shoes he had annually cobbled in Soho, he could still get away with flirting with her.

"I wouldn't say 'nervous' is the right word," she said, twirling her

hair, until she remembered how greasy it was and the fact that she probably smelled like Waffle House and Georgia heat. She sat down at the
table and motioned for him to do the same, because the flirting had
empowered her somehow.

"I really am sorry about Gerry, Deel," Connor said, taking her hand
in both of his, cradling it and covering it completely. Despite the fact
that it was approximately one million degrees that day, Delia hoped he
wouldn't let go anytime soon.

"Yeah, it's been not great. And the funeral was a complete disaster.
I mean, obviously, I'm not handling it super well, I left you that voicemail," she said, her eyes trailing off his face and onto the table in
embarrassment.

"I know I should have called you back sooner," Connor said.
"Or answered. After we broke up, I felt like I didn't know what was . . .
appropriate anymore. Or what was good for me." He quickly added, "Or
for you."

"Well, it's been really hard. Even before Grandpa Gere's heart attack," she said, allowing the honesty to tumble out of her mouth like
vomit.

"It's been hard for me, too, Deel," he said. "Really hard. It feels like . . .
it feels like starting a whole new life, which should be exciting, but . . .
everything feels kind of wrong without you."

Despite her bravery only moments before, Delia felt her eyes well at
this one. This was the moment, the one she had been anticipating for
months.

"Yeah," she managed.

"And when I realized that you had blocked my number, it felt like we
really were done. And I freaked out and in the middle of my workday I
bought a plane ticket and I left the office."

"You left the office in the middle of a workday?" she said. "To come
here?"

"Yeah," he said, nodding, widening his eyes at hers to acknowledge how big of a deal this was. "I had to see you and I had no way of knowing if you were okay or not. I mean . . . you blocked me, Delia. You *blocked* me. Me!"

"I know, I know," she said, leaning into their entangled hands. "I know. I felt like I had to. It seemed like you didn't care." She began to full-on cry, fat tears rolling down her face. Connor pulled his hands off hers, and she immediately regretted allowing herself to get so emotional in front of him.

But he stood up and bent over her, pulling her into as good a hug as two people can possibly have when one is seated and the other is standing. She let him hold her, and she wept into his starchy button-down, reached up and hooked an arm around his neck, feeling the weight of how much she had been missing him. She pulled back to wipe her nose when her snot was dangerously close to her lip, and he sat back down. "Sorry," she muttered.

"Delia, don't," he said, tears in his eyes, too. "Don't." They sat in silence for a few moments.

"I'm just. I'm so glad that you're here," she said, forcing herself to smile like there was still a chance she could make all of this cute.

"I wasn't gonna abandon you in your hour of need," he said, reaching over and wiping a rogue tear on Delia's left cheek. "I wasn't sure how you would handle it, like, if you would receive me visiting well. I didn't want you to read too much into it or whatever, but I'm glad I'm here, too. You obviously needed a friend right now."

Even though the warm, snotty emoting Delia had just done left her in a glow to match even the Georgia heat, she suddenly felt the blood in her veins turn to ice. She felt like her innards were being pulled out of her belly button, and her brain felt like it was made of needles. She opened her mouth, but stopped herself from saying, "What?" because immediately, she understood. Connor was not here to profess his love for her, or because he was actually worried about her. Connor was here because he was scared of being an asshole. The second he realized she had blocked him, that she had turned pristine, considerate, affable Connor into someone worthy of being *blocked*, he simply had to come down to Eulalia, Georgia—on a workday, for God's sake—to right himself in the eyes of a bunch of people he had already discarded. Because he was that insecure, because he was that selfish.

It was then that somewhere inside, Delia knew it would never work. Even if one day she could act like their breakup was a blip, that it happened because they were soul mates who had just met too young, or because he needed to make one mistake because he had been so perfect otherwise, she could never build a life with him after this. She couldn't weld herself to him, because he was too self-absorbed to give her anything to latch on to. If he really loved her, would it have taken her blocking him to make him realize that maybe he should show up for someone who needed him?

And he didn't seem to want to be with her, anyway. She took a snotty, rattly breath and said, "Get out."

Connor pushed his head sideways, keeping his eyes on her. "Excuse me?"

She pointed a finger toward the foyer. "Out," she said.

"Delia—"

"I said get out." Exhaustion rang through her voice. "Seriously. I'm not gonna explain myself. I'm done with wasting words on you, with wasting time on you. And not even on you, on this, like, version of you I've created in my head. I don't hate you or whatever, if that's what you need to hear to leave. But make sure you do. Leave."

He scraped his jaw up off the floor, stood up, pushed his chair in (always mannerly, that Connor), while shaking his head and shouldering his carry-on. He started to walk away slowly, convinced she would walk him out. He was wrong. He turned around as if to say something else, pausing right beneath the "When I Count My Blessings, I Count You Twice" needlepoint hanging above the doorframe, but he just shook his head again and left. Delia crossed her arms over her chest and exhaled, feeling so much that she felt nothing at all.

....

Outside, Ellen looked at the shrub rosebush and sighed, wondered how long she could go without having to ask someone in her family for help. The gardening shed, the one Gerry had built, was right next to the rosebush, and Ellen figured maybe rooting around in there would lend her some direction. She opened the door and pulled the dangling lightbulb string, and it flickered shakily to life. She blinked, her eyes adjusting at a rate that made her feel her age. There were some pots, some bags of seed, some bottles of Miracle-Gro. She didn't know what to do with any of it. She blinked again when she saw something leaning against the wall in the corner. Bagged and soiled at the bottom, a very tall plant edged into focus, its waxy leaves brushing the cement wall. Magnolia leaves.

She stepped closer. Why was there a magnolia sapling in her shed? Was the mystery magnolia planter about to plant one in her yard? Maybe he or she had snuck into the shed to keep it here until the time was right? She touched one of the glossy leaves, wondered how long it had been in here. If it would die in here. There was a floating shelf nailed into the wall next to it. She turned to it and reached up to feel if anything was on it that she couldn't see.

She pulled a manila envelope down. Opened it, slid out a sheet of paper. It was a hand-drawn map, a dotted circle snaking around Eulalia, passing down Myrtle Lane. There were X's all over it: one right where Miss Sparkles had sniffed the mystery magnolia just the other day at the corner, one on Main Street, one on Carter, but mostly they were near her house. Her eyes fully adjusted to the light, and she was able to read the words scribbled in Gerry's hand in the top left corner.

Her heart stopped beating as she read, in messy red ink: "Fred's Bike Route."

·····················

Grant assumed the first drop of rain on his face was his own sweat, but by the time he made it to the old outdoor gym in the park, it was pouring. The sun was still shining bright—the devil beating his wife, everyone in Eulalia said of that sun-shower phenomenon. Probably not something that was okay to say anymore, Grant reckoned. He started doing pull-ups anyway, enjoying the way the rain felt on his bare chest, until he heard thunder and the thought of getting struck by lightning scared him enough to quit. He wasn't actually sure if getting struck by lightning automatically killed you, and if it didn't, surviving a lightning strike would only make him more badass. But he didn't want to mess with his chances, not when he could be called back to the silver screen at any moment.

The finale of his season of *The Bachelorette* had aired the previous night, and Grant was pleased to see social media going haywire over the fact that the winner's two at-home girlfriends had already come forward. He didn't actually watch the episode, though—too many commercials.

He began to jog back home and heard an even louder thunderclap. The air around him darkened. The sound of the rain slapping the thick magnolia leaves was loud enough to penetrate the rap music blasting in his headphones. He rapped quietly to himself, "A *million boinks, I'm a young money boink-ion-aire* . . ." He was concentrating so hard he didn't notice the sound of a car slowing down to match his pace.

He jerked his head up when the horn blasted. Rebecca looked at him through the window and motioned for him to get inside, which he did, shivering as the AC hit his wet skin. "Bell, my savior!" he said too loudly as he struggled to turn his headphones off.

"Jogging in the rain so your tears would blend in? I was worried you'd be a little torn up after last night's finale," Rebecca said.

Grant reached over and snapped the hair band around her wrist. "That's cute that you worry about me, Bell." She rolled her eyes but also tightened her grip on the steering wheel, and Grant smiled when he saw how clearly she was fighting one. But then her face fell, and she turned to look at him. "Grant," she said, "I'm sorry for what I said the other night."

"Ah," he said, looking out into the sheets of rain. "S'okay, Bell. Look, I shouldn't have . . . yeah. No matter how wild you drive me." He grinned his Grant grin and looked at her out of his peripheral vision. She rolled her eyes but smiled.

"Shut up," she said. "You're a dumbass. But me equating it with what Gerry did was just . . . insane. Or what Fred said Gerry did. Or whatever." She squinted and leaned over the steering wheel, trying to see through the storm, and saw a figure with a bike taking shelter under a magnolia tree. She instinctively slowed down to see if they needed a ride, and said, "Oh, shit," when she realized it was Fred.

Fred peered through the rain, and Grant opened the car door and leapt out. Rebecca stiffened, took a breath to ask what he was doing, but then she heard Grant yell, "Pop the trunk!" through the rain as Grant grabbed the bike from Fred. Rebecca pressed the button, and he placed it inside, jogging back to the side of the car and opening the passenger door for Fred, who slid into the seat.

Grant jumped in the back, slamming the door shut and exhaling. "Man," he said. "It's really comin' down out there."

Fred looked uncomfortable in his seat, though whether it was because he was with the grandson of his late secret lover or because of his wet clothes no one knew. He turned to Rebecca, but looked away quickly.

"Thank you," he said.

"Yeah, of course," she said, peeling back into the street and down the road slowly. She looked up from the rain and into her rearview mirror, caught a glimpse of Grant in her back seat. He was looking out the window, drumming on his thighs to the song playing softly on the radio; the music was so quiet under the rain that Rebecca couldn't even tell what it was.

Fred patted his helmet in his lap. "You doin' okay, Grant?" he asked, not taking his eyes off the shiny, dripping plastic.

"Yeah, yeah," he said. "Chillin'."

Fred nodded. Rebecca turned at a stop sign. Fred said, "You know, Grant, I'm real sorry about the funeral."

Rebecca widened her eyes and leaned forward over the wheel, trying to concentrate with all her might on getting her car through the rain, though it was starting to let up. Grant continued looking out the window. "It's true? What you said?"

Time slowed, and the air in the car turned thick and stuffy.

Fred didn't take his eyes off his helmet. "It is," he said quietly.

"What?" Grant asked over the rain, leaning forward. An almost-gasp, almost-sob, almost-laugh escaped Rebecca.

"It's true," Fred said, barely louder.

Grant heard him this time. He focused his eyes on the shoulder of Fred's seat and said nothing. He leaned back and returned his stare out the window. Rebecca debated turning the music up. They arrived at Fred's house shortly, a benefit of Eulalia's tininess. Grant got out and hopped around, pulled the bike out of the popped trunk, ran it up the yard, and placed it on Fred's porch. Fred turned to Rebecca and looked her properly in the eye and said, "Thank you for the ride." She nodded.

He walked up the path in his yard, still tall despite his bend against the rain. Rebecca watched from the car as Grant put out a hand to help Fred up the stairs, but Fred didn't seem to notice and held on to the railing as he made his way up. Finally out of the rain, he turned to Grant, and Grant noticed how loose the skin was around his eyes, how it made him look sad, like Eeyore. Of course, Grant realized, Fred *was* sad, and as they stood looking at each other, the hole in each of their hearts was reflected back perfectly, the same chunk missing.

Grant placed each of his hands on Fred's shoulders and pulled him in close. He felt a little silly, as he had to reach up to do it, Fred still being taller than him. Fred stood stiffly; then Grant felt him relax, felt Fred place his head on Grant's bare shoulder, felt him shake as he began to cry. But it wasn't soft and sloppy like his crying had been at the funeral; it was sharp and quick and jagged. Grant felt tears leak out of his own eyes.

After a moment, the men stepped apart, their internal emotional hourglasses full. Fred turned to his house and Grant bounded down the porch steps, wiping both cheeks with both hands once, then shaking his head like a wet dog as he charged through the rain back into Rebecca's car. He shut her door quickly and exhaled, leaned his head back against the headrest and closed his eyes. Rebecca reached over and squeezed his shoulder.

He kept his eyes closed and his head tilted up, but he crossed his right hand over his body so that it covered hers, resting on his shoulder. "Damn," he said.

"That was . . ." Rebecca's voice trailed off. She didn't know what it was.

"Yeah," he said. He squeezed her hand and uncovered it, sat up straight in the car and opened his eyes. He blinked his eyes wide open and wiggled his shoulders, the way he did subconsciously before he lifted a weight or started running. "Can we go get ice cream?"

Rebecca rolled her eyes, training them on her sunroof, watched the rain slash against it. She drove them to the Cream Dream.

....

The rain stopped, and the other Williams grandson ventured out. Part of what Red loved so much about running was the focus of it, his mind inhabited by only the music he was listening to, the topography of where he was, the sound of his feet on the pavement, his breath and his body. Even though Red worked for YouthLyfe, running provided the most relief from his anxiety, and for that reason, it was his real religion.

That day, he decided to swing by Eulalia High to get a few laps in on the track surrounding the football field. The gate was already open, and he immediately felt the ten-degree temperature rise on the turf. It transported him back to the days of cross-country training camp, and the nostalgia sweetened the suffocating humidity. He rounded the end zone, and through the flickering heat mirage saw a person sitting in the stands, but was too zoned out to give any thought to what sort of Eulalia High football fan would be crazy enough to watch an imaginary game. He feared he might be having a heat stroke when he squinted through his sweat and thought he saw JJ, then felt his beloved run-reverie abruptly end when he realized that he definitely *was* seeing JJ.

"I thought that was you," JJ said. Red climbed up the bleachers and sat on the same bench as his father. Sweat started flowing down his legs like a waterfall. He caught his breath and spit off to the side, which would have horrified Jennifer, but he was glad to do it in front of JJ. It felt like a masculine thing to do, even coming off a "pussy sport" (JJ's words) like running.

"What are you doing here?" Red asked.

JJ sighed. "I'm sitting."

Red nodded as though that satisfied his curiosity and looked out at the empty field with his dad. It hadn't been painted yet for the fall season, and it looked pitiful and brown. "Wait, is this where you've been coming?"

"What?"

"I asked Mom where you had been going every evening since I knew you weren't at work late, but she was really weird about it."

"How did you know I wasn't at work?"

"Because I listen to the show when I'm home sometimes," Red said matter-of-factly.

JJ kept staring at the field. "You do?" he asked.

"Yeah," Red said, shrugging. "It's a good show." Red didn't really think it was a good show, but he liked to hear his dad talk about sports, liked hearing him laugh.

"That's nice," JJ said, but Red could tell he was a thousand miles away. Red guessed JJ came out to this field to relive his glory days, and that made Red feel sorry for him. He also judged him a little. "They used to bring me out here every day in the summertime when I was a kid," JJ said. "I loved being out here with them. When I got older and needed more challenging workouts and had one-on-one training with Coach, I would still come out here with them more 'n anybody else."

"Who?" Red asked.

"Daddy. And Fred," JJ said. Despite the heat, Red felt his blood suddenly run cold. "I think I liked the attention, you know, they thought I was a star. And Fred had been a star himself right here at Eulalia High."

"I know. His jersey was still hanging in the gym when I was in high school," Red said, as though JJ didn't speak of Eulalia High football history often.

"He was a legend," JJ said, tearing his eyes from the field and looking down at his sneakers. "But I think I also loved being with them because it made me feel like I was part of their group. One of the guys. Like I was a man." Red nodded. JJ went on: "They were like . . . their friendship. It felt cosmic or somethin', like they were twins, two halves of the same thing. And I loved seeing that. They would let me laugh along with their jokes like I understood 'em. Shit," he said, spitting just as Red had, even though he hadn't been running. "Feels nasty now, to say that they were like twins."

Red became very still, petrified of saying the wrong thing. "So," he tried. "You do think it's true."

"I don't know," JJ said. "But I know I hate it. I know that I fucking hate it." He paused, then sighed, then took a sharp breath, looking to the cloudless sky. "It ain't right."

Red gulped, but his throat didn't move. Without Jennifer policing his language, Red supposed his dad felt free to really let it rip, to finally express what he felt about men being together like that. Red had suspected it, of course. And now here it was. Confirmation that he fucking hated it.

Red didn't say a word, didn't trust himself to. He didn't know if he would spit, scream, make a horrible joke he disagreed with, or, worst of all, cry. So he just got up and ran away.

....

Hard as Ellen stared at it, she couldn't remember when exactly it had been planted. It was the mystery magnolia by Miss Sparkles's turn-around stop sign, and was about twenty feet tall. She didn't remember the specific neighborhood association meeting called to discuss it, though surely there had been one. Miss Sparkles, relieved to take a break from walking, sat by Ellen's feet and also stared up at the tree.

She felt a strange urge to touch the trunk the way that Grant had run his hand over Gerry's headstone, but she remained motionless. Just because the urge was there didn't mean she actually wanted to make contact with it, to feel the bark beneath her fingers, to stand in its shade.

"Hey, Gram," a panting voice said. Ellen turned around to find Red slowing from a run to a walk. He put his hands above his head when he came to a stop, leaning over from side to side.

"Red!" Ellen said, jangling Miss Sparkles's leash, as though Miss Sparkles had been the reason she was standing in the blazing hot sun. "You have a good run?"

"S'okay," Red said, not making eye contact. He and Ellen started to walk down the street.

"You doin' okay, sweetie?" Ellen asked, more out of grandmotherly habit than anything else. She often used pet names with the grand-kids, but it had always been amped up with Red, and always specific to "sweetie." She couldn't help it, she claimed, because he really was such a sweetie.

"I guess so," he said, wiping some sweat off his forehead. His heart rate had only just slowed, but it picked back up again with anxiety, of which there had been a slight uptick around Ellen ever since the funeral. He didn't care to examine it much, but the easiest piece to identify was the guilt. Although he didn't put words to it, a cloud floated in his brain that told him that he could hurt his family the way that his grandfather had, even though he hadn't been married to a woman for sixty years, which most would argue was a key difference.

It made his whole being hum with nerves to do so, but Red asked, "Are you doing okay?"

She considered this. "I suppose," she said after a moment. "People tell you to take it day by day, but it seems like I need to take it more minute by minute."

Red nodded. "Yeah," he said, hoping that would suffice.

"We were married for sixty years, so the main thing is just that I keep forgetting," she said. "Don't tell your parents that, they'll think I have dementia. But I keep wondering where he is and then I remember."

"Probably because it was so sudden, too," Red said. "It'd be different if he had been sick or something." Ellen nodded. Red thought, *And it would be different if his gay lover hadn't come out at his funeral*, but didn't say that out loud. There were so many things he wanted to ask her: Was she surprised? If she was surprised initially, was it starting to make sense now? If she wasn't surprised, how long had she known or suspected? Had she known when they were young? Did she think Fred was the only one?

As if a grandmotherly spidey sense kicked in, Ellen said, "You know that you can ask me anything you want." Ellen glanced at him and saw that his eyes had widened, and he was staring at his feet as he walked.

"You don't have to ask me anything, either," she said, turning her gaze to Miss Sparkles. "I just know that this is a lot to take in for all of us, not just me. He was your grandfather, and that's important."

Red suddenly felt like a brick had been lodged in his throat. He gulped, and then a question flew out of his mouth that he hadn't realized he was going to ask.

"Do you hate him?"

Ellen frowned and jerked her head back as though Red had taken a swing at her. She shook her head a little to recover herself and said, "Gosh, Red, no. I could never hate him. I could never even consider hating him. I mean. Gosh, sweetie, do *you* hate him?"

"No, no," Red said, turning to her, and Ellen could see in his wide, sweet eyes that he didn't really have the capacity to hate anyone. "Never."

Ellen nodded. "Yes, I suppose he . . . lied, and, well. And I am angry about that. You know, after sixty-some-odd years of marriage, you know you aren't always 100 percent honest with each other about every little thing, myself included in that." She paused, tried to gather her thoughts the way she used to have to gather the grandchildren when they would run wild in the Winn-Dixie. "But this . . . thing, well, right now I mostly see only his pain. Him hiding, what it must have been like to lie to me and to you all, how hard that must have been for him. Makes my heart hurt. Even though sometimes I would like to give him a piece of my mind."

The brick was back in Red's throat, but this time it was threatening to turn itself to tears at any moment, and even though he knew she wouldn't mind, he didn't want to cry in front of Ellen. *He* would mind. But there was no use, because he wasn't going to just let her words sit there, and with his words came the inevitable tears. Squinting as though it were the sun causing them, he said, "That's beautiful, Gram. That's compassion. To me, that sounds like the love of God. For us."

Ellen felt his words immediately tattoo themselves onto her soul, so beautiful did she find them and so true did they ring. It all made her so

proud—he was her sweetie but also a man of God. Without really considering it, she prayed right then that Red would get to experience what
she had with Gerry—what he so beautifully called the love of God.

They were nearing their houses, and he stopped walking. She looked
up at him, and he said there was something else he needed to tell her. He
took a breath and told her the truth. She was very still at first; then she
nodded. She had something to tell him, too. They talked some more,
and then it was time for them both to go inside. Ellen wrapped her arms
around him, even though they were both sweating profusely. She held
him for a long time, while Miss Sparkles sat directly on his feet.

Then Ellen watched her grandson turn around and walk across his
yard, hands shoved in the pockets of his shorts, shoulders hunched the
way Jennifer and JJ hated so much. She turned around, slowly made
her way around the house and into the backyard.

Magic hour was settling around her. The crickets chirped and a
lightning bug flashed, but daylight still clung to everything. She looked
at the garden and she breathed in the air. It smelled green. She saw the
roses, the tomatoes, the squash, the hydrangeas. She didn't know how
to care for them, but they were hers. He had planted them for her. She
looked to the sky, tinted pink, and closed her eyes, felt a warm breeze
pass around her shoulders. She smiled.

....

Wilma felt a quick spike in annoyance upon hearing a knock on her
childhood bedroom door. She was stealing a few moments to herself,
of which she had had so few since arriving in Eulalia almost a week
ago. Her phone was off so she wouldn't hear the ding of Derek texting
her, asking her questions she didn't want to answer, like how her day
was going or what her favorite movie was. Sitting on her bed, looking
around at all the books she loved in high school, the Susan Meiselas
print Ellen still hadn't taken down, it was like she could feel her grief

expanding, like it now had room to breathe away from the rooms her family crowded. Carol Anne popped her head in.

"Is now a good time to go over the headshots?" she asked, entering the room before Wilma could answer, Robert trailing behind, per usual. She lifted Wilma's laptop and camera bag from off the paperback-covered window seat and placed them on the bed next to Wilma. She sat uncomfortably close to Wilma on the bed. Wilma sighed, but opened her laptop, started removing the chip from her camera. Robert sat on the window seat and opened his laptop.

Carol Anne craned her neck so her face was about one inch from Wilma's.

Wilma moved her head away. "Come on, Annie. You're making me nervous."

"Why would you be nervous? Do you not think you got a good shot? I thought you were a professional—"

"No, no," Wilma said, sighing. "I'm not nervous about the photos. I'd just feel better in general if I had a little bit of space."

Carol Anne moved almost imperceptibly to her left with a "Humph!" but then got up and walked over to Robert, bending down to look at his screen. "What are you doing?" she asked him.

Robert smiled at her. "I'm setting up a baby registry for Alice."

Wilma looked up. "You are?" she asked.

"Yes," Robert said, looking up at her, eyes widening. "Oh, I hope that doesn't upset you. I am so sorry, I didn't even think about the fact that this may be something you would want to do." He smacked his hand to his forehead. Carol Anne's theatrics were clearly rubbing off on him.

"Oh, no, Robert, that is so sweet of you," Wilma said, meaning it. "Did you . . . did you run this past Alice?" She tried not to sound skeptical, pretty certain that Alice would not be super interested in asking people to buy her gifts, much as she could use them on her writer's salary.

Robert shook his head. "I just thought I would get it up and running, and then show it to her as a surprise. She doesn't have to use it, but this way, if she does want to, it's all set up."

Wilma put a hand to her chest. "I am so touched that you would think to do that. Carol Anne, don't you think that that is just—"

"Yep, he's thoughtful, are the photos up?" Carol Anne asked, jerking her head from hovering near Robert's computer back to hovering near her sister's, her long, frizzy hair tickling Wilma's shoulder. It made her involuntarily shudder, but she sighed and nodded, turning her screen so it faced both her and Carol Anne.

Carol Anne gasped and touched her hands to her face, as if she couldn't believe she really got to look like this. "Wow," she said.

Wilma nodded. "You look beautiful," she said. "I think I was able to capture the—"

Carol Anne reached forward and jabbed the screen with her long, unpainted fingernail. The *click* made Wilma jump and feel like something was squirming inside of her. "That one must go," Carol Anne said, pointing to a thumbnail where her eyes were half closed.

"Well, I was thinking we'd do this the way we did it last time. We don't need to delete anything, we just need to go through, pick our favorites, and then I'll edit those," Wilma said.

"Delete. It. Now," Carol Anne said, her voice registering in a lower octave. Wilma double-blinked and cast a glance over at Robert, who typed diligently but raised his eyebrows. Wilma sighed and moved the thumbnail to the trash icon on her computer.

Carol Anne pulled Wilma's computer off Wilma's lap and onto her own, blocking Wilma from viewing it. She enlarged a thumbnail of herself in the backyard and sighed with pleasure. She started tapping the Next key, going through them, cocking her head at different angles for some, smiling at others, and nodding with approval for a few. "These are good," Carol Anne said. Wilma wished a small bloom of pride didn't open up within her, hearing that. "I imagine you take self-portraits to put on your profiles for dating websites and apps?"

The small bloom withered and died. "You know I'm not really on those."

"Makes sense," Carol Anne said. Wilma tried to take a deep breath, to ignore the subtext here. Even though Carol Anne had deserved Wilma's sass the other day with the cheese, and even though Wilma's sass was tame compared to what other members of the family regularly doled out to Carol Anne, she still felt guilty hours later, had knocked softly on Carol Anne's door while she knew Robert was on a run and apologized. Carol Anne had sniffed indignantly, prompting Wilma to apologize again and admit that she appreciated Carol Anne setting up the date and acting as a buffer, not only alleviating Wilma's nerves but also making it more fun (even though that wasn't true). This made Carol Anne smile at Wilma benevolently and ensure her older sister that all was well.

But here she was again, possibly referencing Wilma's "stiffness." As if Wilma hadn't felt self-conscious enough on the date. She decided to ignore the situation.

Carol Anne, of course, would not let that happen. "You know, I just meant that the more dates you go on, not only does that up your chances of finding your person just by means of casting the net, it also ups your confidence and your ability to *sparkle* on your dates."

"You know," Wilma said, "you seem to be a lot more concerned about my dating life than I am." An attempt at levity.

Carol Anne sighed and rolled her eyes while she dragged another thumbnail to the trash can. "Wilma, I'm just concerned about the energy you're putting out into the universe, and how that's affecting the energy the universe is giving *you*." Robert squirmed on the window seat.

"Do I seem unhappy to you?" Wilma asked.

"You're lonely, Wilma! It's okay, that's nothing to be ashamed of."

"I really don't know that I am," Wilma said, her voice starting to rise. "I'm fine!"

"Oh, sure, sure, Wilma's fine, Wilma's always fine! No one needs to worry about Wilma because she's so busy worrying about everyone else! No one needs you to be a martyr, you know," Carol Anne said, still clicking through photos of herself, though some of her previous enjoyment had clearly evaporated and her tone was sounding less airy than usual.

Wilma threw her hands up by her shoulders and looked around the room as if for backup. Robert remained more focused on his laptop than ever. "I'm not trying to be a martyr!" she said. "But you'll have to excuse me for not throwing myself headfirst into my dating life less than a week after the death of my father!"

"YOUR father?" Carol Anne roared, slamming a fist down on the mattress, her attention finally drawn completely away from her photos, Narcissus finally able to tear his eyes away from the pond. "Just because I'm not wallowing in grief and living in denial doesn't mean I'm not affected. And I also won't apologize for being the only person in this family who seems to have any kind of grip on the circle of fucking life."

"Who's wallowing? I went on a date! I took your headshots!"

"You went on a date because I forced you to," Carol Anne said. Robert closed his laptop gingerly and slowly started to stand. He opened his mouth to mutter some excuse about needing to leave, but Carol Anne threw a hand up to silence him. He gave Wilma a panicked look and fled the room. Carol Anne continued, "Don't act like you put even a little bit of effort into any part of that evening."

Wilma felt like she had burned her finger on a hot plate. She wished that comment didn't hurt her, but it did. She had tried to look nice, she had tried to make conversation, she had replied to texts and gone on the walk with him. She had even held his hand! And how could this possibly be the thing Carol Anne was fixating on? Wilma and, yes, Carol Anne, too, had just lost their *father*. Their beloved father. And here she was, stuck in this accusation that she was an old maid with no one to blame but herself.

Wilma leaned forward like a feral cat, leaned into the anger she always kept so carefully tucked away. Her face just inches from Carol Anne's, she said, "Just because I don't collect boyfriends—"

"You *know* I've dated women—"

"You're right! Just because I don't collect all people, then," Wilma said, "like they're, I don't know, *scarves,* doesn't mean I don't put effort into my life. Maybe it's more difficult for me to grow close to people because I know that I'll actually care for them. Unlike you, I'm not in the habit of *throwing people away.*"

Carol Anne's jaw dropped, and Wilma could see some sort of wicked excitement dancing in her eyes. Nasty as this was getting, Carol Anne loved a fight, and Wilma usually played it so damn safe. And this wasn't even JJ's usual yoga jab or career insult. Carol Anne and Wilma were in the middle of the fucking ring, and the gloves were off.

Recognizing this, but in no mood to try and make it right, Wilma rolled over to the other side of the bed and stood quickly. She stalked out of the room, leaving Carol Anne stunned. The potency of the moment was unfortunately quickly quelled by Wilma having to stalk back in seconds later to grab her laptop, which Carol Anne tried to protest, but Wilma left the room too quickly to fully hear.

Chapter 12

What's got ya down, cuz?" Grant asked, cracking open a kombucha and downing half of it in one fraternity-star chug. "Is it . . . hormonal?" he asked in a way that sounded dirty.

"Ew," said Alice, who had been sitting alone at the kitchen table in one of Gerry's sweaters, staring into space.

"There is nothing 'ew' about a growing life," he said, setting the kombucha on the table, sitting down, and leaning back in his chair in a way that made Alice nervous.

"Actually, there's a lot of stuff that's pretty 'ew' about it, but I appreciate that you clearly know you're not allowed to say that," Alice said. "Just . . . something about you saying the word 'hormonal' is gross to me. Sorry."

"That's okay," Grant said. Because it was. Acknowledging Grant's general grossness was not the way to offend Grant. Alice pretended to read the news on her phone, though she wasn't retaining anything, and kept flicking back to her recent text exchange with Peter, where she had asked him for space, and he had just "liked" the message, without giving an actual response. She looked back up at Grant a minute later and jumped a little, because he was still staring at her.

"What?" she asked, irritably.

"Okay, whoa with the tone," Grant said. "Like, whoa. If I can't call you hormonal, you can't just, like, freak out on me for wondering what's wrong with you."

"It would seem that there's a lot wrong with me."

Grant sighed. "Well, why don't we start with whatever's going on between you and Big Pete." Alice groaned. Grant continued, "Seriously, you should talk to me. I'm the perfect person to talk about your problems with."

"And why is that?"

"Because I probably will never think about this conversation again, so if it's, like, secret shit, no problem there. I'm a shitty liar, so you'll get an honest reaction, if that's what you need. And there's pretty much nothing you can do that I haven't done, so there's no judgment."

"That's kind of . . . amazing logic," Alice said. "Although I will say you've never gotten knocked up out of wedlock."

"But I would have to imagine that I've done some knocking up," he said. Looking to the heavens, he added, "But thankfully none that I know of."

"Yeah," Alice said. She did want to talk to someone; she wanted a gut reaction, not long-winded advice about what her behavior could mean for her future. Her own idea of her future was muddled enough. "Well. I guess it would maybe seem as though Peter and I have always been in love."

"Common knowledge," Grant said, leaning back and knotting his fingers behind his head.

"Okay, well, I don't know about that, but—"

"It is. You two are soul mate vibes. What's the problem?"

"So the other night we were talking in the field—"

Grant leaned forward in his chair, reuniting all the legs with the ground. He offered a fist for Alice to bump, "Hell yeah, you were. I've heard that about pregnant women."

"Heard what, that we go to fields?"

"No, that you get super, you know . . ." He raised his eyebrows so many times in a row it made Alice's head hurt. "Horny."

"Jesus, Grant," Alice said. "Never mind, this is dumb." She pushed her weight onto her feet to stand, but Grant put an arm out to keep her in her chair.

"Nuh-uh, not so fast, missy," he said. "I'll keep the commentary on your sex life to a minimum, but you can't leave now. I'm too invested."

"Well, anything to entertain you," she said, rolling her eyes. Grant sat quietly, waiting for her to continue. "We had this conversation, basically, like, we didn't figure out any logistics, really, but he told me that he's always loved me and wanted this," she said, waving her arm in a circle around her and her belly, "whatever that may look like."

"Love it, love it," Grant said, nodding.

"And then we were in the car and he got a text from a woman."

"Yiiiiiiiiiikes."

"Yeah."

"Was it . . . ?" Grant gave her a knowing look.

"Was it . . . ?" Alice gave him an unknowing look.

"Was it a nude, Alice, was it a nude photo?"

"Jesus, no," Alice said. "This is Peter we're talking about here."

"Right, right," Grant said. "So, what was it?"

"Well, I didn't want to just, like, read his texts—"

"Very cool of you."

"—but he ended up telling me he had been seeing this woman for a while, but hadn't said anything to her since he found out about the pregnancy."

"Sure, I mean getting the love of your life pregnant is one of the

best reasons to ghost I've literally ever heard," Grant said. When
Alice didn't continue speaking, but did continue to look at Grant
expectantly, he said, "Sorry, go on."

"I mean, that's kind of the whole story."

"I think I'm confused," Grant said. "Where was the part where you
got upset?"

"I got upset then! Because he had just told me all these things about
how he had always loved me and always wanted a life with me, but he
had been seeing someone else."

"Did he tell you he wasn't seeing anyone after y'all hooked up?"

"Well, no."

"Were y'all even talking?"

"Um," Alice said. "He texted me some, but I didn't . . . I didn't respond."

"You GHOSTED your BABY DADDY?" Grant asked. "Jesus, cuz,
sounds like you should be the one apologizing."

"I didn't know what to say! I had a lot to process! I knew I would be
seeing him here in person for Rebecca's wedding and would tell him and
I didn't know how to lie about it until then! I didn't know what to do!
It's kind of a sticky situation to get impregnated by someone who lives
in a different state!" Alice said, eyes wild with self-defense and heart
wild with shame.

"Okay, okay, whoa, sure," Grant said. "The judge will allow it. So,
what, does he like this other girl?"

Alice swallowed. "He says he doesn't."

Grant blinked. "I'm sorry, then, I still don't see the problem."

"Well, I mean, Peter has known about the whole baby thing for days,
and I do think it's unfair to her that he still hasn't told her it's over,"
Alice said, leaning back in her chair and folding her arms over her chest.

"Well, Alice," Grant said, leaning in, eyes dancing with joy for the
absolute serve he was about to land on her. Adopting a mimicky voice,
he said, "He had a lot to process! He didn't know how to lie! He didn't

know what to do! It's a sticky situation to get someone pregnant who lives in a different state!"

Alice smacked his shoulder so hard he yelped. He adopted a kicked-puppy-dog look and muttered through puckered lips, "Ouch." He wiped the look off real fast and turned that thousand-watt smile on her, uncapping his kombucha and downing the rest of it in a gulp. "I think, as your psychiatrist, that we both know what's going on here."

"I thought you were being a judge."

"I'm a Renaissance man, babe."

"Please don't call me—"

"This dude loves you. He told you that, and he told you he wants a life with you, and we both know Peter's no liar. He wouldn't say it if he didn't mean it. Plus, anyone with, you know, *eyes* can see that he's been in love with you for as long as I can literally remember being alive. And I'm still not getting what you're even mad about? For him not waiting at the ready in case you ever decided you wanted to be with him and get pregnant? For not knowing how to perfectly end a relationship you don't know anything about?"

Alice sat there, angry, because she knew that Grant was right. Grant, of all people. To be fair, he wasn't really telling her anything she didn't already know, but it didn't feel great to be forced to reckon with her own temper by her kid cousin.

"The good news is this is all fixable. You freaked out, it's whatever, chicks do it all the time even when they're not pregnant. But you need to make it right. Regardless of if you want to be with him or not, it sounds like you owe the dude an apology." Grant stood up and pushed his chair in, because manners were never not important.

In a move so tender it shocked all the shame, fear, and regret swirling around Alice right out of her, Grant bent down and kissed the top of her head so naturally it was like he was her father and had been doing that all her life. "It's gonna be fine, also," he said. "Everything." He nodded to her stomach and winked at it, which truly only Grant could do without it being the strangest, creepiest thing she had ever seen. Alice sat, dumbstruck. Although deflating Grant's ego often felt like the most important thing the people in his life could do for him, she had to admit, she understood why the producers of *The Bachelorette* had cast him. There really was just something about him.

She leaned her head on the hard back of the wicker chair and looked up at the bumpy ceiling. She knew what she needed to do.

·····················

When she heard someone enter her home office, Jennifer blinked open her eyes, furious. She mashed her finger down with such force on her iPhone screen it was a miracle her hand didn't puncture a hole through the phone, the floor, the ground, and hit the center of the earth. The jab was too forceful for her phone to recognize, and the noise of waves breaking and the occasional seabird chirp continued to fill the room. "Inhale," a woman with a deep, pleasing voice said.

"GODDAMMIT!" Jennifer yelled, which seemed to be her default mode of communicating, any improvement that had been made to her blood pressure instantly vanishing. "I'M MEDITATING!"

"Jesus," JJ said. "I just wanted to know where my tux was so that we could see if it needed to be ironed before the wedding."

"So that I could iron it, you mean?"

JJ shrugged. "I guess. Good Lord, Jennifer. No need for . . ." He waved his hand in a circle, trying to encompass her whole angry vibe. "All that."

"No need for *all this*?" Jennifer said through bared teeth in a quiet voice, which did what JJ would have thought was impossible, in making him long for the yell. "I don't know, JJ. I don't know, *Gerald*. Why don't you ask your peppy little assistant to iron your fucking pants, since she'll be the one unzipping them anyway."

There. It was finally out of her. She had been pissed for what felt like ages, but what pushed her over the edge was that he had prevented her from achieving her goal of calming the fuck down, and Jennifer liked to achieve goals. The woman on the app was telling her to find her inner peace, and she thought she would maybe never be able to do that now, which only made her madder, and so the cycle continued. Across the room, JJ's eyes scrunched in confusion. "What are you talking about?" he asked slowly, in what he hoped was a cautious voice, but, to Jennifer, sounded condescending, which only intensified her rage.

"Oh my God, JJ," she said, blowing right past her mental stop sign that denied permission to say the most hurtful things. "You are such. A goddamn. *Idiot*. You think I don't know about"—and she shook her head wildly, raising her arms to express the most dramatic air quotes to ever have been expressed in Eulalia, and possibly the world—"*Stephie?!*" The woman in her phone said, "Caaaaaaaaaallm," and Jennifer pressed her phone with a force usually reserved for childbirth in an effort to silence it.

JJ blinked, as if doing so would place a new situation before his eyes, would change the channel. Because this whole thing seemed like a mistake. "What are you—"

"Don't even bother denying it. God! I thought I would make it through the boys being home." Jennifer stood up and started pacing, gesticulating wildly. "I thought to myself, 'Jennifer, just wait a few days, *then* you'll confront your cheating husband who *so originally* felt emasculated by you making more money than him.' I'm guessing that's part of it, right? Other than her perky tits and her 'Oooh, JJ, you're so smart' and her 'Oooh, JJ, how do I get to be as successful as you?!' And then your dad died, and I actually felt bad for you. And I felt bad for myself, because you know he was like a dad to me, too. But cheating is a family trait, I guess! But you won't accept that! Wow! I wonder if that has to do with you not being able to face your own goddamn self! And I'm lookin' at your mom and I'm thinkin', you know what? I don't think I want to be *humiliated* like she was. I still have a life to live. And I'm not sure how keen I am to spend the rest of it with a cheater."

Their eyes caught on her final word, and JJ jerked his head back as
though she had slapped him. "I'm not a cheater," he said.

"Oh, please!" Jennifer spat, furious that on top of everything he was
wasting her time with the continuing denial.

JJ sank into the armchair in the corner that was used so rarely the
family often forgot it was there. "Jennifer, I've never cheated on you. I
can't . . ." JJ tried to find the right words, but he was coming up short,
which was typical when it came to his emotions. He felt like he was
drowning, trying and failing to kick and punch his way through rapids.
"How could you . . . think that? How could you think I'm like that . . .
like . . . him?"

"Oh, I don't *think* you're like that, I *know* you're like that. All this
working late, I'm not a fucking idiot, JJ. I followed you after work one
day, if you want to know the truth. And you didn't go to the gym. I
mean, where the hell else would you be going?"

She was leaning forward like a jungle cat about to pounce as she spit
words at him, but she straightened up when they heard the front door
open. Grant walked into the office, and he kept looking back over his
shoulder at Red, following closely behind, looking even more bashful
than usual. This somehow managed to annoy JJ even considering the
situation he was in.

"Hey," Red said, shoving his hands in the pockets of his basketball
shorts and scrunching his shoulders up, the way JJ and Jennifer hated.
They thought they'd solved it with a bribe when he was fifteen, a fishing
trip in North Carolina, but apparently the issue was back. Red drew his
hands out of his pockets before he and Grant sat on the old, small couch
Jennifer had been meaning to reupholster. "Y'all got a sec?" Red asked.

Jennifer had shocked JJ so much that he didn't process that his son
was obviously about to tell them something big. But worry immediately
dimmed Jennifer's anger, especially when she realized how uncharacteristically close Grant was sitting to Red, clearly in an effort to be support-

ive. What could he have to tell them that could be so bad? Then the thought flickered in her mind that maybe he was finally telling them the truth, and a little hope shoved out some of the darkness she had been feeling moments before.

"Sure, sure," she said, wanting to create as peaceful a scenario as she could. If only her meditation hadn't been interrupted, she thought bitterly. Red's neck looked like it was about to burst into flames. Grant tapped on his brother's knee, which did not make him relax. Jennifer lowered herself into the desk chair and leaned against the back. No one spoke for a moment, so Jennifer urged, "What is it, honey?"

Red flicked his eyes to his father, whose face revealed nothing. Oh, God. He felt like he was going to throw up and also like every nerve ending in his body was on fire, and not in the good way like when he and Brady hugged.

"I need to tell y'all something. I know my timing with everything with Grandpa Gere isn't ideal, but . . ." He suddenly had the sensation that he was both floating above his body and, at the same time, stuck beneath a tiny trapdoor at the very center of himself. "But I think I need to just tell you."

Jennifer nodded encouragingly, her eyes so wide they seemed to swallow Red whole when he looked into them, and it was then that he realized that she already knew. And while he wouldn't have guessed that her knowing would make it easier, it did. He kept his eyes on her as he said, quickly but clearly, "I'm gay."

Jennifer's whole body seemed to collapse with relief, but she straightened herself up and immediately rushed over to hold Red in her arms, closing her eyes. "Oh, honey," she said. "Thank you for telling me. Us." She knew to say that because she had read dozens, maybe even hundreds, of articles and parenting blogs about how best to respond to your son coming out. Her head was resting on top of Red's, and she twisted her body to look at her husband. His eyes were wide, and he was just staring at the two of them, his face no longer the blank slate it had been. His mouth was in an O, clearly shocked.

"Oh," he said, closing his mouth.

"JJ," Jennifer said, a prompt but also a warning.

But JJ just blinked. It was like his thoughts were moving through a bowl of Jell-O instead of his normal brain. Grant's instinct to speak up and ease the situation, to make a joke and to make light, immediately went haywire, but per usual, something about his father paralyzed him. He felt jittery but also extremely tired, like he could pass out right on that couch and sleep for a decade. Jennifer could feel her heart rate quicken. Was her husband really about to ruin this moment? If she had been mad at him before, Lord, was she beyond irate now. Red felt certain he would throw up.

JJ said, "Son, I hope . . ." They all leaned forward an infinitesimal amount. "I'm just. I hope that I've . . . I hope that nothing I've done or said ever made you . . . What I said the other day, that was different. You know it's different. You're not . . ."

And then JJ began to cry. He hunched forward, his shoulders heaving up and down. Jennifer still had her arms around Red, bent over awkwardly, as they all watched JJ fall to pieces.

Everyone was rigid as a board while JJ sobbed, unsure what to make of it. Grant was plain confused, but Jennifer, to her own surprise, found hope poking its furry head around in her chest—she knew how much her husband loved their son. Red felt nothing, barely felt like he was even seeing any of it. That blankness was cleared by the largest jolt of emotion, the biggest shock, when JJ stood up, rose out of his own tears, and then awkwardly bent over Jennifer and Red, his bullish arms engulfing them both as he continued to sob.

The relief that Red felt rushed up to meet him, like the swimming hole when he let go of the rope swing. He had done it, and he was safe. Jennifer, JJ, and Red hugged each other, one lumpy mass.

Grant reached out a hand and placed it on the part of Red's hair that he could see, as though he were praying over him. He looked at his family, and he was so proud. Tears sparked his eyes, but he smiled. And he nodded, winked at no one, and said, "Nice."

....

Magic hour, Alice's favorite part of the summer day in Eulalia, when the sun had gone down but it was still light outside. Everything felt softer, the sky was a light pink, and the slight drop in temperature was at least noticeable. She pulled up to the Bells' house in Wilma's Prius, windows rolled down. The Lexus was parked in the driveway.

She took a deep breath and exited the car. She leaned against the side of it, looking up at the house she had eaten countless dinners in and thought about constantly growing up, because Peter had been inside. She looked up to the window on the far right of the house, his bedroom window. She could see that he was lying on his bed, reading what looked to be a comic book, which she would have loved to tease him about were she not there to beg his forgiveness. His legs were stretched out, his left ankle crossed over his right, and she realized that she could be looking at him in that posture for the rest of her life. The thought made her stand up straighter.

She reached into the parked car and turned the speakers all the way up. She had to awkwardly lean in to access her phone, linked to the aux cord because the car was too old for Bluetooth. "Fuck," she muttered, squishing her belly a little. She pressed Play. So loud her ears immediately began ringing, Usher's silky-smooth voice blasted through the speakers, all the way from 2004:

There's always that one person that will always have your heart
You never see it comin' 'cause you're blinded from the start

The front door swung open immediately, and Deborah Bell, wearing a faded church T-shirt and chino shorts, took a step outside, looking like she was ready to yell at someone. She shook her head slightly, surprised, when she realized that it was Alice standing there. Alice, immediately embarrassed to be causing such a ruckus and instantly feeling like she were fourteen, leapt into the car to turn the music down.

"Sorry, sorry, Mrs. Bell," she called across the yard, coming back out of the car and freezing like she was in a game of tag when she saw that Peter had come to stand next to his mother, who looked extremely puzzled. Peter looked pleased, though.

"What are you doing, sweetie?" Deborah called across the yard.

"I'm trying to do, like, a gesture," Alice said. "Of the romantic variety."

"Since when is disturbin' the peace considered to be romantic?" Deborah asked.

Alice opened her mouth to reply, but Peter spared her by tapping his mother on the shoulder, who retreated back into the house with a shrug. He closed the door behind him as he walked toward Alice, hands in the pockets of his basketball shorts. He wore his glasses, which was a nice touch, even though he hadn't known Alice was coming and didn't even know how much she liked his glasses anyway.

"This is s'posed to be a peaceful neighborhood, young lady," Peter said, stopping a full yard away, which did not escape Alice's notice.

"Whoops."

He smiled at her, and she had the same feeling she had when they couldn't quite make sex work in his mother's car all those years ago— that feeling of being completely vulnerable, completely exposed, but also fully at ease and safe. She knew she would still have to make her speech, though.

"I'm so sorry for freaking out on you the other night," she said. "It was totally unwarranted, especially considering that you've been nothing short of basically perfect when I, you know, upended your life." Peter opened his mouth to speak, but Alice shook her head and held up a hand. "I'm really scared, Peter. I don't know what I'm doing. I knew I needed a change, but having a baby, even an accidental one, is a really crazy way to go about it. And you being so good about everything, and us being all in love forever, it just felt too perfect. It felt too good to be true, so then seeing some girl's name on your phone, my mind immediately went to, like, 'Here it is, idiot. Here's the proof. I can't believe you let yourself think that this was gonna just work out for you.' So that's why I freaked out. I know I shouldn't have. You didn't do anything wrong, and I'm sorry."

Peter nodded and took a step closer. Her mouth remained open, and she looked really fucking scared, and that's how he knew she wasn't finished talking.

"As for the other stuff. I meant what I said. I love you. And being with you, and having a kid with you, is kind of, like . . . It's kind of the dream? I think I felt wrong and silly for wanting something so . . . obvious. But I would be an idiot to run away from you and to run away from this. You said you wanted to be a family with me, and I want that, too. Families are crazy—I mean, look at mine. But it's what I want. Even if I find out at your funeral that you were sleeping with your best friend the whole time. I mean, I'd rather that didn't happen. But, yeah."

Peter closed the gap between them and wrapped his arms around her, and she leaned her head against his shoulder and took a rattly, wet inhale, smelling his Peter smell. Tears fell, even though she didn't think she had any more emotion left to express. He rocked her from side to side and scratched her back with his right hand. She pulled back just enough so that she could look up into his lovely face. He smoothed the flyaways that were constantly flirting with the humidity down and tucked them behind her ears. "So should I, like, move to Texas?" she asked him.

He kissed her, and Alice worried that he could feel the snot running down her nose from the crying, their faces smushed together as they were. Then she realized she was pretty sure this meant yes, she should

move to Texas, which meant she had locked him down for life, so she
could actually probably rub as much snot on him as she pleased.

....

That night, Jennifer was sitting up in bed, tapping her iPad, pretending
to see what was in front of her. The national cheer competition was
that weekend, and if she couldn't be distracted by her old team, by the
photo Cheer National had posted of her protégé standing in a circle
with the cheerleaders, heads bowed in prayer, arms around each other,
then nothing would do it. Her heart felt like it was squeezing so tightly
it would explode one minute, then unravel with relief the next.

The tightness came from thinking about her blowout fight with JJ.
She was no longer surprised he had denied her accusation about him
cheating; it was the childish thing to do and that was his speed. But she
didn't know where to go from here.

The unraveling came from the relief that her son had finally told
her the truth about who he was. Jennifer had never really understood
how anyone could have a problem with gay people, especially considering how close she had been with her gay male cheerleaders, and how
fiercely she would defend them if anything homophobic ever dared put
itself in their path. She had always seen the way girls mooned after her
sweet son, a different kind of mooning than the kind she saw for Grant
but mooning all the same. Sure, he was a shy kid, but his unwavering
indifference toward them had painted a picture for her long ago.

Her eyes drifted away from her iPad and into space, and she hoped
that when Red did end up with someone, they would adopt or something
because he would be such a good father, much better than his own. JJ
walked in and shut the door, and she flicked her eyes back to her iPad.
Her shoulders stiffened, but she said nothing. If neither of the kids were
home, he would have slept on the couch, but here he was. He walked
into their en suite bathroom and closed the door.

When he emerged, he got into bed and didn't say anything at first, and Jennifer wondered if they would ever talk about her accusation again. She knew they would, with tempers like theirs, but she pictured the two of them climbing into bed, night after night, their fight nestled between them like a pet, or the pillow wall that would eventually have to come up.

He finally spoke. "I'm proud of him," he said.

"Me, too," she said.

He didn't turn over to look at her, but he reached up and turned off his bedside lamp. "I'm not cheating on you, Jennifer," he whispered to the wall.

It was strange to hear him speak so quietly, even though they were in the only place he ever did. She turned her iPad off as well as her bedside lamp. She slid under the covers and looked up at the ceiling. His breathing slowed almost immediately. She had always been jealous of his ability to fall asleep quickly, regardless of light, noise, or time of day. It wasn't just jealousy now; she felt a heavy smoldering in her chest. There was anger, there was sadness, but mostly she just felt alone.

Chapter 13

Wilma inhaled so deeply it would have been comical had her reasons for doing so not been so very sad. She was sitting in Gerry's truck, parked in his spot at the construction office, her camera in her lap. She was using the dawn's light to drive around different spots in Eulalia, see what photos she could take. Maybe there was some sort of Gerry-centric photography project she could put together. Maybe making something would help.

Her deep breath, unfortunately, did not. No scent of Gerry rushed into her nostrils as she had hoped it would when she inhaled. It just smelled like car, and heat. She had parked under a magnolia tree for shade, but it hardly helped. The heat was making her head feel slow, like she was swimming through her thoughts and her thoughts were made of mud.

The good news was this heat and lethargy provided a kind of padding, and her feelings weren't so spiky and tinged with the potential to hurt. She could think about missing Gerry without feeling the sharpness of the pain, though the thought of how disappointed in her she thought he would be counteracted the softness. She knew that her father always took great pride in how kind Wilma was, especially to their family. She could see how it bothered him when JJ would nag Carol Anne, not that he did it as much in Gerry's presence. Gerry had always been good at handling Carol Anne, a talent Wilma had previously thought she shared with her father.

She wasn't so sure anymore after their blowout fight. When they found themselves in the kitchen together the night before, among the rest of the family, Carol Anne projected an iciness so cold Wilma had wished she had a jacket, before Carol Anne promptly stalked out of the room, while Robert followed behind like a puppy and cast apologetic glances in Wilma's direction. Not that he had anything to apologize for.

Did Carol Anne? There was a part of Wilma, the part that sounded like Delia's and Alice's voices (a.k.a. her biggest defenders, when they weren't too busy dealing with their own problems), that knew that Carol Anne did, in fact, owe her an apology. It was unfair, inconsiderate, and downright mean for her to try to make Wilma feel bad about her behavior toward Derek and dating in general.

That said, maybe it was possible she just had Wilma's best interests at heart? Carol Anne, self-involved as she was, didn't make this particularly easy to believe. Whatever her intentions were, though, Wilma had to admit that the solitude in her days was probably worth examining. It wasn't like Wilma thought that people shouldn't couple up. She was absolutely thrilled for Alice, hopeful that Delia would find someone, and still a staunch admirer of her parents' marriage, regardless of anything outside of it that went on.

But thinking about it, she realized she didn't feel some big absence in her life. Sure, there were some nights when she poured herself a glass of wine and caught herself staring at the blank TV, not having turned it on yet because she didn't really want to passively watch a show; she wanted to talk to someone about her day. She wanted to hear someone tell a story that they were telling just for her. But that wasn't every day;

most days when she came home from shoots, she was so drained that the silence of her home felt like a welcome hug. And she could always call any member of her family, and she had a lot of friends.

Was there something wrong with this, though? Was it not really satisfaction with her life, but a self-protective casing left over from Trey? Was it fear of change, fear of getting hurt? Maybe she had just gotten so used to being alone, she no longer knew what she was missing. And maybe that meant she was missing out on the possibility of a fuller life. Her mortality had appeared in sharper focus to her since Gerry passed. Was this relatively quiet life really what she wanted to do with her limited time?

Now it felt like she had been presented with an opportunity to explore this with Derek. What if she had Derek to chat with instead of the blank TV? She pictured coming home from a shoot and Derek peppering her with the kind of questions he had been asking her over text. She groaned at the thought.

Picturing her little house made her realize her homesickness. It struck her that this was good, this idea that she would be happy to get back to her life, whenever she felt ready to leave Ellen. Maybe it wasn't self-protection or self-sabotage; maybe it wasn't that she was afraid of change. Maybe she had just built a life she liked.

She was growing tired of herself, so she turned her camera on and started clicking through the photos she had taken that day. A magnolia flower, the faded construction company sign. Gerry's UGA Football hat resting on the dashboard, never to be worn again. She stopped when she got to a photo from a few days earlier, the one of Carol Anne and Robert. He was bent down, body looking particularly lanky and awkward, and his lips were pressed into Carol Anne's cheek. The crown of his head faced the camera, but Wilma could still sense the seriousness of his expression, the way his whole body leaned into the kiss.

Wilma couldn't see Carol Anne's face, pressed into Robert's chest, her profile obscured by an arm reaching up to Robert's neck. Her caftan

was slung over her shoulder, and her left foot had popped out of her san-
dal, as she had to stand on tiptoes to hug him. Her hair was a mess from
the way she had tossed it to reach up to him, and her arms were pressed
unflatteringly against him.

But despite all this, something about it plucked a vein in Wilma.
She stared at the photo, trying to figure out what it was, zooming in and
zooming out. After several minutes, it hit her. Carol Anne, for perhaps
the first time, had chosen to ignore a camera when knowingly in the
presence of one. For a small moment, she didn't care about how she
looked, about her headshot, about what would happen if someone saw
a photo of her looking off. She just wanted to hug Robert, and so she
did. Wilma didn't realize she was smiling until she caught herself in the
rearview mirror.

....

When JJ and Jennifer were newlyweds on Myrtle Lane, they almost always took walks in the summertime after dinner, digesting and enjoying
the slightly lessened heat, he sipping a beer, she a Solo cup of wine.
Eventually, they took these walks pushing strollers, then with the boys
scootering and skating around them. Then they stopped taking them
altogether.

It was not evening, and there were certainly no Solo cups. It was
the morning after the blowout fight, after Red came out. Jennifer was
surprised that JJ had suggested a walk, not because she thought it was a
bad idea, but because she, unable to sleep in beside him, staring up at
the ceiling, had been thinking the same thing. It had been a long time
since they had been in sync.

It wasn't *too* hot yet, but considering the early-morning hour, Jennifer dreaded how hot they would all be later, at the wedding. She could
feel JJ walking slower than usual, so she slowed down, too. He had probably tuckered himself out coming up with ways to lie about his affair.

He said, as calmly as he could, "Jennifer, I have never cheated on you. And I frankly cannot believe that you would accuse me of that after what *just* happened with my father."

Jennifer's fists curled into balls, and she tried to make her meditation app's ocean sound crash in her ears, tried to peel her shoulders away from her face. "JJ, you've been lying about where you are. You fall all over yourself anytime that young little . . . *thing* is anywhere near you. Men cheat on their wives with young women all the time, and sometimes not even with obvious people, as we've learned."

"That was a low blow."

Jennifer sighed and stopped walking. "I'm not trying to hurt you here, JJ," she said. "It's just true."

JJ turned to face her. "Well, what's not true is the idea that I'm a cheater."

"Then where have you been going after work?"

"Anywhere!" he yelled, splitting the soft air and turning away from her, stomping a few feet ahead. She glared after him, then quickened to keep up. He growled, then shook out his shoulders, visibly trying to calm himself down. "Anywhere," he said again in a more civilized tone. "I go sit at the football field, I drive around, I do go to the gym sometimes, I've even gone to the movies. I saw *Crazy Rich Asians* twice."

"You knew I wanted to see *Crazy Rich Asians*."

"Yeah, but how am I supposed to want to take you to the movies when all you do is nag me? And yell at me? You're so . . . God, Jennifer, you've always been tough, and it's one of the things I've always loved about you. But for what feels like a long time now, you've just been so . . . *mean* to me."

"*Mean* to you?" Jennifer asked, surprised to hear him say that, and feeling anger beginning to slosh around and rise like water in a tub. "You're the one that's been in a bad mood for the last five years."

"And when are you in a good mood, Jennifer?"

Jennifer could feel her vein pulsing, the one that JJ didn't know to fear. "Why *would* I be in a good mood, JJ? I have a husband who lies to me about where he is because he would rather drive around aimlessly, apparently, than spend an extra second in his own home with me."

"Don't act like you've been in a mood ever since I started skippin' out on coming home early. You've been in a mood for years."

"I haven't been in a mood. I was just *busy*! I was just *doing well*. Can you please acknowledge that *that's* the real issue here?" Jennifer said, suddenly wishing they had a dog just so that she could have a witness to this conversation. Maybe she should have brought Miss Sparkles.

"Well, fine," JJ said. "Sure, you were busy. Too busy for your husband. You made that clear. Don't act like I'm the only one in this marriage who's been blowin' the other one off. You couldn't be bothered to make dinner or, hell, even go to dinner with me ever since you started sellin' houses."

"When was the last time you asked me to dinner?"

"I've asked you to dinner, Jennifer, but I stopped asking because I knew the answer would be no!"

Something inside of Jennifer knocked itself loose and rolled around in her like a pinball. He was right: the answer would have been, and still would be, no. At first it was because she was busy with work, and the idea of having to eat with JJ and pretend to be interested in the station and his bullshit was just a distraction not worth her time. Then, when the idea of being asked to dinner by her husband did gain some luster, he stopped asking, seemed to be too busy stomping around and yelling. So, yes, the answer would have been no. And it felt ridiculous to consider it now because JJ had not shown interest in her in what felt like decades.

She felt empty, except for that damn pinball. She was suddenly very tired, and fully undone. "You're right," she said.

They were still walking, very slowly, about to turn back onto Myrtle Lane, which would make their circle complete. JJ double-blinked, à la Wilma. "I'm what?"

"You're right," Jennifer said quietly. "The answer. Would have been no. Is no now."

JJ nodded, feeling a slight tingle of victory beginning to vibrate in his chest. "So, where do we go from here?" he asked, partially to be generous, as he believed himself the winner of this argument and was curious to hear the ways in which she would promise to be a better wife.

They could see their house, where they had lived for over thirty years, coming into view. It looked almost nothing now like it did then, and Jennifer allowed herself to wish for that beginning, to picture how young and full of hope she had been, they both had been. A knot formed in her throat when she thought about moving into that house, across the street from the doting parents she hadn't had growing up, with a man whose love was so strong and loyal and inextricably bound to her it baffled her almost every day. It wasn't that she thought storms would never come, but she thought they would be strong enough to bear all of them.

She slipped her hand into his and squeezed. He looked down at their intertwined hands, confused, and also feeling his heart soften. While he knew things were bad between them, it never occurred to him that anything could get bad enough to break them, even now. So it really stole the breath from him when she looked up into his meaty face, eyes twinkling with tears, gave his hand another squeeze, and said, "I want a divorce."

....

Alice shifted in her chair for what felt like the thousandth time, trying to find a position that made her go-to summer wedding dress feel less like it was straining to the point of bursting against her belly, even though it wasn't. Delia checked her bangs in her phone's front-facing camera, and Ellen watched her from across the kitchen table, a look of plain disapproval on her face. Wilma and Jennifer made eye contact, looked at Ellen, and laughed out loud. Ellen didn't understand what they were laughing at and didn't ask. Red and Grant peered into the fridge, while JJ paced back and forth. He didn't like weddings, and after the morning he had had, he was approaching the evening with the same enthusiasm he would were he getting a colonoscopy. But this still didn't mean he wanted to be late. He filled up a glass of ice water and placed it in front of his wife.

"Thanks," she said without looking at him.

"No problem, do you need anything else?" he asked, staring at her hands folded on the doily place mat, at the light glinting off her engagement ring. Wilma raised her eyebrows. "Seems we'll be here for a while."

"I can go check on her," Robert, also sitting at the table, said.

"No need," Ellen said, smiling at him. "She's late on purpose. To make an entrance."

Robert nodded. "Well, sure."

"Oh, for God's sake," Jennifer muttered as Carol Anne floated into the kitchen, hands out by her sides as if she would take flight at any moment. She twirled and giggled.

"Annie . . ." Wilma said, double-blinking so ferociously it looked like she had something stuck in her eye.

Carol Anne took a sip of the glass of chardonnay in her hand and stepped intentionally to her left, into the light cast by the kitchen window. The glass made little rainbows dance across the white fabric of her floor-length gown, and Grant and Red had to look away, blinded by the light reflecting off her gold crown.

"Is that . . ." Wilma started to ask.

"Vintage? Yes," Carol Anne said.

". . . one of your wedding dresses?" Wilma finished. Delia and Alice tried to hide their laughter, but the smiles were wiped off their faces real quick when Robert stood up so suddenly he knocked the kitchen chair over backwards.

"Carol Anne," he said, hurriedly bending over to right the fallen chair. "You . . . you can't be serious." Carol Anne blinked and took another sip of her chardonnay, shrugging. The rest of the Williamses froze. "You look gorgeous, of course," he added. "Positively ethereal. Bridal . . . but, well, you're not the bride."

"I was so distraught by the news of Daddy's death that I forgot about Rebecca's wedding and simply didn't pack anything formal," Carol Anne said. "And this was hanging in my closet, and I can't help that I look beautiful in white."

"I don't get what's happening here," JJ said, "and I don't care. Let's go."

"We can't go!" Robert said, more loudly than anyone in the family, including Carol Anne, had ever heard him speak. "You can't go to a wedding dressed like that! It's disrespectful to the bride. And it's the bride's day!"

Carol Anne frowned. "I'm sure Rebecca won't mind."

"I mind!" Robert yelled, bending forward and shaking his hands. "I mind! Carol Anne." He took a deep breath and stood up straight, closed his eyes for a beat, then opened them. "Today. Is. Not. About. You." Carol Anne took a step back, jaw unhinged, as though she had been slapped. "I know you think that most things are, and that's partially on me for always . . . letting you think that. But not this time. You cannot wear that to the wedding because today is not about you."

Carol Anne threw her chin up defiantly and shook her long hair. "You cannot speak to me like that, Robert!" she said.

"I'm sorry, but you have to change," Robert said. "Jennifer, can she borrow something of yours?" Jennifer nodded, eyes wide in awe of Robert, trying not to let a smile show on her face.

"I may have something, too, Aunt Carol Anne," Delia said, getting up and pulling Carol Anne by the hand back into the living room. Carol Anne glared at Robert, but turned on her heel and allowed Delia to lead her, stomping her feet loudly.

No one in the kitchen moved, but Wilma, JJ, Jennifer, and the cousins were all trying their hardest not to laugh. Robert swallowed and looked around nervously, finally landing on Ellen. Fear crept in as he realized he had just berated her daughter right in front of her, in her own house.

But Ellen just looked up at him calmly and said, "Well done."

....

Carol Anne borrowed Delia's (pink) backup dress, and the Williams family got themselves out the door and headed to the church where less than a week earlier everything had gone to shit. After much grumbling from JJ about how it shouldn't be so hard for him to get a parking space at his own damn church, after they all had to wait for Delia to reapply her lip gloss for the umpteenth time and check her hair in the rearview mirror of Wilma's Prius in preparation for the possibility that Rebecca and Justin had attractive, single, male doctor friends, the family began making their way up the church steps, all walking much slower than usual, surrounding Ellen on all sides.

This did not help with the feeling she had had since she woke up that morning, which was that she was suffocating. Surely this was coming from the fact that she would see Tina, Mildred, Greta, and the rest of the town, all in the same place. And the rest of the town, of course, included that one person, the only person, who might be receiving a comparable amount of attention to her. And they wouldn't be receiving separate attention—Ellen knew that everyone would be looking at her, and looking at him, and looking to see if and how he was looking at her, if and how *she* was looking at *him*.

And like Robert had said, today was supposed to be Rebecca's day!

Her sweaty hand held Grant's sweaty hand as she walked up the steps. She had never in her life been so resentful of an undeniable need for physical support. She kept her eyes trained on each step in front of her, and tried not to appear out of breath. She concentrated so hard on this she nearly walked right into JJ, who had stopped at the top step. She would've asked what was wrong, but she didn't have the breath for it.

When she looked up, the first thing she saw was her son's squared shoulders, tension practically radiating off him. The rest of the Williams family had also stopped. She looked past JJ and immediately understood.

You wouldn't know he exposed his face to the sun every day considering how white it was in that moment. And for once, he looked almost small. Fred, who had climbed up the other side of the stairs, which were crowded enough to conceal him, now stood directly in front of the whole family. It was the moment all of them had been anticipating, with varying amounts of time and intensity across the family, for the past week. But now that it was here, no one knew what to say.

Fred gulped, and he bowed a little, placed a hand over his heart. He opened his mouth, and Ellen felt everything, her body, her spirit, stiffen in anticipation. She could form no cohesive thoughts, could articulate nothing. Like she were a puppet, waiting to be brought to life. He nodded and said, "Well, hello."

JJ cleared his throat loudly. The family's fear and secondhand embarrassment of what could fly out of that mouth rendered everyone, except for Ellen, unable to look at him. Ellen would have if she weren't behind him, would have given him one of the mom glares Wilma now imitated so effectively, the one that said he better shut his trap and not make a scene. They were in the house of the Lord, of all places (or at least about to be). There was not a need to cause any sort of upset here, on this day.

Ellen was surprised to find that this instinct to shut JJ up wasn't purely maternal, wasn't purely mannerly. She also felt a lionesque urge to defend Fred, who looked so helpless and sad, and who had been her friend for most of her life. She had no desire to see him publicly humiliated. They had both had enough of that for the past week.

But Fred was in no such danger from JJ, who hadn't cleared his throat to make way for a barrage of insults, but because, horrifying as this was to him, his throat had become a hard ball of tears for the second day in a row, and he was absolutely not about to boo-hoo for Fred the way

he had for his son. It wasn't abnormal for JJ to be confused by his feelings, and the past week would have been overwhelming for even the
most emotionally literate to have handled. And that, he did feel: how
absolutely in over his head he was. He was drowning; it was too much.
He had lost his father, learned his father had lied to him, experienced
his son trusting him with his truth, and been told his wife was going to
leave him.

All this made him want his dad, but of course he couldn't have him.
And on the one hand, here was the next best thing, standing right in
front of him: Gerry's beloved best friend, his brother, his proxy. JJ's second father. But on the other hand, that's not who he was anymore. JJ
couldn't compute this: there he was, Fred, but he was also a stranger.
JJ wanted to go to him, for Fred to clap his hand on his back and tell JJ
everything was going to be okay. But wasn't JJ also supposed to want to
punch him in the face?

For lack of anything better to do, he nudged Red, who stood to his
left, and Alice, who stood to his right, whose eyes were also filled with
tears. Feeling JJ's nudge, Red and Alice both tore their eyes away from
Fred and walked past him into the church. Alice wanted very badly to
give the old man a hug, to tell him that she wasn't upset with him, and
that she understood that she couldn't understand and so she wouldn't
try to, but he was safe with her.

Grant squeezed Ellen's hand as they gave Fred a wide berth and entered the chapel, and her previous resentment melted away. She was
grateful to grip on to something solid. Her breath was coming sharper,
and more jagged, and it seemed that the fear she had woken up with
was coming to a realization. So many feelings were swirling around in
her, and it felt like Grant's hand was an anchor, keeping her from taking
flight.

She was both relieved that JJ had said nothing and made even more
anxious by his silence. If he wasn't going to say something now, who
would later? And what the hell would they say? Seeing Fred, in the

very location where he had changed everything, brought the memory of Gerry's funeral into lethally sharp focus, and she felt that same anger brought on by the coffee machine not turning on roar up inside of her. She felt self-conscious walking into the church, where in reality everyone was facing the front, but her anxiety was telling her every single person had turned around, wouldn't tear their eyes away from her and her family as they processed down the aisle to find a seat on the bride's side.

But like JJ, she also felt bamboozled most of all by the fact that, on an instinctual and habitual level, all she wanted to do was hug Fred. And cry into his lapel, and say, "Can you believe he's really gone?"

They found a pew, thankfully very far away from the front. JJ settled in next to Jennifer and locked his jaw, tried not to think about the reckless urge he had just had to cry again. He twitched his head, as if he could flick the feeling right out of there. This annoyed Jennifer, who tensed her shoulders. JJ clocked this, and tried to move his own shoulders down his back, tried to relax his jaw as Carol Anne was always instructing him to do. He would be on his best behavior, goddammit. He had to. He couldn't lose Jennifer, too.

He leaned down and said quietly into her ear, "Remember our wedding?"

She didn't look up at him, just swallowed and said, "Yes." Because of course she did, but that was also irrelevant.

Red kept looking back as the pews continued to fill and finally spotted Brady walking in with an older woman with an almost exact replica of his face and a tall, white-haired man. Red smiled wide and waved, which made him immediately feel like a loser. Brady smirked and winked.

Music began to play, and the church quieted. Justin, whom Grant noted with satisfaction was still quite skinny, entered from the side and approached the altar, his groomsmen in tow. Peter looked out over the congregation, and when his eyes snagged on Alice's, they both smiled.

Alice gave him a little wave. Delia, watching her sister do this and finding herself misty-eyed, gently patted Alice's tummy, which Alice found strange but nice.

Rebecca's four bridesmaids (all Justin's sisters) began their procession. "Hideous dresses," Delia whispered to Jennifer, who nodded in agreement. The music finally swelled to that familiar tune and everyone stood. Rebecca walked down the aisle, radiant. Delia's eyes filled with tears, not even out of envy, just heartfelt emotion to see the friend she had known all her life glowing in a wedding dress. JJ was horrified yet again to find his eyes had also become wet, though no one could hold a candle to Robert, who was openly sobbing and plowing through the extra-large box of tissues he had hidden under the pew.

Grant felt an unwelcome knot in his throat seeing his neighbor like this. She approached their pew, a big smile on her face. Grant held his breath, waiting for the moment when Rebecca would look at him, and he would wink, and there would be a little twinkle in her eye acknowledging him, because even though she was marrying someone else, there was still, and always would be, something special between them. But her eyes never left Justin as she walked down the aisle—Justin, who was crying so hard (though not as much as Robert was) it weirdly made Grant want to punch him in the face, even though he usually hoped for groom tears anytime he attended a wedding. She made it to the altar, the congregation sat down, and Grant tried to swallow the lump in his throat. He looked around the pews to figure out whom he could flirt with at the reception.

Ellen tried not to turn around and look at Fred, who she guessed was in one of the pews behind. She took a breath and tried to summon the peace she usually felt in church. She fixed her attention on the altar, exactly where she and Gerry had stood some sixty years earlier, making the same promises, filled with the same hope.

The cocktail hour, held on the patio of the Eulalia Country Club while the wedding party took pictures, was almost unbearably hot. Everyone's glasses practically sprayed sweat, the condensation so quick it was like a time-lapse video. Grant and Delia lamented the fact that this meant that their drinks would be watered down, while Ellen listened disapprovingly. Wilma fanned herself with her program, her short hair sticking to her forehead. JJ couldn't find chivalry in this heat; it wasn't easy like in the winter, when he could offer his wife his coat.

The family stood in a circle, closed off from the rest of the party. This was highly unnatural; they all had friends there, and had certainly had more than enough of each other over the past week. But no one wanted to leave Ellen's side, even though she would have been pleased as the melting punch to see all of them scatter and have a nice time.

Robert held an iPad up in his long arms, taking photos of the cocktail hour like he was at the Louvre. Red kept wiping his sweaty palms on his pants and looking through the crowd for Brady, but he wasn't seeing him anywhere. He turned to Grant, who stood to his left. "Hey," he said to his brother in a low voice. "I got a message for you."

Grant raised his eyebrows and cast his eyes over to a small blonde woman wearing a low-cut dress about ten feet away. "Is it from her?"

Red rolled his eyes. "No. It's from your grandmother."

"Oh," Grant said, jerking his eyes away from the woman quickly. "What's up?"

"Gram wants us to meet her at the gardening shed tomorrow morning. Six fifteen."

"Six fifteen? As in the ass crack of dawn?"

"It's her request, not mine," Red said.

Grant sighed. "Okay, then."

"Pass it on to Delia. I'll tell Alice," Red said.

Grant gave Red a look of confusion, but leaned over to his left and started speaking quietly into Delia's ear. Red stepped out of the circle, walked over to Alice, and tapped her on the shoulder.

Finally, it was time to go into the ballroom, which the Bells had decked out with enough flower arrangements that one almost didn't notice the ancient, shabby carpet and the peeling wallpaper looked almost charming. Something about the bliss of the air-conditioning, and the energy of a good party, loosened the chain the Williamses had wrapped around themselves over the week, and they dispersed to greet friends and check out the surroundings. Wilma and Ellen headed to the buffet.

After filling their plates with rubbery-looking chicken and mashed potatoes and okra and buttery rolls, they found a big table and looked around the room, waving their hands in big motions to show the rest of the family where they would sit. But they were all too busy socializing to care. Wilma's eyes finally snagged on Carol Anne, who was holding a glass of champagne and making dramatic hand gestures to Robert, pointing all over the room, undoubtedly telling him about some local production she had been a part of here, or some fabricated story about a past wedding here. Possibly one of her own, even. Robert nodded, then bugged his eyes out at something Carol Anne said, then quickly started laughing after another dramatic hand gesture from Carol Anne. It made Wilma smile.

Just then, Charlie and Deborah Bell made it to Wilma and Ellen's mostly empty table on their round of greeting their guests. Wilma hugged them both, the hugs lasting for a long time. Even though it had already basically felt like it, they were a real family now, and there would be a real person, a mix of all three of them, who would join them soon. Ellen started to get up, but Charlie and Deborah insisted she stay seated and they crouched down to talk to her. The four of them were all smiling like fools.

"I've always loved them," Ellen said after Charlie and Deborah moved on to the next table. Wilma nodded. "Alice is lucky to have such wonderful in-laws."

Wilma took a sip of the wine Grant had placed in front of her on his last walk around the perimeter of the ballroom, scanning for females, while Delia followed behind him, calling him a pig. "Well, Mama, you know they aren't necessarily getting married or anything."

Ellen rolled her eyes. "Want to put some money on it?"

Wilma laughed. "I always thought you disapproved of Daddy's betting!"

"Well, it's not something polite people do," Ellen said. "Or talk about, anyway."

"Okay," Wilma said. "By the way, Mama, can I stay with you for a few days?"

The lead singer of the band approached the microphone and said, "And now, ladies and gentlemen, introducing for the very first time: Dr. and Dr. BAKER!" The ballroom doors opened, and Rebecca and Justin burst in to whoops and hollers and applause.

"What did you say?" Ellen tried to ask over the ruckus while she clapped and smiled politely, leaning closer to Wilma.

"I asked if I could stay with you for a few days!" Wilma yelled back.

Ellen frowned. "Honey, of course you can. You know you don't need to ask me that." Wilma nodded. "And I know it's none of my business, but does this have to do with wanting to see any kind of funeral-plannin' man?"

Wilma grimaced. "Who told you about that?"

Ellen raised her eyebrows. "Who told you I was too far gone to know what was goin' on in my own house?"

"Well," Wilma said, sighing. "No. It doesn't have to do with that, and I don't think I'll be seeing him again, actually."

"Oh," Ellen said. "Well, like I said, none of my business. But if that's the case, I hope you know that I've been gettin' on just fine for eighty-two years, so if you're trying to stay just because you're worried about me, I'll be fine."

"Mama, I know that you don't need me. But maybe I need you, did you ever think of that?" She said it playfully, but they both looked at the table, unable to meet the other's eye. Ellen felt relief flood her limbs, finally felt some oxygen return to her blood after the day's suffocation. Maybe it was just an untrue gift her daughter was giving her, but Ellen thanked God that she could feel needed by someone.

"I'll be right back," Wilma said, standing up and rescuing both of them from having to say anything further. She approached Robert and Carol Anne, who was somehow still telling a story. Robert's eyes flitted back and forth between the two sisters, unsure if it would be better for him to stay or go. Carol Anne immediately stopped speaking and looked dead-on into Wilma's face. She threw her head back and downed the last few sips of her champagne in one fluid motion. She shoved the glass toward Robert, who wordlessly took it and headed for the bar.

"That dress looks pretty on you," Wilma said.

Carol Anne sighed, looking down. "I guess I should just be thankful I'm one of those people who happens to look good in everything."

Wilma nodded. "Listen, Annie. I'm sorry for what I said to you the other day." She looked at her sister, who stared at her blankly.

Carol Anne finally made a motion with her hand. "Go on."

"Okay," Wilma said, taking a breath. "I hear you if you think I try to be a martyr, and I'm sorry if I come off that way. I really do just worry, and . . . anyway. I really do appreciate you setting me up with Derek. He's very nice. Even though your criticism was hurtful, I'm choosing to believe that you actually just have my best interests at heart. And of course, above all, I'm sorry for what I said about you collecting people. That wasn't fair, and you know, I've been thinking about it, and I actually think it's really amazing that we have such different ways of loving people. I know that you really love Robert, and I see the way that he really loves you. And that's a beautiful thing, regardless of . . . anything else. And just because you've found something wonderful with him, and there are lots of lucky people in the world who are able to find something wonderful with a partner, that's not me right now. And I think I'm happy with that. I think I might . . . like that about myself, actually," Wilma said, smiling sheepishly and looking at her shoes.

Carol Anne nodded. She took a big breath, placed her hands on either side of her sister's shoulders. She smiled benevolently and closed her eyes. "I forgive you," she said.

The rest of the family plated up and joined Ellen at her table, and everyone drank and ate as though they hadn't spent the last week stuffing their faces. Red, Delia, and Grant all sat together, pointing out different people across the ballroom they thought had potential for the others, but mostly just teasing each other. Delia only punched Grant's arm twice for his suggestions. Jennifer had to tell herself to calm down, that at this point the last thing she had a right to do was become visibly irritated by how hard JJ was trying to be attentive. Carol Anne ate all of Robert's chicken.

Peter sat at their table, which Alice assured him he didn't have to do. But Rebecca and Justin weren't sitting down, and neither were Charlie and Deborah, and as he told her, "The Williamses are my family now, too. Officially." Alice had blushed and raised her eyebrows, because even though formally their families weren't merging in any kind of marital union, what could represent a merger more than a literal one—a person, coming from the two of them, who had all of them.

Peter passed the salt and pepper, which were little bride and groom figurines, over to Carol Anne when she asked him to, and Alice couldn't believe how normal it all felt. If someone had showed Alice a snapshot of this when she was twelve—of her at thirty-two, pregnant with Peter Bell's child, sitting with her whole family at his sister's wedding—she would have just nodded and said, "Well, of course." But if someone had showed her this snapshot even just a year ago, she never would have believed it.

And yet her twelve-year-old self had prevailed, and it felt as natural as the sand under her toes at the swimming hole. Her thirty-one-year-old self wasn't gone, though; she was there, too. She was saying, "Appreciate this. This was not a guarantee."

"Who ya textin'?" Delia asked, leaning over to her mother, who was texting her neighbor back in Atlanta who was supposed to have been watering her plants but had just got in touch to tell Wilma she forgot, and they were all dead.

"No one fun," Wilma said. Delia winked. "I'm serious," Wilma said, lightly smacking her daughter's shoulder with the back of her hand.

"Yeah, I heard you're done with Death Derek," Delia said.

Wilma shook her head and sighed. "Can't anyone in this family have any secrets?"

Delia leaned her head back and hooted. "Yeah! *Not* having secrets is the problem."

Wilma laughed, too. "I know you were really excited about the idea of Derek—"

"Hold on, not for me! I hardly need a new daddy," Delia said. "I just want you to have fun, is all."

Wilma nodded. "I am. Or trying to, in spite of everything, anyway."

Delia held up her glass of champagne. "To singledom. May it strengthen us, may it bond us with our sisters in arms, and may we get laid along the way."

Wilma guffawed at her daughter's salaciousness, but clinked glasses all the same. She leaned over and wrapped a quick arm around Delia, who didn't pull away, to the surprise of Wilma, who had somehow never stopped expecting Delia's teenage behavior. They squeezed each other.

"All right," Grant said, throwing his napkin on the table and standing up. "It's time to party."

"Hear, hear!" Delia said, also standing up. Red, Peter, Alice, Carol Anne, and Robert followed. JJ extended a hand to Jennifer, who tried not to visibly shudder as she took it.

"Go on, now," Ellen said to Wilma, nodding to the dance floor.

"I don't think so," Wilma said. "Though I am gonna run to the ladies' room. You okay here by yourself?"

"Wilma, I swear—"

Wilma threw her hands up. "Okay, okay," she said, leaving the table.

Ellen, finally alone, looked across the reception hall, and her eyes
caught on Fred, mirroring her across the room, sitting alone, sipping
iced tea. It struck her that she didn't know if she had ever gone so long
without seeing or talking to Fred before these six days. He felt like the
most familiar person in the room to her, and also looked like a total
stranger.

Ellen had been to countless weddings with Fred over the years, and
the night usually ended this way: with Fred and Ellen sitting down.
Gerry and Linda loved to dance, and would always drag Fred and Ellen
to the dance floor with them, but eventually Fred and Ellen would be
excused, and would find a seat together to eat cake and watch their
spouses dance with each other, inexhaustible as they were. A lump
formed in Ellen's throat because it wasn't just one man she missed. She
missed her husband, she missed Linda, and she missed the man sitting
across the room instead of at her table, as he should be.

The weddings and particularly the funerals of the past few years had
made Ellen painfully aware that life would not always hold the four
of them. Once Linda passed on to the other side, that knowledge had
become even sharper. And now, that fear was realized because Gerry
was gone, and her heart felt unbelievably heavy that even though Fred
was still here, he wasn't by her side, sharing her grief. Even though she
claimed to want it, she felt her aloneness like it was a plastic bubble
around her, but knew she shouldn't, and maybe didn't, have to bear
this all by herself. She took a sip of her water and tried to smile when
Wilma returned and cast those concerned eyes on her. Neither of them
said anything.

"Music's loud," JJ said as he and Jennifer swayed on the dance floor.
Neither of them particularly liked dancing at weddings, though they felt

like they couldn't complain considering the dreaded flash mob had been canceled, due to confusion over the YouTube video. But JJ had asked, and Jennifer didn't want to say no, so there they swayed.

Jennifer felt her eyes begin to roll, but she stopped herself. It was a dumb comment, but he had made it just for the sake of saying something to her and she knew it. "Yep," she said in return, not looking up into his face even though she could feel his eyes on her. She looked around the dance floor instead, smiled, and said, "Look at that."

JJ followed his wife's gaze to Alice and Peter, who were swaying with Alice's head resting on Peter's chest. Both of their eyes were closed, so neither could see the other smiling. Something unfurled in Jennifer, and she felt both hope for her niece and her own heartbreak at the same time. But she laughed when JJ nudged her, rolling his eyes, nodding over to the corner, where Carol Anne was striking ridiculous poses with the flower arrangements while Robert stood on a chair taking dozens of pictures of her with the iPad, from each exact angle she wanted.

Red, Grant, and Delia hopped around the dance floor like maniacs, like all their home videos showed they used to do as kids. They took a water break for the slow song, giggling and dizzy from their endorphins and champagne. Delia had the thought that she wouldn't be able to act like this—free—if she were at her own wedding, and gratitude for this, this freedom, washed over her. Grant wondered when they would cut the cake.

Red was sweating as much as he did on his runs. He knew there was some quote about champagne being the drink of the stars, or bottled stars, or something. Whatever the quote was, he felt that he perfectly understood it. Three glasses deep, and it seemed to Red like he was floating in the sky, a heavenly body.

He was looking across the dance floor at Justin spinning Rebecca around in a crowd of their medical school friends when his eyes finally met Brady's. Brady was swaying along with the band, a respectable distance from the throng. The boys smiled at each other, and Red jerked his star-filled head to the door, turned on his heel, and walked out of the country club.

The tables and flowers from the cocktail hour were still out on the patio, and now the string lights actually shined. He heard Brady's footsteps behind him and turned around, smiled big. "Hi," he said.

"Hi there, Red," Brady said. "Your brother got me all caught up on your good news."

"When did you talk to Grant?"

"I saw him on a run, and I had a lot of questions about *The Bachelorette*." Red nodded, and his neck felt funny. It took him a moment to realize it was because there was no flush creeping up. "I'm proud of you, that's fucking awesome. Seriously," Brady said. He took a few steps toward Red, though they still were too far apart to touch.

"Well, I pretty much had to," Red said. Brady narrowed his eyes, started to smile. "I kind of have a crush on this guy, and he told me he doesn't kiss closeted boys."

Like it didn't scare the absolute shit out of him, like he really was made of stars, Red closed the gap between them and looked down into Brady's blue eyes. Red bit his lip and smiled, rooted in the last moment of his existence when he had never kissed a boy. The last of his Before.

Red bent down and pressed his lips on Brady's, and Brady kissed him back, raising his hands to Red's immediately fully flushed neck. Red kept his hands in his pockets, but he felt like at any second they might lift up, and his whole body might follow, taking flight, and he would hover above this wedding, this town, everything.

....

Ellen and the grandkids got up at the designated time the next morning, the cousins battling post-wedding hangovers. Alice, Grant, and Delia would have been grumpy about it, but they were driven by their overwhelming curiosity about why Ellen wanted them up at the crack of dawn. Red came prepared with gardening instructions saved to his phone, and Grant and Delia followed his directions to grab the bigger shovels in the shed. Ellen told Alice to pull down the map from the shelf, guessing that her oldest grandchild would be the quickest to interpret its meaning.

Alice held the map in her hands, blinking as she stepped out of the shed and into the dim, early-morning light. She looked up at her grandmother in confusion. "Gerry kept that here," Ellen said, standing by the open wooden door. "Hidden." She nodded to the shed's back wall, and Alice followed her eyeline to the baby magnolia leaning against the wall. Alice traced her fingers over her grandfather's words, the recognition of his handwriting confirming what her grandmother had just told her. "Fred's Bike Route."

"What is it?" Delia asked, coming to stand by her sister and craning her neck over the paper. Grant looked over Alice's other shoulder.

"I don't get it," he said.

"Grandpa Gere . . . he planted all the mystery magnolias," Alice said.

"The mystery magnolias that the neighborhood people are always getting their panties in a wad over?" Grant asked.

Alice nodded. "He planted them along Fred's bike route."

"Always been Fred's favorite," Ellen said quietly. Red stood next to his grandmother and kept his hands shoved in his pockets.

Delia burst into tears. They looked at her, alarmed. "That's so . . . that's so," she said in between sobs. "That's so beautiful," she finally managed to get out. "Or . . ." She looked up into her grandmother's eyes and sniffled. "Sorry . . ." she said.

Ellen shook her head. "No need," she said. "I rather agree with you."

The five of them set off toward the end of Myrtle Lane, the opposite end from where Miss Sparkles's turn-around stop sign was, where that mystery magnolia had been planted for years. None of them spoke. Red carried the sapling, cradling it close to his stomach, and craned his neck so the branches wouldn't poke his head. They got to the spot marked on the map, the only remaining spot where there was no magnolia tree. Alice double-checked that it was correct. Grant and Delia set to work digging a hole, both of them sweating in the morning heat.

"Think we're good?" Grant finally said. Red consulted his phone and nodded. The five of them gathered wordlessly around the hole, and Red placed the tree in it. Grant and Delia started shoveling the dirt back in, and Red and Alice got on their knees to help push the dirt along with their bare hands. Ellen kept watch over them and the street, on the lookout for meddling neighbors, not that she would have any sort of defense were any of them to come across her and her grandchildren at that point anyway. Besides, for the first time since Gerry passed, she felt in her gut and in her bones that they were all being watched over already.

"Yo, Gram," Grant said, extending the shovel over in Ellen's direction. "You wanna handle the last clump?" Ellen looked at the shovel and she looked at her grandson. She nodded and shuffled over.

He handed her the shovel, and she used it to gently push the last bit of dirt back into the hole. Grant joined Red and Alice on their knees, and they all patted the dirt around the tree. Delia wiped the sweat off her forehead and backed up a couple paces to admire their work.

They all simply stood there, and even though they didn't mean to, they stood in order of age. They looked at the young, vulnerable tree. Ellen knew that she would be gone before she would ever see it grow big, and thought about how Gerry and Fred would have known that, as well. Alice thought about Fred passing these trees on his bike every day, the simultaneous secrecy and openness of it, and Grant admired the size of the romantic gesture. Delia thought about the strength of the love something like this required. Red just looked and realized that he felt less alone than he ever had.

They all went back home and sat around the kitchen table for a few minutes. Ellen brewed a big pot of coffee, and everyone drank a cup, even though their sweat hadn't cooled yet. Delia, whose eyes were already starting to swell from her crying, couldn't resist berating Red about where he went off to last night. All five of them laughed as Grant made an impassioned plea to Alice to name her baby after him, which she refused to agree to, but did promise (truthfully) to consider.

Eventually, the cousins went back to their beds, but Ellen and Miss Sparkles went to the front porch. They sat in a rocking chair and waited for their friend to pass by on his bike.

Acknowledgments

The first thank-you goes to the person who made it all happen: my agent, my friend, the first person I spoke to every day for three years over our shared cubicle wall, the incomparable Andrianna deLone. I'm lucky to know exactly just *how* lucky I am to have her as my partner in all this. Thanks also to Michael and Marilyn Yeatts, and Sean deLone.

I am so hugely grateful to get to work with Randi Kramer, the most terrific editor an author could ask for. I am so grateful for her smart notes, the perfect combination of calm and excitement she brought to this process, and her warmth. It felt like the Williams family was just waiting to be loved by her.

The Publications Department at ICM Partners is made up of the most special, fun, and smart people on the planet. I can't believe I convinced them to hire me, let alone represent me. Special thanks to Kristyn Keene Benton and Kari Stuart, for being my North Stars as I navigated life from ages twenty-three to twenty-eight. Thanks to Esther Newberg for allowing me to witness her general badassery, for purse day, and for her help with this process. Thanks to Zoe Sandler for keeping it real while also being radically kind. Thanks to John De Laney, who truly slays all day. I am so grateful to know Boaty Boatwright, the kindest, wisest, most fabulous woman in New York City. And thanks to Josie Freedman and Alyssa Weinberger!

It's difficult to articulate my gratitude for Sloan Harris, even though I'm supposedly a writer or whatever. He gave me a chance when no one else would, and he has lifted me up every day since. He and Jenny Harris have made me feel like I have family in New York, and I could not be more thankful to know them.

Thanks to Molly Bloom, Vincent Stanley, and Michelle McMillian at Celadon for making this into a real thing! And a pretty one, too.

My gratitude to Celadon extends to Rachel Chou, Jennifer Jackson, Anna Belle Hindenlang, Liza Buell, Jaime Noven, and Sandra Moore.

Thank you to Eboni Rafus-Brenning for her smart notes. Thanks also to Mary Beth Constant for going through this thing with a fine-tooth comb.

Thank you to Matt Murphy for my author photo! And to Morgan Mabry and Evan Zimmerman.

As a student, I had many wonderful teachers who encouraged my writing, and I cannot overstate their impact. Special thanks to Jennifer Dracos-Tice at Westminster and Dr. Maggie Zurawski and Reginald McKnight at the University of Georgia. I must also thank my fourth grade teacher, Julianne Schaaf, whose encouragement was an integral part of all this.

Big thanks to Heather Karpas: my most trusted reading buddy, my career counselor, my idol, and the older sister I never had.

Thanks to Alexa Brahme for understanding.

Thanks to Katie Baumberger, who has been here through it all. Someone is staring at you in personal growth.

I would never have had the confidence or inspiration to actually try to be a damn writer if it wasn't for my Morton girls. Thanks especially to Sarah Raymer, Katherine Green, Mary Luttrell, Lauren Buss, Abby Kovan, and Mathilde Tribou for the early reads and encouragement.

Thanks to Laney Mallet for holding down the fort here in the city with me. Gracy Juba, you should probably call me back.

I'm so grateful for my friendship and literary sisterhood with Sydney Jeffay.

I didn't expect to meet my soul mate folding scuba jackets in SoHo Women's, but that's where I met Ethan Carlson. I wrote the first draft of this book over the pandemic, and none of this would have happened if we hadn't consumed a concerning amount of wine together, held each other accountable to write every night, and fueled each other's dreams. I am so grateful to have had him to celebrate with at every step this took in the right direction, and there is no one I would rather have been standing with at the corner of Eighty-Seventh and York when I got the life-changing phone call.

I am so lucky to have gotten to run around New York City all these years with Scott Nugent and Patrick Kelley, and am so thankful for their friendship and support.

Thanks to Tim Dalton, for a lot, but especially his patience.

This book and its dumb author do not exist without Adrienne Crow, Alex Oliver, Ali Pattillo, Kaitlyn Nugent, and Caroline Ellis. Their encouragement, support, loyalty, and love are the luckiest parts of my life, and it's too big and too tied to everything for me to put into words.

Huge thanks and love to Anita "Nina" Baker, who taught me how to read.

This book is about family, and I am so thankful for mine. Thanks to Howard Shook for being a writer first and paving the way. Thanks to Alise Shook for always telling me I should make a career out of what I loved, and for making me love storytelling. I love Mary Martin Shook more than anyone on the planet. Thanks also, of course, to Georgie, Roo, and Max.

Last, but certainly not least, I am so thankful for all four of my grandparents, and especially my maternal grandmother, Maryann Martin, whom I'm so lucky to still have.

CELADON
BOOKS

Founded in 2017, Celadon Books, a division of
Macmillan Publishers, publishes a highly curated list
of twenty to twenty-five new titles a year. The list of
both fiction and nonfiction is eclectic and focuses
on publishing commercial and literary books and
discovering and nurturing talent.